GRAHAM
MASTERTON

Scarlet
Widow

HEAD
ZEUS

Scarlet Widow

GRAHAM MASTERTON trained as a
newspaper reporter before beginning his
career as an author. Graham's credits as
a writer include the bestselling horror novel
The Manitou, which went on to become
a successful film starring Tony Curtis,
and the Katie Maguire crime series, which
became a top-ten bestseller in 2012. *Scarlet
Widow* was inspired by Graham's many
visits to New England and is the first in a
new series, introducing eighteenth-century
apothecary Beatrice Scarlet.

Also by Graham Masterton

For Kinga Kaczanów
who loves science
with love

Scarlet Widow

Prologue

Early on Easter morning, after a long and painful labour, Beatrice gave birth to a baby girl. When she heard her crying, she felt as if she had rolled away the stone and miraculously come back to life.

'She's beautiful,' said Goody Rust, holding her up for Beatrice to see her. 'Dark hair, just like yours. But she has her father's eyes, don't you think?'

'Be careful to cut the cord short,' put in Goody Kettle. 'We don't want her to grow up a strumpet!'

Beatrice sat up a little, her curls damp with perspiration and her mouth dry. The early-morning sunshine blurred her vision, so that the crowd of friends and neighbours in her bedchamber seemed like an ever-shifting shadow-theatre. Seven of them had sat around her all through the night, feeding her with groaning cakes and beer and comforting her when the pain had been at its worst. Now they were chattering and laughing and passing the baby around from hand to hand.

Goody Rust sat down on the bed next to Beatrice and plumped up her pillows for her. 'I'm certain that her life will be a happy one,' she said, gently. 'You know what they say, that the tears of grief always water the garden of happiness.'

'I've wrapped up the afterbirth for you,' said Goody Greene. 'I'll take it down to the kitchen so that Mary can dry it for you.'

Beatrice smiled and said, 'Thank you.'

'Here, lie back,' said Goody Rust. 'I'll clean off all that hog's grease for you, and then you can get some sleep.'

'Let me just hold her before you do,' said Beatrice. The baby was passed to Goody Rust and Goody Rust laid her in her arms.

The baby's eyes were closed now, although Beatrice could see her eyes darting from side to side underneath her eyelids as if she were already dreaming. She touched the tip of her nose with her fingertip and whispered, 'Who are you, my little one?'

One

On Christmas morning, on their way back from church, they came across a cherub kneeling in a doorway.

She wore a halo of knobbly ice on her head and on her back a thin frost-rimed blanket had given her white folded wings. Her milky blue eyes were open and her lips were slightly parted as if she were about to start singing.

Beatrice's father stood looking at her for a long moment, then he reached out and gently touched her shoulder.

'Frozen solid,' he said. 'You carry on home, Bea. I'll go back and fetch the verger.'

Beatrice hesitated, with the snow falling silently on to her bonnet and cape. She had seen dead children in the street before, but here in this alley that they had taken as a short cut home, this girl made her feel much sadder than most. It was Christmas Day, and the church bells were pealing, and she could hear people laughing and singing as they made their way along Giltspur Street, back to their homes and their firesides and their families.

Not only that, the girl was so pretty, although she was very pale and emaciated, and Beatrice could imagine what a happy life she might have had ahead of her.

'Go on, Bea,' her father told her. 'There's nothing more anybody can do for her now, except pray.'

Two

That afternoon, over their roasted beef dinner, her father said, 'I wonder if it would ever be possible to preserve your loved ones when they pass away, exactly as they were when they were alive?'

'What on earth do you mean, Clement?' asked Beatrice's mother, spooning out turnips on to his plate.

'I mean, like that poor little girl that Bea and I came across this morning. She was only frozen, of course, so her remains won't last for long. But supposing you could petrify people or turn them into wood? Then you could keep them with you always.'

'Oh, Clement, what an idea! I couldn't have a wooden statue of my mother sitting at the table with us! It would give me a fit!'

He smiled and shrugged and said, 'Yes . . . yes, you're probably right. But one could do it with a pet, perhaps. A cat, or a dog. Then your child could play with it *ad infinitum*.'

Beatrice put down her spoon.

'What's the matter, Bea?' her mother asked her. 'Aren't you hungry?'

'I can't stop thinking about that girl,' said Beatrice. 'If only somebody had given her something to eat and a fire to keep her warm.'

'Bea, you shouldn't upset yourself. She's in heaven now, and Jesus will be taking care of her.'

Beatrice said nothing. She didn't want to contradict her mother. But although she was only twelve years old, and she had never been brought up to think any differently, she couldn't help wondering if heaven were really real, or if it were just a story that was made up to make us feel better about people we had lost. Perhaps when you froze to death you felt cold for ever after.

Three

'Come here, Bea,' said her father, appearing in the kitchen doorway, with the sun behind him. 'I have something wonderful to show you!'

'Oh, *please*, Clement!' her mother protested. 'Her breakfast is ready!'

'This won't take long,' said her father. His eyes were lit up and he was smiling, the way he always did when one of his experiments worked out well.

'That's what you said when you made that so-called volcano,' her mother retorted. '"This won't take long!" and the poor girl came back two hours later reeking of sulphur as if she had been to hell and back!'

She coughed, as if the very memory of it irritated her throat.

'Only five minutes this time,' said her father. 'I swear it, on my dear mother's life.'

'Clement, you know very well that you *detested* your mother, and in any event she passed away years ago.'

But Beatrice settled the argument by pushing back her chair and going across the kitchen to take her father's hand. 'What is it, papa? Have you made that lightning?'

'No, no, Bea. I haven't quite managed to make that lightning yet. I will, I believe, but this is different! Come and see for yourself.'

Beatrice looked at her mother pleadingly, and after a moment she waved her hand at her and said, 'Go on, then! But only five minutes because your porridge will grow cold!'

Beatrice and her father went out through the scullery and crossed the small high-walled herb garden hand in hand. The garden was planted in neat triangles with absinthe and fennel and lavender and rosemary and sweet cicely. It was a summer morning, already warm, and the fragrance of the plants was so strong that it made Beatrice sneeze.

'Bless you!' said her father. Then, looking down at her and smiling, he said again, much more quietly, 'Bless you.'

He ushered her into the whitewashed outbuilding at the back of the house. This was where he ground up all the herbs and spices for his customers, and prepared his medicinal mixtures, and where he worked on what he called his 'mysteries'. It was cool and dark in there because the windows were very small and grimy. Three of the walls were lined with shelves, and every shelf was crowded with flasks and apothecary bottles filled with pink and green and amber liquids, as well as china spice jars labelled ginger, galingol, saffron, pepper, cloves, cinnamon and nutmeg. There was a strong smell in here, too, but unlike the aromatic smell in the herb garden, it was pungent and musky. It always put Beatrice in mind of far-off places where men wore turbans and women wore veils, and everybody flew around on carpets like in the *Arabian Nights*.

'You will not believe this, Bea, when you see it,' said her father, guiding her over to the workbench at the end of the room. The surface of the bench was cluttered with pots and pans and candle-holders and all kinds of strangely shaped glass retorts. Right in front was a canoe-shaped copper container, rather like a fish kettle, which was half filled with viscous yellow oil.

Beside this container, Beatrice's father had spread out a brown cotton cloth, although it was humped up in the middle and there was plainly something hidden underneath it.

'You remember at Christmas, when we found that poor frozen girl in Bellman's Alley, and I spoke to you of turning animals into wood, so that a real animal could become a toy?'

Beatrice nodded, her eyes wide. She said nothing, because whatever her father did always surprised her. He had once magnified a drop of water and shone its image on to the wall to show her all the microscopic living creatures that swarmed inside it. Another time, he had made sparks fly from his fingertips, as if he were a wizard. He could make liquids change from green to purple and then back again, and iron filings crawl across a sheet of paper like spiders, and he could snuff out lighted candles without even touching them. He had even made a dead frog jump off his workbench and on to the floor.

He took hold of one corner of the cloth. 'What you are about to see, Bea, is a scientific marvel that man has sought for centuries to achieve! Even the greatest alchemists of ancient Egypt were unable to fathom how this could be done!'

Beatrice couldn't help laughing. Her father was normally very sober and undemonstrative, and when it came to talking to his customers his face was unfailingly grave. He was good-looking, in a slightly foxy way, with prematurely grey hair brushed straight back from his forehead and a neatly trimmed moustache and beard. He usually dressed very formally, but this morning he was in his shirt-sleeves, without even a collar.

'I give you – the Wooden Rat!' he exclaimed, and whipped the cloth away.

Standing on the bench, staring at Beatrice with beady black eyes, was a large brindled rat. Beatrice squealed and jumped back, holding her apron up to her face. She was terrified of rats.

Only two weeks ago, when visiting her friend Lucy in Cock Lane, they had heard screaming from her baby brother Rufus. They had rushed into his nursery to find out what was wrong and discovered that a huge grey rat had climbed into his crib and was biting at his face.

'Don't be frightened, Bea!' said her father. 'This fellow can do you no harm at all!' With that, he picked up the rat and knocked it against the side of the workbench. It was completely rigid, and it made a tapping sound as if it were carved out of solid mahogany.

Beatrice still stayed well back, frowning. 'Is it real?' she asked. 'It has fur, and whiskers, and real teeth!'

'It is quite real, my darling! I trapped it myself in the water butt in the garden!'

'So what did you do to it? How did you make it all woody like that?'

'Aha! First of all, I put it to sleep by placing it inside a glass flagon and extracting all the air, so that it could no longer breathe. Then, when it had expired, I gently simmered its body for two days in this linseed oil. After that, I removed it from the oil, and drained it, and washed it, and allowed it to cool, and here it is, completely harmless, a plaything instead of a pest!'

'It's *horrible*,' said Beatrice. 'I wouldn't want to play with it!'

'Very well, yes, I can understand that, Bea, it's a rat. I chose it for my first experiment because it was vermin. But one could equally turn kittens or puppies or baby rabbits into wooden toys and they would be far more charming.'

'No, they wouldn't! How can you say that? Kittens and puppies and baby rabbits? That would be so *cruel*!'

Her father looked taken aback. 'One would only use unwanted animals, Bea, and strays. What would happen to them otherwise? Either they would starve or they would be tied in a sack and thrown into the river. At least the animals chosen for this treatment would pass away painlessly, and after they had passed away they would continue to bring pleasure and amusement to any child who owned them, for years to come.

'Here,' said her father, holding out the rat. 'Feel it, stroke it. It won't bite you.'

Beatrice reluctantly prodded the rat with her fingertip. It felt completely hard and its fur was sharp and bristly, like a scrubbing-brush.

'It's *horrible*,' she insisted.

'Well, yes, that's as may be. It's a rat, after all. But it's a rat that looks exactly as it did when it was alive – *exactly* – and that's another use for this treatment. Taxidermy.'

Beatrice shook her head to show her father that she didn't know what 'taxidermy' was. She was only twelve, after all.

'Taxidermy is when you stuff dead animals and mount them, so that people can put them on display. You know, like stags' heads, and parrots, and fish in glass cases.'

'Oh, yes,' said Beatrice. 'There's that stuffed greyhound, isn't there, outside Shephard's Coffee House? That always used to frighten me. I used to think it might suddenly come alive and chase after me.'

Her father smiled. 'Yes, but wouldn't you agree that it's a very queer-looking greyhound indeed? All lopsided, with a crooked tail, and a very silly grin. That's because it takes tremendous skill and anatomical knowledge to restore a dead animal's natural shape and features, and very few taxidermists have the ability to do that.

'This way, however,' he said, and held up his solidified rat, '*this* way, any creature will look exactly as it did when it was living and breathing.'

He paused, and then he said, 'Perhaps one day one might be able to do the same with people. You know, if you had lost a loved one . . .'

'*Papa*,' Beatrice admonished him.

'No, of course,' said her father. 'It was just a thought.' He turned the solidified rat this way and that, then set it down on his workbench. 'You really don't like this, then? I thought perhaps you might.'

Beatrice emphatically shook her head.

'Well, you're much more like your mother than me,' her father told her. He put his arm around her shoulders and kissed the top of her hair. 'Your mother wouldn't hurt a bottle-bee.'

They went back outside, into the herb garden, and her father locked the outbuilding door behind him. As they walked back towards the kitchen door, they heard her mother coughing again, more persistently this time. When they went inside, they found her leaning over the sink and wiping her mouth with a handkerchief.

'Nancy, that cough sounds worse,' said Clement.

She pumped water into the sink to wash away the spit that she had coughed up. 'I'm all right, Clement. It's this summer cold, that's all. You know how weak my chest is. Are you ready for your breakfast, Bea? What did papa have to show you?'

'It was a rat turned into wood. It was *ugh*.'

'A real rat?'

Beatrice sat down at the kitchen table and her mother brought her over a bowl of porridge.

'Bea didn't care for it much,' said her father. 'But I'm trying to find a way for people to preserve living creatures exactly as they are, forever.'

'Is that possible?' asked Nancy. 'I didn't think that anything could last forever.'

Clement stayed in the doorway, watching her, without saying anything. Beatrice glanced up at him as she ate her porridge and she couldn't understand why he looked so concerned.

After a few moments he said, 'I had better finish dressing, my dear, and open up the shop. I will have customers beating at the door before I know it.'

'I'll make you some tea,' said Nancy, and coughed, and then coughed some more.

Beatrice was woken up in the early hours of the morning by her mother's coughing. Through her bedroom wall she heard her father talking to her, and the creaking of their bed, and then she saw a light outside her room as he went downstairs. She heard the pump squeaking in the kitchen as he drew her some water.

She climbed out of bed and cautiously opened her door and went across the landing to her parents' chamber. Her mother was sitting up in bed, propped up by pillows. She looked deathly white and was pressing a handkerchief to her mouth. She was obviously about to say something, but then she started coughing again. Beatrice came around the bed and stood patiently next to her until she had stopped.

'Don't come too close to me, Bea,' said her mother, wiping her mouth. 'I don't want you to catch whatever it is that ails me.'

Even though her mother had scrunched up her handkerchief into her fist, Beatrice couldn't help noticing that it was spotted with pink.

'Mama, I should go for the doctor.'

'There's no need for that. Your father is making me up a mixture to ease my cough. I need sleep more than anything else.'

She coughed again, and this time she retched into her handkerchief, and it was flooded red with blood.

'Papa!' called Beatrice, in a panic. '*Papa!*'

She heard her father hurrying up the stairs. He came into the chamber in his long white nightgown and gently moved her to one side so that he could sit on the bed next to her mother. She coughed again and sprayed his nightgown with speckles of blood.

'Bea, please bring me a cloth,' said her father. 'Anything will do. You'll find some in the bottom drawer there.'

Beatrice pulled open the drawer and took out a small linen tablecloth, which he unfolded with a shake and gave to her mother. She coughed some more, holding the cloth over her mouth, but she brought up no more blood, only pink-streaked sputum. Her father held her shoulders as she sat struggling for breath, her chest rising and falling with a sharp crackling sound.

'How do you feel now?' he asked her after a while, and she nodded, although her eyes kept darting around the room as if she couldn't understand what she was doing there.

He turned to Beatrice and said, 'Bea, there's a cup of water on the kitchen table, as well as a green glass bottle. Would you please bring them up here? And a spoon, too.'

When Beatrice had climbed back up the stairs, carrying the cup and bottle, her father helped her mother to sip a little water. After that, he gave her two spoonfuls of the emerald-green medicine that he had prepared. 'There, my dearest. Betony water and lungwort, mixed with a little honey. That should ease the rheum on your lungs. Try to get some sleep now. You should feel much better in the morning.'

He helped her to lie down and turn on her side, and he drew the pale yellow blanket up to her neck. The chamber was warm and stuffy, but she was shivering and perspiring and her teeth were chattering.

He took Beatrice back to her room. 'She is so much *worse*,' said Beatrice, worriedly, looking across the corridor at her mother lying in bed. 'This morning she said it was only a cold. Why is she coughing up blood?'

'I believe she may have the consumption,' said her father. 'Let us pray not, but we will see how she feels in a few hours' time. The physic I have given her should help.'

'Will we have to take her to the hospital?'

Her father said, 'St Thomas's? No. I can treat her here at home just as well as any of the doctors in that cesspit. But before you go back to sleep, Bea, do ask God to take care of her, won't you, and make her well again?'

Beatrice nodded and hugged him. His beard prickled her cheek and she thought of the rat, with its bristly fur, and then she thought of what her father had said about preserving people. She could see her mother staring at the candle beside her bed, her beautiful mother with her dark curls spread out across the pillow. She didn't want to think about losing her, or what would happen to her if she died.

Her mother started coughing again and so her father kissed Beatrice on the forehead and went back to his chamber, and closed the door.

Beatrice climbed back into bed and lay there for a long time with her eyes open. It was hard to say a prayer, with her mother continually coughing, let alone sleep. When she did eventually doze off she dreamed that she walked into the parlour to find her mother sitting by the window, holding up her embroidery hoop. As she approached her, however, she saw that her needle was poised but her hands were motionless.

'Mama,' she heard herself saying, in a blurry voice. 'Mama!'

But her mother didn't answer, or even turn to look at her. Before she was halfway across the parlour, Beatrice realized that her mother was dead and that her father had turned her into wood.

Three weeks later, Beatrice awoke one morning and the house was silent.

Her mother had been coughing and coughing almost continuously for days and nights on end, but now she seemed to have stopped. Outside, on Giltspur Street, it was warm and windy. She could see waste paper flying past her upstairs window and hear the muffled cacophony of street peddlers shouting and cartwheels grinding on the cobbles. Inside, however, the air was stifling and there was no sound at all.

She drew back her blankets and went across to her parents' room. Her father was kneeling on the floor beside the bed, his head bowed, holding her mother's hand. Her mother was lying on the pillow with her eyes closed, perfectly still, not breathing.

'Papa?' Beatrice whispered.

Her father turned to her, and she had never seen anybody's face look so stricken.

'Mama is with God now, Bea,' he told her. 'From now on, it's just you and me, with nobody to care for us but ourselves.'

Four

The day of Nancy Bannister's funeral was warm, but gloomy, with low grey cloud. Before the service she lay on view in the parlour, dressed in a white woollen shroud with her head resting on a white woollen pillow, as required by the Burial in Woollens Act.

Beatrice approached the coffin with her father holding her hand. Without a word he lifted the flannel that covered her mother's face. Beatrice pressed her hand over her mouth. She could scarcely believe that this figure was her mother. Her face was the colour of ivory, and her eyes were as deep and dark as two inkwells.

'Don't be alarmed, Bea,' said her father. 'Your mother is in heaven now, smiling and laughing. This is nothing more than the body that bore her suffering for her.'

The coffin was carried from the parlour into the street outside, where a hearse drawn by two black horses was waiting to take it the short distance to St James's Church in Clerkenwell Close. A silent procession set off, led by the balding young parson, the parson's mute, and a feather-man with a tray of black ostrich feathers balanced on his head. It began to feel like rain.

In the church, in a high, sing-song voice the balding young parson extolled Nancy's virtues as a wife and a mother and then commended her soul to God. The church echoed so that it sounded as if three parsons were all talking at once. The bell was rung six times, as was customary for a woman. Afterwards, the bearers took Nancy's coffin down to the crypt to join more than two hundred others from St James's parish who slept together in the darkness.

The rain didn't start to patter down until the funeral guests had returned to the house, and then it began to dribble down the windows like tears. Nancy's sisters, Jane and Felicity, served tea and cinnamon cake, while Clement handed round glasses of port wine. His hand trembled as he did so, and his face was so ashen with grief that he looked ill.

'Now you shall have to be the lady of the house, young Beatrice,' said her Aunt Felicity. 'No more schooling at Mrs Tutchin's, I imagine.'

'Not a bit of it,' said Clement. 'Bea shall carry on with her classes, just as before.'

'But, Clement! How on earth will you *manage*? You don't look at all well, if you don't mind my saying so! I don't want to be back here before Christmas for another funeral!'

Clement shook his head. 'Every young girl needs French, and mathematics, and logic, as well as cookery and plain-work. But Bea shall help me with the business, too. She has always shown a great aptitude for mixing medications, ever since she was old enough to hold a spoon. She preferred it to baking biscuits with her mother. One day, you mark my words, she will be London's first and most celebrated female apothecary.'

'A female apothecary? I can hardly see *that* being acceptable! Especially one so young and so pretty! How many gentlemen will feel comfortable coming to a female apothecary, especially if they have any kind of *private* ailment?'

'I doubt if it will be any fewer than those who ask me every day of the week for calomel lotion. It's never for themselves, you see. It's always for a "friend".'

Beatrice said, 'Calomel lotion? That's for the French disease, isn't it, papa?'

'Oh! I'm quite shocked!' Aunt Felicity exclaimed, throwing up her black-gloved hands. 'The girl is no more than twelve. What does she know of the French disease?'

'Actually, I'm thirteen in three weeks' time,' said Beatrice. 'And papa has never made a secret of people's illnesses and where they catch them from.'

Clement put his arm around Beatrice's shoulders and gave her an affectionate squeeze. When he looked down and smiled at her, though, she saw more pain than hope in his eyes, and she could tell how much he was suffering.

As summer gave way to autumn, and then to winter, Beatrice tried to keep up her attendance at Mrs Tutchin's academy every day. Mrs Tutchin was young and blonde-haired and almost skeletally thin. She was the wife of a banker, although she was childless herself. There were nine girls in the class altogether and Mrs Tutchin taught them manners and deportment, and how to speak colloquial French, and how to add up and multiply. She also showed them how to sew on buttons and embroider, and how to bake a lardy cake with raisins folded into it.

Beatrice loved the academy because Mrs Tutchin was so gentle and soft-spoken and smelled of diluted rosewater. She was patient with all of her girls, but especially sympathetic to Beatrice because she knew how much she missed her mother. Sometimes, when Beatrice was bent over her sewing, she would come and stand behind her and gently rest one of her bony hands on her shoulder, as if she were reassuring her that her mother was watching over her.

Every week, though, it became harder for Beatrice to find the time to attend the academy, even though Mrs Tutchin's house was only three streets away, at the top of Snow Hill. Now that it was colder, and it was growing dark so early in the day, her father was becoming more and more depressed and erratic in his behaviour. He had started drinking – only in the afternoons at first, with his dinner, but then he started to take a glass of genever before he opened the shop, and more glasses throughout the day, from a brown stone bottle that he kept hidden under the counter. Almost every evening he would fall asleep in his armchair in front of a gradually dying fire, and every night she would hear him stumbling upstairs to bed when the fire had turned to ashes and he had woken up shivering.

Almost every morning she would have to wake him because he was still snoring thickly when it was time for him to open up the shop – wrapped up tightly in his blankets but fully clothed and crusty-eyed and reeking of stale alcohol.

He would open his eyes and stare at her as if he didn't know who she was. Then he would sit up and croak, 'I'm sorry . . . I'm so sorry, Bea. It won't happen again, I swear to God.'

Once he had washed himself and changed his clothes and come downstairs to eat breakfast with her, he was almost back to his old self again, especially if she served him oatmeal gruel with butter and wine in it. By then, however, it was often too late for her to go to Mrs Tutchin's and her father would coax her to stay at home and help him prepare his medicines because he had such a backlog of prescriptions waiting to be filled, and so many customers who were beginning to lose patience with him.

'I'm blessed by God to have such a clever daughter,' he said to her almost every day, kissing her on the top of her head. 'If only your mother could see you now!'

Beatrice would put on a long linen apron and a stiff linen bonnet, and her thick wool cloak, too, if it was cold, because there was only a small wood-burning stove in the outhouse to keep her warm. Then she would sit all alone for most of the morning, making up pills and powders and lotions and bottles of various cordials, following the recipes in her father's dog-eared notebooks.

Some of the medicines took her hours. One of Clement Bannister's most popular cure-alls was Mithridate, which was claimed to be effective against poisoning and animal bites and even the plague. It contained over fifty ingredients, which Beatrice had to measure out in very precise quantities – including opium, cardamom, frankincense, saffron, ginger, anise, parsley and acacia juice. Once measured, they all had to be pounded together in honey. Almost as popular was Venice Treacle, which had sixty-four ingredients – roots, herbs, peppers, even bitumen and animal parts, like roasted adders – although it was much more expensive.

Apart from these, Beatrice had to mix up a mouthwash of dried marigold petals and erigeron, as a remedy for chronic toothache. For nosebleeds, she would stir together comfrey and plantain water, sometimes adding yarrow.

Every time she smelled the pungency of yarrow leaves, she thought of the song that her mother used to sing to her when she put her to bed. If she wrapped yarrow leaves in a handkerchief, her mother had told her, she would wake up in the morning and know who she was going to marry.

Thou pretty herb of Venus' tree,
Thy true name it is Yarrow.
Now who my husband he will be
Pray tell me thou tomorrow!

She could almost hear her mother's clear, high voice, and it was so hard to think of her lying in the crypt of St James's Church, dead, cold, and in darkness.

One of her father's best-selling preparations was Bannister's Patented Hair Invigorator, but she hated making it because it smelled so rancid. For this, she had to boil up houndstooth leaves in water, with a little oil and salt added, and then mould a poultice with pig fat which she had to buy at Smithfield Market, just up the street. The balding customer was supposed to spread this on his scalp overnight, covered with a hot towel, and wash it off in the morning.

She didn't like making calomel lotion, either, because the mercury in it stained her fingers black. It was supposed to cure the French disease, or syphilis, but she had seen for herself the effects on those men who had used it for any length of time. Their gums were rotted red-raw, all their teeth had dropped out, and their jawbones were so decayed that they could hardly open their mouths to speak.

All the same, they still came into the shop and begged her father in mumbling voices for more because they believed they were taking too little of it, rather than too much.

On the last Monday of the year, Beatrice was rolling out a long pipe of pills when Clement pushed open the outhouse door with a bang that made her jump. He stepped unsteadily inside, bringing with him a gust of icy-cold air. Behind him, snow was falling fast and thick and silent. The walled herb garden was blanketed with snow and Clement had snow melting in his hair and in his beard.

'Bea, my darling!' he cried out. 'Why aren't you at Mrs Chew-chin's?'

'Papa – the door! It's freezing!'

'What? Oh, yes, I'm sorry! Can't have my daughter catching her death! My lovely daughter sent by God!'

He came up to the workbench and stood next to her, swaying slightly.

'Papa, have you been drinking again? I hope you've locked up the shop.'

'What? The shop? Yes, yes, I've locked it! Locked it securely! Locked it up tight as a drum!'

'Perhaps we'd better go into the house. I was going to give you mutton for your dinner, with boiled potatoes and carrots. But you can have bread and cheese if you'd rather.'

She started to rise off her stool, but Clement laid his hand on her shoulder and gently pushed her back down.

'What are you doing?' he asked her. He frowned at the long rope of dry white paste that she had rolled out on to a blue Delft tile, ready for cutting up.

'I'm making those carminative pills you asked me for. You said they were urgent, because you'd run out of stock.'

Clement leaned forward and sniffed. 'Ah, yes. Peppermint and fennel and anise, guaranteed to settle the stormiest of stomachs. Good girl. Blessedly good girl. But you can stop for now.'

'I thought you needed them in a hurry.'

He tilted his head from side to side as if he had a stiff neck. 'You're not at Mrs Chew-chin's?'

'No, papa. Don't you remember? You wanted me to stay here and make you some carminative pills and some lung syrup.'

22

'Did I? Well, even if I did, you don't have to. Not any more. You can stop now. You can put aside your pestle and we'll do something much more amusing instead. Something to make us laugh instead of cry.'

He stared at the workbench for a few long seconds without saying anything, his eyes unfocused. Then he looked back at Beatrice and said, 'I'm so tired of crying, Bea. I don't want to cry ever again. I was standing in the shop. I was standing in the shop and that woman came in. What's her name? She always wears green. She came into the shop and said she needed something for melancholy.

'I was just about to suggest my tincture of borage when my throat choked up as if I had swallowed thistles and tears began to roll down my cheeks. Right in front of her. She was nonplussed, but I couldn't stop myself. I thought, this woman is asking *me* how to cure melancholy? Me? When I'm still wracked with grief for your mother. *Wracked*, that's a strange word, isn't it, wracked? Wracked, wracked, wracked! But it feels exactly as it sounds.'

'Papa—' Beatrice put in, but her father carried on talking as if he hadn't heard her.

'She said that her husband had recently passed away and that she had been suffering from deep depression ever since. Do you know what I told her? I told her the truth. I told her that there *is* no cure. I told her that she could drink three bottles of my tincture of borage every day until her face turned green to match her coat and her bonnet. But there is no cure. Not for death, Bea. Not for death.'

Beatrice reached out for him and held both of his hands. 'Papa, you should come into the house and have something to eat. Your hands are so cold! I could make you a hot drink of chocolate, if you like.'

23

'Chocolate?' he said. 'What good is chocolate?

Then he stared at Beatrice intently and asked, 'Why aren't you at Mrs Chew-chin's?'

'You wanted me here, papa. Now come back into the house.'

'We shall entertain ourselves!' he said, loudly, like an impresario addressing a theatre audience. 'Today, we shall make lightning! And smoke that changes colour! Smoke! And fire! Today, we shall tear paper into a thousand pieces and make those thousand pieces dance like a snowstorm! We shall melt pewter spoons into puddles! We shall set off explosions so loud that we will be deaf for a week thereafter! But we shall laugh! And dance! And we shall make ourselves as happy as we ever have been!'

Still holding on to Beatrice's hands, he performed a slow, shuffling dance, nodding his head and tunelessly humming as he did so.

'Papa, you need something to eat,' said Beatrice, tugging her hands free. 'Come on into the house.'

'Ah,' said Clement. 'Now I remember why I came out here to find you! I've run out of gin and I need you to go to The Fortune and buy me another bottle!'

'Papa, you really don't need any more! You've drunk enough already today.'

Clement opened the outhouse door again and stared out at the snow. The silence was overwhelming. Not only did the snow deaden the sound of carriage wheels, and keep the street peddlers indoors with their rattles and trumpets, but it had stopped the driving of livestock through the streets. It was like London seen in a dream.

'Bea,' said her father, 'I can't carry on without it. It's deathly cold in the shop and yet my shirt is drenched with sweat and my hands have been shaking so badly that I can barely measure out a powder. Please, my darling. I know that I shouldn't, and I promise you that I will start tomorrow with a clean slate and not drink another drop.'

Beatrice blew out the decorative brass lamp she used for heating opium. 'You have made that promise every day, papa, but still not kept it.'

'I know, my sweetest one. I know I have. But tomorrow I swear that I will, and every tomorrow thereafter. Today, though, please go to The Fortune and fetch me another bottle. Here—' he dug into his pocket and produced a sixpenny piece. 'You might as well fetch me two bottles to save you going out again later.'

'Papa—' she said, but still he continued to stare at the snow falling. It blew in through the doorway and curled across the wooden floor.

'I don't want to beg, Bea. Please don't make me beg. But if you won't do this for me, I fear that I shall die.'

Beatrice stepped out into the snow and closed the outhouse door. Her father took out the key, but his hands were trembling so badly that he was unable to fit it into the keyhole. Beatrice took it from him, locked the door, and handed it back.

'Don't tell me that I was sent by God,' she admonished him, as he was about to open his mouth. 'If I go to buy you more gin, I was more likely sent by Satan.'

'You are my angel, Bea. You know that, don't you? My angel and my saviour. And you look so much like your mother. You could be her, resurrected, risen from the crypt.'

Beatrice was tempted to tell him not to speak like that because it upset her to be constantly reminded that her mother was dead, and it frightened her to think of her coming alive again. She had nightmares about her suddenly appearing in her bedroom doorway, looking the same as she had when she was lying in her coffin in the parlour, her eyes dark and hollow, her hands as shrivelled as chamois gloves that had been left in the rain.

She helped him into the house. He stumbled into the parlour and sat down heavily in his armchair, close to the fireplace, shivering uncontrollably. The cinders in the hearth were still glowing so Beatrice prodded them with the poker, and scooped on more coal from the scuttle.

She knelt down and blew on the fire until a few small flames began to lick up between the coals, but her father opened his eyes and said, 'What? Haven't you been to The Fortune yet? Never mind the fire.'

Beatrice took no notice. Her father stared at her with increasing desperation, clutching the arms of his chair as if he were afraid he would fall out of it, but she waited and kept her eyes on the fire until she was satisfied that it was well ablaze and starting to crackle. Then, without a word, she went out to the hallway and took down her thick brown woollen cloak, and put on her bonnet.

'Bea!' called her father, as she opened the front door.

She didn't turn around, but said clearly, 'I won't be long, papa, I promise,' and stepped out into the street.

Five

The snow was whirling down furiously now and there was hardly anybody else about. A few carriages were making their way slowly through the gloom, like ghost carriages, their horses' hooves slipping on the icy cobbles. Beatrice couldn't remember it ever having been so cold.

At least the snow covered the heaps of household rubbish on the pavements and made the street appear reasonably clean, although the outline of a dead dog was still visible and there was a pale brown stain of raw sewage wending its way along the gutter.

She put up her hood and made her way to Pye Corner, blinking against the snowflakes that caught on her eyelashes. The Fortune of War public house was only six doors down, past a mercer's and a grocer's and a small shop that had been a bookstore and stationer's until October, when the owner had died of what his physician had described only as 'teeth'.

Two small children were huddled under a filthy quilted horse-blanket in the bookshop doorway, a boy and a girl. The boy was asleep, but the girl stared hollow-eyed at Beatrice as she passed, although she said nothing. Even Beatrice's mother, at her kindliest, had told Beatrice that it was impossible for them to feed and shelter all the destitute children that they saw in the streets, but Beatrice made up her mind that after she had taken her father his bottle of gin she would come back and give these children mugs of hot parsnip soup, which she would make herself.

The Fortune of War stood right on Pye Corner. Halfway up its sooty brick frontage perched a small gilded statue of a boy, the Golden Boy of Pye Corner, who been put up there to mark the furthest extremity of the Great Fire of London, nearly three quarters of a century before. This morning he had a little pyramid of snow on top of his head.

Beatrice pushed open the door and went inside. She hated coming in here because it was dark and filled with pipe smoke and crowded with drunken men who would wink and leer at her and grin at her with their gappy teeth. The shouting and laughter were deafening.

'And a welcome to you, my gorgeous little darling!' called out a greasy-looking porter with a huge floppy cap and a bulging grey waistcoat. 'Come here, sit on my lap why don't you, and make a lonely man happy!'

He hooted with amusement and slapped his thigh, and all of his friends cackled, too. 'You couldn't find your pizzle, Jack, if it was tied to the end of your nose!'

Beatrice went up to the counter, where the red-faced publican was pouring out glasses of brandy. He gave her a smile and asked, 'What's it to be, then, Mistress Bannister? Another bottle of genever?'

Beatrice put down her sixpence. 'Two, please, Mr Andrews. Papa says it will save me coming out twice.'

'Oh, he's a thoughtful man, your papa,' said the publican sadly. 'Wait there for a minute, I'll have to go down to the cellar for it. These fellows here have been drinking me dry this morning. It may be good for business, but I won't be sorry when this snow lets up and they can all go back out to work.'

He lit a lamp and then opened the cellar door behind the bar and went down into the darkness. Beatrice stayed where she was, with her elbows on the counter and her hands ostentatiously pressed against her ears so that the men around her would see that she wasn't listening to their coarse banter about pizzles and jilts and pulling the pudding.

She was still waiting for Mr Andrews when somebody tapped her on the shoulder. She turned around and saw that it was Robert, a skinny young boy of about fifteen with wiry blond hair who worked at The Fortune as a pot-boy and cleaner. She liked Robert because he was handsome, in spite of his raging red spots, and whenever she came into the pub he always talked to her and made her feel pretty and grown-up.

'Hey, Bea, you're not back for *more* of the jolly old gin?' he asked her.

'Papa needs it for his tonic,' said Beatrice. 'He mixes it with marigold and betony water to keep away colds.'

'Oh, you don't say so?' Robert smiled. 'Keeps away colds, does it?' He was wearing a floor-length leather apron and he reached into the pocket and produced a thin twist of paper.

'Barley sugar?' he asked her. 'John Welkin give me some for helping him carry in some stiffs.'

He snapped the stick of barley sugar in half and offered her some, but she shook her head. She loved barley sugar, but John Welkin was a resurrectionist and she didn't want to put anything in her mouth that a resurrectionist might have handled.

Robert bit off a piece and rattled it around between his teeth. 'When I say stiffs, they're *proper* stiff, most of them. Stiff as boards! They fell through the ice on the river last night, drunk as lords, and they're all frozen solid.'

'That's so horrible! I don't know how you can bear to touch them!'

'Nah, they're not so bad. At least they don't pen-and-ink. Not until they thaws out, any road. And some of them have pennies in their pockets, which Mr Welkin lets me keep. Do you want to come and see them? He got a fair good catch this morning, and there's not just drunks. There's two kids, too, who were trying to skate, and their mother who tried to save them. You should see her face! She looks like she's still screaming at them!'

'No – no thank you. I'd rather not.'

'Oh, come on, Bea! You never saw such a sight! It's better than a freak show! And it's free!'

Beatrice had seen dead bodies carried into the back room at The Fortune of War more than once, especially after low tide. Her father had told her that the pub had been officially appointed by the Royal Humane Society for the 'reception of drowned persons' found in the Thames. If their bodies went unclaimed, the surgeons would come round from St Bartholomew's Hospital to see if they were suitable for dissection. If they were, resurrectionists like John Welkin would be paid 'finishing money' for their trouble, sometimes as much as four guineas.

Her father had told her all this in a strangely distracted way, which had made Beatrice wonder if he was secretly thinking of buying a body for himself in order to solidify it, like that bristly brown rat. She had changed the subject and said that she needed to tend to the suet pudding that she was boiling.

Robert shrugged and said, 'Please yourself. I'd best be gathering up some pots in any case.'

He went over to the nearest table and started to collect up dirty tankards and glasses. As he did so, however, the porter in the huge floppy cap heaved himself up from the bench where he was sitting and approached the bar.

'Well, now, my pretty little lamb!' he exclaimed. He was swaying with drink and he came to stand so close that Beatrice could smell the urine that soaked his britches. He turned to her, grinning, and then without warning he hooked his arm around her waist and wrenched her roughly towards him. His eyes were yellow and his brown teeth were crowded together like some neglected graveyard.

'You could give me a kiss, my little innocent, couldn't you? What harm would a kiss do? About time somebody introduced you to the pleasures of the flesh, wouldn't you say?'

Beatrice tried to wrench herself away from him, but he tightened his grip around her and laughed, so that she could feel his spit on her face.

'Come on, my little charmer! Don't deny that you want to!'

He tugged her closer still, but as he did so Robert crossed over to the counter and promptly put down all the tankards that he had been collecting up. Without a word he came around from behind Beatrice and punched the porter on the right ear. The porter shouted out, '*Shite*!' He let go of Beatrice and lurched heavily back against the counter, his floppy cap falling over his eyes. Robert punched him again, on the bridge of the nose. Blood spurted out of both his nostrils and sprayed over his filthy grey waistcoat.

'You maggot!' the porter snorted, dragging off his cap and pressing it against his nose to stem the blood, 'I'll cut your tallywags off for that!'

Three or four other porters rose from their seats and gathered around Robert, with threatening looks on their faces. They were all just as ugly and filthy and just as drunk.

'*You*,' said one of them, pointing at Robert with a blackened fingernail. He looked as if he were smiling, like a clown, but he had deep horizontal scars each side of his mouth, as if somebody had dragged a butcher's cleaver sideways between his lips. 'You are on your way to get your neck wrung, boy!'

Robert glanced quickly from one of the porters to the other. The greasy-looking porter reached into his waistcoat pocket and produced a large clasp-knife, which he opened up with an elaborate flourish, like a conjuring trick. Blood was still running from both of his nostrils and he had to lick his upper lip every now and then to stop it dripping down his chin.

'You'll be singing a different tune from now on, sunshine,' he said. He gave a bubbly sniff and then he added, 'A very *high* tune, like a maiden, because that's what I'm going to turn you into!'

Robert edged back, his fists half raised to defend himself, but he didn't seem to know what to do. Beatrice felt her heart beating against her ribcage and she was so frightened that she was breathless. Five drunken meat-porters would probably do far more than hurt Robert, they would probably murder him – and they would probably hurt her, too. She suddenly thought of a dead woman she had seen lying in Hosier Lane once, her face bruised crimson and her petticoats dragged up around her waist, and a wooden shovel handle thrust up her.

She tried to grab Robert's hand. He didn't seem to understand what she wanted him to do and she had to snatch at it a second time before he took hold of it. He stared at her wide-eyed and said, '*What?*' but she said nothing at all. She pulled him away from the counter and across the bar towards the pub's back door.

The porters shouted, 'Oi! Oi! *Oi!* You come back here, you little shite-cock!' But Beatrice and Robert scrambled through the door together and Robert slammed it behind them. He turned the key in it and bolted it top and bottom. He was just in time. Two or three seconds later the porters crashed into it, so that one of its panels was split. There was a moment's pause and then they crashed into it again, but it stayed firmly in its frame.

'*Open up!*' they roared. They sounded more like ferocious beasts than men. '*Open up this damned door or else!*'

Beatrice and Robert stayed where they were, staring at each other, not daring to speak. The porters kicked at the door and then they battered a chair against it, but after a few more desultory kicks they gave up. Beatrice could hear voices. It sounded as if Mr Andrews might have come upstairs from the cellar.

'What are we going to do?' she whispered. It was gloomy and very cold out there in the corridor, and there was a sickly sweet smell which made her stomach tighten. It reminded her of church.

Robert was about to say something when there was a sharp, quick knock at the door.

'Robert? Are you out there, Robert? Can you hear me?'

'Mr Andrews! I'm out here with Bea, the 'pothecary's daughter!'

'What's been happening, for God's sake? There was five or six fellows in here and they claim that you attacked them. They was bent on tearing you limb from limb if they could.'

'I was defending Bea's honour, Mr Andrews!'

'What with, a double-headed axe? There's more blood on the floor than Symond's slaughterhouse!'

'Mr Andrews!' Beatrice called out. 'Have they gone now, those men?'

'Yes, my darling, I threw them all out. But if I was you, I'd leave through the yard, and back-slang along the alley to your place. If you go out by the front door, you may well find them waiting for you round the corner. They're very drunk, to say the least, and I wouldn't want you to come to no harm.'

'One of them was trying to make Bea kiss him,' said Robert. 'That's the only reason I lammed him.'

'We'll talk about that later,' Mr Andrews told him. 'Open the door so that I can give Mistress Bannister her two bottles of gin, and then she can go.'

Robert shot back the bolts and unlocked the door. Mr Andrews appeared, his cheeks even redder than usual. He handed Beatrice a coarse hessian sack with two heavy earthenware bottles in it, which clinked as she took them.

'Give your papa my very good wishes,' he said. 'But also tell him he won't never find the answer to his sorrows in Geneva. Only here at home, in London.'

Beatrice said, 'Thank you, Mr Andrews,' very quietly. She understood exactly what he was saying, and she felt better for his sympathy. He was one of the few people who seemed to understand how lonely she felt, and how hard she had to work to help her father, and how worried she was about his drinking.

'You'll have to come through the stiffatorium, I'm afraid,' said Robert. 'But don't you worry. There's none of them can hurt you, not in here.'

Beatrice hesitated, but then she thought about the drunken porters who might be waiting for her in the street outside and nodded, and followed him into the large back room. It was even colder in here, so that her breath smoked, and the only light came from a single high window. The walls were damp and flaking, with black patches of mould on them, as if they had caught the diseases of the people who were brought in here day after day.

This morning there were nine bodies altogether – five men, two women and two children. They were lying on trestle tables against the walls and on blackboards just above them the names of their resurrectionists had been scrawled in chalk, to lay claim for bringing them in. Three of the men were still dressed in coats and britches, although their shoes had either fallen off or been removed, revealing holes in their stockings or dirty bare feet. Two of them were dressed in grubby woollen shrouds, and one of the women, too, was wearing a shroud, but hers was much cleaner, as if she had just been lifted from her coffin. The other woman wore a heavy grey skirt with layers of tattered petticoats underneath, and black button-up boots with worn-down heels.

Each of their faces was concealed by a flannel duster – not to give them dignity, but to spare any visitors the sight of their collapsing features as they decomposed. Although the room was so chilly, and most of the bodies had been recovered from an ice-cold River Thames, the smell was still so strong that Beatrice pulled up her sleeve to cover her nose and mouth and tried not to breathe too deeply.

'Take a squint at this one!' said Robert, lifting the duster from the face of one of the men. The man was cross-eyed, with patchy ginger hair, and his tongue was sticking out sideways, as if he had died while trying to make his friends laugh.

'Please – I don't want to,' said Beatrice, turning away 'I just want to get home.'

'How about this young lady – she was the one who tried to save her children from drowning!'

Beatrice couldn't help but look. The woman was white-faced, very young, no more than nineteen or twenty, with a pointed nose and the razor-sharp cheekbones of somebody who had never had enough to eat. Her brown eyes were staring at the ceiling and her mouth was stretched wide open.

Before Beatrice could turn away, the woman let out a high, breathy whine, which ended in a squeak. Beatrice jumped away in fright.

'She's *alive*! Robert! She's still alive!'

Robert took hold of her hand again and gave it a shake, as if to shake the silliness out of her. 'Nah, Bea, don't worry, they often does that. It's the gas in their bellies. You can come in here some summer evenings when it's warm and they've been lying here all day and they'll all be whistling and farting and moaning and complaining. It's like they're saying, what are we doing here dead, when we should be in the bar, having a pint of ale and playing ombre?'

He lifted the duster that covered the face of the woman in the shroud and peeked underneath it. 'Don't know why they brought *this* one in, though. She's a bit far gone for the surgeons, I'd say.'

Again, Beatrice didn't really want to look, and yet she couldn't resist it. Even though the bodies disturbed her so much, and their smell made her feel so nauseous, she found that they fascinated her. How had they died? Why had they died? That cross-eyed man, who had probably had a heart attack in mid-guffaw, or that panicky-looking young woman, caught forever in a soundless scream – she and Robert could stare at them and make remarks about them, but they would never be able to explain what had happened to them. They were all here, all nine of them – but they were all gone, too.

She nodded towards the woman in the shroud. 'Why is she wearing that funeral gown? She looks as if she's all ready to be buried.'

'That's because she *was* buried once,' said Robert. 'Either that, or laid out ready. John Welkin never says where he gets them and the surgeons never ask. There's been plenty dug up from churchyards, and even some gone missing from people's front parlours while they was lying on view.'

Beatrice stepped cautiously forward, her sleeve still pressed against her nose and mouth. The woman was lying directly under the window, so that she was illuminated by the cold, colourless light reflected from the snow outside. That made her look even whiter and even more ghostly than she already was. As she came closer, Beatrice could see that her eyes had fallen in, and her cheeks were hollow, and the skin around her mouth had shrunk so much that she was lipless.

'Bet they'll boil off her flesh and use her for a skelington,' said Robert. He lifted the duster a little further, revealing the woman's hair. It was dark, and wavy, and immediately she saw it, Beatrice realized who the woman was.

'*Put it back*!' she shrilled.

'What?' he said.

'That flannel! Put it back! Cover her face up!'

Robert frowned, and hesitated, but then he did as he was told and dropped the duster back over the dead woman's face.

'I have to go home!' said Beatrice, and started to cry. 'I have to go home now! I have to tell papa!'

'Bea, what's the matter?' Robert asked her. He tried to take hold of her shoulders to calm her, but she twisted herself away from him and went to the door that led out to the back yard. She tried to turn the key, but she was holding the hessian bag in one hand and the lock was too stiff.

'Robert – please – I have to go home! I have to tell papa!'

Robert unlocked the door for her. Outside, the yard was cluttered with beer casks and wooden boxes full of empty glass bottles. It was still snowing, thick and fast.

'Bea—' said Robert. 'I don't understand! It isn't me who's upset you, is it?'

Again he tried to take hold of her arm but she pulled away from him. Her mouth was turned down in misery and her eyelashes were stuck together with tears.

'That's my mama, Robert!'

'What?'

Beatrice pointed back into the room. 'That's my mother! Your precious John Welkin, who lets you keep dead men's pennies, he's stolen my mother out of her coffin!'

With that, she stumbled across the yard and tugged open the rickety back gate.

'Bea!' called Robert, but then she was gone. He heard the gin bottles clanking in her bag as she ran along the alley. 'Bea!'

He stood in the snow for a few moments. Then he went back inside. The nine dead bodies were all there waiting for him. He went over to the body of Beatrice's mother and stared at her. He tried to see if there was any likeness, but she was so emaciated that it was hard for him to imagine what she must have looked like when she was alive. He was still standing there when Mr Andrews came in.

'What are you doing, you young laggard? There's pots to be washed and the floor to be swept and I need you to take a message to St Thomas's for me!'

Robert said, 'Yes, Mr Andrews. Sorry.'

Then, as he followed Mr Andrews back into the bar, he said, 'Do you believe that God ever plays games with us, Mr Andrews?'

Mr Andrews turned around and frowned at him, as if he were an idiot. 'Of course God plays games with us. What do you think we're here for?'

Six

She beat furiously at the back door of her house and called out, 'Papa! Papa! Let me in! Papa! Let me in!'

It seemed to take him forever to realize where she was. Eventually, however, she heard him coming along the hallway. He unlocked the door and opened it, and stared in bewilderment at her standing in the snow.

'What are you doing back here? Why didn't you come in the front way?'

She threw herself at him, and gripped his coat tightly, and sobbed so hard that she could hardly breathe. Her father patted her on the back and said soothingly, 'What is it, Bea? What's happened? Come on, tell me. Why are you crying like this? Has somebody hurt you?'

He closed the back door and steered her inside, into the parlour, where the fire was blazing. She stood in front of it, quaking.

'You brought my genever, then,' he said, taking the hessian sack and setting it down on the side table. 'So why are you so upset, my darling?'

'It's mama,' wept Beatrice, her chest heaving with distress. 'Mama is lying in The Fortune.'

Her father sat down in his armchair and drew her close. 'I don't understand you, my darling. Mama is in heaven. You know that.'

Beatrice emphatically shook her head. 'I don't mean her soul. I mean her body. Her body is lying in The Fortune, with all the bodies of drowned people.'

'Bea, listen to me. Your mother's remains are lying in the crypt of St James's. They can't be in The Fortune, of all places. You must have made a mistake.'

Beatrice opened her eyes wide and almost screamed at him. '*They stole her body*! *The resurrection-men*! *They stole her body and they're going to boil it down until she's nothing but a skeleton*!'

'Ssshh, shh!' said her father, holding her wrists to restrain her. Then he looked at her very intently and said, 'You mean it, don't you? It *is* her.'

'She looks so *sad*,' Beatrice wept. 'What are we going to do-o-o?'

Her father stood up and started to button up his coat. 'We're going to go and claim her, that's what we're going to do. We're going to take her back and have her reverentially returned to her coffin. And whoever took her, we'll have him brought before the courts and punished for grave robbery. Come on.'

'We should go by the alley,' said Beatrice. 'Some drunken men were causing trouble in the bar and they might still be out in the street.'

'Don't you worry,' her father told her. 'It takes more than a gang of rowdy tosspots to frighten me.' He lifted down his heavy brown cloak, shrugged it over his shoulders and fastened the clasp. Then he put on his three-cornered hat and held out his hand. 'Come along, Bea. Be a brave girl.'

Beatrice reluctantly took his hand. She was desperate to rescue her mother's body from that terrible chilly room at the back of The Fortune, but she wasn't at all sure that she wanted to see her again, the way she was now, so fleshless and so irrevocably dead. The decomposing woman who was lying on that trestle table with a flannel over her face – that wasn't the same mama that she prayed to every night. The mama she prayed to was warm and laughing and lively, with sparkling eyes.

They went out into the snowy street and started to walk towards Pye Corner. The two children who had been huddled in the bookshop doorway had gone now and Beatrice felt a pang of regret that she hadn't taken them any hot soup.

Her father sensed something and asked, 'What? What is it?' but she shook her head and said, 'Nothing.' Her mother had said, '*We may wish to, Bea, but we can never save them all. Only the Lord can do that.*'

They reached The Fortune of War. Clement was just about to push open the doors when a harsh voice called out, 'Oi! You there! Yes, *you!*'

Clement turned round. The greasy-looking porter in the floppy cap was sheltering in a doorway on the opposite side of the street, along with the man with a smile like a clown, and three more of his drunken friends.

'Not *you*, you lobcock!' the porter shouted. 'That pretty little troublemaker beside you, that's who I'm talking to! That sweet young baggage who had me knocked in the smeller and then thrown out before I could finish the tank I just paid for!'

He came staggering out into the street and was almost run down by a two-horse chaise that came rattling round the corner. 'Bastards!' he screamed at it, shaking his fist. '*Baaaasssssstards!*' When the chaise had disappeared into the snow, however, he straightened himself up, tugged down his bloodstained waistcoat, and continued to cross the road with the weaving determination of the very drunk. His friends followed, weaving and swaying in the same way, so that the five of them looked as if they were making their way towards them across the deck of a ship.

Clement said to Beatrice, 'Get inside. I'll deal with these fools.'

But Beatrice clung to his cloak and begged him, 'Don't, papa! Leave them! It doesn't matter! They won't come inside, Mr Andrews won't allow them!"

'No,' said her father. 'I'll not have you terrorized by anyone, especially ruffians like these. You're my angel, remember? My angel and my saviour.'

Beatrice looked up at him and she could see that he was having difficulty focusing on her. It was then that she realized that he was almost as drunk as any of the porters.

'Papa, come inside, please!'

By now, however, the greasy-looking porter had come right up to them and was standing with his fists on his hips and his legs wide apart to keep his balance. The dried blood on his upper lip made him look as if he was wearing a black moustache.

'Do you know what I wanted?' he said, in a soft, slurred voice, which was all the more threatening for sounding so reasonable. 'A *kiss*, that was all I wanted! Nothing more! Just to show how highly I thought of her. I wasn't asking for a wapping.'

'You're foxed,' said Clement. 'Be on your way, you and your friends, before I have you locked up for menacing.'

'Do you know who I am?' the porter demanded.

'No, I don't, and I don't care, either.'

'Well, you should care, because they call me Sticker.'

'I told you, I have no interest whatever in who you are, or what they call you. Leave us be.'

Clement opened the door wider and tried to push Beatrice inside. At that moment, however, the porter took three clumsy steps forward and appeared to punch Clement in the chest, three times, and then to punch him twice in the stomach. Clement gasped, and lifted one arm as if to protect himself, but it was too late by then. He dropped on to the doorstep like a marionette with its strings suddenly cut.

'*Papa*!' cried Beatrice. She knelt down beside him, but as she did so the porter tilted forward and hit her, too, so that she fell back and struck her head against the door jamb. He was about to make a grab for her arm when the door was pulled opened wider and Mr Andrews appeared, brandishing a long mahogany cudgel.

'What in the *name* of Jesus!' he exclaimed, and then, '*You* again, you slubberdegullion! I thought I told you to stay well away! Robert, run for the constable!'

'Don't you dare to speak to *me* like that!' the porter retorted. 'Not unless *you* want sticking, like this fellow!'

He held up his right hand and waved it from side to side, and it was now that Beatrice could see that he was holding a bloodied clasp-knife, and that his fingers were glistening with blood, too. Although she was stunned from knocking her head, she managed to lean forward and drag back her father's cloak. His coat and waistcoat were soaked with warm blood, and his blood was beginning to run across the doorstep and into the snow, staining it pink.

'You've stabbed him!' she cried. 'You've stabbed him! Mr Andrews, he's stabbed my papa!'

'That's it!' said Mr Andrews. He stepped over Clement and confronted the porter, swinging his cudgel. 'My boy's gone for the constable and you'll be dangling for this!'

The porter's friends pulled at his clothing. One of them was so drunk that he fell sideways into the snow, and said, 'Shit!' The others said, 'Come on, Sticker, you've done it good and proper this time! Come on, leave it! Come on, before the horneys gets here!'

The porter hesitated for a moment, still defiantly holding up his clasp-knife, but his friends pulled at him again and he ostentatiously shut away the blade and followed them back across the street. The snow was falling so thickly now that they had all disappeared in seconds.

Beatrice was trying to turn her father over so that she could see his face. Mr Andrews knelt down beside her and said, 'Let's take him inside and see how bad he's been hurt. Duncan! Charlie! Give us a hand here, would you!'

Three men lifted Clement off the step and carried him into the bar, where they cleared a table and laid him down. His eyes were closed and his face was grey. Blood was sliding from the sides of his mouth and his breathing was shallow. Mr Andrews unbuttoned his waistcoat and his shirt, which was soaked with blood.

'Can somebody fetch me some rags?' Mr Andrews called out, and a middle-aged woman untied her apron and said, 'Here, Dicky, use this.' Beatrice recognized her as Molly, the wine-seller, who was usually walking up and down the streets with her basket of bottles.

There was so much blood leaking out of Clement's chest and stomach that Molly's apron was rapidly soaked, too. Beatrice could see that the porter had stabbed him in the chest – two shallow wounds in his breastbone, but a much deeper wound between his ribs – and had then stabbed him twice in the lower left side of his stomach. The wounds in his stomach were gaping like the mouths of dying fish and there seemed to be no way to stop them bleeding.

Beatrice was trembling with shock. She laid one hand on her father's forehead and said, 'Papa! Papa! Can you hear me, papa? It's Bea! It's your angel, papa!' But her father's eyes remained closed and only a single bubble of blood came out from between his lips.

Molly had brought some muslin rags from behind the bar and Mr Andrews folded them up and pressed them hard against Clement's chest wound.

'Come along, 'pothacree, don't give up on us now,' he said, but Beatrice caught him looking up at Molly and his expression was grim.

'Can't we take him to the hospital, Mr Andrews? He needs a surgeon, doesn't he? Somebody to sew up all of those cuts.'

Mr Andrews pressed his fingertips against the right side of Clement's neck to feel his pulse, then he bent his head close to Clement's face.

'I think it's too late for that, Mistress Bannister.'

'What?'

'I do believe your father's passed away. He won't need to go to St Barthomolew. He's on his way to see St Peter.'

Beatrice stared at her father and she knew with a dreadful sinking sensation that Mr Andrews was right. A subtle change had come over his face – an emptiness, which he had never had before, even in his deepest drunken sleeps. He might have been comatose with gin but he still had colour in his cheeks and he always looked as if he might open his eyes at any moment and say, 'My God! My head! Where am I?'

Not now, though. He had left her, and the body that was lying on this table was as dead as her mother in the chilly back room.

She backed away. As she did so, one of the men in the bar said, 'Look at you, girl! He got you, too! Didn't you feel it?'

Numbly, Beatrice turned around. 'What do you mean?' she said. 'What do you mean he got me, too? He only made me bang my head.'

But the man pointed to the floorboards where she had been standing, and there was a trail of blood. Panicking, Beatrice opened her coat and looked down at herself. There was no blood that she could see on her dark blue gown, but now that the man had brought it to her attention she could feel wetness on her legs and her petticoats. She lifted up the hem of her gown and saw that there were rivulets of blood running down her calves. She looked across at Molly and said, 'Look!' in the faintest of voices, and then she collapsed.

When she opened her eyes, she found she was lying on a bed in a small upstairs bedroom. Outside, it was beginning to grow dark, although it looked as if it had stopped snowing. There was a jug and a basin on a washstand on the opposite side of the room, and a woodcut of St Sebastian, the martyr, tied to a tree and bristling with arrows, his eyes rolled up towards the heavens.

She sat up. Her coat and her gown and petticoats had all been hung over the back of a chair, and she was wearing nothing but her shift and corset, although she was covered with a thick knitted blanket. She lifted the blanket and saw that her shift was stained with blood, although it had dried now. So the porter *had* stabbed her. He must have been holding his clasp-knife in his hand when he pushed her. He couldn't have cut her too badly, however, because she didn't seem to be bleeding any longer.

He had killed her father, though. Her father was actually dead. She lay back and covered her face with her hands, although for some reason she couldn't cry. She felt completely dry, as if she had no tears left.

She was still lying there when she heard footsteps coming upstairs and then a knock at the door, although it was open.

She stayed where she was, with her face still covered. She didn't want the next part of her life to start happening, not just yet.

'How are you feeling, Bea?' asked a kindly woman's voice. 'You look just like one of them saints lying on a tomb.'

Beatrice took her hands away from her face. Molly had her head tilted to one side and was smiling at her sympathetically.

'We're all so sorry about your dear papa. Such a good man. Always had time to listen if you was sick with some pox or other, and always ready to give you a cordial even if you didn't have the chink for it.'

She sat down on the side of the bed. She had a large wart on her upper lip and very thick eyebrows. She took hold of Beatrice's hand and said, 'Dicky Andrews says he'll help with all the arrangements, if you want him to. But you probably have relatives, don't you? Aunts and uncles, someone you can turn to. All we want you to know, darling, is that you won't be left to do everything on your own.'

Beatrice didn't know what to say. She still couldn't cry, but she felt so exhausted that she couldn't even find the words to tell Molly why she and her father had come to The Fortune, and that her mother's body was lying in the back room. She was so tired that she could have closed her eyes and fallen asleep forever. At least if she did that she would see her parents again.

'The constables came,' said Molly. 'We told them what happened, and who done it. They know the fellow, so they'll probably grab him sooner or later. He'll be dancing on nothing when he does.'

'I can't work out where he cut me,' said Beatrice, lifting up the blanket again.

'Well, you'll forgive me, darling, but I took the liberty of looking, and he didn't.'

'But where did all this blood come from?.'

Molly squeezed her hand. 'You lost your mama, didn't you, so you had nobody to tell you. But what it is, you've started your flow.'

Beatrice frowned at her. She didn't understand.

'You've fallen off the roof,' said Molly. 'You've had a visit from auntie.'

'What?'

'You're a woman now, Bea, my darling, in more ways than one.'

Seven

'As much as I would like to, Beatrice my dear, I simply cannot take care of you,' said her Aunt Felicity. 'Our house is full to capacity already, what with my brother's family now that he is bankrupt, and my father who is in his dotage. I would, believe me, if only I had the room, but I believe you will be far more comfortable with your cousin Sarah in Birmingham.'

Beatrice said nothing. She was standing in the parlour in front of the fire, which had burned low now so that it was reduced to hillocks of hot white ashes. Apart from Aunt Felicity the funeral guests had all left. There were glasses and plates to be washed and dried and put away, and the floor to be swept, and then she didn't know what she would do, except lock the front door and climb the stairs to bed, like she used to do when her father had drunk too much and dropped off to sleep in his armchair.

Aunt Felicity's chaise was waiting outside in the early afternoon gloom, ready to take her back to her house on Blackheath, south of the river. She was anxious not to leave her return too late because of the snafflers who came out on the road when it began to grow dark.

'You will have to sell the business,' she said. 'It should fetch a fair amount of money, though, and that will pay for your fare to Birmingham and cater for your needs for quite some time to come. I have a lawyer friend at Lincoln's Inn, Mr Lacey, whose clerks can manage the sale for you.'

'Thank you, Aunt Felicity,' said Beatrice. 'You've been very kind to me.'

She had met her cousin Sarah Minchin only once before. Sarah had come down from Birmingham to stay with them when Beatrice was seven or eight years old, and she remembered her as a tall, sharp-nosed woman who had seemed to find everything in life disagreeable – her bed, the food that Beatrice's mother had served her, the smell of the London streets, the weather, even the dresses that Beatrice had been wearing.

'A young girl should always look obedient and demure,' she had said of a red pinafore that Beatrice's mother had made for her. Beatrice had had no idea what 'demure' meant, but she had assumed it meant sour-faced, like cousin Sarah.

When Aunt Felicity had left Beatrice went into the darkened shop and looked around at all the gleaming bottles arranged on the shelves. It was so silent. The smell of herbs and spices permeated everything, even the wooden counter. She found it almost impossible to believe that her father was dead and that her life here was all over. She had always imagined that she would be working with him until he retired, and that the Society of Apothecaries would accept her as a member, even though she was a girl, and that one day she would be running the business herself.

Her father had taught her so well that she believed she could almost run the business now, on her own, but she knew that it was impossible.

She went back into the parlour and started to clear up. Only fifteen mourners had come to the funeral because the snow had made it so difficult to send letters to all of his old friends and acquaintances who might have wanted to pay their respects, and equally difficult for any of them to travel here. He had been laid to rest in the crypt of St James's, next to her mother, whose body had been retrieved by the constables from The Fortune of War.

As she carried a candle up the narrow stairs to her bedroom she stopped halfway and started to sob. She stood there, gripping the banister rail, with tears running down her cheeks, trying to swallow her grief and almost choking on it.

In a city of more than seven hundred thousand people, she had never felt so alone in her life.

Cousin Sarah was there to meet her when the stage chaise arrived mid-afternoon at the Rose Inn in Birmingham. It was a very cold day, but bright, and the coach had made good time from Selly, which had been their last stop for refreshment and changing horses.

A broken spring had held them up the day before at Banbury, but it had taken them only three days to cover the hundred and twenty miles from London. Beatrice had been able to afford fivepence for an inside seat, and she had been glad of that, especially on their first day, when they had been overtaken by a ferocious hailstorm as they passed through Watford and the passengers on the roof had been chilled and soaked through in spite of their heavy cloaks.

Beatrice didn't recognize cousin Sarah at first, not until she came pushing her way through the crowd in the courtyard, calling out, 'Beatrice! Beatrice! *Here*, you silly girl! *Here*!' as if she were calling a pet dog.

Cousin Sarah was not nearly as tall as Beatrice remembered her – in fact, she seemed tiny and very thin. Under her plain black bonnet she had a face like a ferret, with close-together eyes and protruding front teeth. She was wearing a dark grey cape and grey suede gloves.

'Thank goodness you're on time!' she exclaimed. 'I thought I might catch my death if I had to wait out here any longer! My goodness, girl, you look appallingly *wan*! You're not *sickening* for something, are you?'

'I'm just tired,' said Beatrice. Although cousin Sarah was so prickly she found it an unexpected relief after the journey to be met by somebody who cared about her, and she was very close to bursting into tears again.

The postilion heaved down her brown leather trunk from the roof of the coach and a toothless porter dragged it over to her, grinning. 'Jeremy!' snapped cousin Sarah, turning around. 'Jeremy, where are you? That *boy*!'

A young man of about seventeen appeared from out of the crowd, wearing a thick bottle-green coat and a black cocked hat. He was tall and well-built, with wavy brown hair that reached almost down to his shoulders. Beatrice thought he was quite handsome, although his lips were rather full and red, as if he had been illicitly eating strawberries, and his eyes were a little sly.

'This is my youngest son, Jeremy, your first cousin once removed,' said cousin Sarah. 'Jeremy, this is Beatrice, my dear late Clement's girl, and you must make her feel at home.'

Jeremy lifted his hat and gave Beatrice a deep mock-bow. 'You're welcome to Birmingham, Beatrice,' he told her. 'I hope you're happy here. You'll find it exceedingly dull after London, I expect, but we'll do our best to keep you amused.'

'Jeremy, behave yourself,' snapped cousin Sarah. 'The poor girl is recently bereaved and the *last* thing she is looking for is amusement.'

They left the courtyard and went out to the road where their carriage was waiting, a plain maroon chaise with a worn-out leather top. Two tired-looking horses stood between the shafts and up on the box sat an elderly coachman with a tall hat and mutton-chop whiskers who looked even more exhausted than the horses. Jeremy lifted Beatrice's trunk on to the back and they all climbed in.

'Wup,' said the coachman, with a desultory shake of the reins, and the horses went shambling off.

'You've brought only this one piece of luggage?' asked cousin Sarah.

'Aunt Felicity is sending more on,' Beatrice told her. 'The rest of my clothes, and all of my father's books and his laboratory equipment.'

'What on *earth* would you want those for?'

'I could mix medicines for us, whenever we have need of them.'

'*You*? The very thought! You're only a child!'

Beatrice thought of what Molly had said to her, about becoming a woman, but she didn't like to argue. Instead, she said, 'Papa showed me how to make all kinds of tonics and cordials and pills, for almost any ailment you could think of. And how to make magic tricks, like candles that you can never snuff out, no matter how hard you blow on them, and little pieces of paper that can dance by themselves.'

Cousin Sarah blinked at her disapprovingly. 'You're newly orphaned, Beatrice. I hardly think that frivolities like that are very becoming during your period of mourning. Or, indeed, *ever.*'

Beatrice couldn't help thinking that her father would have loved her to carry on with his 'mysteries', especially if they cheered her up. But she turned her head away and said nothing. Even if she was a child, she was old enough to accept that it was very generous of cousin Sarah to have offered to take care of her. More than that, she knew that she had absolutely nowhere else to go.

Birmingham seemed so small to Beatrice after London, but it was very much cleaner. Although every chimney around the town was smoking furiously, a strong wind was blowing from the high snow-covered moors to the west, so that the air smelled quite fresh. The main street was roughly cobbled and very steep, crowded with market stalls and lined on both sides with shops and houses. The pavements were much wider than in the City, and better swept, but Beatrice couldn't help noticing that most of the shoppers who were walking up and down them were very unfashionably dressed. Most of the men still wore full wigs and ankle-length coats, and only a few of the women wore wide-hooped farthingales.

Their labouring horses pulled them slowly uphill, with the coachman occasionally wheezing '*Wup! Wup!*' to them, without much optimism. They reached High Town and then turned up towards Pinfold Street where cousin Sarah lived. As they turned, she pointed out a grand baroque church on the crest of the hill, built in gleaming white limestone. 'That is where we worship, Beatrice. St Philip's. You will be able to say prayers there for your poor papa.'

Beatrice gave her a fleeting smile, although she didn't need to go to church to say prayers for her father. She spoke to him all the time, wherever she was, inside her head – and he spoke back to her. She could still hear his voice, and hear him laugh.

They drew up outside cousin Sarah's three-storey house, in the middle of a terrace of five brick-fronted houses which faced directly on to the street.

'Here,' said cousin Sarah, as Jeremy helped them down from the carriage. 'This will be your home now, Beatrice, for the rest of your life.'

Although the house looked narrow and nondescript from the outside, it was spacious inside, with high ceilings and tall windows that looked out over a small apple orchard at the back. Cousin Sarah showed Beatrice the parlour, with its formal furniture and chiming ormolu clock and slightly distorting mirror over the fireplace. Then she took her into the dining room, with its shiny mahogany table and empty shield-back chairs, and finally into the kitchen, where a fat, black-haired woman in a long white apron was perspiring freely and boiling up a leg of mutton in a large black pot.

'This is Elizabeth,' said cousin Sarah. 'Elizabeth, this is Beatrice. I am sure the poor girl must be hungry after her journey. Perhaps you would cut her some gammon, and some slices of bread, and pickled onions.'

Elizabeth lifted up her apron and buried her face in it to mop up the perspiration. When she dropped it again she said, 'I've yet to start the fish soup, Mrs Minchin.'

'You'll manage, Elizabeth,' cousin Sarah replied, although Beatrice thought that it sounded more like an order than an expression of confidence. 'Besides, when she is rested, and changed, Beatrice will assist you. Our scullery maid, Jane, is away this week in Edgbaston for her mother's funeral, and our housemaid, Agnes, is out shopping. You can peel potatoes, can't you, Beatrice? And your mama must have shown you how to set a table.'

They left the kitchen. Beatrice glanced back and saw Elizabeth scowling as she ladled the scum with a slotted spoon from the surface of the boiling mutton. 'Come along, Beatrice,' said cousin Sarah. 'I will show you to your room.'

They climbed the main staircase until they reached the landing. Cousin Sarah touched the tip of her finger to her lips and then pointed to the door on the left-hand side. 'That is Roderick's room. We are always very quiet when we go past Roderick's room.'

She paused, and when she saw that Beatrice didn't understand what she was talking about, she said, 'Roderick, my husband. Your cousin-in-law. Not long after Jeremy was born he was kicked in the head by a horse and since then he has suffered from a very *unpredictable* demeanour. So we do our best not to disturb him.'

'I see,' said Beatrice, although she couldn't imagine what cousin Sarah meant by 'a very *unpredictable* demeanour'.

They climbed another staircase, steeper and narrower. On the topmost floor there were two large bedrooms and a much smaller room, facing the back of the house.

'Oliver's room and Charles's room,' said cousin Sarah, opening the doors to both the larger rooms. 'They are away at the moment, Oliver in India and Charles at university.' She opened the door to the smaller room. 'This will be where *you* live, Beatrice.'

There was just enough space in this room for a single wooden bed with a blue patchwork quilt, while under the window stood a pine table with a jug and a basin on it, for washing. The only other furniture was a small bow-fronted wardrobe, with two drawers underneath. There wasn't even a chair.

On the wall beside the bed hung a framed engraving of a bearded man in a long blue cloak. 'St Philip,' said cousin Sarah. 'A great worker of miracles. Did you know that he was crucified upside down? But he still kept on preaching, even as he hung there.'

At that moment, Jeremy came up the stairs, lugging Beatrice's trunk. It bumped loudly on every tread and cousin Sarah hissed, '*Ssshh*! We don't want your father to have one of his fits.'

Jeremy said, 'He's asleep, mother. I looked in on him.'

'All the same, I don't want you waking him up. At the moment I have quite enough to cope with.'

Jeremy left the trunk on the landing and went back downstairs, deliberately whistling as he went.

'That boy,' said cousin Sarah. 'He'll be the death of me one day.' She looked around the room. 'I'll leave you to unpack, then. Once you've done that, come down to the kitchen and help Elizabeth. We have seven for dinner tonight, from the parish council, and she always gets herself into such a panic when she has to cook for more than four.'

She went to the door, but then she stopped and said, 'Before I forget . . . the proceeds.'

Beatrice frowned at her. 'What proceeds?'

'The proceeds from the sale of your father's business. Felicity told me that you realized quite a reasonable sum. Two hundred and forty-three guineas, I believe, after your lawyers and auctioneers had both been paid.'

'Yes,' said Beatrice.

'You brought the money with you, I assume?'

'Yes. Aunt Felicity said that you would have a strongbox to keep it safe.'

'Well, yes, because I will depend on it to pay for your board and lodging, not to mention your clothing and any other incidental expenses that may arise in the coming years.'

'I'll bring it down for you, cousin Sarah, so soon as I've changed.'

Cousin Sarah gave her a ferrety smile. 'Don't be too long, then. And put on something plain, with an apron. I don't care

for frivolous dress in this house, and besides, you have work
to do.'

Before she left she took the key out of the door and held it
up. 'In case of fire,' she said, and dropped it into her pocket.
'Wouldn't want to have you locked in here, would we, with
your bed ablaze, and us unable to get in to save you?'

That evening, after she had bid goodnight to the last of her
dinner guests, cousin Sarah came downstairs into the kitchen.
She was wearing a plain blue satin round gown and her hair
was tightly braided.

In the scullery, Beatrice and Agnes, the housemaid, were
already starting to wash the plates and cutlery, while Elizabeth,
the cook, was sitting at the table, scouring her pots as if she
had a grudge against them.

Agnes, when she had returned from shopping that afternoon,
had turned out to be a small, busy girl with a large bosom
and a protruding bottom and a round face with a button nose
and two of her front teeth missing. She got on with her work
without any fuss, and spoke in a very matter-of-fact way, but
her Birmingham accent was so thick that Beatrice had difficulty
understanding what she was talking about.

'Burt-triss, joos bring me the plights from the tie-bull, would
you?' she asked, as she tipped an enamel jug of hot water into
the sink.

Cousin Sarah stood watching them for a while and then she
said, 'I'm retiring now. I will see you in the morning, Beatrice
– I hope you sleep well. Agnes – my tea at half-past six, please.
I have much to do tomorrow. Elizabeth, the caper sauce was
very thin, and the Reverend Bute had a fish bone in his soup
which almost choked him.'

Elizabeth said nothing, but banged down her iron pot.

'Goodnight, cousin Sarah,' said Beatrice. 'And thank you.'

Cousin Sarah gave her a thin, self-satisfied smile, as if Beatrice had complimented her for her saintliness, and then left them to finish clearing up. It was past nine o'clock now and Beatrice was feeling deeply weary. Three days of being jostled in a coach, jammed in with five other people, had made her ache all over, especially her back.

'You go on oop now, Burt-triss,' said Agnes, as Beatrice started to dry the soup tureen. 'Me and Elizabeth can finish the rest. Look at you, girl, you're worn ragged.'

Agnes gave her a lighted candle and Beatrice tiredly climbed the stairs to her bedroom. She paused on the first landing and listened. From Roderick's room came harsh, irregular snoring, but on the other side she heard cousin Sarah's voice, speaking very low and very fast, as if she were giving instructions to somebody in a hurry.

Beatrice tiptoed over to cousin Sarah's door and leaned close to it in an effort to make out what she was saying. All she heard, though, was, '. . . *name of the Father, and of the Son, and of the Holy Spirit, amen.*' This was followed by the creaking sound of cousin Sarah climbing into bed.

Beatrice went up to her own room. When she opened the door she found that it was so cold in there that she could see her breath, and so dark outside that she could see her reflection in the blackness of the window, a pale ghost staring in at her. She didn't undress before she got into bed, although she pulled off her mob cap and unbuckled her shoes and loosened the strings of her corset. She buried herself in the patchwork quilt and lay there, huddled up, shivering, too cold even to cry. The flannelette sheets were rough and damp, as if they hadn't been dried properly after washing.

For a while she could still hear clattering echoes from the kitchen downstairs, but after twenty minutes or so the house became silent and she fell asleep.

She dreamed that she was back in the corner of the chaise as it jolted and bumped its way towards Banbury. She was almost overwhelmed by the huge hooped gown of the woman sitting next to her, and the bony knees of the man sitting opposite kept jabbing into hers. Outside, the landscape was beginning to grow dark and a few large flakes of snow were tumbling down. In the distance she could see leafless elm trees, with inky crows perched in them.

The woman turned to her and it was Molly, from The Fortune of War. She winked at Beatrice and said, 'You've fallen off the roof, my darling. Fallen off the roof.'

The next moment there was a juddering crash and her bedroom was suddenly filled with light and dancing shadows. She twisted around in her quilt and sat up in bed, her heart beating hard. For a few seconds, she couldn't work out if she was still dreaming or if this was real.

Standing in her bedroom doorway, holding a long candle in his hand, was a wild-looking man, completely naked. His hair was as bouffant and grey as a dandelion-clock, and his eyes were glittering and deep-set under his forehead. He was bony and emaciated, except for his stomach, which was so swollen that his navel protruded. He was leaning forward and grasping his erect penis tightly, as if he were afraid that if he let go of it he would lose his balance and fall over.

'Well! Well! The Lord and all of his seraphic host be praised!' he exclaimed, his eyebrows rising and falling suggestively with every word. 'My dearest Sarah told me that we would be having a young girl for a house-guest! But she didn't tell me how comely you would be!'

He took one staggering step towards her, and then another.

'Throw back your coverlet, my dear, and let a frozen fellow feel the warmth of your bed and your body!'

Beatrice shrank away from him, pulling her quilt up to her neck. He stood by the side of her bed, candle in one hand and penis in the other, and ostentatiously licked his lips.

'We shall have such a night together, you and me!' he told her. 'You shall give me children, to be my obedient heirs, and I can dispossess those treacherous sons of mine who seek to rob me of my fortune!'

Beatrice said, '*Cousin Sarah,*' but she was so frightened that she could only manage a whisper. She cleared her throat as the wild man took another step nearer and was about to shout out, 'Cousin Sarah!' when Jeremy appeared in the doorway, with his own candle-holder raised. He was wearing a nightcap and a long white nightshirt.

'*Father*!' he snapped, as if he were talking to a disobedient child. 'What are you doing in here? Go back to your bed this instant!'

The wild man cried out, 'Wooo!' and pivoted around, startled, letting his candle fall to the floor. He nearly fell over sideways, but Jeremy seized his scrawny arm and pushed him back towards the door.

'Quick, Bea! *Beatrice*! The candle!' he said. Beatrice climbed out of bed and picked it up, just as the proddy rug was beginning to smoulder.

Jeremy pulled and pushed Roderick downstairs. All the way down, Roderick made a high keening sound in the back of his throat, more like a disobedient dog than a man, and when he had returned him to his room, Jeremy slammed his door quite loudly. None of this seemed to disturb cousin Sarah, however – or else she was used to it. Beatrice sat on the side of her bed holding the candle until she heard Jeremy coming back upstairs.

'I'm *so* sorry for that!' he told her. 'He didn't hurt you, did he? His mind has gone completely.'

'I'm all right,' said Beatrice, trying to sound brave, although she was shivering from cold and shock.

Jeremy sat down on the bed next to her. 'If he ever bothers you again, you must cry out for me immediately. I'll always come at once. You should really lock your door at night.'

'Your mother took the key away. She said it was too much of a risk to lock the door, in case of fire.'

'Oh, she has a terror of that. Her own parents died in a fire when she was young. She saw them beating at their window with their hair alight and there was nothing she could do to save them.'

'That's terrible!'

'Well . . . she was taken in afterwards by her aunt, which is why she felt duty-bound to take *you* in. She has little natural sympathy for other people, Bea, I know that, but she strongly believes in doing her Christian duty.'

Jeremy put his arm around her shoulders and said, 'There... are you feeling better now? I'll tell you what I'll do, I'll bring you a wooden wedge that you can push under the bottom of your door at night so that father can't get in.'

'Thank you,' said Beatrice. 'But what if there *is* a fire?'

'I'll kick the door open and rescue you, don't you worry about that.'

Jeremy took the candle-holder from her and she climbed back into bed.

'Sleep well, Bea,' he said, with a smile. 'You and me, we're going to be great friends, you wait and see.'

He leaned forward and kissed her on the forehead. Then he stood up and left the room, quietly closing the door behind him. Beatrice pulled the blankets tightly around her and lay in the darkness with her eyes open. She almost wished that she believed in ghosts, so that she could feel her mother bend over her as she always used to.

'*Goodnight, mama,*' she whispered. '*Goodnight, papa.*'

But there was no answer, and outside the city of Birmingham was silent except for somebody drunkenly singing in the street.

Eight

She first saw Francis on the morning of 17 March, as they returned from the Sunday morning service at St Philip's – Beatrice and Jeremy walking in front, while cousin Sarah followed a few steps behind with Mrs Shelley, their widowed neighbour, whose stiff black skirts bustled noisily on the pavement when she walked and who never stopped talking about how unfortunate she was.

'Why did the Lord pick on *me*, of all people? What did I ever do to deserve such wretchedness?'

It was a chilly morning but the sky was clear, apart from a long thin streak of cirrus cloud, and already the plane trees were budding green.

'You fell asleep in the sermon,' said Jeremy.

'I did not,' Beatrice retorted. 'I simply closed my eyes so that I could give all of my attention to what the Reverend Bute was saying instead of watching you pulling all those foolish faces at me.'

'What was it about, then, the sermon?'

Beatrice tilted up her nose and didn't reply.

'Go on, then,' Jeremy persisted, 'if you were concentrating your mind so hard, what was it about?'

'It was about shepherds.'

'No, it wasn't. It was about lepers.'

'Well, there's an echo in that church. Lepers, shepherds. Shepherds, lepers. They both sound nearly the same.'

'They don't at all. And shepherds' fingers don't fall off. Well – perhaps in the winter, if they get frostbite.'

They rounded the corner into Bell Street, and as they did so they found that a party of twenty or thirty people was obstructing the pavement – men, women and children. They had all just come out of a large house overlooking the main market square and they were talking and laughing and shaking hands. Beatrice thought she had never seen people look so cheerful on a Sunday morning. Perhaps it was because they hadn't been to St Philip's and had to sit through the Reverend Bute's interminable sermon about lepers.

'He put his hand inside his cloak, and lo! when he pulled it out, it was leprous like snow. And God said, "Put your hand back inside your cloak," and lo! when he pulled it out a second time, it was restored like the rest of his flesh.'

Beatrice and Jeremy had to walk around these people, into the road, and Beatrice could hear cousin Sarah tutting loudly behind her and saying, 'Really! They have no consideration for the church, and no consideration for others, either.'

One of the men heard her, because he stepped aside to let cousin Sarah pass and said, 'My deepest apologies, Mistress Minchin.'

Beatrice turned around, and when she did so she became aware of a tall young boy standing next to the man who had just apologized. He was staring at her, this boy, as if he knew who she was and exactly what she was doing here. Not only that, he looked as if he was upset because she hadn't chosen to acknowledge him. He was dark-haired and very thin, and dressed entirely in black except for the tight white knotted handkerchief around his neck. Beatrice thought he was really quite handsome, but very gangly, as if his arms and legs had suddenly grown longer overnight but his body hadn't yet caught up with them. It was the expression in his eyes, though, that really caught her attention. Saintly, almost. She could almost believe that he understood everything she was feeling: how lonely she was, how much she was grieving for her mama and papa, and yet how hard she was trying to make the best of her new life here in Birmingham with cousin Sarah.

'Who was that?' she asked cousin Sarah, looking back over her shoulder.

'Geoffrey Scarlet,' she snapped. 'He owns the bookshop in the High Street and lives over the Swan Tavern. He publishes a weekly newspaper, the *Birmingham Journal*. Tittle-tattle, most of it.'

'I meant that boy who was with him.'

'Don't turn round, girl. We don't want them to think that we have the slightest interest in them – which, of course, we don't. They're Nonconformists. That means they don't agree with the traditions of the church, or respect its authority. There's far too many of them in Birmingham. It's a *hotbed*. We have more Quakers than you can shake a stick at, and Radical Dissenters, too. I can't think what the world is coming to.'

Beatrice looked over her shoulder again. She could see that the boy had stepped out into the road in order to watch her as she walked up the street.

'Do you know his name?' she asked cousin Sarah.

'Whose name? What are you talking about?'

'The boy.'

'I said don't turn round! He's Geoffrey Scarlet's son, Francis. Why on earth would you want to know that?'

'She's smitten!' hooted Jeremy. Then, to Beatrice, 'You are

smitten, aren't you? Smitten with Francis Scarlet! Of all the noddies!'

'Of course I'm not,' said Beatrice. 'He did stare so, that's all, and I was wondering why.'

Jeremy tapped the side of his nose with his finger and winked. 'Perhaps *he's* smitten with *you*, young Bea! Not that I'd wish you such bad luck!'

Over the months that passed, Beatrice saw Francis almost every Sunday. As soon as he saw her walking home from St Philip's after communion he would step out of the crowd of Nonconformist worshippers on the corner of Bell Street and stare at her until she reached Lea Lane. She would glance back at him now and again, over her shoulder, and give him a quick, coy smile.

Cousin Sarah would catch Beatrice glancing behind her and would turn round herself, to see what she was looking at.

'Beatrice? That Scarlet boy isn't giving you the eye again, is he?'

'I'll go back and lamp him, if you like,' said Jeremy, turning round, too.

'Oh, Jeremy, don't be foolish!' Beatrice told him. 'I was turning round because I couldn't hear Mrs Shelley talking to your mother and I thought we might have left them behind.'

'Now then, Beatrice!' cousin Sarah admonished her. 'There's no call for cheek!'

Now and again, Beatrice saw Francis in the town, too. He was always with his father, or his mother, or one of his sisters, so they couldn't stop to talk to each other. Beatrice usually had Jeremy with her, too. She was beginning to like Jeremy, but he hardly ever left her alone. If cousin Sarah sent her to the grocer's for salt, or butter, or down to the butcher's for pig's liver, Jeremy would insist on coming with her. He would even carry her basket, ignoring the derisive hoots of his friends. 'Going shopping, Jere-*mary*?'

Wherever she was in the house, upstairs or downstairs, he always seemed to be there, too, offering to help her with whatever she was doing, whether it was cleaning the cutlery or changing the beds or shaking out the rugs. Either that, or he was simply watching her.

He was funny, though, and most of the time he was cheerful. He showed her how to play the Game of Goose, on a coloured board with sixty-three squares.

'If you land on a goose, you'll be rich and successful,' he told her. 'If you land in a bad place, like an alehouse, then you'll be miserable and poor. Like me, I always end up in the alehouse.'

'Oh, don't say that,' said Beatrice.

Jeremy shrugged and smiled. 'When you've been living here with my mother long enough you'll probably come and join me. Better to be drunk than downtrodden.'

One morning in mid-July, when cousin Sarah was attending a church meeting, and Agnes was out in the garden hanging up the washing, Beatrice took the key from the hook in the kitchen and went down to the cellar. All her father's equipment had been stored down there – his jars of dried spices and glass retorts and bottles of poison and vitriol – but it was his notebooks that Beatrice was looking for.

She found them in a wooden box at the very back of the cellar, wrapped in sacking. There were five books in all, bound in brown leather, and each of them was crowded with her father's neat, tiny writing. He had described in detail all the preparations that he had mixed up for hectic fever or milk leg or *lupus vulgaris*. Not only that, he had written up all of his 'mysteries', his scientific experiments, such as making dead mice run across the room, or chicken feathers spontaneously catch fire, or a person's hair rise up from their head as if they had seen a ghost.

She took the notebooks up to her room and hid them under her bed, but almost every night she took one out and read it until she was too tired to read any more, or cousin Sarah came halfway up the stairs and called out, 'Beatrice! Put out that light at once and go to sleep!'

When she read her father's words she could almost hear him talking to her, and hear him laugh the way he had done when he surprised her with one of his magic tricks. She touched the lines that he had written with her fingertips and whispered, 'I love you, papa, wherever you are.'

One year passed, and then another, and another. As time went by, Beatrice took over more and more of the domestic chores and by the time she reached her fifteenth birthday cousin Sarah often left her in charge of the whole household while she went to visit her sister or her friends, often for two or three days at a time.

Just before Christmas that year Agnes became pregnant by the son of a local carter, although she told nobody but Beatrice. She begged Beatrice for pennyroyal oil from her father's stores, in order to bring on a miscarriage, but Beatrice refused to let her have it. She knew from her father's books that a pregnant prostitute from Bow had once asked him for pennyroyal oil. Even though she had taken only two small spoonfuls of it, it had been enough to poison her and she had died. Agnes kept on begging her, but Beatrice continued to say no, and in the end Agnes fell on the frozen cobbles in the market and lost the baby naturally.

Beatrice continued to see Francis quite often, although they still hadn't had had the opportunity to speak to one another. Strangely, it didn't seem to matter. They would exchange in passing looks that seemed to Beatrice to convey everything they needed to know about each other. There was always an expression on Francis's face that said, 'One day, we will be together, you and me, but I can wait for that day.'

Jeremy was sent off to London to study law under an old friend of his father's at Lincoln's Inn. However, he returned less than six months later, with a letter from his father's friend saying that 'the process of law should not be regarded, as Jeremy regards it, as an entertainment on a par with bear-baiting'.

Early one evening in May, after a long day of baking bread and boiling laundry and shaking out rugs, Beatrice wearily climbed up the stairs to her bedroom to wash and to change her clothes for supper. She undressed, hanging up her gown and laying her petticoats on the bed. She filled up her china basin with water from the jug, but before she washed she went to the window and looked down at the garden and the apple orchard.

The sun was sinking, but it had filled the whole of the garden with golden light, so that it looked like the Garden of Eden in the hand-coloured print that hung on the wall in the hallway. And here she was, standing by the window with the sun shining on her skin, as naked as Eve.

She wondered if she would ever be happy – as happy as she had been with her father and mother – or whether her life would continue to be an endless succession of daily chores and duties, with church on Sundays. Standing in the sunlight, though, she had a feeling that her future was calling her and that somewhere beyond the hills to the west, where the sun was sinking, she would find the happiness that she had lost.

It was then that she heard a creaking sound behind her. She turned around and saw that while she had been staring out of the window, her bedroom door had been opened, and Jeremy was standing on the landing outside, looking at her.

She seized her petticoats from the bed and bunched them up to her neck to cover herself, feeling her cheeks flushing hot.

'Jeremy! What are you doing? Stop staring at me! Go away!'

Jeremy was clearly embarrassed that she had caught him out, but he shrugged and gave her a lopsided smile and said, 'What does it matter? We're going to be married soon anyway.'

'Who says we're going to be married?'

'My mother, of course. She has your life all mapped for you. What do you think she's going to do now that she's getting old? She'll be forty-three next Easter! She'll need somebody to run the house for her, and to give her heirs. She didn't take you in out of the goodness of her heart, you know.'

'I'm not going to marry *you*!'

'Then who? Who would you find to take any interest in you, apart from me?'

Beatrice didn't answer, but closed her door and pushed the wooden wedge underneath it. She waited, listening, but after a while she heard Jeremy going back downstairs.

She turned back to the window. The sunlight had gone now and the sky was growing dusky. '*Who would take an interest in you?*' Jeremy had asked her, and she couldn't help thinking of Francis and the way he looked at her when they passed each other in the street.

Nine

Cousin Sarah called out, 'Elizabeth! Agnes! Jenks! I want you all in here right away! You too, Beatrice!'

They gathered in the dining room. It was raining outside, quite hard, and Beatrice could hear the rain rattling through the branches of the apple trees. It was gloomy, too, for an early April afternoon.

On the polished dining table stood a tall glass confectionery jar half filled with tarnished brown coins, pennies and farthings, and a few silver sixpences. Cousin Sarah was standing on the opposite side of the table with her arms folded and her lips tightly pursed.

Beatrice had been brushing cobwebs off the bedroom ceilings and she was still holding her ostrich-feather duster. Agnes stood next to her, her sleeves rolled up and her forearms reddened halfway up to her elbows from plunging them into the washtub. Behind them stood Elizabeth, smelling of sweat and suet, and Jenks, a young man who did odd jobs around the house, dug the garden and tended the horses. Jenks kept swivelling his eyes around the dining room and sniffing. He was the oldest son of one of the local metalworkers, but his father had considered him too much of a liability to be working with molten iron and so had found him employment with Sarah Minchin.

Beatrice could see all of them in the slightly distorted mirror behind cousin Sarah's back, and somehow the subtle flaws in the glass made them look like strangers pretending to be them.

'I am deeply disappointed in one of you,' said cousin Sarah. 'All of you must be aware that I collect coins in this jar, which I donate every Easter to the destitute in St Philip's parish. What you may *not* know is that I count them at the end of each week, after our Sunday meal.'

They glanced at one another sideways. Jenks was probably the only one of them who couldn't guess what cousin Sarah was going to say next.

She picked up the jar and gave it a single sharp shake. 'When I counted the contents of this jar last Sunday, it contained two pounds seven shillings and sixpence. When I counted them today, I found that I had only two pounds one shilling and twopence. Since I do not believe that coins can spontaneously evaporate, or that this house is haunted by thievish spirits, I have no option but to conclude that one of you has been stealing. Six shillings and fourpence, to be exact. Six shillings and fourpence! And what would any of you do with such a sum of money?'

Agnes instantly put up her hand. 'If you please, Mrs Minchin, it weren't me what took it.'

'Oh, no? So why are you in such a rush to deny it?'

'Because I don't want you believing it might have been me, because it weren't.'

'So who else could it have been? It must have been one of you. That money didn't disappear by magic. Elizabeth? Didn't I hear you complaining that you needed new shoes? Six shillings and fourpence! That would buy you a good stout pair of shoes, wouldn't you agree?'

'Yes,' said Elizabeth. 'But I didn't steal your money, ma'am, and I will swear to that on the Holy Bible.'

'Jenks!' snapped cousin Sarah. Jenks blinked at her and cupped his left hand around his ear to show her that he was listening.

'Have you been dipping your hand into my jar of coins, young man?'

Jenks frowned at his hand, turning it this way and that. It was obvious that he didn't understand what she meant.

'Have you taken any of my money, Jenks? Have you been helping yourself from out of this jar?'

Jenks vigorously shook his head. 'No, Mrs Chimney. Not me.'

'*Minchin*,' cousin Sarah corrected him, but Beatrice could tell by the way she closed her eyes that this wasn't the first time, and wouldn't be the last.

Then cousin Sarah said, 'Well! Since none of you will confess to taking my money, but one of you must have done, then all of you will have to pay it back. Elizabeth, Agnes, Jenks – you will each have threepence deducted from your weekly wages until the loss is made up, and from you, Beatrice, I will take a shilling from the proceeds of your father's business.'

'But *I* didn't steal any of your money, cousin Sarah!' Beatrice protested. 'Why should I have stolen it, when I have so much money of my own?'

'You do *not* have money of your own, Beatrice. The proceeds from your father's business are under my trusteeship now, to recompense me for taking care of you, and believe me, that money will not last forever. What then? Will I throw you out on to the street? Of course not.'

'But I still didn't take any money out of your jar!'

Cousin Sarah shrugged. 'I believe that you probably didn't, my dear. But if the true culprit refuses to come forward and confess, what choice do I have? Why should the poor and the hungry of this parish have to suffer because one of you is so dishonest? Why should *they* go without shoes, or food for that matter? Goodness me, six shillings and fourpence would buy them three whole pigs, or a dozen rabbits.'

Elizabeth said, 'Threepence a week, ma'am? I have my own family to feed.'

'I'm sorry, Elizabeth, but my mind is made up. Or would you rather I called for a bailiff? Please get back to your chores, all of you. If any of you wish to come to me privately and admit that you stole my money, you may do so at any time. In the spirit of Christian charity I will not have you arrested, but I will expect you to return it.'

They left the dining room and went downstairs to the kitchen. Elizabeth was shaking with anger. 'I have never in my life done a single dishonest deed!' she protested. She picked up her pastry-pin and clubbed the ball of pie dough that she had been rolling out on the kitchen table, as if it were cousin Sarah's head, 'For Mrs Minchin to accuse me of such a thing and then to take threepence out of my wages! It's scandalous!'

'Well, it weren't me, nee-thuh,' said Agnes. 'If I thought that I could foind another jub, Oi'd walk right out of that door and not come back.'

Jenks scratched his head and shrugged. 'I never took it. What would I spend it on? Besides, I didn't even know she had it. Or did I? I can't remember if I did or not.'

'Perhaps somebody came into the house from the street and stole it,' said Elizabeth. 'The front door's often left ajar, isn't it, when Agnes is sweeping up?'

'That doesn't really make sense,' said Beatrice. 'If a thief had come in from the street, they would have taken the whole jar, wouldn't they? I think it's somebody in the house, because they thought they could take a few coins without them being missed.'

'There's nobody, is there, apart from us, and Mr Roderick, and Master Jeremy?'

'Well, we shall have to see,' said Beatrice.

'And what does that mean, pray?' demanded Elizabeth. 'I'm still going to be short by threepence a week. And I can't see Mrs Minchin explaining to my children why they have to go a day without milk.'

Cousin Sarah spent Thursday and Friday night away with friends in Edgbaston. A woman she had known since childhood was dying of typhoid fever. She returned early the following afternoon, and Agnes took her a cup of tea and some biscuits, but after less than an hour she called them into the dining room again.

The glass confectionery jar was standing on the table in front of her, but this time it was empty. She had counted out all of the pennies and halfpennies into shilling piles and stacked up ten sixpences to make a crown.

'Are you *mocking* me?' she asked them. None of them answered.

'Are you deliberately trying to provoke me into having you dragged in front of a court and imprisoned?'

'I'm sure I have no idea what you mean, ma'am,' said Elizabeth. 'Mocking? How?'

'Can't you *guess*, Elizabeth, or are you a noodle? The sheer barefaced impertinence of it! There is yet more money missing from my jar! Three shillings and sevenpence-halfpenny, to be exact! I insist on your telling me *now* which one of you has stolen it!'

Agnes started to sob. 'I don't know who took it, Mrs Minchin, and that's the God's honest truth.'

Jenks did nothing but blink and look confused.

'I am at a loss!' said cousin Sarah. 'I have never *known* such barefaced dishonesty, not in all of my life!'

'Your fingers, cousin Sarah,' said Beatrice. 'Look at your fingers.'

'*What?*'

'Look at your fingers. You see those stains?'

Cousin Sarah slowly raised her hands. Her right thumb and fingertips were speckled with purplish-brown blotches, and in the palm of her left hand there was a much larger blotch. She wiped her hands against her apron but the blotches wouldn't come off. She wiped them again, much harder. If anything, though, they looked as if they were growing darker by the second.

'*What?*' she repeated. 'Where did these come from? What have you done to me?

She wiped them even more furiously, again and again. 'Beatrice! What is this? Did you do this? What have you done to me? *Beatrice!*'

Beatrice went up to her and took hold of her hands. 'It's lunar caustic, cousin Sarah. It stains your skin for a while, but it doesn't harm you. The surgeons use it in the hospitals for healing wounds and papa used to sell it to people who wanted to get rid of warts.'

'But, *how?* What? How did it get on my hands? How will I remove it?'

'It comes from the coins. While you were away, I took them out of the jar and I soaked them all in lunar caustic, and then dried them, so that they were all covered in silver salts. I thought that anybody who tried to take them would get black stains on their fingers, like yours. I'm sorry. I was going to tell you what I'd done, I promise. I thought you'd think it was clever. I didn't know that you would be counting them out so soon.'

Cousin Sarah looked down at her hands again. The blotches on her fingertips had darkened even more until they were almost black. 'I suppose you went down to the cellar,' she said. She was so angry that she kept twitching, as if she were about to have an epileptic fit. 'I should have thrown all of your father's bottles away, shouldn't I? All of those potions and all of those powders and all of that – hocus-pocus.'

'Ma'am?' said Elizabeth, and then, *'Ma'am?'* even more emphatically. She raised both of her hands, palms outwards, so that cousin Sarah could see that she had no black stains on her fingers. She nudged Agnes with her elbow and Agnes did the same.

'Go on, Jenks,' said Elizabeth. 'Show Mrs Chimney your hands.'

'Very well,' snapped cousin Sarah. 'It appears that I might have misjudged you. You can go now. Get back to your work.'

'You won't be taking threepence a week, then, ma'am?'

'No, of course I won't, since you appear not to be responsible. Beatrice – how can I remove these dreadful stains? It's our parish sewing class tomorrow morning. I can't possibly teach young girls embroidery with my fingers all black like this.'

'Papa used to use spirit of hartshorn.'

'In that case, I trust that you have some.'

'I don't know, cousin Sarah. I'll have to go down to the cellar and look.'

'And if you haven't?'

'The apothecary in the High Street will probably stock it. Or, when papa ran out, he used piddle.'

'He did *what?'*

Beatrice blushed. Her father had always talked to her so straightforwardly that she often forgot that other people could be more prudish. Whenever his hands were stained with lunar caustic he would urinate into a bowl and wash his hands in it, so that the ammonia would bleach out the silver.

She was just about to explain this to cousin Sarah when Jeremy passed the dining-room doorway, very furtively, almost on tiptoes. He had almost reached the front door when one of the floorboards creaked.

'Jeremy!' said cousin Sarah, without looking round. 'You're not going out, are you, Jeremy? I need you to come to Mrs Jupp's with me and carry those sacks of old clothing that we collected for the poor.'

Jeremy stopped, but kept his back turned. 'I can't, mama. I've arranged to meet Frederick.'

'Frederick can wait. I can't possibly carry all of those sacks by myself.'

'You can get Jenks to do it, can't you?'

'I could, yes. But there's another reason I want you to come with me. I very much want you to meet Mrs Jupp's youngest daughter, Grace.'

'Oh, *please*, mama! You're not trying to marry me off again, are you? It was that hideous Rebecca Buckland the last time. I would rather have walked down the aisle with an Old Spot pig than with her! Get Jenks to lug your sacks for you.'

He carried on down the hallway, towards the front door, but cousin Sarah went after him. She caught up with him just as he lifted his hand to open the latch.

'Show me your fingers,' she said.

Beatrice went out into the hallway to see Jeremy jamming both his hands into his armpits.

'Show me your fingers!' cousin Sarah demanded.

Reluctantly, Jeremy held out both his hands.

'You *thief*!' she screamed. 'Taking my money like that! How did you *dare* to do such a thing?'

'I didn't take your money! I'll lay a wager it was Agnes! Jingled her pocket, have you? I'll bet you it was her!'

Cousin Sarah clutched his wrist and forced him to hold up his black-stained fingers. 'You can't deny it! This is the proof! Your cousin Beatrice covered the coins with caustic! Look – *see*! – it stained *my* fingers, too! Now, give me my money back, this instant, you ungrateful devil!'

'Ungrateful? Ungrateful? What do I have to be grateful for? You give me half a crown a week and expect me to live like a lord!'

'If you didn't spend every penny in the Old Crown, drinking ale with those feckless friends of yours, perhaps you might save some of it! Now, give it back to me!'

Jeremy reached inside his sagging coat pocket and brought out a heap of pennies and sixpences. He dropped them one by one into his mother's cupped hands, but while he did so he was staring not at the coins but at Beatrice, unblinkingly, and the look in his eyes was one of fury.

For the next three days Jeremy avoided her. When they did have to meet, passing each other on the landing or sitting together at the dining table for supper, he refused to look at her or speak to her. His fingertips remained stubbornly blotched with black, as did cousin Sarah's. They had sent Agnes to the local apothecary to buy some spirits of hartshorn and for a whole afternoon the house reeked of ammonia. But they had left it too late to rub off the stains and they had become indelible.

Cousin Sarah wouldn't say if she had also attempted to rub them off with 'piddle', and Beatrice didn't dare suggest it again, but that probably wouldn't have worked, either. They would just have to wait until they wore off.

On Thursday afternoon, after a fine rain had finished falling and a weak sun had begun to shine, cousin Sarah asked Beatrice to go with Agnes to the haberdasher's in the High Street for green silk thread and needles, and then to the barber's for a pound of orange-scented hair powder.

Beatrice and Agnes walked through the High Town arm in arm. The street was crowded and the sun was shining so brightly off the wet cobbles that they were dazzled. That was why Beatrice didn't see Jeremy lurching out of the doorway of the Old Crown tavern and pushing his way through the throng of shoppers towards them. Suddenly, though, he appeared in front of them, with his wig tilted to one side and brown beer stains down the front of his camel-coloured coat. He was so drunk that he kept staggering to one side as if somebody were repeatedly shoving him.

'You! You *nose*! Thought you were clever, did you, little Mistress Bea-hive, marking that money? The trouble you got me into! I could've swung for that if it had been somebody else's money and not my own mother's! I could've been twisted!'

Beatrice said, 'I'm sorry, Jeremy.'

'You're sorry? You're *sorry*? What good to me is sorry? She says she's going to write me out of her will! What am I going to live on when she croaks? I thought you and I were going to be married! Some wife *you* turned out to be!'

'Honestly, Jeremy, I didn't know it was you who was taking it.'

'Who the purple-spotted pig did you *think* it was? The servants would've have been too scared, or too stupid, or both!

And my dear demented father wouldn't know a bender from a button!'

Agnes pulled Beatrice away from him and said, 'Leave her alone, Master Minchin. She only did what she thought was right.'

But Jeremy lurched towards them with his hand raised. He was shouting so loudly and so hoarsely, almost screaming, that shoppers were turning to look at him. Spit was flying from his lips. 'You know what I should do to you for snitching on me like that? I should cuff you till your nose bleeds! That's what I should do! A bloody nose for a bloody nose!'

Agnes tried again to pull Beatrice away, but when she stepped back, Beatrice lost her footing on the cobbles and almost fell over. She was saved, however, by somebody catching her from behind and helping her back up on to her feet again. She turned around and saw to her astonishment that it was Francis Scarlet, the boy who had been staring at her on Sunday morning.

'Are you all right?' he asked her gently, and when she nodded, too surprised to speak, he turned to Jeremy and said, 'Don't you dare to touch her! Do you hear me? Go back to your beer and leave her in peace!'

Jeremy lurched sideways again and stared at Francis with unfocused eyes. 'You—' he slurred. 'You, you *whippersnapper*! I shall *have* you!'

Francis let go of Beatrice's arm. He took two steps forward and pushed Jeremy in the chest, very hard, with the heels of both hands. Jeremy lost his balance and fell heavily backwards, on to his shoulder, with his legs flying up in the air. He rolled over into the gutter, which was still running with dirty rainwater, and lay there, stunned, blinking up at the sky.

Beatrice pressed her hand over her mouth. She didn't know what to say. Two of Jeremy's friends had emerged from the

Old Crown to find out where he was and when they saw him sprawled in the gutter they hooted with laughter.

'Help me up, you cods' heads!' he shouted at them. 'Help me up!'

Agnes was laughing, too, but Beatrice said, 'Oh, *no*! Oh, this is terrible! He's never going to forgive me for this.'

Francis smiled at her and shook his head. The look in his eyes was strangely old for his age. Beatrice could imagine that Jesus had looked at his disciples with the same kind of expression – caring, strong, but infinitely tolerant.

'Don't worry,' he said. 'I'll take care of you. I'll take care of you always.'

With that, he turned round and walked off up the hill. Beatrice stood and stared after him until he had disappeared into the crowds of shoppers. Cackling with laughter, Jeremy's friends had by now heaved him on to his feet and all three of them were zigzagging back across the street to the tavern. Jeremy didn't even look round at Beatrice and Agnes. He was so drunk he had probably forgotten why he had crossed the street in the first place.

'Well!' said Agnes, still smirking. 'I do declare!'

But Beatrice couldn't speak. She had the most extraordinary feeling, as if the whole world had begun to revolve slowly around her – clouds, rooftops, trees, shops and people – but that she was standing totally still at its centre, suspended in time. She was deaf to all the noise in the High Street, shoppers chattering to each other and carriage wheels grinding and street traders shouting.

All she could hear in her head was Francis saying, 'I'll take care of you. I'll take care of you always.'

The next time Francis spoke those words to her, those very same words, was on the day they were married, on Saturday,

14 May 1750, in Geoffrey Scarlet's parlour over the Swan Tavern in the High Street.

According to law, their marriage banns had been read three Sundays in a row at St Philip's church, but they exchanged their vows here, in front of Roger Fulton, justice of the peace, a large, overflowing man with the loudest laugh that Beatrice had ever heard in her life, and all of their friends from the Nonconformist congregation. Beatrice wore her best blue velvet dress and a new lace bonnet.

Geoffrey Scarlet made a long and complicated speech about devotion, and awakening, which nobody really understood, and then they all sat down to a cold supper of roast meats and pies.

Of all her relatives, only cousin Sarah came to see her married. None of the others had been ready or able to make the arduous journey from London, and Jeremy had gone late the year before to join his brothers in Manchester, where they had started up a shipping business to the East Indies. Jeremy had forgiven her long ago for the telltale stains on his fingers, but Beatrice suspected that he had never forgiven her for not responding to his advances.

Cousin Sarah came up to her and took hold of her hands. 'I shall miss you, Beatrice. The house will be very empty without you, especially now that Roderick has gone, God bless his poor demented soul.'

She paused, and then she added, 'I have been sharp with you sometimes, and expected much from you, but believe me I have grown to love you as my own daughter. There are fifty-two guineas left of your father's proceeds, and you shall have them, as my wedding gift.'

Beatrice didn't know if she should thank her or tell her how parsimonious she was – but it was her wedding day and she was so happy that she couldn't find it in herself to be resentful. She kissed cousin Sarah's cheek and for the first time she was aware of how withered she had become, and how bony she was, as if all of those years of being so mean-spirited had dried her out.

'God thanks you, cousin Sarah,' she said. 'And I thank you for taking care of me.'

That night, when Beatrice came into the bedroom in her long white nightgown, her hair hanging loose around her shoulders, she found Francis standing by the window, staring at his own reflection. The spare bedchamber over The Swan overlooked the hills behind the city, so that the window was utterly black.

He turned round. Since she had first seen him on that Sunday morning all those years ago he had grown very thin, with a long, chiselled face and a straight, pointed nose. He put her in mind of one of those bony, attenuated saints painted by El Greco, especially because he still had those dark, compelling eyes. His eyes were both pious and understanding, but somehow sad, and when at last he had come to admit that he had loved her, ever since he first caught sight of her, she had been unable to resist the way he looked at her, as if he could see right into her heart – what troubled her and what aroused her.

Tonight, though, his expression was unexpectedly rueful.

'What's the matter?' she asked him. 'I haven't done anything to upset you, have I, my darling? We've been married for less than half a day!'

'No,' he said, 'it's me. I have been a poor husband to you already.'

She came up to him and clung on to the sleeve of his night-shirt, frowning. 'Francis, what's wrong?'

'I have done something without consulting you, because I was afraid that you would try to dissuade me. I'm truly sorry.

I should have shown more courage, and more belief in you. But it is something that I have been burning to do for years now, and now that I have found a wife I believe that it is the right course for me to take.'

'Francis, what on earth is it? Tell me! You're making me feel frightened now!'

He gently wound one of her ringlets around his finger, around and around. 'I have booked us passage to America. There is a small community in New Hampshire which is in need of stated supply – that is, a temporary pastor – and I have agreed to go.'

'*America*?' exclaimed Beatrice. 'Oh, Francis! What have you done?'

'If you really don't want us to go, my dearest, I'm sure I could find a ministry here, in Birmingham.'

But then Beatrice thought of the time that she had been standing at her bedroom window, watching the sun go down behind the hills, and she remembered the feeling that one day she would follow it and find happiness.

'No,' she said. 'I am your wife now, Francis, and where you go, I shall go, too.'

Ten

'Goody Scarlet! Goody Scarlet! It's the pigs!'

Beatrice looked out of her kitchen window to see Mary running along the back fence where the sunflowers grew. She set down the large bowl of flummery that she had been stirring and went to the door, just as Mary came bursting into the hallway. Mary's cheeks were bright red and her mob cap was askew.

'It's the pigs, Goody Scarlet! All of them! Dead as doornails!'

'God preserve us,' said Beatrice. She followed Mary outside and hurried along the garden path to the pig-pen, which stood at the side of the house. It was surrounded by a waist-high wooden fence made of sharpened stakes and against the wall stood a lean-to shed crammed with straw for the pigs to sleep in at night and keep themselves warm in the winter.

Mary had gone out to feed the pigs only a few minutes before, but her wooden pail of Indian corn and potatoes and turnip peelings was now tipped out across the grass. Lying motionless on the rough dry mud were five fully grown Berkshires, a boar and four sows, their eyes still open but with blowflies already crawling in and out of their mouths and into their snouts. With their black bodies and white blazes they looked like five stranded whales. The ripe smell of pigs was overwhelming.

Beatrice unlatched the gate and went inside. Gathering up the hem of her plain blue linen skirt, she crouched down beside the nearest sow. She ran her hand along her sides and lifted up her hind legs, but she couldn't see any obvious injuries. She looked up to Mary, and said, 'Here, help me turn her over'.

With a complicated thump, the two of them heaved the four-hundred-pound sow on to her left flank. The blowflies rose up in an irritated cloud, but quickly settled again. Beatrice examined the sow's side and back, but still she couldn't find any wounds or lesions or animal bites. She stood up and went across to the other four pigs. There appeared to be no marks on them, either. In any case, she thought, even if they had been stabbed or beaten with cudgels or bitten by some wild animal, it was unlikely that all five of them would have died without setting up a squealing that she would have been able to hear from the kitchen, or even the parlour. And if they had been shot, surely she would have heard the crack of the muskets?

'What do you think did for them, Goody Scarlet?' asked Mary. She was a plump, gingery girl with curly ringlets, only fifteen years old, although she had been helping out in the Scarlet household since she was twelve.

'I can't tell, Mary, not just by looking at them,' said Beatrice. 'They have no marks on them, do they? And if somebody has deliberately killed them, why did they do it? We have no enemies that I know of. Who would do such a thing to spite us? And if it was Indians looking for food, why didn't they carry them away – or drive them away while they were still alive? That would have been easier, wouldn't it?'

It occurred to her that it might well have been Indians, but Indians who were seeking revenge rather than provisions. The Penacook tribe still bitterly resented the English settlers for driving them off the land that had once been theirs, and they would raid the village every so often. If that were the case, though, they would have been much more likely to enter the house and kidnap Beatrice and Mary for ransom, and maybe take little Noah, too, who was still asleep.

She didn't mention this thought to Mary, however. The poor girl was upset enough as it was.

'What can we do now?' asked Mary. 'Should we butcher them? We should butcher them, shouldn't we, before the meat becomes maggoty? It's so hot today.'

'No, Mary,' said Beatrice. 'Not until we know what killed them. It could have been the scour, or another infection much worse. If we were to eat their meat, we could suffer the same fate as them. When Francis returns I'll have to see what he decides. My Lord, he's going to be mortified. We paid more than two pounds ten shillings a head for these poor creatures.'

There was nothing more that she could do for the moment, not without discussing it with Francis. If the pigs had been the victims of some disease, she had no idea what it could have been, although she had treated many sick pigs in the past. Pigs with long-term illnesses would visibly waste away, but it would take them weeks, if not months, before they died. Acutely sick pigs would invariably vomit or suffer from copious diarrhoea.

She went back out through the gate, with Mary following her. As she was latching the gate, she glimpsed a bright reflected sparkle in the boar's open mouth, as sharp as a star.

'Wait, Mary,' she said, and went back into the pen. She bent over, and when she pried the boar's lips open wider, she saw that there was a small triangle of broken mirror stuck to its thick grey tongue. She carefully picked it out, wiping it on her apron, and then she held it up so that Mary could see it.

'What's that?' asked Mary.

'It's a little piece of looking-glass. I can't think what it was doing in his mouth. Surely he wouldn't have tried to eat it.'

'Oh, my Lord,' said Mary, and pressed her hands together as if she were praying.

'What's the matter?'

'You know what they say, Goody Scarlet, about a piece of broken mirror on your tongue. That's the Devil's Communion.'

'The Devil's Communion?' said Beatrice. 'I've never heard of that before.' She went over to one of the sows and opened up her mouth, too. Right at the back of her tongue she saw another shard of mirror. She left it where it was and examined the other sows. All of them had fragments of mirror on their tongues, of different shapes and sizes, some of them curved, some of them thin and pointed like knife blades. Whatever mirror they had come from, it must have been smashed with considerable violence.

'Satan's work, this is,' said Mary. 'The Devil makes mock of the holy communion by placing a piece of a broken looking-glass in your mouth instead of a wafer. Your own vanity cuts your tongue, see, so that you drink your own blood instead of the blood of Christ.'

'And who told you that?' asked Beatrice. She came out of the pen again and fastened the gate. She was trying to keep calm but her heart was beating fast beneath her stays and she was feeling very hot and breathless.

'The pastor himself told me,' said Mary.

'You mean the Reverend Scarlet? My husband?'

'Yes, Goody Scarlet. When I was much younger. He said that it was to teach me not to be too proud of my appearance.'

A ruffed grouse suddenly burst out of the orchard, off to their left, squittering in panic as if it had been disturbed by Satan himself, loping away through the apple trees.

Eleven

Francis was much later than she had expected in returning home, and the clock in the parlour had chimed eight before Beatrice heard his shay rattling and squeaking down the rutted drive. The sky had turned mauve and it was still very warm, although over to the west an ominous bank of black cloud was building up. Scores of brown bats were flying around the house to catch the insects that were rising up into the evening air.

She came out with a lantern. Francis was backing Kingdom into the carriage-house so that he could unfasten his harness and lead him into the paddock beside the orchard. It had been a long journey from Bedford, twenty-two miles, and both Francis and Kingdom were covered in a fine whitish dust, like ghosts.

'Thank the Lord you're back,' she told him.

He looked at her quizzically.

'What's wrong?' he asked her.

'You'll have to come and see for yourself, my darling.'

'No, tell me. Noah's not sick, is he?'

'Noah's quite well. It's the pigs. Mary went to feed them this morning and found every one of them dead.'

'*Dead?* How? What's happened to them? How can they all be dead?'

He led Kingdom to the paddock and then accompanied Beatrice around the back of the house to the pig-pen. He stood staring at the dead pigs for a few seconds without saying a word. Then he said, 'Please, my dear,' and held out his hand for the lantern. He swung open the gate and went inside, shining the light over each of the animals in turn.

'They don't have any injuries, or at least none that I can see,' said Beatrice. 'But every one of them has a piece of broken looking-glass on its tongue. Mary said that when she was younger you told her a story about such a thing. The Devil's Communion, that's what she said.'

'Did you remove them?'

'I took out just the one piece, for you to see.'

'You didn't take it into the house, I hope?'

'Yes, why? Did I do wrong?'

'You weren't to know, my dearest. But we must remove it from the house at once. It is a piece of Satan's mirror, through which the Devil can see *us* as clearly as we can see ourselves.'

He looked around at the pigs and shook his head. 'This is plainly the work of some witch.'

'A *witch*? You really think so?'

'Believe me, Bea, Satan is still doing everything he can to prevent us from establishing our faith in this country, and as usual he is using weak and immoral people as his instruments. We were discussing it only today, at the parish meeting, and trying to decide what steps we could take to defend ourselves.'

'But why would anybody kill our pigs? What would be the point of it?'

'I really don't know, my dearest. Perhaps it's because I'm a pastor. Shake the roots, Satan surmises, and the whole tree will tremble and all of its fruit fall to the ground and spoil.'

'You don't *really* think it could have been a witch?' asked Beatrice. 'I mean, look what happened in Salem. So many poor women were hanged for witchery but every one of them was shown in the end to be innocent.'

'I know, yes,' said Francis. 'But this is quite different. What happened in Salem was common hysteria. There was no material evidence, only hearsay.

'But here, look, we have the material evidence lying before us, and nothing could be more material than five dead pigs. They have no marks on them, have they? They show no sign of sickness. But they all have these pieces of looking-glass on their tongues. What other conclusion can we come to?'

They stood for a few moments longer looking at the pigs and then walked back along the garden path. Beatrice went into the kitchen and Francis followed her. 'So what can we possibly do?' she asked him. 'If this person is so determined to do us harm, witch or not, how can we protect ourselves?'

Francis went over to the kitchen table where Beatrice had left the triangular piece of mirror. 'Is this it?' he asked. He bent over it so that he could see his eye reflected in it, but he didn't touch it. 'Our first urgency is to bury this outside so that Satan is unable to see where we are or what we are doing. Once that is done, I will bless this house and pray to the Lord to be our shield against anyone who wishes us evil.'

He picked up a damp grey cotton rag from the side of the washtub and wrapped it around the piece of mirror. He took it outside, with Beatrice carrying the lantern for him so that he could see his way. It was completely dark now because the clouds had rolled right over to the eastern horizon, so that no stars were visible. Using the garden trowel, Francis dug a hole in the earth next to the paddock fence and dropped the piece of mirror into it. Kingdom came up to the fence and whinnied, as if he were asking them what they were doing.

'There,' said Francis. 'We have blindfolded his Satanic Majesty, at least for now. Tomorrow morning early I will ask Jubal to help us burn the pigs to ashes.'

'Burn them? Can't we just bury them?'

'The blowflies will have laid their eggs in them, and their larvae will hatch, and when those larvae in turn become blow-flies they will carry the Devil's infection in their spittle. If they enter the house and settle on our food, then *we* could be infected with it, too.'

'What about the witch?' asked Beatrice.

'I will make discreet enquiries of the men in the village, and perhaps I can ask you to do the same among the women. I know how much they like to gossip. Maybe some goodwife has overheard her neighbour spreading slanders about us, or seen her behaving strangely – brewing up unusual potions or talking to dogs or suchlike.'

'It's not someone we *know*, surely? I can't think of anybody who would wish us ill.'

'I'm keeping an open mind, Bea. There are several women in this village who are not malevolent in themselves but have the weakness of character to lay them open to being suborned by Satan. Goody Merrow, for one, or the Widow Belknap. I passed the Widow Belknap's cottage last week and heard her singing to her goat. A *love* song, too, as if that on its own were not profanity enough.'

Once they were back in the kitchen Beatrice patted some of the dust from the shoulders of his coat and said, 'Why don't you change out of those clothes, my dear, and I will serve up our supper? Go in to see little Noah, too. He was out in the garden most of the day, picking strawberries for me. I think he ate as many as he picked, but we have more than enough for our meal tonight.'

She stoked the wood-burning Franklin stove to warm up the big iron pot of chicken stew that she had made that afternoon, while Francis went up to their chamber. She could hear him creaking about upstairs before he eventually came down wearing his banyan, an ankle-length cotton gown with a blue diamond pattern on it, which he usually wore in the evening, or when walking through the orchard seeking inspiration for his sermons.

'Did you see Noah?' asked Beatrice as they sat down at the table.

Francis nodded. 'He is a blessing from God, Bea. Such an angelic little boy. I do not know if I could ever forgive myself if some harm were to come to him because of me.'

'No harm will come to him, Francis, not so long as I am here to watch over him, I promise you.'

'I don't know, Bea. It's not just our pigs. At our meeting today, I heard of many disturbing things that have been happening in our parish lately. John Mechison said that in Dover five newborn infants have died within the past three weeks for no accountable reason. Several orchards in Ipswich have been stricken by some blight that blackens all of their fruit, both apples and pears, and in Londonderry dozens of cattle have fallen sick. It is almost as if the very air we breathe has become tainted.'

He looked across the table at her, and in the candlelight Beatrice saw something in his eyes that she had never seen before, even when they first set sail for New England. Uncertainty.

She laid her hand on his, and then he laid his other hand on top of hers, but it seemed to her that he was seeking reassurance for himself, rather than for her.

'I confess that I am frightened,' he said. 'I know that God will shield us, but I wish I knew against *what*. It is the unknown that unsettles me the most.'

Beatrice ladled chicken and asparagus and potatoes into his bowl. Then she cut a quarter of fresh rye loaf for him and passed it over, with the brown stone jar of butter.

Francis clasped his hands together, closed his eyes and bowed his head. 'Dear Lord,' he said, 'we thank Thee for this day and for this sustenance. We thank Thee for all of Thy blessings and humbly ask for Thy deliverance from whatever evil is arrived at our door. Amen.'

That night it was so hot and airless in their bedchamber that they left the window wide open. Beatrice was exhausted and her back ached from planting nine long rows of beans and cutting asparagus, but she found it impossible to sleep. She couldn't help thinking about the dead pigs with the fragments of mirror stuck to their tongues, and who might have given them the Devil's Communion. At the same time, however, she couldn't help asking herself how such a communion could possibly have killed them.

Beatrice believed in God and Satan, but her father had brought her up always to question the inexplicable. *Just because you can't work out how something is done, my little Bea, that doesn't necessarily mean that it's magic.*

She was reminded of St Luke's account in the Bible of the Gadarene swine – when Jesus exorcized a man possessed by demons by transferring them into a herd of pigs, which then all rushed over a cliff and drowned in a lake. Maybe the slaughter of *their* pigs had been a deliberate mockery of Jesus's demonstration of His power over evil. But unlike the Gadarene swine, she could not see any reason why their pigs had died, apart from witchcraft, or imagine who might have killed them.

For all she knew, that same person might be creeping around their house even now, in the darkness, carrying a bagful of broken mirrors. In the morning, she might find all of their geese and chickens dead, or Kingdom lying dead in his paddock.

She listened, but all she could hear was an owl hooting and the endless scissoring of insects.

She had only just fallen asleep when she was woken up again. Francis had reached across the bed in the darkness and lifted one side of her nightgown. She opened her eyes, but she didn't move, and she continued to breathe steadily, as if she were still sleeping.

He cupped her right breast in his hand and gently tugged at her nipple, which stiffened and knurled. Then he ran his fingers down her side, making her shiver when he reached her hip. But still she lay motionless and still she kept on breathing deep and slow. *She is not dead, but sleepeth.*

He parted her thighs and lifted himself up so that he was kneeling between them. Then, with a struggle, he reached behind him and pulled his nightshirt over his head and dropped it on to the floor. She couldn't see him in the darkness but she felt him as he leaned forward and guided himself into her. She was warm and slippery by now, and he slid in easily, until she felt the crispness of his hair pressing against hers.

'Bea?' he said, so close that she could feel his breath on her face.

'What is it, Francis?'

'I love you,' he said. 'I love you till death.'

She reached her arms around him and kissed his nose before she found his lips.

'And I you, my dearest,' she told him. 'And I you.'

Twelve

Soon after the sun came up the following morning, their labourer, Jubal, and his younger brother, Caleb, dragged the dead pigs out of the pen and across to the far side of the rough triangular field behind their vegetable garden.

There they built a pyre of shagbark hickory branches and heaved the bodies on top of it, covering them up with more branches. Then they poured whale oil over them, but before they set them alight Francis opened the mouth of every one of them and carefully removed the pieces of mirror, which he dropped into a blue cotton offertory bag, ready for burying next to the piece he had buried the evening before.

Mirror glass might be blackened by smoke, but it wouldn't burn, and through every fragment Satan would be able to spy on them.

Both Francis and Beatrice had busy mornings ahead of them. Francis had to go to the village to see to the needs of Goody Jenkins, who was dying of consumption, while Beatrice had to dress and feed Noah and then turn her attention to sewing and knitting and ironing her aprons and Francis's shirts. She also had fresh bread to bake and beans to be trimmed and salted.

All the same, they stood side by side in the field for a while to watch the fire crackle, and the smoke rise up through the trees, with shafts of sunlight playing through them as if they were the windows of a church.

'We will have to replace these poor animals,' said Francis. 'We won't be able to last through the winter without hams and bacon and lard.'

'Can we afford them?' asked Beatrice. The pigs themselves had caught fire now, with a strong smell of scorching hair, and she held up her apron over her face because the smoke was making her cough.

'Jubal!' she called out. 'When you and Caleb have finished, come into the kitchen for breakfast.'

She started to walk back to the house, where Mary had already pegged out Noah's freshly washed clouts on the line outside the kitchen.

It was going to be another hot day. The only clouds in the sky were thin and wispy, and she could hear the soft, feverish drumming of grouse in the woods. She had never before thought that the sound of them beating their wings like that was threatening, but this morning she felt as if it had a renewed urgency about it. *Watch out! Watch out! Evil is about!*

They had almost reached the door when they heard the jingling sound of a horse and saw a stockily built man riding towards them down their driveway. He was dressed all in brown, with a floppy brown Monmouth cap, and a brown shirt and brown leather sleeveless jerkin. His britches and his boots were brown and even his horse was a shiny chestnut colour.

'Reverend Scarlet!' he shouted out in a rasping voice. 'Reverend Scarlet!'

Francis and Beatrice waited while he came jogging up to them. It was Henry Mendum, a dairy farmer whose estate lay to the north-east of the village. He was one of the wealthiest and most influential of Francis's congregation. He was hot, because he was so fat and was riding at a trot, but his face was always a dark shade of crimson. His head put Beatrice in mind of a large joint of rare roasted beef, but she was never uncharitable enough to say so, even to Francis. His pale green eyes were bulging and his forehead was bursting with perspiration.

'Reverend Scarlet! It's a disaster!' he said as he heaved himself out of the saddle. 'I shall be ruined!'

'What's happened, Henry? Please, my dear friend – come inside. It's much cooler.'

'My Devons, reverend! My pedigree Devons!'

Henry Mendum tied his horse to the split-rail fence and followed Beatrice into the house. She led him through to the parlour, where Mary was sitting, sewing a smock. Mary stood up and curtseyed, and Beatrice said, 'Please, Mary, bring Mr Mendum a glass of apple juice, would you?'

Henry Mendum dragged out a handkerchief from his pocket and mopped his face. 'They have all fallen sick! All twenty-nine of them! When the girls went to milk them this morning, they found them all lying around on the ground, labouring for breath!'

'So, what ails them?' asked Francis. 'I don't see how I can help you. I know very little of cattle, I regret, except for what is said in the Bible about them.'

Henry Mendum sat down in one of the wheelback chairs and took the glass of apple juice that Mary offered him. He drank it thirstily and then belched, and belched again, and wiped his mouth with his handkerchief, and sniffed.

'I thought at first they might be suffering from the grass staggers,' he said. 'Some of my Linebacks were affected last spring, but that was when the grass was new and very lush because of the rain. My Devons, though, they've all been feeding well and there's no sign around them that they've been thrashing, so as far as I can tell they have not been having convulsions.

'It is not the scour because they have passed no foul movements, and it is not the pasture bloat. Neither are they infected with lungworms or sucking lice.'

'Did you send for Andrew Pepperill?'

'That cow-leech? I wouldn't trust Andrew Pepperill with a dying rat. Did you hear what he did to Goody Bradstreet's cow? Bled it, purged it, blistered and fired it, and caused it more pain than any sickness could have done, and still it died. My Devons are far too valuable for such mistreatment.

'No,' he said, 'I believe that you might be the only man you who can help me, Reverend Scarlet. I strongly suspect that what has happened to my Devons may be the same thing that has befallen your pigs.'

'I'm sorry? You know about our pigs?'

'Well, of course, my dear reverend. The whole village knows about your pigs.'

Mary quickly picked up Henry Mendum's empty glass and said, 'More apple juice, sir?' Her cheeks were blushing almost as crimson as his.

'*Mary*,' said Beatrice.

'Yes, ma'am?'

'When you went to the village yesterday afternoon for basket salt, who did you speak to?'

'Only Goody Pearson, when she served me.'

'And did you tell Goody Pearson about our pigs, and how we found them dead?'

'I may have mentioned it. Yes, I believe I did.'

'Oh, Mary! For pity's sake! Did you tell her about the mirrors?'

Mary nodded, blushing even more than before. Beatrice put her arm around her shoulders and gave her an affectionate squeeze. 'You are a noodle, aren't you? You might as well have told the *Gazette* as Goody Pearson!'

Henry Mendum said, 'Don't be hard on the girl, Beatrice. It is better to be aware that the Devil is among us, wouldn't you say?'

'But did any of your cows have pieces of broken mirror on their tongues?' Beatrice asked him.

Henry Mendum shook his head. 'No, no they didn't. But my cows are not yet dead, so perhaps they were spared the unholy communion that was given to your pigs, and only cursed.'

'They have no obvious sign of injury?'

'None. Having said that, though, they are still far too sick even to stand up – and there is something that I would ask you to come and look at, reverend, and tell me what you make of it. Something that disturbs me greatly.'

'What is it?' asked Francis.

'I think you need to see it for yourself,' said Henry Mendum, lifting himself out of his chair. 'I am by no means a superstitious man, reverend, and I would very much dislike to be accused of having an imagination.'

Francis took out his pocket watch. 'Very well,' he said. 'I think that Goody Jenkins will be able to postpone her passing for a little while longer.' He went out into the hallway and took down his wide-brimmed pastor's hat. He was wearing his long black vest over his loose white shirt, but the day was too warm for him to put on his coat.

Beatrice stood up and said, 'Francis, let me come too.'

Henry Mendum looked across at Francis with one bushy eyebrow lifted, as if to say why on earth should we take your wife with us? How could a woman possibly know anything about cattle sickness? Besides, she must have plenty of unfinished chores here at home.

Beatrice saw the look on his face and said, 'My father was a man of science, Henry. He taught me from a very early age never to accept anything at face value. Some things that appear at first sight to be supernatural can quite often turn out to have the most humdrum of explanations.'

'Your pigs all died with broken mirrors on their tongues,' Henry Mendum retorted. 'If that wasn't some witch's work on behalf of the Devil, what would be your humdrum explanation of that?'

'I confess that I don't know yet,' Beatrice told him. 'We might well have the Devil to blame. But I see no harm in considering other possibilities, more commonplace. After all, why would God allow the Devil to do such a thing to us? It is not as though we are lacking in piety. Perhaps we have sinned without knowing it, but I cannot think how.'

'Sometimes God teaches us lessons *before* we have sinned,' said Henry Mendum darkly. He didn't explain himself further, but Beatrice had heard the gossip about him and Goody Greene, a young widow who lived on the outskirts of the village, not far from his farm.

'Well, I think Beatrice *should* come with us,' said Francis. 'Who knows? What she learned from her father could be helpful, as it was with our chickens.'

'Your *chickens?*'

'Yes. Twenty or thirty of our chickens went lame last spring, and some were unable to walk at all. I had no idea why, and I had resigned myself to destroying them all. But it had been raining almost constantly for weeks and Beatrice discovered that the chickens' feed had become waterlogged and mouldy.'

'Well, that was humdrum enough. And what was her humdrum remedy for that?'

'It was very simple, Henry. She gave all of the birds a dilution of molasses to clean the mould from their stomachs, and then she fed them on crushed oyster shells to strengthen their bones, and almost all of them recovered and were soon strutting about as healthy as you please.'

'Hmm,' said Henry Mendum, with his mouth turned down. He was refusing to be impressed. 'I think you will see that my Devons have been stricken by something far more alarming than mouldy feed.'

Beatrice gave him a conciliatory smile, but he wouldn't smile back or give her anything more than a cross, sideways glance.

Francis went outside and called Caleb to bring Kingdom out of his paddock and harness him up to the shay. Beatrice, meanwhile, told Mary to take care of Noah for her until she came back, and to feed him his mush, then she buckled on her black leather shoes and wrapped her fine yellow shawl around her shoulders, the one with the tassels. Francis helped her to climb up into the shay and they went jolting off down the driveway. Henry Mendum rode up ahead of them, his large buttocks bouncing up and down in his saddle, snorting and wheezing almost as much as his long-suffering mare.

'Why is Henry in such a state, I wonder?' asked Beatrice as they reached the end of the driveway and turned left towards the village. 'He's so thick-skinned, usually, and he fought with the militia, didn't he, once? I've never seen him in such a bad temper and so fearful.'

'Well, we shall find out soon enough,' Francis told her. He paused, and then he said, 'It's one thing to believe in Satan, Bea, but it's quite another to be presented with material evidence that he really exists. It's just the same whenever God makes His presence known to us by some sign or other. No matter how faithful we are, it still shakes us to the very core.'

'Yes, my dearest,' said Beatrice. She was used to Francis's little sermons. In the three and a half years that they had been married she had learned that he composed them to help himself cope with the apparent contradictions of daily life, as much as for his congregation.

As they approached the village, with its sloping green, they could see the meeting house clock tower rising above the oak trees. Then, next to the meeting house, a higgledy-piggledy row of salt-box houses, and Goody Pearson's store, and the smithy run by Rodney Bartlett. His hammer was ringing on the anvil as loud and monotonous as a funeral bell.

They clattered past the village and down the two-mile track that led to Henry Mendum's dairy farm. It was breathlessly hot and Beatrice fanned herself with the calico fan she had made at the beginning of the summer. On either side of them the trees rustled and whispered, as if they were gossiping about them. *Where are they going, these people? What are they doing?*

Beatrice had never before had such a feeling that something momentous was about to happen, and she prayed that it wouldn't be something dreadful. She looked up at the ink-blue sky and wondered if God were watching them as they rattled between the trees, and whether He was caring for them or teaching them the consequences of being so proud and self-reliant.

She glanced at Francis and gave him a smile. Francis smiled back, but without much conviction.

Henry Mendum rode ahead of them between the avenue of hickory trees that led up to his farm. The sprawling white farmhouse stood on top of a hill, surrounded by milking-sheds and feed stores and barns. Like many prospering farmers around Sutton, Henry Mendum had enlarged his house again and again with lean-to extensions, especially on the northern side, where the store rooms were cooler for keeping cheese and salted beef.

The farmyard overlooked three hundred and fifty acres of grazing and alfalfa and orchards. Beyond, Beatrice could see for miles over woods and rocky outcroppings, all magnified by the heat, as if she were looking at them through a shiny window. She could even see the granite promontory eight miles to the north called the Devil's Pulpit, but she thought it more sensitive not to point it out to Francis as he helped her down from the shay.

A lanky slave in stripy pants and a fraying straw hat came loping out from the stables. He took Henry Mendum's mare from him and patted her nose.

'Sheesh, Mr Mendum, sir, this poor crticher look like she ackshly meltin'.'

'Give her a good rub-down, Joshua,' said Henry Mendum. 'I took a bath myself only last week, but in this heat I am quite minded to take another. Come on now, follow me.'

He drew out the silver-topped walking stick that was tucked under his saddle girth and waddled ahead of Francis and Beatrice down a long tussocky slope, grunting with every step he took and occasionally stumbling. At the foot of the slope they reached a fenced-off pasture. It was speckled with daisies and so green that it appeared almost unreal. Henry Mendum opened the gate and they all went through. On the left-hand side of the pasture two herdsmen and a snub-nosed young girl in a mob cap were standing together. At first the scene looked idyllic, but as they approached they could see the brown Devon cows lying in depressions in the long grass all around them, each beneath its own cloud of flies.

'How are they faring, Matthew?' Henry Mendum called out.

Matthew was grey-haired and sunburned, with crinkled eyes and a face like a dried-out wash leather. 'No worse, I'd say, sir. But no better, neither.'

'I've asked the Reverend Scarlet and his wife to take a look at them.'

The two herdsmen respectfully bowed their heads and the snub-nosed young girl picked up the hem of her skirt and curtseyed.

Francis looked around at all the cattle lying on their sides, panting. 'Merciful heaven,' he said. 'This is like one of the plagues of Egypt.' One or two cows tried to raise their heads, their eyes rolling, but they soon dropped back down again.

'The plagues of Egypt, reverend, were sent by God,' said Henry Mendum. 'You wait until you see what I have to show you now. Then you will have to ask yourself who sent *this* plague.'

Beatrice knelt down in the grass beside the nearest cow and held its jaw in her hand, squeezing open its mouth so that its tongue slid out. As Henry Mendum had said, there was no sign of any fragments of broken mirror, nor any indication that its tongue had been cut to make it swallow its own blood. But it had not been vomiting, either, and there was no foam around its lips which would have shown at once that it was suffering from one of the common cattle diseases.

'God bless you, you poor creature,' said Beatrice, laying her hand gently on its shoulder. 'God bless you and make you well.'

'Come with me, if you really want proof that the Devil has been here,' said Henry Mendum.

Thirteen

They climbed to the far corner of the meadow, where the grass was much shorter and patches of rough grey granite protruded through the turf. Five cows were lying on their sides in a circle here, nose to tail. Three of them were shuddering and groaning like sick old women and trying to lift up their heads, but two of them looked very close to death, with their eyes misted over.

'There,' said Henry Mendum, pointing with his stick to the ground beside them. Beatrice looked down and saw a complicated pattern of hoof prints, as if the cows had been dancing. But these hoof prints had not been pressed into the grass, they had been *burned*, scorching the grass black and brown, as if not only had the cows been dancing but their hooves had been on fire while they did so.

Francis crouched down and cautiously touched one of the prints with his fingertips. Immediately he said, '*Ouch*!' and furiously wiped his fingers on the grass. He held up his hand and Beatrice saw that his fingertips were red and blistered.

'Are you all right, reverend?' Henry Mendum asked him.

'Yes, yes. It's nothing,' said Francis, flapping his hand. 'But how could your cows have left prints like these? I see no charring on their hooves, nor anything caustic they might have stepped in.'

'That's because these prints were not made by my cows,' said Henry Mendum, emphatically. 'They *look* like cow hooves, I grant you, but they are not as large as these cows would have made and they are far wider splayed.'

Beatrice bent over and picked a dandelion that had been burned by one of the hoof prints, and sniffed it. It had a sickly, rotten odour, but it also produced a burning sensation in her nostrils and the back of her throat, like essence of cloves. It reminded her of something, but for the moment she couldn't think what.

'What does it smell of?' asked Henry Mendum. 'Does it smell of hell?'

'I'm not sure,' said Beatrice. 'But it does smell strangely familiar.'

'It *should* smell of hell, because these hoof prints are those of a goat, and a very large goat at that. More than that, this is a goat that walks on two legs instead of four. See how close together the impressions are, and there is no variation between the front and back hooves.'

He turned to Francis. 'As I said, reverend, I would not care to be accused of having an imagination, but these are the hoof prints that a man would make if that man did not have feet but hooves like a goat.'

'You mean Satan,' said Francis.

Henry Mendum waved with his stick at the hoof prints, as if to say, what else could they be?

Francis looked around the field. 'Could it not have been a goat? Goats can pass on sicknesses to cattle, can they not?'

'Not with such suddenness,' said Henry Mendum. 'This happened within only a few hours. And if it was a goat, and if it was sick enough to infect my cattle, where is it? Surely it would be lying here along with the rest of the herd.'

Beatrice walked slowly around the circle of five cows. It looked to her as if they had been dragged into this arrangement on purpose, although the grass was too short for her to be sure. Perhaps the circle had some mystical significance. Five cows to represent the four elements plus the power of the human spirit? Or the five wounds of Christ? Or the five sides of a satanic pentacle?

Francis came up to her and laid his hand on her shoulder. 'This is very grave, Bea,' he told her. 'Our pigs could have been killed by some human agency, I'll grant you. It could have been some witch directly commissioned by Satan, or some ill-intentioned person trying to summon Satan by doing his work. But look at the sorry condition of these cows, and these hoof prints . . .'

'You really think that the Devil was here, in person?'

'What other explanation can there be?'

'I don't know, Francis. I can't think of one. But we need to be cautious before we start blaming witches. You said yourself that what happened in Salem came about from hysteria and that all those poor women were hanged even though they were innocent. We don't want to become infected with such a madness here in Sutton.'

Henry Mendum came over to join them, dabbing his sweaty face with his balled-up handkerchief. 'Well?' he demanded. 'What can be done? If these poor beasts fail to recover, it will cost me hundreds of pounds. And what if Satan returns and spreads this sickness to all of my other cattle?'

'I will pray for you, Henry,' said Francis. 'I will pray for you and I will ask God to show us mercy. I don't know what we could have done to deserve the Devil walking among us, but on Sunday when we all pray together we must ask Him for forgiveness.'

'Is that all? Is there no way we can sprinkle the fields with holy water or some such, so that Satan can't trespass on our property?'

Francis shook his head.

'What if we weave rowan twigs into our fences?' Henry Mendum persisted. 'That might deter him. Or boil up some witch-bottles?'

'Let us begin with prayer first, Henry, and see if that will protect us. I am not really in favour of using witchcraft against witchcraft, no matter how benign its intention. To do that is an admission that we believe in it, and if we show that we believe in it we will give Satan and his minions even more power to harm us.'

'How can we *not* believe in it when all of your pigs are stone dead and my Devons are dying all around us?'

Beatrice left them talking and walked slowly over to the fence at the very edge of the field, where there was a wide flat outcropping of bare granite. The goat-like hoof prints crossed the rock diagonally, from right to left, and then disappeared into the longer grass and weeds on the other side of the fence. What puzzled her was that the fence was far too high for a goat to leap over. No goat that she had ever seen, anyhow. She wasn't tall, but when she stood on tiptoes the upper rail was on the same level as her up-tilted chin.

She turned round to see if Francis or Henry was watching her. When she saw that they both had their backs to her, she reached into her dress and pulled out her pocket. She took out a white linen handkerchief, unfolded it, and laid it flat on the rock on top of one of the hoof prints. Then she stepped on it, pressing her shoe down hard so that as much as possible of the black tarry substance was imprinted into the linen.

Making sure that Francis didn't see what she was doing, she picked up the handkerchief and folded it up again so that none of the mark was visible. Then she tucked it back into her pocket, along with her keys and the button-thread and the ribbon she kept in it, and the small red-bound book of prayerful thoughts.

She rejoined Francis and Henry Mendum and together they climbed the slope back up to the farmhouse.

'Can I offer you refreshment?' asked Henry Mendum.

Beatrice would have loved a cool glass of spring water, but Francis said, 'No, thank you, Henry. We both have much to do and as soon as I have seen to Goody Jenkins I will go to the meeting house and say prayers for you.'

'Thank you, reverend. I'll need them. Who can guess what Satan is scheming to do to us next.'

As they approached their house Francis and Beatrice were surprised to see a black four-wheeled calash standing outside. Its black folding top was raised, like a giant widow's bonnet, so that it was impossible to see who was inside, but it was harnessed with two horses, one black and one grey, which were being held by a young man wearing a faded grey hunting shirt and black britches and a black three-cornered hat.

As they circled around in front of their carriage-house this young man raised his hat and bowed his head.

'Were you expecting a visitor?' asked Beatrice as Francis helped her down from the shay.

'Of course not, my dear. I have far too many appointments to keep today.'

Francis walked across to the young man holding the horses. As he did so, little Noah came running out of the front door, closely followed by Mary, who called out, 'Noah! Noah! Come back and let me wipe your mouth!'

'Mama!' cried Noah, holding up both hands. He was only seventeen months old and still not steady on his feet, and as he ran up to Beatrice he pitched forward and bumped his head on the ground. He started to cry, even though he was wearing his pudding cap, so Beatrice picked him up and cuddled him and gave him a kiss.

'There, silly!' she said. 'You didn't really hurt yourself, did you?'

Noah had curly brown hair and a heart-shaped face and anybody could see that he was Beatrice's son, but his eyes were dark and soulful like his father's. Sometimes when he was lying in his crib she caught him looking up at her and the expression on his face was so deep and knowing that she could hardly believe he was only a toddler.

Francis was saying to the young man, 'Good morning! Who has come to call on us, if I may ask?'

The young man didn't answer, but gesticulated wildly with both hands, as if he were being attacked by a wasp. His face was spattered with cinnamon-coloured freckles and his lips were very red. His lips were *wet*, too, because he licked them, and then licked them again, but still he didn't say a word.

'Can you not speak?' Francis asked him.

The young man nodded furiously, almost shaking off his three-cornered hat. Then he turned to the calash and let out a loud screeching sound, more like a barred owl than a human being. Francis took a step back and raised his hand to Beatrice, warning her to keep well away.

Then, however, with a sharp creak, the black collapsible top of the calash was folded down and a man stood up from his seat in the back. He was wearing a grey linen tailcoat and a vest and britches to match, and although he looked no more than thirty-five years old his wig was grey, too. He climbed down to the ground and came up to Francis with both hands held out, as if he were greeting a long-lost friend.

'The Reverend Francis Scarlet, I assume?' clear and resonant, like an actor, and with a cultured English accent.

'Yes, sir,' said Francis. 'But you have me at a disadvantage.'

The man came closer and clasped Francis's hands. 'I have heard much about you, reverend. Your reputation has spread far wider than Sutton. And this is your lovely wife, Beatrice? And your infant son?'

He released his grip on Francis's hands and walked over to Beatrice. He smiled at her, warmly and indulgently, and then at Noah. 'You have been crying, my little soldier! That will never do!' He produced a bunch of keys from his vest pocket and shook them in front of Noah, saying 'Here! What do you think of these?'

Noah buried his face in Beatrice's neck. Beatrice said, 'He is a little shy of strangers, sir. I'm sorry.'

She couldn't help thinking that whoever this stranger was, he was extremely handsome. Although he wasn't as tall as Francis, he stood very upright and he had a deep, strong chest. His forehead was broad, his nose was straight, and he had a firm, determined jaw. There was something in his eyes, too, that she found appealing – a hint of mischief, which was rare among the pious, hard-working men of Sutton and its surrounding farms.

The man turned back to Francis and again held out his hand. 'Jonathan Shooks, reverend. I think you might describe me as a doctor of sorts. This is my loyal assistant, Samuel. As you have already discovered, poor Samuel is incapable of speech. What he lacks in loquacity, however, he makes up for with willingness and wit. Don't you, Samuel?'

Samuel nodded again and uttered another bird-like noise.

'So how can I be of service to you – Mr *Shooks*, is it?' asked Francis. 'You appear already to know who I am. I can only assume that you have come here for something specific.'

'Well, as I said, I am a doctor of sorts.'

'We have a physician already in Sutton, Doctor Merrydrew. All our medical needs are well catered for.'

Jonathan Shooks continued to smile, as if he found the conversation amusing. 'In a manner of speaking, Reverend Scarlet, I *am* a physician, and in the course of my career I have treated both men and women and what you would no doubt call the beasts of the field. But more than that, I am a doctor of natural medicines, of herbal and ritual remedies, and most importantly, of *spiritual* cures.'

'I still fail to see what I can do to assist you, Mr Shooks,' said Francis. 'What is it you want of me?'

'I want nothing of you, reverend. Quite the opposite. It is what I can offer to you and your community.'

Francis said nothing. Mary wiped Noah's mouth with a muslin cloth and then took him from Beatrice and brushed his frock straight. He had stopped crying now and he stared at Jonathan Shooks with tears clinging brightly to his eyelashes.

'Come along, reverend,' coaxed Jonathan Shooks. 'I have heard that a shadow is falling across this village and some of the farms hereabouts. The same noxious shadow has fallen over several settlements in Massachusetts and Maine, and caused a great deal of suffering. Animals dying, crops blighted. Children taken sick.'

'Well, yes, I'm aware of that,' said Francis. 'But Sutton is a prayerful community and I'm sure that we can see to our own salvation. The Lord has never abandoned us before and He will not do so now.'

Jonathan Shooks shrugged and kept on smiling. 'I am sure that He won't. In fact, what do you think has brought me here this morning? I can purge Sutton of all of the malign influences that threaten it, be they Devil, or demons, or disease. It is what I do, Reverend Scarlet. It is my profession. To put it simply, I can exorcize your village and make it whole again.'

Fourteen

Francis invited them into the parlour. Before he sat down Jonathan Shooks circled slowly around the room, peering at the samplers on the walls and the engraving of Jesus casting the moneylenders out of the temple, and then at himself in the looking-glass over the fireplace. The glass was slightly flawed, so that it twisted one side of his face.

'Would you care for tea, Mr Shooks?' asked Beatrice. 'Or perhaps a cup of cider?'

Jonathan Shooks brushed his shoulders and straightened his cravat and then he turned to Beatrice and gave her a disarming smile. 'Tea, please, if it's not too much trouble. And if your girl would be kind enough to take some water out for Samuel.'

'He's more than welcome to join us,' said Beatrice.

'Samuel is not very comfortable in company, I regret. He will be happy enough outside, thank you, taking care of the horses.'

Beatrice ushered Mary into the kitchen. While Mary filled the kettle and put it on the hob, Beatrice set out a tray with cups and plates and took snickerdoodles and bishop's bread out of the larder. Noah climbed on to a chair to watch and she snapped a snickerdoodle in half and gave it to him. He wasn't usually allowed to have treats in between meals but for some reason Beatrice felt particularly protective towards him today.

Something about Jonathan Shooks unsettled her, even more than his talk of a 'noxious shadow'.

Mary warmed the porcelain teapot and spooned out tea. While Mary's back was turned, Beatrice lifted out her pocket and pulled out the folded handkerchief with the hoof mark imprinted on it. She tucked it into the left-hand drawer of the pinewood hutch, behind the cutlery tray. She would have time to examine it more closely after Noah had been put down to sleep this evening, before Francis had returned from his parish meeting. She had never hidden anything from Francis before, but she didn't want him to think that she was questioning his beliefs. If you believed without question in the existence of God, then you believed equally in the existence of the Devil.

When she returned to the parlour Jonathan Shooks was saying, 'Yes, reverend, I was in the shipping business originally, for a company in London, and on their behalf I travelled the world very widely. I visited India and Arabia first, and then I crossed the Atlantic to New Granada and Guatemala and Puerto Rico. On each of my journeys I spoke out of natural curiosity with the priests and shamans of many different religions and cultures, and gradually I came to realize what my true calling was.'

Beatrice set the tray down on the side table. As she was pouring out the tea she became aware that Jonathan Shooks was talking to Francis but was staring all the time at her. She passed him a cup and then offered him a plate.

'I have snickerdoodles or bishop's bread, Mr Shooks. Or plain pound cake, if you would prefer it.'

'I am happy with a slice of bishop's bread, Goody Scarlet.'

Why is he smiling at me like that? she asked herself. *What is so diverting about tea and cake? Or has he seen something in me that amuses him?*

'Of course, there are many beliefs,' said Francis. 'There is, however, only one true God, and it is that God who will be our salvation.'

'There is only one true Devil, too,' replied Jonathan Shooks. 'Our difficulty here in New England is that he does not always appear in his familiar guise, so it is much more difficult for us to recognize him.'

'I'm not sure that I understand what you mean.'

'This is the New World, reverend, where the Devil does not necessarily answer to the name of Satan and can manifest himself in ways that are unfamiliar to pastors such as yourself. Here, Satan has countless different faces and countless different names, and it can take very different procedures to identify him, and very different incantations to send him back where he came from.'

'I can't see that it matters what he calls himself or what form he takes. Evil is evil, by any name. God will know him, even if I don't.'

Jonathan Shooks took a sip of his tea and then put down his cup. 'My dear reverend, why does the church have such a variety of prayers and collects? Each is specific to our needs on any given day, because the Lord cannot tell what perils we face unless we tell him. But what if we ourselves don't know what those perils are?'

'I still don't follow you,' said Francis. 'If pigs mysteriously die and cattle collapse, if apples rot on the trees and children unaccountably fall ill, that seems to me like the work of Satan, no matter what he calls himself.'

'But how can you tell for sure?' Jonathan Shooks persisted. 'What if Satan appears in the shape of a screeching bird of prey, whose every screech brings death to those who hear it? Or a headless woodsman with doors in his chest that open and shut with a sound like the chopping down of a tree? Or a figure made out of broken mirrors – mirrors that glitter in the forests in the dead of night? Are these all manifestations of Satan? Or are they some other demonic spirits quite unallied to Satan – spirits from some other hell of which you may know nothing at all?'

Francis glanced at Beatrice uncomfortably. She could see how much he disliked Jonathan Shooks and everything that he was saying. Francis hated his faith to be challenged, and although he believed in the Devil he had no time for folk stories about goblins or banshees or men who turned into wolves. But Jonathan Shooks had mentioned broken mirrors and because of that alone she could tell that Francis was going to hear him out.

Francis said, 'God created everything on this earth, Mr Shooks, even those spirits that have chosen the path of evil. No matter how ignorant I may be of the different forms in which the Devil may come to us, I am confident that God will protect us.'

Jonathan Shooks sipped some more tea. 'If that is how you feel, reverend, then I admire your faith. May I say, though, that should you encounter anything that you find both menacing and inexplicable I would like you to feel free to contact me, if only for help in identifying what it might be. In my experience, the Lord can help us far more expeditiously if He knows exactly what threats we face.'

Beatrice knew that, for Francis, this came very close to blasphemy. As far as Francis was concerned, God was all-seeing and all-knowing and if He chose not to save us from disease or death or any other misfortune, He must consider that we deserved it.

Jonathan Shooks had taken a bite of his bishop's bread now and was chewing it slowly and methodically, and she could see by the light in his eyes that he understood just how much he had discomfited Francis, and with how much pleasure he was waiting for him to answer back.

Francis cleared his throat and tried a variety of expressions before he said, 'Thank you for your offer, Mr Shooks. I expect to have no need to call on you, but all the same I appreciate your concern.'

Francis and Beatrice stood in the doorway to watch Jonathan Shooks climb back into his calash. Samuel let out a high screeching noise to start the horses, and shook the reins, and as the calash wheeled around in a semicircle Jonathan Shooks picked up his grey tricorn hat from the seat beside him and lifted it into the air in farewell. Like every other gesture he had made since his arrival, there seemed to Beatrice to be a hint of mockery about it. *Goodbye, you innocents, you have no idea what storms are on their way.*

'Well,' she said, as they went back into the parlour. 'What did you make of him?'

'I'm not at all sure,' said Francis. 'Either he is a self-deluded fanatic or else he is a very devious man indeed. It may be uncharitable, but I have to say that I didn't care for him at all.'

'Well, I think that he told us only half of the story,' said Beatrice. 'There is much more to Mr Shooks than meets the eye. And I have the feeling that this is not the last we will see of him, by any means.'

Francis laid one hand on her shoulder and kissed her forehead. 'You have unusual perception for a woman, my dearest. Sometimes I must confess that it disturbs me.'

'I'm your *wife*, Francis,' she insisted, looking up at him. 'I never want to cause you any unease. Your happiness and your comfort are all that I care for, yours and Noah's. I'm here to serve you, like any good wife.'

Francis took out his pocket watch. 'Heavens! I must go at once! I have so much to do! Goody Jenkins could well be at her Saviour's breast by now! And I have to meet Richard Moffatt about the accounts!'

As Francis put on his coat Beatrice went into the kitchen and picked up Noah. 'Give your father a kiss and say "bye-bye".'

Francis gave Noah the quickest of kisses and then hurried outside, calling out, 'Caleb! Caleb! Fetch round the shay for me, if you will! As quick as you like!'

Beatrice carried Noah into the parlour and across to the looking-glass over the fireplace. 'Who's *that*?' she asked him, pointing to his reflection. 'Is that Noah's little friend? Why don't you wave to him?'

Noah rested his head shyly against Beatrice's shoulder, but watched himself out of the corner of his eye. Beatrice found herself staring at her own image and for a few long moments she felt as if she were staring at a stranger – a stranger much younger than herself. While the men of Sutton usually appeared to be much older than they really were, in their powdered wigs and high-buttoned waistcoats, the women all contrived to stay as youthful as possible, even the older matrons in their forties. Beatrice didn't have to try. She looked no more than twenty, although she was seven years older than that. She was slight and narrow-waisted, but very full-breasted, which was emphasized by the tightness of her corset. She had dark brunette ringlets and her eyes had intensely blue irises, as blue and speckled as lapis lazuli. Her nose was short and up-tilted, and her lips always looked as if she were pouting. When she was a young girl her father had teased her by telling her that she looked like a cherub – a pretty cherub, but a cherub who was sulking because God had given her brown hair instead of gold.

Staring at herself, she found it hard to believe that she was now the wife of a minister, and a mother, and the mistress of her own house. But she couldn't help feeling a flush of guilt that she was so proud of what she had achieved and so vain about her looks. She hoped that her vanity hadn't somehow contributed to the death of their pigs and the sickness of Henry Mendum's cattle. The Lord was very quick to punish those who thought too much of themselves.

Her thoughts were interrupted by the sound of Francis rattling off down the driveway. She needed to stop daydreaming and return to her duties. As she carried Noah back through the doorway, however, she glanced back at her reflection, almost furtively, and she couldn't stop herself wondering what Jonathan Shooks had thought of her. He had stirred some feeling inside her that she had never experienced before. Was it apprehension, or was it attraction, or was it some curious mixture of both?

She turned away, but when she did so the slight distortion in the mirror made her look as if she were secretly smiling to herself.

Early in the afternoon Beatrice and Mary walked into the village. A soft, warm breeze had sprung up and the trees were rustling and dipping all around them, as if they were curtseying. It was less than half a mile, but they made very slow progress because little Noah insisted on walking on his leading-strings most of the way, and every now and then he would stop and pick up something that caught his attention, like a twig, or a pebble, and either Beatrice or Mary would have to take it away from him before he put it into his mouth.

After a while Mary picked him up and carried him, even though he started to grizzle.

'We should put him in a wheelbarrow,' she said. 'If we can push potatoes around on wheels, why not children?'

They reached the village and climbed the steeply sloping green to the meeting house. Beatrice wanted to make sure that the grass in the graveyard had been scythed, and the brick path weeded, and that the floor had been swept ready for Sunday's services. Noah was still whining so she went inside alone. The interior of the two-storey meeting house was very plain, with no stained-glass windows or ornaments or pictures of Jesus. Its box pews were as simple as cattle stalls and its high pulpit was bare and unadorned. All the same, it was filled with sunlight, and utterly silent, and Beatrice stood still for a moment and closed her eyes and whispered a prayer.

'*Dearest Lord, please forgive us for any arrogant thoughts that have entered our heads, and protect us from evil. Amen.*'

She went back outside. Mary had put Noah down now and he was tottering around the gravestones, trailing his leading-strings behind him. The newest stone marked the recent burial of Mercy Quilter. Beatrice had known Mercy well, and liked her. She had died in April during the difficult birth of her seventh child, at the age of thirty-three. Her gravestone recorded that she was 'Eminent for Prayerfulness, Watchfulness, Zeal, Prudence, Sincerity, Humility, Meekness, Patience, Diligence, Faithfulness & Charity'. Beatrice remembered her more than anything for her wicked sense of humour, but that would not have looked well on her gravestone.

'Come along, naughty little Noah!' she called him. 'I have to go down to see Goody Holyoke, and if you like you can play with little Eliza.'

They walked across the slanting green towards the Holyoke house, which was one of the larger dwellings in Sutton, with two tall chimneys and a pillared porch. At the far end of the green three small boys were climbing on a cannon, a relic of the French and Indian War, and Noah stopped to stare at them enviously. In the end Mary had to pick him up again and carry him.

They had nearly reached the other side of the green when a plump young woman appeared from the doorway of one of the salt-box houses next to the Holyokes'. She came hurrying along the track, holding up her skirts with one hand and keeping her cap on her head with the other. Beatrice recognized her as Jane Saltonstall, the wife of Andrew Saltonstall, the shoemaker.

As she reached them, Goody Saltonstall stopped and pressed her hand to her breast to get her breath back.

'Jane – what's wrong?' asked Beatrice.

'I'm going for the doctor,' Jane panted. 'Although your husband might be needed just as much.'

'Why? What's happened?'

'Judith Buckley's twin babies, Apphia and Tristram. They're both awful sick. But there's a sign above their cribs. A cross, upside down. It looks as if the Devil himself has left his mark.'

Beatrice said, 'Bring Doctor Merrydew, Jane, as smartly as you can. Mary, I want you to take Noah directly back home. If there is sickness around, I don't want him to catch it.'

'And what will you do?' Mary asked her.

'I'm the minister's wife,' said Beatrice. 'If Satan really has come calling, I need to see for myself.'

She walked quickly along beside the white picket fence until she came to the Buckley house. The front door was open and there were four or five women crowded into the narrow hallway, all of whom Beatrice knew well.

'It's a curse come upon us, Goody Scarlet,' said Goody Rust, a thin woman in her fifties who had always told Beatrice that she believed in witches. 'Somebody in this town has sinned and we are all having to pay the price for it.'

Goody Cutler beckoned Beatrice to a room at the back of the house. It was stifling and dark and Beatrice smelled sickness as soon as she stepped inside. There was one large bed on the left-hand side, covered with a patchwork quilt, where Nicholas and Judith Buckley slept. Against the opposite wall stood two basketwork cribs and in each lay one of the twins. Judith Buckley and one of her cousins were leaning over them and Judith's cheeks were glistening with tears.

On the white plastered wall between the cribs a large black cross had been daubed – an inverted cross, over two feet high.

'Oh, Goody Scarlet,' sobbed Judith. 'Oh, look at them, my babies!'

Both children were naked except for cotton clouts. Beatrice remembered that they had been born in late February, so they were just a few days over six months old, although they were very small for their age. Their eyes were closed and they were pale and sweating. Now and then their fingers twitched, as if they were having nightmares.

'There was nothing wrong with them at all this morning,' said Judith. 'They were bright and laughing and they took their feed without any trouble. At eleven I put them down for their sleep, but three hours later they still hadn't woken up, and when I came in to see why they were sleeping for so long, I found that they had both brought up their milk and soiled their clouts. And there was *this*.'

She pointed to the upside-down cross.

Beatrice went up to the wall and examined the cross closely, although she didn't touch it. It appeared to have been painted with the same tarry substance that had been used to make the hoof marks in Henry Mendum's pasture and when she leaned closer and sniffed it she detected that same irritating clove-like smell. If the Devil had come into this room to make the Buckley twins sick, then it was the same Devil who had infected Henry Mendum's cows.

'You saw nobody around the house or on the green?' she asked Judith. 'You heard nothing?'

Judith shook her head. 'I was baking and then I was mending. Please ask the Reverend Scarlet to come and pray for them. I couldn't bear it if they died. I think I should die, too.'

Beatrice looked down at Apphia and Tristram. 'Try to give them a little water each, Judith. Little and often. Doctor Merrydew will know why they have such a fever and give them a medicine for it, a posset of marigold probably. But water will help for now.'

'They won't die, will they?'

Beatrice looked at the cross again. She didn't fully understand why, but it disturbed her more deeply than any omen had ever disturbed her before. 'No, Judith, I pray not. But I have a feeling that we are being played with, although I don't yet know why, or by whom.'

'It's Satan,' said Goody Rust from the doorway. 'Somebody in this village has called on the Devil to take revenge on us, and I know who it is.'

'You have no proof of that, Goody Rust,' said Judith, in a quiet, panicky voice, almost as if she were worried that they could be overheard.

'What more proof do I need?' Goody Rust demanded. 'She has a sharp tongue for everybody and not a week goes by without her making false accusations about this person or that. Only last week she told Roger Parminter that she would see him in hell, for no other reason than his dogs had chased after hers. And what poisonous potions she cooks up in her kitchen, goodness only knows.'

'You're talking about the Widow Belknap,' said Beatrice.

Judith frantically waved her hands to shush her. 'She's told me so many times that my babies are unnatural because they had fits when they were being born, both of them, and both stopped breathing.'

'What's unnatural about that? They both survived, thank God.'

'She said that they should have died, by rights, but that God blew life back into them to show that it was *He* who decided who was punished, not Satan.'

Beatrice didn't ask why Satan should have felt that he was justified in taking the lives of the newly born twins. Unless both had been very premature, Judith would have conceived them while her husband Nicholas was away in Boston for two months on legal business. That was the gossip, anyhow. Nobody had dared suggest it to Judith's face because Nicholas was so well respected, and so was John Starling, who might well have been the father.

Beatrice said, 'Well, Goody Rust, if you're right about the Widow Belknap, if she really has called on Satan to punish us all for our sins, then all I can say is, may the Lord preserve us.'

At the same time, however, she was thinking: maybe the Widow Belknap didn't *need* to call on Satan. Maybe the Widow Belknap had enough knowledge of poisons to bring sickness and death to the local community without any help from the Lord of the Flies. After all, there were plenty of highly dangerous herbs that were native to New England – herbs that even her father wouldn't have known about, like Jamestown weed and thorn apple and devil's trumpet.

She suddenly thought of her father, and her mother, too, lying side by side in their caskets in St James's Church in Clerkenwell, and she felt a pang of homesickness and grief that she thought she had long ago managed to bury, and tears unexpectedly sprang to her eyes.

Fifteen

Francis must have seen her hurrying down the driveway towards the house because he came out of the front door and walked quickly to meet her.

'Bea, my darling!' he called out. 'What's wrong?'

'You must come quickly!' said Beatrice, pressing her hand against her chest to get her breath back. 'It's the Buckley twins, Apphia and Tristram! They're sick close to death and somebody has painted a sign on their bedroom wall, an upside-down cross! Doctor Merrydew was on his way to them, but they need you, too!'

'An upside-down cross?' said Francis, taking Beatrice by the hand and leading her up to the house. 'Do they have any idea who painted it?'

'No. But it was made of the same tarry stuff as the hoof prints in Henry Mendum's meadow. It even *smelled* the same.'

Francis obviously didn't think to ask her how she knew what the hoof prints had smelled like. Instead, he asked, 'Was anybody seen around the house before the children fell sick? Has anybody made threats against the Buckleys?'

'No. But some of the women are blaming the Widow Belknap. They say that she's been behaving very vengefully of late, for no particular reason. Well, you said yourself that you heard her singing to her goat. Goody Rust believes that she's called up the Devil.'

'In that case, I must attend to them at once,' said Francis. 'Mary, if you would kindly take care of Noah until we return. Caleb! *Caleb*!'

Caleb appeared around the side of the house, his hands full of witchgrass which he had been pulling up out of the garden. 'Yes, reverend?'

'Please harness Kingdom for us, would you, as quick as you can!'

After a short while Caleb came back, leading Kingdom at a trot. He harnessed him up quickly between the shafts of the shay and they headed off down the driveway towards the village. Beatrice turned around in her seat to see Noah waving them goodbye.

'There is something very *dark* happening here!' Francis shouted over the clattering and creaking of the shay and the syncopated drumming of Kingdom's hooves on the hard-baked mud. 'It may not be the Widow Belknap herself who has made the Buckley children fall sick, but as I said before, she could well be one of those weak-spirited people whom Satan picks to manipulate, like a puppet-master makes a puppet dance!'

Beatrice didn't reply. She believed in the Devil as much as she believed in God, and she respected Francis's faith. But the smell of those hoof prints and that upside-down cross had brought back the long-ago smells of her father's laboratory – coal tar and cloves and civet oil and sulphur. It was hard for her not to wonder if there was a human poisoner at work here rather than His Satanic Majesty.

She said nothing, though, because it was possible that Francis's appeals to God might well save the Buckley children and she didn't want him to think that she doubted him, because she didn't. She didn't want God to think that she doubted Him, either.

As they drove around the green Beatrice saw to her surprise that Jonathan Shooks's black calash was standing outside the Buckley house. Its top was folded down and its two horses were grazing on the grass beside the path. Samuel was holding the horses' reins and as Francis and Beatrice drew up beside him he lifted his three-cornered hat and gave them a sweeping, exaggerated bow, as if he were imitating his master.

When they had climbed down from their shay he let out a high-pitched screech and pointed towards the Buckley house.

'Mr Shooks is inside, I presume?' asked Francis, and Samuel nodded vigorously.

They went in. The hallway was still crowded with six or seven goodwives, all of whom curtseyed when Francis edged his way past them.

'So glad to see you, Reverend Scarlet,' said Goody Rust. 'We need God's representatives today and no mistake.'

Inside the children's bedchamber it was warm and airless and smelled of sick, and something else, like faeces, only sweeter. Jonathan Shooks was standing over Apphia's crib, his hand pressed against her forehead. He looked up when Francis and Beatrice came into the room and gave them a sad, solemn shake of his head, as if to say that there was very little hope of the children surviving.

Doctor Merrydew was sitting on the Buckleys' bed, rummaging in his brown leather bag. He was portly, red-faced, with a bright russet wig that clashed with his cheeks. He was wearing a long mustard-coloured waistcoat with dinner stains on it, and wrinkled white stockings.

'Ah! Reverend Scarlet!' he said in his hoarse tin-whistle voice. 'What are we to make of *this* devilry, then?'

He nodded towards the inverted cross on the wall behind the children's cribs. Francis went across to it and stared at it for a few seconds, his eyes narrowed, lifting his hand towards it but not touching it. Then he looked down at Apphia and Tristram. They were both as white as wax and bubbles of pink froth had dried around Tristram's lips.

'My God,' he said. 'I cannot imagine who could have wished these little ones such harm. Whoever it is, though, they are plainly trying to intimidate all of us. First the pigs, then the cattle, now the children.'

'They can't breathe, can they?' said Beatrice. 'What will you give them, doctor? They need something to clear their lungs.'

'I was looking for some fumitory,' Doctor Merrydew told her. 'Ah, yes, here it is – I thought I had some. We can burn it here in the children's bedchamber and it should help their respiration. Quite apart from that, it will exorcize any evil spirits that might still be lurking.'

He took out a small cotton bag and shook out of it a handful of dry, wispy herbs which looked almost like smoke already. 'Goody Buckley, would you be kind enough to bring me a plate for burning these in, and a lighted spill? And please tell your girl to wipe that unholy symbol off the wall. I can't think what foul mixture has been used to paint it, but it smells like the Devil's own excrement.'

Beatrice said, 'Have you no lungwort, Doctor Merrydew?'

'These children don't need lungwort, Goody Scarlet. Lungwort will only make their breathing more laborious.'

'My father always used to recommend lungwort for people who had fluid on their chests.'

'I'm sure he did, my dear. But lungwort has no *spiritual* properties, does it, unlike fumitory? It is not only physical sickness that we have to clear from this room, but demonic mischief. You, as a pastor's wife – you should know that better than most.'

While Goody Buckley went off to the kitchen to find a plate, Beatrice turned to Jonathan Shooks. He was staring at her just as he had stared at her before when he was taking tea with them at the parsonage. She couldn't decide if he couldn't take his eyes off her because he found her attractive, or if he were regarding her with caution, as if her presence threatened him in some way.

'So, what brought *you* here this morning, Mr Shooks?' she asked him. The boldness in her voice made him smile, but he didn't look away.

'I was on my way to the Penacook Inn, Goody Scarlet, which is where I am staying for the time being. I saw these good ladies in obvious distress, so I stopped and asked them if I could help them in any way. But they had already called for the doctor, so it was not for me to intervene.'

'What would you have done, if it had been left to you?'

He looked down at the children again, and shrugged. 'Well, I have seen similar symptoms many times on my travels. High fever, trouble with breathing. There are several different cures, depending on what manner of ill spirit has caused the symptoms, and why.'

'So, in your experienced opinion, Mr Shooks, which particular "ill spirit" has made these children so poorly?'

'It is not for me to contradict the good doctor, Goody Scarlet. Nor your reverend husband.'

Beatrice was about to tell Jonathan Shooks that if he had any idea what had infected Apphia and Tristram, and how to make them well, then he had a duty to tell them. But Francis frowned at her as if to suggest that he didn't approve of her provoking him and that she should hold her peace. She could almost have believed that Francis was jealous.

At that moment Goody Buckley brought in a large copper bowl and a burning wax taper and handed them to Doctor

Merrydew. He tipped the herbs into the bowl and set them alight. The bedchamber quickly filled with pungent blue smoke, which made everybody cough, including the children.

Meanwhile, Goody Buckley's serving girl, Meg, came into the room with a wooden pail of sudsy water and a scrubbing brush and scrubbed the upside-down cross off the wall.

Jonathan Shooks stayed where he was, next to Apphia's crib, saying nothing, although it was clear to Beatrice from the expression on his face that he had very little respect for Doctor Merrydew and his fumitory treatment.

'You are going to *pray* for these children, Reverend Scarlet?' he asked at last, flapping at the smoke with his hand.

'Of course,' said Francis. 'That is why I came here.'

'Well, I very much hope you know what it is that you are praying for. Or, rather, what you are praying *against*. The good doctor here obviously has no idea or he wouldn't be choking us all with a herb that was commonly used to exorcize Old World demons, like Asmodeus and Pazuzu, but will have absolutely no effect on New World spirits.'

Francis glanced over at Beatrice, but Beatrice kept her eyes on Jonathan Shooks and said defiantly, 'You have come here to pray for Apphia and Tristram, Francis. That's all. It doesn't matter what has caused their sickness. All that matters is that they recover. God will listen.'

Jonathan Shooks raised his eyebrows slightly, but didn't say anything.

'Please, Reverend Scarlet,' pleaded Goody Buckley. 'Please pray for them. I can't bear to see them suffering like this.'

Francis bent his head and clasped his hands together and closed his eyes.

'Dear Lord God, whatever unclean spirit has entered our children Apphia and Tristram, we beg Thee to cast it out and to make them well again. We humbly ask also for your protection against those who seek to intimidate us and to make us question our faith. Keep us safe, O Lord, and help us to remain steadfast. And deliver us from evil, amen.'

'Amen,' said everybody in the smoke-filled room, even Jonathan Shooks.

Doctor Merrydew closed his leather bag and said, 'We should leave the children now for three or four hours. By early this evening they should be showing signs of recovery. I will call again before it grows dark.'

They all shuffled out of the room and outside on to the green. The fumitory smoke billowed out of the hallway after them and was caught in the shafts of sunlight that slanted down through the oak trees.

Goody Rust came up to Francis and said, 'What about the Widow Belknap? You're not going to let her go unpunished, are you? The Lord only knows what she might do next.'

'We can't be sure that it was Widow Belknap who made Apphia and Tristram sick,' said Francis. 'I have grave suspicions about her, certainly, but what proof do we have?'

'Huh!' said Goody Rust. 'It's a pity there's no pond in this village! Otherwise we could duck her and see if she floats! That would be proof enough!'

Goody Buckley approached them, still coughing from the fumitory smoke. 'Please, reverend – please make the Widow Belknap lift whatever curse she has put on them. I cannot think how grief-stricken Nicholas will be if he returns from Durham to find our dear twins dead.'

Beatrice looked across at Jonathan Shooks. He was standing by his calash now, one hand grasping the folded top as if he were ready to climb up into it and leave, and yet he was waiting and listening to what they were saying.

'Reverend Scarlet!' he called out, as Francis and Beatrice walked over to their own shay.

'Yes, Mr Shooks?' said Francis, without turning around.

'As I told you, I am staying at the Penacook Inn. So, please, don't hesitate to send word for me if you need me.'

Francis didn't answer, but held out his hand so that he could help Beatrice to climb up into her seat.

Sixteen

They drove over to the north-east corner of the village green, to a ramshackle collection of smaller home-lots that belonged to artisans and smallholders and Sutton's poorer residents. The green here was deeply rutted with cart tracks and pungent with horse manure, but the Widow Belknap's house stood well back from it. Her triangular front yard was wildly overgrown with flowering weeds – yarrow and dame's rocket and fleabane, with purple flowers and pink flowers and flowers that looked like enormous white daisies.

The house itself was five-sided and oddly proportioned, with a lean-to kitchen and dairy at the back. Its clapboards had been painted pale yellow but years of freezing winters and baking summers had cracked and faded them, and the window frames were rotten.

Francis said to Beatrice, 'Wait here,' and handed her Kingdom's reins. As he was about to climb down from the shay, however, the front door opened and the Widow Belknap came outside, her left hand raised to shield her eyes from the sun.

'Reverend Scarlet!' she called out in a piercing voice. 'Are you visiting your flock today? Have you come to bring me some unexpected news from God Almighty?'

She was quite a tall woman, very thin, and although she was a widow she was not yet forty years old and looked even younger. She was wearing a stiff black linen cap over her tangled blonde hair and a black ribbon around her neck. Her gown was black, too, but scooped very low, with a cameo attached to the front.

Beatrice thought that the Widow Belknap was beautiful, in a strange, almost unearthly way. Her face was perfectly oval, with a straight, thin nose. Her eyes, however, were huge and green and she always made Beatrice feel that she was being stared at by a very inquisitive cat.

Francis stepped down from the shay and took off his hat. 'Good day, Widow Belknap. Are you keeping well?'

'What do you want, Reverend Scarlet? Don't tell me you've come to offer me a better seat for Sunday services, away from those wriggling children.'

'I would, if only I could, Widow Belknap, but you know how crowded we are. No, I have come about Apphia and Tristram, the little Buckley twins.'

'I have heard that they are ailing. Why come to me? Your wife knows more about medicinal remedies than I do.'

'I haven't come looking for a cure. To be quite open with you, I've come looking for whoever was responsible for making them so sick.'

The Widow Belknap stayed where she was, her hand still lifted to shade her eyes. She licked her thin pink lips, as if she had thought of something that irritated her but she was going to have the self-control to keep it to herself. The fragrance of her overgrown front yard reminded Beatrice of her father's herb garden, especially since so many bees were droning from one flower to another.

She could almost hear her mother singing, *'Thou pretty herb of Venus' tree, Thy true name it is Yarrow.'*

Francis said, 'Several members of my congregation have

reported that your behaviour has been less than sociable of late, to put it mildly.'

'Several members of your congregation have been less than sociable to *me*, Reverend Scarlet, not to put it mildly at all!'

'What do you mean by that?'

'I mean that they have been gossiping behind my back, mostly accusing me of behaving waspishly with their menfolk. They call me witch and their children toss rocks at my windows. Harriet Mendum said that I should be locked up or exiled from the village altogether, and Judith Buckley said to my face that I should be taken out to the whipping-post and publicly whipped. But is it *my* fault, reverend, if I am a single woman, widowed by fate? Just because I am single, may I not converse in a friendly manner with some other woman's husband? Must I speak only to my goat?'

'There is a difference, Widow Belknap, between a friendly manner and flirtation.'

'And you think I don't know that? But they are all silly, vindictive women and I would have thought they had enough to do, baking their bread and pickling their pork and spinning their yarn, without wasting their time inventing vindictive rumours about an innocent and well-meaning neighbour!'

Francis said, 'I'm sure you recall what Paul wrote in his epistle to the Ephesians.'

'Not offhand, no. I have to admit that I don't.'

'He wrote, "Let all bitterness and wrath and anger and clamour and slander be put aside from you, along with all malice".'

'Well, perhaps you should remind the goodwives of Sutton of that,' said the Widow Belknap. She came down her pathway, bending down as she did so and tearing up a bunch of weeds. She crossed over to the green and went up to Kingdom, patting his flank. He had been chewing at the rank, rutted grass, but when she offered him the weeds he lifted his head and ate them out of her hand.

'There, you fine fellow,' she said. 'Those taste better, don't they?'

Beatrice watched her for a while as she fed Kingdom more weeds. Then she said, 'The Buckley twins are very ill, Widow Belknap. In fact, they look very close to death.'

Widow Belknap stared up at her with those green feline eyes. 'Are you suggesting that *I* know what made them so sick?'

'Well, *do* you? If you know of a cure, it could be for your own protection. I very much fear for your safety if they die.'

'People can think whatever they like about me, Goody Scarlet. I don't have to make excuses for myself or the way I lead my life. What are you going to do? Call for Constable Jewkes to arrest me? Apart from the fact that he's always in his cups and wouldn't be able to find me, what charge could he possibly bear against me?'

She paused for a moment, and then she said, 'You should remember this, the two of you. It is just as dangerous to take the name of Satan in vain as it is to gainsay God.'

'And what do you mean by that?' Francis demanded. 'Are you telling me that you would call on Satan to punish those who are backbiting you? That would be deserving of arrest!'

As he said that a scruffy-looking black bird appeared in the open doorway of the Widow Belknap's house. It hopped along the path, uttering two plaintive cries as it did so. The Widow Belknap held out her left arm and the bird fluttered up and perched on it, cocking its head from side to side. Kingdom snuffled and took a nervous step sideways, away from it, but the bird itself didn't seem to be at all daunted by Kingdom.

'He's a black parrot,' said the Widow Belknap. 'His name is Magic and he's very tame. A seafaring friend of my late husband gave him to me. He said that he found him on some island in the Indian Ocean.'

Francis waited for her to answer his question, but all she did was coo to her parrot and stroke its head.

'Do you know of the Devil's Communion?' he asked sharply.

'I've heard of it. Isn't that when Satan is supposed to take your soul with a piece of broken looking-glass instead of a communion wafer? Your own self-adoration ensnares you.'

'Have my wife and I ever spoken ill of you, Widow Belknap, or done you harm?'

The Widow Belknap didn't look at him but turned her eyes towards Beatrice and smiled. Her utter repose made Beatrice feel strangely vulnerable and unsettled, and she began to wish that they could just leave now and drive back home.

'Oh,' said the Widow Belknap. 'You're referring to your pigs.'

Beatrice could see that Francis was clenching and unclenching his fists, as he always did when he was anxious, but he was holding his ground in front of the Widow Belknap, his chin defiantly lifted.

The black parrot gave another sad cry. The Widow Belknap made kissing noises to it and then she said, 'Have you thought, Reverend Scarlet, why *you* were the first to be stricken by misfortune, before Henry Meldum or the Buckleys?'

Francis frowned. 'No, I can't say that I have.'

'Don't you think that it might have been done to demonstrate right from the very beginning how *impotent* you are? You might be God's own messenger here in Sutton, but if *you* were powerless to safeguard your pigs from the works of Satan, how can we possibly expect you to protect the rest of us from harm?'

'It is not me who protects us, but God,' said Francis. 'I am only a man, I admit, with all of a man's weaknesses. But God will answer me when I pray to Him, and should He consider us worthy of His protection then I am sure that He will afford it to us.'

'In that case, amen,' said the Widow Belknap. She turned her back on them and walked back towards her front door. Halfway there, she shook the black parrot off her arm, as if she were tired of it. It flapped on to the ground with a harsh, resentful squawk.

'Well?' said Francis, as he climbed back into the shay and took the reins. Just as he did so, the Widow Belknap slammed her front door very hard.

'She certainly bears a grudge against us all,' said Beatrice.

'Perhaps she's justified. You know yourself how malicious some of the women's gossip can be, and how petty. Look at all that business when Goody Roper thought that Mercy Gardner had stolen her bodkin. It was only a bodkin, but she accused her of all sorts of immorality.'

They passed by the Buckley house. The fumitory smoke was no longer billowing out of the front door, but Goody Rust was still there, standing with her arms folded.

'Well?' she called out. 'What did the witch have to say for herself? Did she admit her witchery?'

'How are the children?' asked Francis, deliberately ignoring her question.

'No worse, but no better.'

'Tell Goody Buckley that I shall pray for them constantly. I shall come back later to see if they're recovering. Let us give Doctor Merrydrew's nostrum some chance to work – and let us give God a little time, too, to show them His mercy.'

*

On the way back to the parsonage Francis said, 'I confess that I am deeply confused by all of this, Bea. And very troubled. What if the Widow Belknap is right? What if our pigs were killed to show the whole community how – how *ineffectual* I am?' Beatrice noticed that he didn't used the word *impotent*.

She laid her hand on top of his and said, 'Francis, my love. You are both strong and brave. Simply coming out here to New Hampshire took so much courage and belief in yourself. Don't let some sharp-tongued Joan discourage you.'

Francis took out his watch and looked at the time. 'I have an important meeting this morning with Major General Holyoke. We have to discuss the case against Charles and Maria Hubbard for fornication before we empanel the jury. I'm more than ten minutes late already, so you'll have to forgive me if I take you home and then leave immediately.'

'Go now,' Beatrice suggested. 'I can walk from here.'

'No, I won't hear of it,' said Francis and shook Kingdom's reins to hurry him up. Kingdom, however, was walking more and more slowly, and thirty yards before they reached the turning on the Bedford road that led to their driveway he lurched to one side between the shafts of the shay, as if one of his front legs had given way.

Beatrice thought for a moment that he might have tripped on a rock or stepped into a pothole. The road had become much more furrowed after two months of heavy and persistent rain in March and April, followed by week after week of hot, dry weather.

Francis shook the reins again. 'Come along, boy!' he urged him. 'Come along, Kingdom!' But then Kingdom took three or four more steps and collapsed on to his knees, almost tipping the shay over on to its side. As it was, it ended up tilted at a sharp upward angle. Francis climbed down from his seat and helped Beatrice to climb down, too. Then they both went to see what was wrong with Kingdom.

'Lord preserve him!' said Francis. 'He's having a fit!'

Kingdom was quaking and jerking, and his eyes were rolling. With each convulsion, Beatrice could see the muscles rippling underneath his shiny skin. He was breathing in quick, harsh gasps and his tongue was lolling out of the side of his mouth. Instead of its usual healthy pink, his tongue was crimson.

'What could be ailing him?' asked Francis. 'He was in such good fettle yesterday, and when I took him down to Bedford he was trotting so fast that I had to rein him back!'

'I don't know what it is,' said Beatrice. 'But if you can manage to unfasten his harness, I'll run for Jubal and Caleb.'

Kingdom was jolting even more violently now. The only time that Beatrice had seen a horse jolt like that was when their mare, Sheba, had been struck by lightning during an electric storm and she had danced around the middle of the field with sparks crackling in her mane. When they had examined her afterwards, however, her tongue had been dark grey, which in horses was a sign of shock. She couldn't think why Kingdom's tongue was so red.

She laid her hand against his neck, trying to soothe him. He stared back at her, his eyes bulging, almost as if he were pleading with her to stop these uncontrollable spasms.

'Hush, Kingdom,' she said. 'I promise you I won't let you die.'

With that, she picked up her skirts and hurried towards the house, shouting out for Jubal and Caleb.

She was halfway there when she felt a sudden gust of hot wind, and the oaks that lined the driveway dipped and rustled, in the same way that the apple trees in the orchard had rustled after their pigs had died. She slowed and turned her head, although there was nobody there that she could see, even if it had sounded as if Satan were running away through the undergrowth.

Between them, Francis and Jubal and Caleb lifted Kingdom on to the cart that they usually used for carrying hay or potatoes or lumber boards. It took them almost ten minutes because Kingdom weighed at least a thousand pounds and kept kicking and twitching, but at last they managed to heave him on to his side and Jubal lashed him to the cart with ropes.

'Take him to the barn,' said Francis. 'See if he'll accept a little water.'

As Jubal and Caleb dragged the cart down the driveway, Beatrice took hold of Francis's hand and said, 'This is more than ill fortune, my darling.'

'So, what do you think it is? Did the Widow Belknap put a curse on us?'

'I don't know. But I'm sure that somebody has deliberately made Kingdom sick to show us how defenceless we are.'

Beatrice trusted in Francis. She knew how purposeful and strong he could be. But she thought that he was much too ready to blame Satan for what had been happening in Sutton. She met regularly with most of the goodwives in the village and she had seen for herself how malicious the residents of this small community could be to each other. Every day was not only a round of endless hard work, but a struggle for survival against drought, against snow, against Indians, against inexplicable diseases. People were quick to bear their neighbours ill-will for the slightest misdemeanour, real or imagined, whether it was slander or stealing or sexual impropriety. The case that Francis should have been discussing with Major General Holyoke this afternoon was the charge of fornication against Charles and Maria Hubbard. Though married, their first baby had been born too soon to have been conceived in wedlock and they faced a fine of fifty-nine shillings, and possibly a whipping, too.

'I should send Caleb for Rodney Bartlett,' said Francis. 'He knows more about horses' afflictions than anybody else in the village. More than Andrew Pepperill, anyhow.'

'Let me look first at my father's books,' Beatrice suggested. 'He was often called to treat animals as well as people.'

'Bea – your father's books are not the Bible. What is affecting us here in Sutton is a spiritual malignancy. You can't lift a satanic curse with dandelion and burdock.'

'Francis – I'm not challenging your faith, my dearest. But God creates remedies as much as Satan creates sickness. God cannot be taking care of every single one of us at every single minute of every single day.'

'You don't believe that He does?'

'No . . . how can He? Instead, He has given us the means to treat ourselves. I know you don't believe in the Doctrine of Signatures – that God gave certain plants a similar appearance to the organs that they can heal, like liverwort and bloodroot. But why do you think some plants are so effective in curing our ills? God made them so, and gave us the wit to discover what they do.'

Francis still looked uncertain, but he said, 'Very well. In the meantime, I'll see if the smith can tell us why Kingdom is so distressed.'

Caleb brought Rodney Bartlett, the farrier. He was huge, six foot five at least, with a bald head covered in short silver prickles and a lumpy face that looked as if a sculptor had moulded it out of terracotta and then punched it very hard because it had turned out so ugly. In spite of his ogre-like appearance, however, he was the gentlest man in the village and he always spoke softly and quietly, as if he were apologizing for some offence that he might have caused.

He came into the barn where Beatrice was kneeling on the straw, stroking Kingdom's neck, with Francis standing close by. It had been nearly an hour since Kingdom had first collapsed and now he was trembling uncontrollably. He had vomited several times, a greenish-grey slime, and his hind legs were streaked with tawny diarrhoea.

Beatrice had leafed quickly through her father's notebooks, trying to find anything he had written about sick horses, but none of his notes were in any kind of order and the only horse remedy she had been able to discover was a poultice of Epsom salts for a hoof abscess.

'Goody Scarlet,' said Rodney Bartlett respectfully, and then hunkered down beside her, his tan leather apron creaking as he did so. He laid both hands against Kingdom's flank, feeling his heart beating, and then he looked into his eyes and inspected his tongue. Kingdom jerked even more violently when Rodney Bartlett touched him, as if he were frightened.

'He's dying,' said the farrier. 'I would say that he's been poisoned, but I couldn't tell you by what. Whatever it is, it's done for him. His heart's slowing down and his lungs are filled with bad humours.'

'Is there nothing we can do?' asked Francis.

'Not that I know of,' said Rodney Bartlett, standing up. 'Has he eaten anything unusual today, apart from his feed?'

'He was grazing on the village green,' said Francis. 'Apart from that, the Widow Belknap fed him a handful of weeds from her garden, but that was all.'

'Do you know what weeds they were?'

Beatrice shook her head. 'Nothing harmful, so far as I remember. Fleabane, and yarrow, and Joe Pye weed – and Joe Pye weed is medicinal, isn't it, not poison at all?'

'I think a curse is far more likely,' said Francis. 'That woman is determined to wreak havoc on this community and she has called on the Devil to help her.'

Rodney Bartlett nodded. 'The Widow Belknap has had a sharp tongue lately, no doubt of that. She stopped outside my smithy last week when I was beating a horseshoe and asked me outright if I was ringing the bells of hell.'

At that moment Kingdom gave a terrible shudder and let out a long, high-pitched wheeze, like a collapsing bellows. His eyes misted and then he lay still. Beatrice laid her hand on his shoulder and said, 'Oh, my poor Kingdom!'

She stood up and as she did so she saw that little Noah was standing just outside the stable, with a frown of bewilderment on his face. Immediately she hurried over and took his hand.

'Come on, my darling, away from here.'

Beatrice tugged Noah back to the house almost as fast as he could trot, even though he kept turning his head around, trying to look behind him. She knew that he was too young to understand death, but at the same time she wanted him to remember Kingdom running around his paddock in the sunshine, not lying on his side in the stable, stiff and milky-eyed and plastered in filth.

'*Pim*-pom!' said Noah anxiously, which was his way of saying 'Kingdom'.

'It's all right, my darling, God has called poor Kingdom to the horses' heaven.'

They had almost reached the front porch when Beatrice caught sight of a figure standing at the far end of the driveway under the shadow of the oak trees. She slowed, and then stopped, trying to make out who it was. The figure was tall, so it was probably a man, but it was wearing a long dark brown cloak with a hood, so it was impossible to tell for sure.

In its left hand it was holding a staff, which gave it the appearance of a pilgrim, or even of Death himself, for who would wear such an all-enveloping cloak on a sweltering hot day like this?

Noah pulled at her hand and said, 'Mama! Mama!' but Beatrice stayed where she was, staring at the figure with a growing sense of unease. She felt like approaching it and demanding to know who it was and what it wanted, but at the same time she thought that it might be wiser if she didn't, especially since she had Noah with her.

The figure stood there, not moving. Its face was completely hidden inside its hood, so that Beatrice was unable to tell if it was staring back at her or not.

'Ma-*ma*!' Noah repeated, pulling at her hand even more persistently.

Just then, Francis and Rodney Bartlett came out of the stable. Beatrice waved to Francis and called out, 'Francis!'

Francis was talking to Rodney Bartlett and at first he didn't hear her, so she called out '*Francis*!' again and pointed towards the end of the driveway. Francis looked, but the figure had vanished. There was nothing to be seen but the dry rutted track and the oak trees glittering in the sunshine.

'What is it, my dearest?' asked Francis as he approached.

'There was somebody standing there. Right *there*, at the end of the driveway, wearing a cloak. Man or woman, I couldn't tell.'

Francis looked again. 'Whoever it was, they're not there

now. It was probably just a tinker, or a maunder, perhaps, wondering if it was worth begging us for alms.'

'I don't know. It frightened me. It was almost as if the Angel of Death had arrived to take away Kingdom's spirit.'

'Horses don't have spirits, Bea,' Francis said gently.

'Well, you can believe that, if you like. But I think Kingdom did. He was such a dear, sweet creature.'

They all went into the house and Francis called Mary to pour out some cider for them and bring them a plate of never-stale cookies.

'I've noticed more beggars around than usual,' said Rodney Bartlett. 'Sailors, a lot of them were, but trade's been so bad they can't find a ship to sail on.'

'These are evil days,' said Francis. 'It seems that we are being tested to the very limit. How could Kingdom simply fall down and die like that?'

Beatrice said nothing, but Kingdom's symptoms had made her even more convinced that what was happening in Sutton was the deliberate work of a human man or woman, even if they were inspired by Satan. If she could find the time this evening, she would go through her father's notebooks again, and she would also go back to the stable to see if there was any evidence that Kingdom had been poisoned rather than cursed.

Dusk began to gather and as it did so the brown bats began to whirl around the roof. Rodney Bartlett drained the last of his cider and they went outside to see him mount his big piebald horse. The sky was damson-coloured and the chirruping of insects was almost deafening.

Just as Rodney Bartlett shook his horse's reins, however, they heard a rattling from the end of the driveway. A four-wheeled wagon was approaching and Beatrice saw that it was being driven by Goody Cutler's second son, Ambrose.

Ambrose drew up beside them. His face was red and he was sweating profusely, so that his white shirt was sticking to his chest.

'Reverend Scarlet!' he panted. 'The Buckleys ask you to come at once! Their babies are close to death! Doctor Merrydew has said that he can't save them and they beg you to pray for God's mercy!'

Seventeen

When they went through to the Buckley children's bedchamber they found that Nicholas Buckley was there, too, his clothes still dusty from travelling back from Durham. He was a small, dark, grave-looking man with eyebrows that met in the middle and a hawk-like nose. He was standing close to Judith as she gently patted little Apphia's forehead with a muslin cloth.

Both Apphia and Tristram were breathing in shallow, clogged-up gasps. Now and then one of them would stop breathing altogether and everybody in the bedchamber would fall silent, waiting anxiously for them to start up again. Goody Jenkins was sobbing quietly in the kitchen. She sounded like a kitten mewing for milk.

'Where's Doctor Merrydew?' asked Francis.

'The good doctor took his leave of us twenty minutes ago,' said Nicholas Buckley. 'He said that he had done his best, but there was no other cure that he could think of and he was late for his supper. That's why we sent for you.'

Francis looked down at Apphia and Tristran. 'I thank you for your faith in me, Nicholas, but I have to confess that my prayers have done no more good than Doctor Merrydew's fumitory smoke.'

'*Please*,' Judith begged him. 'I could not bear to lose them. *Please*.'

'Of course I will pray for them again,' said Francis. 'I have to tell you, though, that for you to lose these two dear children may be the will of God. Sometimes, for no reason that we can understand, He wants them back in heaven almost as soon as He has sent them here.'

'Are you trying to tell me that I'm being punished?' asked Judith.

Francis shook his head. 'There are many reasons why the Lord calls children back before their time, Goody Buckley, and it is not for us to know them all.'

Beatrice glanced at him. Considering that Judith was asking him obliquely if she should blame herself for having Apphia and Tristram as a result of her adulterous affair with John Starling, she thought that his words were deeply kind and forgiving. She knew plenty of other pastors who would have told her that she was a trull and that to lose her two children was all that she deserved.

Francis stood between the children's cribs and clasped his hands together.

'Dear Lord,' he said, 'I implore of Thee yet again to grant both Apphia and Tristram a longer life on this earth, that they may fulfil their duties to Thee and bring joy to Thy servants Nicholas and Judith. We ask Thee in all humility to show Thy sympathy and generosity and spare them from death this day, and for many days to come. Amen.'

He stepped back. Nicholas and Judith both repeated *'amen'* under their breath, but it was clear from the stricken look on their faces that they didn't believe that God would respond. Tears were streaming down Judith's cheeks and she had her hand clasped tightly over her mouth to stop herself from sobbing out loud.

Beatrice felt a tightness in her throat, too. She wished now that she had argued much more forcefully with Doctor

Merrydew and insisted that he give the children an infusion
of lungwort instead of filling their bedchamber with fumitory,
but it was too late now. Even if Doctor Merrydew had any
lungwort, which she doubted, Apphia and Tristram were too
close to death for it to do them any good. It would take at
least an hour to prepare an infusion, and the children were
too sick to chew the leaves, which were very slimy.

Francis started to recite Psalm 103: '*Praise the Lord, my
soul, and forget not all His benefits, who forgives all your sins
and heals all your diseases, who redeems your life from the pit
and crowns you with love.*'

As he did so, however, Beatrice heard voices in the hall, where
six or seven goodwives were still crowded, and after a moment
Jonathan Shooks appeared in the doorway. He was wearing his
light grey linen tailcoat and his light grey wig, and was carrying
a brown leather satchel. He looked across at Beatrice as he came
in and gave her a quick, knowing smile, as if they shared some
secret, but then immediately went over to the children's cribs.

'I can see that their condition is very much worse, Goody
Buckley.'

Judith nodded, but she was too upset to be able to say
anything.

Francis spoke up. 'Mr Shooks! This is Goodman Buckley,
Mr Shooks – the children's father. Nicholas, this is Mr Jonathan
Shooks—'

He paused, and then added, 'Mr Shooks claims to have some
special talent for curing the sick. Which is why, I presume, he
has returned here this evening.'

Jonathan Shooks held out his hand to Nicholas Buckley.
'I am truly sorry that I have had to make your acquaintance
under such distressing circumstances, sir, but I assure you that
I have come here with the intention of doing good.'

'Can you save our children, sir?' asked Nicholas. His lower lip was quivering.

'I can only try. The Reverend Scarlet doubts my abilities, I'm afraid. But I will tell you what I told him, that I have travelled almost all around the world and I have learned that the Devil manifests himself in different forms wherever you go. To beat the Devil, sir, you have to know what shape he has taken on. The Devil in New Hampshire bears little resemblance to the Devil you knew in England, just as the plants and animals here are different and the Indians speak languages of which we know nothing and observe rituals we cannot comprehend.'

'I am not at all sure that I understand you,' said Nicholas. His voice was tight-throated with emotion. 'All I ask is that Apphia and Tristram do not die.'

'If I may have a brief word with you in private,' said Jonathan Shooks. 'Meanwhile, Goody Buckley, if you would be so kind as to bring a full kettle to the boil.'

Beatrice asked, 'What are you intending to do, Mr Shooks?' She didn't want to say that the children were probably past saving, not in front of the Buckleys.

'I am not making any promises, Goody Scarlet,' said Jonathan Shooks. Again he gave her that amused, conspiratorial look, almost as if they had once shared a bed together without anybody else knowing. 'However, I will do my utmost to dismiss what possesses them.'

He left the room. Nicholas Buckley gave his wife a reassuring kiss on the cheek, and squeezed her hand, and then followed him.

Beatrice went back to the children's cribs. Their breathing was even harsher now and little Apphia's lips were a pale turquoise. Judith went to the kitchen to put a kettle on the stove. When she returned she came and stood close to Beatrice

156

and looked down at her children with infinite sadness in her eyes.

'This man, this Jonathan Shooks, whoever he is – can he really cure them?'

'We don't know, Judith,' said Francis. 'But if he can, it will only be with God's approval.'

Beatrice said nothing. She didn't want to crush Judith's hopes by saying no, she didn't believe that Apphia and Tristram could be saved, but neither did she want to raise them by saying yes.

After two or three minutes Jonathan Shooks and Nicholas Buckley returned. Judith Buckley looked at her husband as if to ask him what they had talked about, but Nicholas simply shook his head to show her that he didn't want to discuss it. Jonathan Shooks appeared very calm and confident. He opened his leather satchel and took out six or seven thin pinewood sticks, wrapped in paper.

'Is the kettle boiled, Goody Buckley?' he asked. 'If so, please bring me two bowls of hot water, as quick as you can.'

When Judith Buckley had gone back to the kitchen he unwrapped the sticks, and Beatrice saw that they were Chinese fire inch-sticks, which her father had sometimes used for lighting his pipe. Judith returned with two white china bowls filled with steaming water, which Jonathan Shooks put down on the three-legged stool beside the children's cribs.

He used one of the candles beside the cribs to lit the inch-sticks, one after the other, so that they flared up brightly, crackling as they burned and giving off pungent yellow smoke.

'This is the fire that the Devil fears, the Devil in the woods,' he recited, as if he were talking to himself. 'This is the smoke that makes the Devil choke, the Devil in the trees.'

After each inch-stick had burned down about halfway he dropped them into the bowls of hot water, three inch-sticks in each one. They spluttered out and when they had done so he stirred the water with his fingertip.

'This is the brew that the Devil cannot swallow. It will catch in his throat so that he will run away to seek out fresh water and his minions will follow. Begone, Devil. Begone and never return!'

Again he stirred the bowls of water with his fingertip, but this time he was testing it to make sure that it had cooled down. 'Goody Buckley,' he said, 'please pick up your daughter and seat her on your lap. She must drink this water to clear her lungs of the Devil's contagion.'

Judith Buckley did as he asked her and lifted Apphia out of her crib. Apphia's arms and legs were as disjointed as a doll's and her head flopped forward, her blonde curls damp with perspiration. Jonathan Shooks carefully cradled her head in his left hand, tilting it back a little while he poured the inch-stick water between her lips, one sip at a time.

It seemed to Beatrice that it took almost an hour for him to empty the bowl, but it was probably no more than five or ten minutes. Apphia spluttered a little after she had finished it, but Jonathan Shooks patted her on the back and she took several deep breaths. Her lungs were still crackling with fluid, and she still didn't open her eyes, but she was alive.

Judith laid her back in her crib and picked up Tristram. Jonathan Shooks repeated the procedure with him, patiently tipping the second bowl of inch-stick water into his mouth, a little at a time, until that was empty, too.

When he had finished, Jonathan Shooks looked at Beatrice again, but this time his expression was much more of a challenge. *Now we'll see who can make the Devil turn tail, Goody Scarlet, your sainted husband or me.*

'What do we do now?' asked Nicholas.

Jonathan Shooks stood up. 'There's nothing more that we can do tonight except wait until your children show signs of recovery. I shall return at first light and give them more fire-stick water, and then again around noon tomorrow. But they should be much improved by then.'

'I shall pray for them, too,' put in Francis. Beatrice went over and stood beside him to show her support. He put his arm around her shoulders and smiled at her, but she could tell that he was upset. Jonathan Shooks had come into the Buckley home with his incantations and his inch-sticks and completely undermined Francis's authority in front of his own parishioners.

Jonathan Shooks left them, climbing into his hooded calash so that Samuel could drive him off into the darkness, with only a dimly flickering coach-lamp to light his way. Francis and Beatrice stayed for another half-hour, but since the Buckley twins both seemed to be breathing more easily and had stopped their spasmodic twitching, they decided to leave and to call back the following morning.

As Beatrice went to the front door Judith caught at her sleeve.

'Thank you and the Reverend Scarlet for being so kind,' she said. 'I'm sure that the pastor's prayers have helped just as much as Mr Shooks's remedy.'

'Well, we shall see,' said Beatrice. She paused, and then she said, 'Do you know what it was that your husband and Mr Shooks spoke of, before Mr Shooks treated them?'

'I asked Nicholas but he would not tell me. Perhaps he will when the twins are well again. *If* they get well again, please God. Perhaps Mr Shooks was warning him not to hold out too much hope.'

'*Bea*!' called Francis out of the darkness. Ambrose Cutler had brought his wagon around so that he could drive them home.

Beatrice called back, 'Coming, Francis!' There was nothing more she needed to say to Judith, although she gave her one of those looks that women share when they accept that they have to be patient – but only in the certain knowledge that they will eventually get their own way.

'So how did Shooks expect those children to be cured with nothing more than hot water and inch-sticks?' asked Francis, tossing down his quill-pen.

They were sitting in their parlour after supper. Beatrice was finishing a sampler while Francis was trying to write this Sunday's sermon. His theme was 'how to appeal to God's mercy', but Beatrice noticed that he had fiercely crossed out almost as many lines as he had written.

'My dearest, I have no idea,' she told him. 'We don't even know if they *will* be cured yet, do we? For all we know, they could have passed away by now, God forbid.'

'I know it's uncharitable of me to say so, but I really dislike that man,' said Francis. 'He has such a *smugness* about him. Whenever he walks into a room, he makes me feel as if I'm twelve years old and that I have no understanding of religion at all. I don't like the way he looks at you, either.'

'I can't say that I've noticed.'

'Well, it's salacious. That's the only way that I can describe it.'

'Why, Francis! I do believe you're jealous!'

A few minutes after nine o'clock Francis announced that he was going upstairs to bed. Beatrice told him that she had to bring up some washing from the back yard that Mary had forgotten, but that she wouldn't be long in joining him.

There was very little washing hanging up on the line, only two shirts and some of Noah's clouts, and once she had collected them under her arm Beatrice went to the stable, where Kingdom's body was still lying on its side in the straw.

He looked stiff and strange, with his legs sticking out straight, like a horse that her father had turned into one of his wooden animals. His stomach, however, was hugely swollen and he was beginning to smell cloying and sweet. She knelt down and used one of Noah's clouts to gather up some of the diarrhoea-caked straw from under his tail. Then she did the same for the straw that was covered in his dry green vomit.

Holding up her lantern, she peeled back his lips and looked into his mouth. Underneath his tongue and between his back teeth she discovered six or seven dark green needles, although they were so well chewed that it was difficult to tell what they were. She picked these out and wrapped them up, too.

She looked down at Kingdom for the last time. Francis had instructed Jubal and Caleb to cremate him at the end of the field the next day, to destroy any traces of satanic infection, in the same way that they had cremated the pigs. It seemed as if, day by day, their secure and happy lives were going up in smoke, although she had no idea who could bear them such ill-will. She was seriously fearful that one of the family might be next, either Francis or herself, or even little Noah.

She walked briskly back across the yard to the house. She had to will herself not to break into a run, for the night all around her was black and noisy with the grunts and screams of nighthawks.

*

Just as dawn was beginning to lighten the sky outside their window, Francis turned towards her and slipped his hand up underneath her thin linen nightgown. She was already awake but she had been lying still, thinking about Apphia and Tristram and how Kingdom had collapsed between the shafts of their shay.

'Francis—' she said, but he had cupped his hand around her left breast and was gently rolling her nipple between finger and thumb, until it stiffened.

'*Francis*—' she repeated, more insistently, as he dragged up her nightgown and tried to turn her over on to her back. Her mind was too filled with questions and anxiety to think about making love.

'I *need* you, Bea,' he said hoarsely. It didn't sound like a demand. It was more of a plea for help.

'Francis, please,' she said. As he lifted himself over her, however, she stopped trying to resist him and lay back on the pillow and parted her thighs so that he could kneel between them. He was her husband, after all, and if he needed her, then how could she deny him? He was only showing her how much he loved her.

She closed her eyes as he entered her. He pushed himself into her as far as he could go and leaned forward to kiss her. He kissed her again and again, but his lips were very dry and rough and his breath smelled of the onions he had eaten yesterday evening. She turned her face away and closed her eyes, although he continued to kiss her neck.

'What would I do, Bea?' he asked her. He was pushing himself into her again and again, unusually hard and unusually quick, and was starting to pant. 'I don't know how I could live without you.'

In spite of his exertions, she could feel that he was beginning to soften. He slipped out of her, and although he managed to cram himself back inside her again, using his fingers, it was hopeless. After two or three more pushes he lost his erection altogether and he was gone. He rolled off her and dropped heavily on to the bed beside her.

'*Francis*,' she said, stroking the stubble on his chin. 'Please don't feel badly, my love. You have so much to worry about apart from making love.'

'It's that Jonathan Shooks,' said Francis. He pulled at his softened penis in frustration, stretching it up as if he wanted to strangle it for letting him down.

'Don't let him concern you, Francis. It amuses him to taunt people, you know that.'

'It's no use, Bea! I can't stop seeing his face, even when I close my eyes! The way he smiles at me, so self-satisfied, as if he's a personal friend of God and chats to Him intimately – while I can do nothing more than call out to Him from the next room, so to speak, through prayer, and only hope that He can hear me.'

He paused for breath, and then he said, much more quietly, 'Shooks makes me think the most unchristian of thoughts.'

'Tell me, Francis. If this is affecting you so much, I have the right to know what it is.'

Francis bit his lip. 'I found myself hoping that the Buckley children would not survive, so that it would prove to the whole village that Jonathan Shooks is nothing but a charlatan. Can you believe that I allowed such a thought to enter my head?'

'Oh, Francis. You shouldn't let him trouble you so! He is very much travelled, very experienced, and he has a very bold way about him. But you are just as strong as he is, and you are true to your beliefs. If he is nothing but a boaster, then God will eventually reveal him for what he is.'

'I don't know. What disturbs me about him most of all is that he might be much more skilled at dealing with the Devil than I am. He hasn't shaken my belief in God, Bea, but he has shaken my belief in myself.'

Beatrice pulled down his nightshirt to cover him up and then drew the sheets over him, up to his neck, and kissed him.

'It's still very early,' she said. 'Hold me in your arms and let us sleep a little more. Try not to think any more about Jonathan Shooks. I know you think that his presence belittles you, but perhaps he will prove himself to be your ally rather than your enemy.'

Beatrice slept for another half-hour. A little after five o'clock she gently disengaged herself from Francis's arms and eased herself out of bed. He was deeply asleep now and softly snoring. She went to the window and drew back the crewel-work drapes, which she had embroidered herself. The morning sun was casting long shadows across the paddock where Kingdom had grazed, until yesterday.

She felt sad, but this new day also made her feel more determined. If she could find the time, she had the dried-out traces of Kingdom's illness to examine, as well as the tarry samples from Henry Mendum's field. Her father had often analysed his customers' vomit, or their urine or their stools, to discover what they might have eaten or drunk to make them fall ill, and she was fairly confident that she could do the same from the evidence that she had collected.

She took off her mob cap and shook her dark hair loose. She crossed her arms in front of her, grasping her nightgown, and she was just about to lift it off when she saw one of the long shadows in the paddock detach itself, amoeba-like, from the rest of the shadows and move across the grass.

She could see now that it wasn't a shadow at all but the figure in the long brown cloak that she had seen yesterday, standing at the end of the driveway. It paused for a moment, as if it were staring up at her window. Then, using its staff as if it were poling a flat-bottomed boat, it quickly walked away and disappeared underneath the trees. As it did so, she heard a bird screeching.

Beatrice stayed by the window for over half a minute, wondering who the figure was and if it would reappear. She turned around and looked at Francis. She considered waking him up, but now that the figure had gone there was really no point to it, and he needed his sleep.

She turned back to the window but all she could see was Mary, walking up the driveway in her apron and flappy yellow bonnet. She could hear Noah singing in his crib, as he almost always did when he first opened his eyes in the morning. It was time to get dressed and go downstairs and set her dough for baking today's bread.

By the time she came down to the kitchen Mary had already taken Noah from his crib and changed him, and was feeding him bread soaked in milk. He bounced up and down in his baby chair when he saw her and cried, 'Mama!' so that a wet lump of bread dropped out of his mouth and on to his smock.

'Come on, Noah!' Beatrice chided him. 'Don't be such a messy puppy !' She went over to the hutch to fetch a mixing bowl. She usually had her own breakfast much later, about ten o'clock, after she had finished her baking and any other early chores that had to be attended to, such as mending and scouring the pewter and preserving the pears that she and Mary had collected from the orchard.

On the hutch beside her mixing bowls she saw a small brown paper package, tightly tied with hairy string and sealed with blobs of green wax.

'Mary?' she asked, holding it up. 'Where did this come from?'

Mary wiped Noah's mouth and turned around. 'Oh, *that* – I don't know, Goody Scarlet. I found it on the front step when I came in. I don't know who could have left it, but you'll see that it has your name on it.'

Beatrice turned the package over. On one side of it *Beatrice Scarlet* was written in a scrawly copperplate hand. That in itself was very unusual, since most of the letters and packages she received were addressed to *The Reverend Francis Scarlet, His Wife*. She shook it. It made a dull rattling sound, but she couldn't begin to guess what was in it, so she took a knife out of the cutlery drawer and cut the string.

Inside the brown paper wrapping there was a plain cardboard box, and when she opened it she found a teardrop-shaped glass bottle with a triangular glass stopper.

She lifted the bottle up to the light. There was no label on it, but it was filled with an amber-coloured liquid.

'What is it?' asked Mary. 'It looks like perfume, doesn't it?'

'There's only one way to find out,' said Beatrice. The stopper was fastened with thin silk thread, like a clarinet reed. She cut through it and tugged out the stopper with a glassy squeak.

'Well?' said Mary.

Beatrice was cautious about smelling the contents of the bottle. She knew that there were several poisons that could cause unconsciousness, and even death, if they were inhaled, such as camphor and spirits of hartshorn, and if this package had been left on the doorstep by somebody who wished her harm then she needed to be very careful. Why anybody should wish to poison her, she couldn't imagine – but then she couldn't imagine why anybody would want give her a gift of perfume, either.

She sniffed, and then sniffed again. The bottle definitely contained perfume, and it was a perfume she recognized because it was very popular among the wealthier women around the village. Henry Mendum's wife, Harriet, wore it – and very liberally, too. It was a strong blend of musk, amber and jasmine, and it was called Queen Margot's Perfume, after the queen of France who had first blended it. Beatrice never bought perfume herself, but she knew that this one was very expensive, more than ten shillings a bottle.

She passed it across to Mary and let her smell it.

'It's wonderful,' said Mary. 'But who would have bought it for you?'

Beatrice replaced the stopper and put the bottle back in its box. She didn't want Francis to come down and smell it because she could think of only one man who had looked at her flirtatiously of late, and who appeared to have enough money to buy her perfume, and that was Jonathan Shooks.

It also occurred to her who the mysterious figure in the brown hooded cloak might have been. She had heard a bird-like screech as it had vanished into the trees, but perhaps that screech had not been a bird at all. Perhaps it had been Jonathan Shooks's mute carriage-driver, Samuel.

Eighteen

It was another hot morning, although thick white cumulus clouds were piling up like giant cauliflower curds behind the trees to the west of Sutton and Beatrice could hear the distant grumbling of thunder.

She was out in the garden cutting asparagus when she heard a wagon around the front of the house. After a few moments Mary came out and said, 'Ambrose Cutler is here, Goody Scarlet! He says that he's come to take you and the reverend into the village to see the Buckley children!'

Beatrice gathered up the asparagus stems in her apron and hurried towards the kitchen door. 'Does he have news of them? Are they recovered?'

'Much better, so he says.'

Francis was already sitting on the side of the bed pulling on his stockings when she went upstairs to their bedchamber.

'This is good news, isn't it?' she said, as she took down her new blue linen bed-gown.

'Yes, it is,' said Francis. 'At least it shows that my malicious thoughts about Jonathan Shooks had no ill effect on the children, thank God.'

Ambrose drove them down to the village. A small crowd was already gathered outside the Buckley house, although there was no sign yet of Jonathan Shooks's black calash. Francis helped Beatrice down from Ambrose Cutler's wagon and they went inside. Some of the women clapped their hands as Francis appeared and two or three of them curtseyed and said, 'Reverend'.

In the Buckley twins' bedchamber they found Judith holding Apphia in her arms, while Tristram was still in his crib. Both children were flushed, with reddened cheeks, but they were awake and they looked much better, even if they did appear bewildered by all the people crowded around them.

Nicholas came away from the side of Tristram's crib. He grasped Francis's hands and shook them as if he were never going to let him go. His eyes were filled with tears.

'The Lord has answered you, Reverend Scarlet! I don't know how I can thank you! Look at them both! They have both taken milk and Apphia has even managed a spoonful or two of apple sauce.'

Beatrice took Apphia in her arms. She was hot and sticky, and she smelled of sick, but she looked up at Beatrice and gave her a bashful smile.

'Do you think that Mr Shooks's remedy helped at all?' she asked Nicholas.

Nicholas shook his head. 'I don't see how. He made a drink of inch-sticks dropped into hot water! How could that cure anybody? But there is plenty of proof in the Bible that people can be cured by the power of prayer. Apart from *your* prayers, reverend, Judith and I prayed almost all night.'

'Well, we're delighted that Apphia and Tristram seem to be so much improved,' said Francis. 'I will say another prayer for their complete recovery.'

Beatrice smiled and handed Apphia back to Judith. As she turned around to leave, though, Jonathan Shooks appeared in the doorway. His wig was dusty and his face looked drawn, as if he had just returned from a long and arduous journey.

He looked quickly around the room and his eyes fixed almost immediately on Beatrice.

'Mr Shooks!' said Nicholas. 'I am very pleased to see you, sir!'

Beatrice thought that Nicholas didn't sound pleased to see him at all. He spoke in quick, nervous blurts and as he spoke he continuously wrung his hands together.

'How are the children this morning?' asked Jonathan Shooks. 'They appear to be much more lively.'

'Yes, well, much better, thank you,' said Nicholas. 'It seems that the Lord has answered our appeals.'

Jonathan Shooks went over to Tristram's crib. He placed his hand for a moment against Tristram's forehead and said, '*Hmmm*.' Then he went over to Judith and held his hand against Apphia's forehead, too.

'Good,' he nodded. Then he lifted up his brown leather satchel and said, 'I've brought more Chinese inch-sticks. If you would be kind enough to ask your girl to boil some water for me, Goody Buckley?'

'As I say, sir, we thank you for your concern,' put in Nicholas.

'But?' said Jonathan Shooks. He paused in the middle of unbuckling his satchel. 'I sense a qualification, sir.'

'Yes, you do. I – we, my wife and myself, that is – we don't think that any more of your remedy will be necessary.'

Jonathan Shooks frowned. 'Your twins *are* improving, sir, there's no doubt of that. But the cause of their improvement is the infusion that I gave them, which is gradually flushing out their lungs. They are both still feverish, though, and their breathing is still laboured. They have some way to go before we can consider them fully restored to good health.'

'You believe that they need further doses of your inch-stick water, Mr Shooks?' Beatrice asked him.

'Of course. You can all see for yourselves how effective it has been. But they are not well yet and it would be folly to stop the treatment now.'

'Well, you *would* of course say that, under the circumstances,' said Nicholas.

'I'm sorry, Mr Buckley?' replied Jonathan Shooks. 'I'm not at all sure that I follow you. Why would I say such a thing if it didn't happen to be true?'

Nicholas turned to appeal to Judith. 'I've been turning this over in my mind all night, when I wasn't praying for the twins to recover. I think that I am being played for a fool and that Mr Shooks here has taken advantage of our babies' sickness to deceive me.'

'My dear sir, why should I deceive you?' asked Jonathan Shooks. 'To what possible end? Your children's lives are at a stake here – these twins. Surely their survival is priceless.'

'Yes, it is. Priceless. That is why the Reverend Scarlet asked for nothing from me, saving my trust in God.'

'So you believe that I am gulling you, sir? Is that it?'

Nicholas was so emotional that he couldn't speak, only press his lips tightly together and furiously nod his head. Judith laid one hand on his shoulder and said, 'Nicholas? I don't understand, either. Even if it *was* the prayers that worked, and not the water, how is Mr Shooks deceiving us?'

'The inch-stick water *does* work,' said Jonathan Shooks. 'Believe me, Goody Buckley, if I had not given your twins my infusion, they would never have lasted the night. We would be arranging two funerals this morning, not arguing about the merits of further treatment.'

'And the reverend's prayers had no effect, I suppose?' Nicholas challenged him.

'I hold nothing against prayer, sir,' said Jonathan Shooks.

'Prayer can be very beneficial when you feel that you have nowhere else to turn. But in this case, you and your goodwife *did* have somewhere to turn. You could turn to me, and my wider knowledge of the unfamiliar guises in which Satan and his attendant demons can appear in foreign lands. And, of course, how to dismiss such demons.'

'For which I had to pledge you twenty acres of land,' said Nicholas.

'*What*?' said Judith. 'What do you mean? Twenty acres of land is more than half of all we own!'

Jonathan Shooks raised both hands, as if he were surrendering. 'Yes, Goody Buckley. I *did* ask your husband for twenty acres of land. The demons who have made your children so sick would accept no less. I think you can count yourself lucky that they didn't demand every single daywork.'

'These demons wanted *land*?' asked Francis sharply.

'Why should that surprise you?' asked Jonathan Shooks. 'Come along, reverend, you and I talked about this before. Satan is trying his best to repossess this country before you can spread the Christian religion too widely and the demons who infected these unfortunate children were acting on his behalf. They were probably using some misguided human agent, as you said yourself.'

'Yes, the Widow Belknap,' said Goody Rust from the hallway.

'Something similar has happened in many European countries,' Jonathan Shooks went on. 'In Poznań, in Poland, Satan was so alarmed at the number of churches being built that he sent demons to lift up a hill and drop it into the river Warta so that the whole city would be drowned. Fortunately, the demons were surprised by a rooster crowing and the hill landed in the middle of a wood. But the hill is still there today. I have seen it for myself.'

'So what are their names, these demons, and what do they look like?' asked Francis.

Jonathan Shooks put his fingertip to his lips. 'It would be very unwise of me to utter their names now, Reverend Scarlet. Not here, with these children present. If the demons hear their names, they may very well think that they are being summoned back here, and the consequence of that could be fatal. I promise that I will tell you later, in private, and also how you may recognize them when you see them. Which, believe me, you will. Satan has not finished with Sutton yet.'

Nicholas said, 'I believe in Satan, Mr Shooks. But I also still believe that you took advantage of me in a moment of great weakness. What will happen to my twenty acres if I make them over to you? Will the demons farm it? Or will *you*? Or will you sell it for a profit?'

Jonathan Shooks gave him a thin, humourless smile. 'I regret to say that what happens to your land will no longer be your business, sir. I have done what you begged me to do, which was to bring back your two beloved children from the very edge of their open graves. I made it patently clear to you that twenty acres was my price for doing it, and that I could not do it otherwise.'

Tristram began to cough and to whine for breath. Judith lifted him out of his crib and called out, 'Jane, please put a kettle on to boil!'

Nicholas, however, said, 'No, Jane, don't! These children don't need water with burned-out sticks in it. They need prayer.'

Jonathan Shooks turned to Beatrice. She had never seen such a complicated expression on a man's face before. He didn't say anything to her, but he was staring at her intently, his eyes narrowed, as if he were trying to transmit his thoughts directly into her brain. She thought that he looked anxious, but at the same time he looked frustrated, too. She felt that he wanted her to explain to Nicholas that he was making a very serious misjudgement and that unless he changed his mind his twins were in imminent danger of dying. Two precious lives, for the sake of what? A few acres of cornfield?

'Mr Shooks?' she asked him. He stared at her a moment longer, but he still didn't say anything to her. He gave a slight shake of his head and then turned away.

She was deeply puzzled. Why should Jonathan Shooks think that *she* could have any influence on Nicholas, out of everybody here? Perhaps he had somehow discovered that she was well acquainted with medical remedies and that she would know that his 'inch-stick water' actually worked? In truth, she had never come across it before and had no idea whether it might be effective or not. Even if it were, and even if she were sure of it, it wouldn't be easy for her to tell Nicholas that it wasn't Francis's prayer that had saved his children. Not in front of Francis, anyhow. His confidence had been shaken more than enough by Jonathan Shooks.

'You're adamant, Mr Buckley?' asked Jonathan Shooks.

'Yes,' said Nicholas.

'Well, to put it kindly, I think you're a fool. I sincerely hope that your twins survive without further treatment. If they do, however, I shall still come looking for my recompense because it was my ministration that saved them.'

'You can come looking all you like, Mr Shooks. I have spent all of my life working those acres and I will not be tricked out of them.'

Judith started to cry again – deep, painful sobs. Beatrice went over and held her very close.

'Shush,' she whispered. 'Shush.'

'They're going to die, aren't they?' wept Judith. 'My poor, dear babies! They're going to die!'

'Shush,' Beatrice soothed her, and then, very close to her ear, while everybody else in the house was talking loudly, she said, 'I'll come back this afternoon with something to help Apphia and Tristram get better. Don't tell Nicholas, though. Don't tell anybody.'

She glanced across at Francis, who gave her a hesitant, uncomprehending smile.

'Don't even tell God,' she whispered.

Nineteen

Young Ambrose Cutler drove Beatrice home on his wagon, but Francis stayed in the village to visit Major General Holyoke and discuss the forthcoming court cases.

That afternoon, Francis had been invited to go to Henry Mendum's stables to choose a replacement for Kingdom. After he had heard about Kingdom's death, Henry Mendum had sent a message to Francis saying that, among other horses, he had a strong three-year-old bay that would make an excellent driver and that he could let him have it for £7 instead of £9, which it was probably worth.

Jonathan Shooks had stalked out of the Buckley house without saying another word and Samuel had driven him away immediately. Because of that, Beatrice hadn't had the opportunity to ask him if it was he who had sent her that bottle of Queen Margot's Perfume. She had no fear of asking him, although she wasn't at all sure what she would have said if he had admitted that, yes, that it *had* been him. Would she have dared to ask what he expected in return – if anything?

As Ambrose circled the wagon around to make their way back to the parsonage, Beatrice saw that the Widow Belknap was leaning over her front fence, with her black parrot, Magic, perched on the gatepost beside her. She was wearing a brick-red dress with a matching bonnet, and was smoking a clay pipe.

'Do you mind turning down that way, Ambrose?' she asked him. 'I want to have a word with Widow Belknap.'

Ambrose turned the wagon around again and drew it to a halt outside the Widow Belknap's house. The Widow Belknap blew smoke out of the corner of her mouth and said, 'Well! Good day to you, Goody Scarlet! You've been to visit the Buckley babies, I presume? How are they?'

'Better, for the time being, anyhow,' said Beatrice. 'Unlike our horse, Kingdom, who died yesterday, not long after we had stopped here to talk to you.'

The Widow Belknap took another puff at her pipe. 'I heard about that, yes. Very unfortunate.' She paused for a moment, and then she said, 'You don't blame *me* for it, do you? You and that holy husband of yours?'

'We don't know *what* caused his death, Widow Belknap. Not yet, anyhow.'

'Well, don't worry, you can blame me if you like! Everybody in Sutton blames me for every misfortune that befalls them, great or small, and I'm really quite used to it. In fact, the more my neighbours fear me, the more they stay out of my business and leave me alone, which is just the way I like it.'

'Please – I am not accusing you of anything,' said Beatrice. 'But I shall be trying to discover why it was that poor Kingdom died so suddenly, and if I *do* find evidence that he was killed with malice, I believe that I shall also find proof of who was responsible.'

'Oh, really?' said the Widow Belknap. 'I don't know how you expect to do that, Goody Scarlet, but you don't alarm me one bit. As I say, I am quite used to being blamed. All I can say is that anybody who makes false accusations against me had better be prepared to accept the consequences. I don't answer to the gossips of this village, nor to you, nor your saintly husband. I answer only to my own conscience and the Powers that Be.'

'Oh, yes? And what does that mean? The Powers that Be?'

'Whatever you take it to mean, Goody Scarlet. You're a pastor's wife, aren't you? Haven't you been reading your scriptures lately?'

'There are powers of good mentioned in the Bible, Widow Belknap, but there are many powers of evil, too.'

The Widow Belknap didn't answer that, but sucked on her pipe again, although it had now gone out. Even if she had caused Kingdom's sudden seizure – whether by curse or by poison or by satanic spell – she clearly had no intention of admitting it.

Beatrice said to Ambrose, 'Thank you, Ambrose, let's go,' but just as they lurched forward she caught sight of a mass of pink and purple flowers by the Widow Belknap's front porch. She hadn't noticed them before because they were growing so deeply in the shade.

'Stop, please!' she said, and Ambrose pulled on the brake. 'That's lungwort! *There*, Widow Belknap, by your door! *Pulmonaria.*'

The Widow Belknap turned around to see where Beatrice was pointing. 'Oh, yes. I call it "spotted dog" myself, but yes, you're right. Lungwort.'

'Do you mind if I take a few leaves?' asked Beatrice. 'I thought I would have to go all the way to the woods to find some.'

'I suppose so. What do you want them for?'

'I want to make an infusion to treat the Buckley twins. Their lungs are all clogged with fluid and lungwort will help them to breathe more easily.'

'You want me to help you to cure them? I thought you suspected me of making them sick.'

'*Was* it you who made them sick?'

'You're very barefaced, Goody Scarlet. Do you seriously think that if I had done I would confess to it? My life may not be a happy one, but I have no desire to lose it just yet.'

Ambrose Cutler said, 'I'm sorry, Goody Scarlet, but I can't tarry here much longer. I have chores to be doing at home.'

'Well?' said Beatrice.

The Widow Belknap smiled. 'All right, pick some leaves if you want some. Take as many as you like.'

Beatrice lifted up her muslin petticoats and climbed down from her seat. 'If it was you who made those children ill, Widow Belknap, God will see this as a gesture of redemption.'

The Widow Belknap stared at Beatrice with her green feline eyes and gave her an eerie smile.

'You know what your trouble is, Goody Scarlet? A pretty young woman like you – you've been married to a man of God for far too long.'

As soon as she arrived home Beatrice went through to the kitchen to fetch Ambrose some jumble cookies for his trouble. While she was wrapping them up in a cloth, she asked Mary to fill a copper pan with water and put it on the stove to simmer.

Mary picked up one of the floppy green silver-speckled leaves that Beatrice had laid in a heap on the kitchen table and cautiously sniffed it. The leaves gave off a sappy, fresh fragrance, like comfrey or cucumbers.

'You're not thinking of making *soup* with those, Goody Scarlet?'

'An infusion, Mary, to save two little lives. I will show you how to make it yourself, in case any of your family ever get sick with consumption, or the croup.'

'I must hang out the wash,' said Mary. 'The bread's almost ready, by the way.'

That morning Beatrice had left the house with Francis before her dough had proved, but while she was away Mary had rolled it out for her and put the loaves into the oven to bake. Mary had boiled all the laundry, too, and swept the floors, and peeled and chopped a whole barrel of quinces, ready for jelly-making. Because she had done all this, Beatrice at last had a little time to examine the residue of Kingdom's sickness and the tarry substance that had looked like the Devil's hoof prints.

She didn't expect Francis to be home until late, and although she felt guilty about making these tests without telling him what she was doing, she didn't want him to think that she, too, was questioning his authority. She was his wife, and she loved him, and she respected his absolute trust in God. When they knelt beside their bed at night and prayed, she would often open one eye to watch him and wish that her own faith burned as brightly as his.

'Noah!' she called. 'Go out in the yard and play, my darling! Mary's out there, hanging up the sheets!'

Noah toddled out into the sunshine. Beatrice meanwhile went to the musty-smelling leather-bound chest at the end of the hallway and took out her father's notebooks, as well as a bottle of pure alcohol and three glass flasks, all wrapped up in grey tissue paper. Back in the kitchen, she half-filled two of the flasks with warm water and then pushed the clouts that she had used to wipe up Kingdom's vomit and diarrhoea into them. To the flask with the vomit she added some of the dark green needles that she had found under his tongue and between his teeth.

Into the third flask she tucked the linen handkerchief with the tarry hoof print on it, and then poured half a cupful of alcohol into it. She had guessed from its strong naphtha smell that the hoof print was mainly composed of coal tar, even though it was mixed with other substances, and she knew that coal tar was insoluble in water. Her father used to make a mixture of alcohol and coal tar for the treatment of chronic skin complaints, like psoriasis or St Anthony's Fire.

She stirred all three flasks with the handle of a wooden spoon and then waited for a few minutes for the solids to dissolve. While she did so, she looked out of the kitchen window at Noah sitting next to Mary while she hung up the wash, playing with her clothes pegs. He was tapping them together and then throwing them as far as he could across the grass.

She felt sad for him – and sad for herself, too. It had taken her nearly five years before she had first fallen pregnant, even though she had prayed every day for a child and regularly taken solutions of red clover and motherwort. Since Noah's birth she still hadn't fallen pregnant a second time, even though she wanted so much to give him brothers and sisters. Most of the goodwives in Sutton had at least five children and some had seven or eight, or even more. Goody Knowlton had eleven.

Beatrice knew that Francis wanted more children. He considered it his duty to set a good example to his parishioners and multiply. But he had always been considerate and understanding and if he was disappointed by her inability to conceive he tried not to show it. He had reassured her several times that Noah was a blessing and that God might have some other mission for her apart from motherhood.

She sniffed the flask of diluted vomit first. She was relying mainly on her sense of smell to find out if Kingdom had been poisoned. Her father had encouraged her to open every jar and bottle that crowded the shelves of his apothecary and breathe in the contents until she could identify them with her eyes closed, as he could.

The vomit water smelled distinctly like tonquin beans or vanilla. She knew that tonquin beans could make you very sick if you ate too many of them, although many wives used them for flavouring cookies and cakes. They were also supposed to have magical properties. When she had been trying for Noah, Goody Rust had told her that if you held a tonquin bean in your hand and made a wish, your wish was supposed to come true, and only a month afterwards she had conceived.

The Widow Belknap was familiar with poisons and herbs and magical potions. Perhaps she had fed Kingdom a handful of tonquin beans along with the weeds that she had torn out of her garden? But Beatrice doubted if she would have been able to feed him enough to stop his heart – and she could detect another smell in the liquid, much more pungent than vanilla, which put her in mind of cat's urine or leather.

She sniffed the diarrhoea water and that smelled similar, although not as strong.

She opened up her father's notebooks and flicked through page after page until she came to a chapter that he had written about 'Equine Ailments'. His writing was tiny and crabbed, but very neat, and at last she found what she was looking for: 'Vegetation Toxic to Horses & Cattle'.

Wm Chandler ask'd me to come to Islington to see to his piebald mare which was suffering from palpitations of the heart and sickness. By the time I arrived at his property it was too late and the mare had expired. It was clear however the cause of death. His gardeners having trimmed his yew hedges had thrown the cuttings into the field where he keeps the mare and she had eaten them. The vanilla smell was most distinctive on her breath and her mouth was still filled with yew leaves and berries, both of which are toxic to horses. Less than 6 lbs of yew leaves can kill an adult horse in less than 5 mins, even quicker in the winter, when the toxin is stronger.

Her father had painted a watercolour picture of the yew leaves that had poisoned Mr Chandler's mare and they were almost identical to the slimy green leaves Beatrice had found in Kingdom's mouth.

She knew now what had probably caused his death, but she was still frustrated. She had hoped that if she discovered *how* he had died, she would be able to tell if somebody had poisoned him on purpose, and if so, who. But she would have to go back to the village to see if there were yew bushes growing in the Widow Belknap's garden, and even if there were, she would have no absolute proof that it was the Widow Belknap who had fed them to him.

She glanced out of the window and saw that Mary had almost finished pinning up the wash, so she turned to the third flask. She took out the linen handkerchief and sniffed the alcohol inside it, which had now been turned pale amber by the dissolving coal tar.

The smell was very complex, but when she closed her eyes Beatrice could detect several other notes in it apart from coal tar and cloves. She was sure that there was civet oil, which gave off an odour even more like cat's urine than the yew leaves. There was sulphur, too, which reeked like rotten eggs. There was also an aroma that was cloying and very sweet, but which she found hard to identify. She guessed that it was molasses. There must also have been some strong acid or alkali content which had burned Francis's fingers when he had touched it, but it had no smell.

When she had finished she poured all three liquids away and rinsed out the flasks. The pan was simmering now, so she quickly chopped up the lungwort leaves and lowered them into the water. They would take about an hour and then she could strain them and take the infusion down to the Buckley twins.

She needed to find out more. The coal-tar mixture that had been used to make the hoof prints and the upside-down cross had obviously been intended to look and smell like the marks of the Devil, and there was no question that they had badly frightened most of the villagers who had seen them. However, they had finally convinced Beatrice that Sutton was being threatened by a human man or woman, and not by Satan, or a demon, or even anyone acting on Satan's behalf.

If this viscous brown concoction had really been left behind by Satan, it would surely have been some evil substance exuded from his own demonic glands, and she doubted that she would have been able to determine what it was made of. It was highly unlikely that it would have been a mixture of coal tar, civet musk, sulphur and refined sugar beet, which were all ingredients that could be bought at any grocery store or pharmacist's.

Once she had put away the flasks, and washed the clouts, she spent a few minutes leafing quickly through her father's notebooks in search of any entry about Chinese fire inch-sticks and whether they could really be used to ease lung congestion.

She was still reading what he had written about betony, and how it helped to cure shortness of breath, especially when mixed with honey, when she heard a light carriage approaching the parsonage, very fast. There was a jingle of traces and then somebody frantically banged the knocker at the open front door.

'Reverend Francis! Reverend Francis! You must come quick! It's hellfire, reverend! Hellfire!'

Twenty

Beatrice immediately closed the notebook and hurried out into the hallway. She thought she had recognized the young man's voice, even though it was hoarse with panic. It was Nathaniel, the youngest of the five sons of George and Elizabeth Gilman. The Gilmans owned a large farm that lay to the north-west of Henry Mendum's property.

Nathaniel was a broad-shouldered, well-fed, round-faced boy of nineteen, with a tangle of blond curls and blue eyes and freckles. He had obviously been working in the fields because he was wearing a broad-brimmed hat, his shirt-sleeves were rolled up, and his stockings and the knees of his cotton britches were stained with sandy orange soil.

'Where's the Reverend Scarlet?' he asked. 'I have to fetch the Reverend Scarlet!'

'Nathaniel, calm yourself!' said Beatrice. 'The reverend isn't here at the moment, he's gone to Henry Mendum's to buy us a new horse.'

'Then I'll have to go and find him! My father said to bring him back home with me at any cost!'

'What's the matter, Nathaniel? What's happened? Is there anything I can do?'

'It's the Devil, Goody Scarlet! He's come to *our* farm now! Three of our slaves are dead and one nearly! He's burned

186

them alive, in hellfire!'

'Dear God, Nathaniel, that's terrible! But how do you know it's the Devil?'

'Because of the cross that he's marked on the wall of the barn, a topsy-turvy cross!'

'Is it painted, this cross, in some kind of tar?'

Nathaniel nodded furiously, as if he were doing his best to shake his head off. 'My mother said there's no doubt about it. It's the same as the cross they found in the Buckleys' house.'

'In that event I'm coming with you!' said Beatrice. 'Just let me tell Mary to look after Noah.'

'But father said I needed to fetch the reverend!'

'I understand that, Nathaniel. But I know as much about this as the reverend does, if not more. Take me first to your farm and then go to Henry Mendum's to find my husband.'

She told Mary that she was going out again, and gave Noah a quick kiss. Then she took down a linen shawl and went outside. Nathaniel was waiting with a two-wheeled carriage and a scruffy-looking roan. He helped her to climb up into the seat and they went trotting briskly off towards the village.

'When did this happen?' asked Beatrice.

'The burning? Less than an hour since. I was up in the five-angle field when I heard my father shouting. I looked up and saw smoke coming from out of the barn and father running towards it, and then my brothers and some of the field-workers, too. By the time we got there, though, it was much too late. There was nothing we could do to save them. Well, one slave called Quamino was still alive, but he's been badly burned. Prince and Cumby and Isum, they were all three dead already.'

'Before this happened, did you see any strangers near the barn?'

Nathaniel shook his head. 'I was working too hard, Goody Scarlet, bent over, planting potatoes. If the Angel Gabriel himself had flown right over my head, I wouldn't have noticed him.'

The Gilman farm lay across a sloping valley, with maple woods on the north-west side and a shallow river meandering down the middle of it. The farmhouse and all the other outbuildings were halfway up a hill in the north-east corner where the ground began to rise towards Henry Mendum's property.

As they jolted down the narrow stony path, Beatrice could see that hazy grey smoke was still drifting out of one of the barn's doorways. Apart from black soot smudges above its side windows, however, like devilish eyebrows, the building didn't appear to have been extensively damaged.

They arrived in the yard, where George and Elizabeth Gilman were gathered with the rest of their sons and most of their farm-workers and slaves. These included three African women, one of whom was wailing uncontrollably and beating herself with her fists, and four or five African children. The other two African women stood silent, but they both looked miserable and bewildered and their cheeks were streaked with tears.

'What, no reverend?' said George Gilman, stepping forward to help Beatrice climb out of the carriage. 'You are very welcome here, Goody Scarlet, but it is your husband that I have urgent need of, rather than yourself.'

Unlike his sons, George Gilman was a slight, wiry man, with a beaky nose and a shock of grey hair. He was never still, however, and endless hard work had made him very prosperous. He reminded Beatrice of one of those clockwork figures that continually rushes around from one side of the room to the other, and she always thought he ought to have a key sticking out of his back.

'Nathaniel,' said Beatrice, 'if you would be so good as to go up to Mr Mendum's farm, you should find the reverend there.'

George Gilman flapped his hand at Nathaniel to indicate that he should go and then said to Beatrice, 'Has Nat told you what's happened here?'

Beatrice nodded. The stench of charred wet hay was making her eyes water, but she was glad that it was strong enough to mask the smell of cremated human flesh.

'He said that some of your slaves have been burned. And a cross painted on to the wall, upside down. There was a cross painted like that on the wall of the Buckley children's bed-chamber when they were taken ill.'

'We heard about that, of course,' said Elizabeth Gilman. She was just as small and sharp-featured as her husband and it seemed almost impossible to Beatrice that she had given birth to so many strapping sons. 'It's the Devil walking among us, no question of that. Either the Devil himself or one of his disciples, naming no names.'

'First it was your pigs, Goody Scarlet,' said George Gilman, counting them off on his fingers. 'Then it was Henry's Devons. Then the Buckley children. Now our poor slaves. But we heard how the reverend's prayers saved the Buckley children's lives.'

Beatrice said, 'Yes, I'm sure that his prayers are helping their recovery, but—'

'What else could it be? It's the power of prayer. It's too late to save our unfortunate slaves. But I am very much hoping that the reverend will be able to call on the Lord to protect the rest of my family, and our livestock, and all of our remaining slaves. It will be very costly to replace them if I lose any more.

Two hundred pounds each, at the very least. More, if their teeth are good.'

'How were your slaves burned?' asked Beatrice. 'Nathaniel told me that one of them has survived. Is he able to talk?'

'Quamino? No, he is being tended to, but he is still unconscious. Whether he will last much longer is anybody's guess. I can show you those who died. We still haven't cut them down yet. I thought it was essential for the reverend to see them *in situ*, as it were.'

'George!' said Elizabeth Gilman, 'I don't think that Goody Scarlet will thank you for showing her. You will give her bad dreams.'

'Well, yes, of course, you're right, my dear. Goody Scarlet, why don't you and Elizabeth go into the house and take some tea while we're waiting for the pastor to appear?'

Beatrice stayed where she was. 'If you don't mind, Mr Gilman, I would very much like to see your dead slaves.'

'I warn you, it's not a pleasant sight. Elizabeth's quite correct. I shouldn't even have suggested it.'

'Thank you for warning me. But I have mentioned to you before, have I not, that my father was an apothecary in the City of London? I have seen every kind of disease and injury that you could imagine, and many that you wouldn't want to imagine, including some truly terrible burns. It takes a lot to turn my stomach, believe me.'

'Well . . . very well. But if the Reverend Scarlet berates me for it, you will have to tell him that you twisted my arm.'

'He won't complain, sir. Honestly. My husband respects my strength as much as I admire his.'

Accompanied by two of his tousle-headed sons, Adam and Augustus, George Gilman led Beatrice into the barn. The hay was only smouldering now, but its smell was so strong that

Beatrice tugged a handkerchief out of her pocket to hold over her nose and mouth.

'I sent for Constable Jewkes, too, but so far there's no sign of him,' said George Gilman over his shoulder. 'I think we can all guess why that is.'

Beatrice didn't answer. She knew that Constable Jewkes would probably be drunk, even though it was early afternoon, but she didn't want to say anything uncharitable.

George Gilman stopped in the middle of the barn. Bales of hay were stacked high on three sides, but it was mostly the hay on the left-hand side that had been scorched black, nearly to the roof. It was still sullenly smoking, although George Gilman and his sons must have thrown scores of bucketfuls of water over it, because it was sodden. The discarded buckets were still lying scattered around on the floor.

George Gilman touched Beatrice's arm and said, 'There,' and pointed upwards. Beatrice lifted her eyes and directly above her she saw the three burned slaves. They were suspended among the rafters by ropes, almost twenty-five feet up. All three of them had their arms spread out wide as if they were flying, and they were lashed to rake handles to keep them that way.

They were all naked, but they had been charred so badly that their skin was hanging in tatters, so that they looked as if they were wearing ragged black clothes. Underneath the tatters their flesh was scarlet and raw. Their legs were drawn up under them, with their knees bent, but Beatrice knew that this was only because the heat had made their tendons shrink. She had once seen the victims of a fire on a coal barge on the Thames and they, too, had all been crouching in this monkey-like posture.

The slaves' mouths were stretched wide open, baring their brown and yellow teeth, and their ash-grey tongues were hanging out. Their eyes were open, too, but the pupils had turned milky-white because they had cooked.

George Gilman pointed to a star-shaped scorch mark on the floor. 'Quamino wasn't strung up, like those three. He was kneeling right there, with his hands together like he was praying, although he was all bound up with rope so that he couldn't move. He was on fire, too, but of course we were able to throw water over him because he was down on the ground, within reach. The other three . . . they didn't stand a dog's chance.'

He looked up again. 'I think you can understand why I wanted the reverend to see these poor fellows before I brought my ladders and cut them down. It's my belief that they were strung up like this on purpose. A blatant act of blasphemy, that's my belief. And that's why I'm sure the Devil did it, or one of the Devil's disciples.'

Beatrice stared at the three black figures with their arms stretched out wide. 'It looks like the Crucifixion, doesn't it? Jesus and the two thieves, on crosses, with one disciple kneeling and praying in front of them.'

'Exactly!' said George Gilman. 'That's the way I see it, anyhow. I believe the Devil has deliberately done it to mock our Redeemer, right at the very moment of His Redemption!'

George Gilman was so agitated that he jerked his arms this way and that, and paced around in circles, and kept taking his wig off and putting it back on again. He was one of the more fervent members of the Sutton congregation and he often helped Francis to organize prayer meetings and Bible study groups, as well as giving readings from the Psalms every Sunday.

'Your poor slaves,' said Beatrice. 'They must have gone through such agony!'

'Yes, indeed, I'm perfectly sure that they did! But the Devil has done much more than burn four undeserving slaves. He has put the torch to everything that our faith means to us! I don't think there's any mistake about it, Goody Scarlet! The rascal is trying to hound all of us God-fearing folk out of Sutton, maybe out of New Hampshire altogether, or at the very least he's trying to make us renounce our religion.'

'Nathaniel mentioned an upside-down cross.'

'Ah, yes, the cross! As if we needed any more proof!' George Gilman stalked across to the opposite side of the barn, where the doors were closed. Daubed on the raw pine planking was a cross, inverted like the cross in the Buckley house, but painted much larger, nearly three feet high, with much thicker tar.

Beatrice went up close to it and sniffed it. It smelled the same as the Devil's hoof prints, of cloves and coal tar and civet oil and sulphur and molasses. If there was any difference, it smelled a little more sulphurous.

'You see?' said George Gilman. 'We're dealing with the Devil and there's your evidence.'

Beatrice looked back up at the three burned bodies, spinning very slowly among the rafters with their knees half-bent and their arms outstretched. *No*, she thought, *we're not dealing with the Devil. I almost wish we were, and that Francis could exorcize him with prayer.*

We're dealing with somebody very much more inventive than the Devil, and more evil, too. The Devil is evil by his very nature, whereas this person has chosen to be evil.

Francis arrived about forty minutes later. By the time Nathaniel Gilman had reached Henry Mendum's farm, he had already left it and ridden their new horse to Rodney Bartlett, the farrier, to be re-shod.

Beatrice was sitting in the stuffy farmhouse parlour with Elizabeth Gilman. Mistress Gilman had served her tea, but she had taken only two or three sips of it. She was beginning to grow anxious because her lungwort infusion would be ready and she needed to take it to the Buckleys. She could only hope that the twins had continued to recover – whether they had been saved by Jonathan Shooks's inch-stick remedy or by Francis's prayers, or a combination of both.

As soon as Francis arrived George Gilman led him into the barn to see the burned slaves suspended from the rafters. They spent more than ten minutes in there while Beatrice and Elizabeth waited for them in silence, their tea growing cold. When he came into the parlour Francis looked shocked and confused, and he immediately came over and took hold of Beatrice's hand.

'*You* saw them, too?' he asked her. 'You shouldn't have done, my dearest. It was too dreadful for words.'

'I'm all right, Francis, really,' said Beatrice. 'I saw far worse in London when I was a child.'

'Dear God, it's hard to imagine anything worse than those three poor wretches!'

Francis turned to George Gilman. 'Has anybody threatened you, George, or made demands?' he asked. 'I can't think why anybody should have tried to intimidate you like this.'

'Isn't it enough that my faith has been mocked?' George Gilman demanded. 'My faith is all I have! I came to America because of my faith! I married Elizabeth and raised a family because of my faith! Here, in my prosperity, is the proof of my faith! Every breath that I have ever taken has been in the service of God, and what has the Devil done to me this day? He has tried to burn my belief to ashes!'

The long-case clock in the hallway chimed four and Beatrice said, 'I need to get back home, Francis, if Nathaniel will be good enough to take me. Will you stay here, or will you come with me?'

'I will remain here for a while,' said Francis. 'I can help George to bring down the bodies and prepare them for burial. They may have only been slaves, but they were still God's creatures and they deserve my prayers.'

Elizabeth took Beatrice by the hands. 'Thank you for coming, Beatrice. I'm sorry that it was under such dreadful circumstances.'

Beatrice wrapped her linen shawl around her shoulders and went outside. She was climbing up on to Nathaniel's wagon when young Augustus Gilman appeared round the side of the house. 'Father? It's Quamino. He has just this minute passed away.'

Beatrice stepped down again. 'I would like to see him, if I may.'

'Bea – do you think that's wise?' asked Francis. 'Haven't you seen enough horrors for one day?'

'Francis, if I am to help you to fight this evil, whatever it is, I need to look it in the face.'

Francis said nothing, but looked across at George Gilman, who simply shrugged and said, 'Lead on, Augustus.'

Augustus took them round the house and across a red-brick yard to the stables. Behind the stables, with their own small gardens, there was a row of cottages where the Gilman's nine slaves lived, with their wives and children. Most of them were standing outside the cottage at the farthest end of the row, sobbing and wailing.

A young woman in a black headscarf and a plain grey cotton dress was standing inside the open door of the cottage, with three small children clinging around her. She hadn't been crying, but Beatrice thought that she had never seen anybody looking so bereft.

'This is Quamino's wife, Sally,' said Augustus. 'Quamino is right inside here.'

Inside the cottage there was only a single room with three wooden chairs and a table and a wide bed under the window. Quamino was lying on the bed covered by a blood-patterned sheet. His face was puffed up with yellowish blisters and his hair had been burned to crisp white ash.

Beatrice approached the bed and looked down at him. It was suffocatingly hot inside the cottage and the smell of stale cinnamon and sweat was overwhelming. When she bent over the bed, however, and inhaled deeply through her nostrils, she picked up several other aromas – pine resin, and naphtha, and a sulphurous odour, too.

'Come away now, Bea,' said Francis from the doorway.

'I won't be a moment,' said Beatrice. She folded back the sheet so that she could see Quamino's chest. The upper part was covered with suppurating yellow blisters, like his face, but lower down his flesh had been burned so deeply in places that his ribs were gleaming through. Around his armpits she could see a white crusty tidemark that looked like salt. She licked the tip of her finger and touched it, and almost at once she felt an intense burning sensation, as if she had pressed her finger against a smoothing-iron. She hastily wiped it on her shawl. It was quicklime. She could guess now what had happened to Quamino and his fellow slaves. They had been stripped naked, tied up, and then liberally plastered in a thick blend of pine resin, quicklime and naphtha, and probably saltpetre, too.

The Devil hadn't done this, not unless the Devil was a chemist. This was Greek fire, or sticky fire. Her father had once mixed some up to burn out a hornets' nest that was too high up to be knocked down with a pole.

Beatrice drew back the sheet over Quamino's body and stepped out into the sunshine. Chickens were strutting up and down outside the cottages and somewhere a dog was barking. Francis said, 'Well? Have you learned anything? Do you have any idea who might have killed him?'

Beatrice turned to Quamino's widow, Sally. Although she had three children, she couldn't have been older than twenty-one or twenty-two. She dropped her gaze when Beatrice looked at her so that she wouldn't appear disrespectful.

Beatrice laid a consoling hand on her arm and said, 'I'm sorry. I know you tried your best to save him, but there was nothing that you could have done. He was burned by a kind of fire that not even water can put out.'

She wasn't sure that Sally understood her, but she nodded, even though she still didn't raise her eyes.

Francis frowned and said, 'Bea? What do you mean? What kind of fire is it that water cannot put out?'

'The fire of hell, reverend,' George Gilman put in, before Beatrice could answer. 'The fire that the Devil keeps stoked for all eternity to punish sinners and threaten the pious.'

'So it *was* Satan who did this?' asked Francis.

'In a way, yes,' said Beatrice. She didn't want to contradict George Gilman to his face or to give the impression that Francis had a wife who was too outspoken.

She climbed up on to Nathaniel's wagon so that he could drive her home. Just before they reached the carved wooden archway across the entrance to the Gilman farm she saw Jonathan Shooks approaching them in his calash, from the direction of Penacook. She heard him call out to Samuel to slow down and as their carriages drew alongside each other he raised his tricorn hat to her.

'Goody Scarlet!' he greeted her. 'Fancy seeing you here!'

'I should say the same to you, Mr Shooks.'

'Well, I received news that something untoward had occurred here and so I came at once to see if there was anything that I could do to help.'

'If you can describe the burning alive of four of Mr Gilman's slaves as 'untoward', sir – then, yes, something untoward *has* happened. My husband is here to pray for their souls.'

'Ah, that's good. We all know how effective your husband's prayers can be.'

'There is no call for sarcasm, Mr Shooks.'

'Please – I hold nothing but admiration for your husband's faith. Is there any indication who might be responsible for this atrocity?'

'I thought *you* were the expert on colonial demons, Mr Shooks.'

Jonathan Shooks took a breath, as if he were about to answer back, and perhaps accuse *her* of sarcasm, but all he did was to nod and give her a smile that said '*touché*' and then rap with his cane on the side of his calash. Samuel let out one of his unearthly screeching noises and Jonathan Shooks went rattling off.

Back at the parsonage, Beatrice strained the pale green lungwort infusion through a muslin bag and then poured it into an earthenware bottle, which she corked.

She wrote a note to Judith Buckley, explaining that she should give each of the twins two tablespoons once every three hours, and that she would call into the village tomorrow to see how they were improving. She gave the bottle to Mary so that she could take it to the Buckleys on her way home.

'And, Mary, please don't drop it! You know what a butter-fingers you can be!'

'Yes, Goody Scarlet. No.'

As Beatrice turned to go back into the house, she caught sight of the tall figure in the brown hooded cloak standing at the very end of the driveway, in the darkest shadows underneath the trees. She shouted, '*Mary*!' but Mary was too far away now to hear her. She thought of running after her, but then she heard Noah tumble over in the kitchen and start to cry.

She went to the kitchen and picked him up, and carried him out to the porch. By now, though, Mary had reached the end of the driveway and the figure had vanished.

Twenty-one

It was almost dark by the time Francis returned home, riding their new horse, Uriel. He had been named for the archangel of healing, one of only four archangels who could stand in the presence of God. Beatrice came out with a lantern to help him see his way round to the paddock.

'There, he's going to be a fine strong driver,' said Francis, patting Uriel on his glossy reddish-brown flank. 'It was very generous of Henry to let us have him for such a reason-able price. It proves that there are still good people in this world.'

'How are Henry's cattle?' asked Beatrice as they walked back into the house.

'Well – they're all recovered, he says. Even the worst of them, he says, that were very close to death.'

'So your prayers *did* work, after all. So much for those who would say that you have lost your connection to God.'

Beatrice blew out the lantern and then they went through to the parlour, which was lit by four sconces on the walls. 'Are you hungry?' she asked. 'I have had no appetite at all after what I saw today, but you should eat.'

Francis shook his head. 'I couldn't, Bea. I keep thinking of what agony those poor men must have suffered. George is so devout and yet it doesn't seem to enter his mind that slaves can feel pain as keenly as the rest of us. He seems to worry more about their value than their souls.'

He hesitated, and then he said, 'Besides, there is something else that has greatly disturbed me.'

Beatrice took hold of his hand, but he turned his head away as if he were ashamed of himself.

'What is it, Francis? Tell me.'

'Henry Mendum. He told me that his Devons had recovered, but only after a visit from Jonathan Shooks. Apparently, Shooks dosed the cattle with some elixir, and spoke some incantation over them, and only a few hours afterwards they began to revive. Yet you and I saw for ourselves, didn't we, how desperately sick they were? I know little of animal husbandry, Bea, but I would have given them very little chance at all.'

'Francis, you must not allow Jonathan Shooks to unsettle you so much! You don't get upset when Dr Merrydew relieves somebody's fever, do you? Or if Rodney Bartlett cures a horse of the staggers?'

'Of course not, because *they* don't make me feel that my prayers are completely ineffectual, in the way that Jonathan Shooks does. They regard my prayers as a spiritual supplement to the practical work that they do, not as some Old World irrelevance.'

'Francis, God is not an Old World irrelevance. God is relevant the whole world over!'

'You know that and I know that. But now that Jonathan Shooks has healed the Buckley children, and Henry's cattle, I suspect that more and more people in the village are beginning to doubt my ability to protect them, and are turning to him. "The Reverend Scarlet knows nothing of the demons that plague us here in the colonies." "The Reverend Scarlet couldn't even stop them from slaughtering his own pigs, or causing his own horse to drop dead in its tracks, right in front of his nose!"'

'Oh, Francis, the people of Sutton know you and love you too well. They wouldn't speak like that about you.'

Francis gave a quick, bitter shake of his head. 'When their own families and their own livelihoods are threatened, Bea, people will turn on anybody.'

The next morning, very early, Mary came bursting into the house when Francis and Beatrice were still in bed and called up the staircase, 'Goody Scarlet! Goody Scarlet! Are you awake yet?'

Beatrice threw back the sheet and climbed out of bed. Francis lifted his head from his pillow, blinking, his hair sticking up at the back like a cock's comb.

'What is it?' he blurted. 'What's wrong?'

Beatrice ran downstairs in her nightgown and bare feet. Mary was standing in the hallway, biting her lip with anxiety.

'What's happened, Mary?' She prayed that it wasn't another dreadful atrocity like the Gilmans' slaves.

'Little Tristram Buckley, Goody Scarlet . . . he looks as if Jesus is just about to take him!'

'We'll come directly. Give us a few moments to dress and harness the shay. The Reverend Scarlet brought home a new horse yesterday evening.'

'I saw it in the paddock. I can harness him for you while you get yourselves ready.'

'How is Apphia? Is she bad, too?'

'No, no. It's only Tristram who's so sick. Goody Buckley is beside herself.'

'You'll take care of Noah, won't you, while we're gone?'

'Of course I will, Goody Scarlet. I'll guard him with my life.'

Francis was almost dressed by the time she came back upstairs and she quickly stepped into her petticoats. She had to ask Francis to lace her corset for her because Noah had woken up and started crying and Mary had gone to attend to him.

'Not tight enough!' she told him as he fumbled with the laces.

'Dear God, Bea, I don't want to squeeze the very life out of you!'

They hurried outside. Mary had harnessed Uriel and tethered him to the split-rail fence beside the driveway. Uriel was restless. Although it was warm this morning, the sky was slate-grey and thundery, and serpents' tongues of lightning were flickering on the horizon towards Bedford.

Francis clicked his tongue and Uriel set off along the driveway at a trot, his head held high. Even if Henry Mendum had upset Francis by appealing to Jonathan Shooks for help in curing his cattle, he had sold him a very handsome young bay.

When they arrived at the village green there were only three or four women gathered by the front door of the Buckley house. It was nearly six o'clock now and every woman in the village had her morning duties – baking and washing and scouring the rooms and preparing the family breakfast. Francis and Beatrice went into the house and the second they stepped into the hallway they heard a terrible, heart-tearing cry of anguish.

The cry was so shrill and so agonized that at first Beatrice thought it was Judith, but when she entered the children's bedchamber she saw that it was Nicholas, who was standing next to Tristram's crib holding the little boy pressed to his chest. His face was a mask of anguish, his mouth dragged downwards and tears sliding down his cheeks. When he opened his eyes and saw Beatrice and Francis he could only choke out, 'Why,

Lord, *why*? Why have You taken this poor innocent child, who has done no harm to anyone?'

Beatrice went over to Judith, who was holding Apphia close to her. Apphia was sobbing, too, although she was still wheezy and struggling for breath. Judith's eyes were almost blind with tears and her mouth was puckered tightly, but she was silent.

'You gave them the lungwort?' asked Beatrice in a gentle voice.

Judith nodded. 'They both took it, and at first they both seemed better.'

She had to pause for a moment to swallow her emotion, but then she said, 'At midnight I gave them more, and still they both appeared well. But when I came in to see them this morning Tristram was gasping for air.

'Several times he stopped breathing altogether, but then he would start again. I tried to give him some more lungwort, but he couldn't swallow it. It was then that I saw Mary passing the house and I asked her to send for you.'

Nicholas laid Tristram gently back on his horsehair mattress. It was damp with sweat and stained with urine. Beatrice leaned over him and felt for his pulse, but there was none. She lifted his eyelids, one after the other, but his pale blue eyes were staring only at heaven. Last of all, just to make sure, she asked Judith for a hand-mirror. She held it close to Tristram's face, but there was no clouding of breath on it.

Nicholas stood close beside her with his fists clenched, looking both miserable and angry.

'That *witch*!' he said, with his nostrils flaring. 'I shall have that witch burned at the stake, I swear to God!'

'Nicholas,' said Francis, 'this is a case for the court, not for revenge. Besides, what proof do you have that the Widow Belknap was responsible for this?'

'Who else could it be? Who else has the ability to make children sick unto death without even entering their bedchamber? Who else is always so vindictive and constantly makes such threats against us?'

'Nicholas, if you have any accusation to make against the Widow Belknap you should send for Constable Jewkes.'

'That tosspot? He's more than likely still in bed, or under the table, or in a ditch, or wherever he fell asleep last night. No – I will speak to her myself. I want to hear from her own lips why she harboured such hatred for us that she took away the life of our beloved boy.'

Beatrice said, 'Nicholas, you should be careful. I have no reason to suppose that you are right and that it was indeed the Widow Belknap who put a curse on Tristram, but at the same time you should beware of making an enemy of her.'

'I'm not afraid of her witchery,' said Nicholas. 'I'm going to go and confront her now, this minute!'

Francis caught at his sleeve, but he twisted it away and pushed through the goodwives crowding in the hallway. There were many more women gathered in the house now, and outside on the village green, too. Beatrice followed Nicholas through the front door and as she did so she saw that Jonathan Shooks had arrived and was just stepping down from his calash. Today he was wearing a coat of a much darker grey, as if it had been cut from the thunderous clouds above their heads. When he saw Beatrice he gave her his usual smile of acknowledgement, part appreciative and part mocking.

Nicholas stalked to the far corner of the village green, to the Widow Belknap's house. By the time he reached it, rain had started falling, fat heavy drops that rustled into the weeds and flowers of the Widow Belknap's front garden.

Beatrice came close behind him as he marched up to the

porch, and both Francis and Goody Rust came close behind her, as well as Jonathan Shooks and William Rolfe, the shoemaker, who had happened to be walking past and was obviously keen to find out what the fracas was all about.

A large brass knocker hung on the Widow Belknap's green-painted front door, in the shape of a snarling wolf's head. Nicholas took hold of it and banged it hard, three times. Almost immediately, the door opened and the Widow Belknap appeared, wearing the same brick-red gown that Beatrice had seen her in yesterday. Her black parrot, Magic, came strutting out, too.

'What's this?' she asked, looking from one of their faces to the next. 'Have you all come to pay me a social call? If so, I regret that I am freshly out of cake.'

'I am come about my baby son, Tristram, you witch!' said Nicholas. His voice was wobbling with anger. 'I am come to ask why you took his life. If you had wanted to take your revenge on us, for whatever reason, why could you not have asked for money, or some other recompense in kind, or even taken *my* life – but not the life of a child who had so many years to look forward to?'

There was a very long silence, during which the Widow Belknap stared at Nicholas unblinkingly. He started to repeat his accusation, but she interrupted him and said, 'I can hear what you are accusing me of, Mr Buckley. However, I had no involvement in it whatever. How could I have taken your baby's life when I was here in my own house all of yesterday and all of last night? And why would I want to? I would have thought you had enough trouble with your own wife without accusing *me* of any misconduct!'

'You can't deceive me, you witch!' Nicholas retorted. 'Every-body in the village knows that you have no need to leave your lair to spread your mischief! You can send that infernal black bird of yours, or one of your cats, or simply a wraith that flies invisible through the darkness, with breath that can suffocate anybody who happens to have displeased you!'

The Widow Belknap looked him up and down with her intense green eyes, as if she were trying to decide what size of coffin he would need.

'How *dare* you come to my door and slander me so?' she replied, although her voice was much quieter and more controlled than his. 'How *dare* you?'

'Because there is only one person in this village who could have wanted to inflict such harm on our family, and there is only one person in this village who is *capable* of it!'

'You nocky!' spat the Widow Belknap. 'Do you really think that I could ever be so exercised by the empty-headed gossip of your wife and her knotting-circle that I would go to the extent of murdering one of your infants? Why would I risk my life for such petty vindictiveness? Do you think I *want* to be hanged, or burned, or floated in a pond?'

'Then who else made my children so sick?' Nicholas lashed back at her. 'Who else would have painted a cross upside down on their bedchamber wall, in brimstone and treacle? My son was murdered by a procurator of the Devil, and there is only one procurator of the Devil in Sutton, and that is *you*, Widow Belknap!'

The Widow Belknap's eyes narrowed and she pointed a long finger directly at his face. 'If you ever call me such a name again, Nicholas Buckley, the flesh will be boiled from your bones and you will be reduced to broth! So go away and think about *that* while you're burying your baby boy!'

'Widow Belknap—' said Francis, stepping forward. 'I am sure this has been nothing more than a simple misunderstanding.

Mr Buckley has just lost his youngest son and it is natural that he is very overwrought. Let us please make peace with one another. You remember what Peter said? "Be ye all of one mind, having compassion, one of another. Love each other as brethren, pitiful and courteous."'

'This witch killed my son!' said Nicholas. 'I shall see her burned, I promise you!'

'Not before *you* have been turned into a mess of pottage, Nicholas Buckley!' said the Widow Belknap. 'Now, get off my property, all of you, before I call the constable and have you arrested for trespass!'

Jonathan Shooks came up and laid a hand on Nicholas's shoulder. 'Come away, my dear fellow. You're playing with fire with this woman, believe me.'

Nicholas pushed his hand away. 'And what about *you*, Mr Shooks? Was I not playing with fire when I invited you to treat my children? On the one hand I have this murdersome witch, and on the other I have you and your Chinese fire-sticks and your deals with demons. I don't know which is the worser!'

'I made it clear to you that I could protect your children,' Jonathan Shooks persisted, his voice dropping even lower and steadier. 'Only, however, at a price.'

'Yes – twenty acres, more than half my land! That land is my *life*, Mr Shooks, as much as my family!'

'Well, yes,' said Jonathan Shooks with an understanding nod. 'And now I realize that it was more than you were prepared to sacrifice. Unfortunately, you can see what your refusal has led to. If you had deeded that land over to me, I could have come to an arrangement with Satan's proxies and your infant son would still be alive today.'

'Don't you have any idea what you were asking me to do?' demanded Nicholas. 'You were asking me to strike a bargain with the Devil! The *Devil* – the embodiment of everything evil! It flew in the face of everything that I have ever believed in! You were asking me to choose between my family and my God!'

'My dear sir, we all have to come to a deal with the Devil sooner or later in our lifetimes. In a world full of moral ambiguity, it is the only certain way in which we can guarantee our survival.'

Nicholas was confused and breathing hard, as if somebody had been chasing him. 'Very well,' he said. 'Supposing I were now to change my mind, and say *yes*, I *will* come to such an agreement? Supposing I *do* deed over those twenty acres? What would prevent this proxy of Satan from coming back later and demanding even *more* land, until I had no property left to my name at all?'

Jonathan Shooks folded his arms and looked at him with another of those expressions that Beatrice found impossible to read. It was like a tolerant adult looking at a child who persisted in being awkward – but at the same time it was very highly charged, as if his tolerance had limits and those limits were very close to being reached.

'You would have to trust me, Mr Buckley,' he said. 'The only guarantee that I can give you is my word.'

'But what about Satan? I don't doubt that I can trust *your* word, but if you are striking a bargain with a proxy of Satan, how far can I trust *his* word? Satan is a liar by nature!'

'Mr Buckley – I warned you what would happen if you didn't agree to the terms of my arrangement, and very sadly it has. You still have a chance to save Apphia, and your wife, and the remainder of your family and servants. Time, however, is running very short. The hourglass is rapidly emptying even as we speak.'

'Mr Shooks,' put in Francis. '*Was* it the Widow Belknap who caused the Buckley children to fall ill? If so, we should simply have her arrested and tried for her crime.'

Jonathan Shooks looked down at the stony brown roadway for a moment, as if he were trying to summon up all his reserves of patience.

'My dear reverend, you have to understand that what is happening here in Sutton is very much more complex than that. This is not simply a case of a vengeful woman who has the ability to cast malevolent spells.'

'Then what is she? And what is her place in this, if any?'

'I suppose you could best describe her as a facilitator for the underworld – a go-between, what the Spanish call an *intermediaro*. Proving such a thing to the satisfaction of a court, however, even to the most superstitious of juries – no, that would be well nigh impossible. The days of Salem are long gone.'

When Jonathan Shooks said that, Nicholas turned on his heel without a word and started to walk back down to his house. Jonathan Shooks made no attempt to follow him. Instead, he let out an exaggerated sigh and said, 'Such a pity. Such a great, great pity! That fellow is a fool to himself.'

Beatrice didn't know what to say to him. She didn't trust his motives in demanding twenty acres from Nicholas Buckley, but at the same time she didn't trust the Widow Belknap, either. While Nicholas had been confronting the Widow Belknap in her porch, and accusing her of murdering Tristram, Beatrice had been carefully studying the various plants and bushes in her flowering weed garden. She had seen several medicinal herbs, such as Solomon's seal, which was used to take away bruises 'caused by women's wilfulness in stumbling upon their hasty husbands' fists'.

There was eyebright, too, and costmary and marigold, all of which could be used to treat a variety of ailments, from colic to worms. Almost in the centre of the garden, however, a yew bush was growing, dark and even more pungent now that it had started to rain – one of the thickest yew bushes that Beatrice had ever seen.

Twenty-two

They were only halfway home when there was a deafening detonation of thunder directly above their heads and the trees all around them began to thrash and sway, as if they were trying to uproot themselves and run away. Uriel snorted a few times, but Francis managed to calm him down and keep him trotting straight ahead. Whenever it had thundered, Kingdom used to slew violently to one side of the road, or sometimes he would stop altogether, shivering with terror.

'What do you think?' asked Beatrice, as she and Francis sought shelter in the porch. The rain was lashing down much harder now and Caleb came hurrying around to the front of the house to unharness Uriel and lead him to his paddock.

'Don't seem to frighten him, this thunder,' said Caleb, tugging affectionately at Uriel's mane. Caleb himself was soaked but he didn't seem to mind. At least the rain was warm.

'Maybe that's because I named him for an archangel,' said Francis. 'There must be plenty of thunder in heaven, especially when the Lord is angry.'

'And what about you, Francis?' asked Beatrice, as she went in through the front door and took off her bonnet. 'Are *you* angry?'

'Of course I'm angry! But it's righteous anger, not pique! An innocent child has died and I don't know how, or why!'

'We must try to think about it calmly and with logic,' said Beatrice.

'How can we, when there is nothing logical about it at all? Jonathan Shooks seems to be suggesting that Satan was responsible, or at least some proxy of his, but I can't work out if Tristram's death was natural or supernatural, or something of both. I have no way of telling if those children had simply picked up some common childhood sickness, like weaning brash, or if somebody poisoned them on purpose or deliberately gave them an infection – or if indeed a deal really *was* done with some demon or other, which is what Jonathan Shooks would have us believe. Then again, Jonathan Shooks stands to profit handsomely from this, whatever the cause. Twenty acres, to say the least.'

Beatrice went through to the kitchen where Mary was slowly stirring a kettle filled with cream and milk and water to make cheese.

'Did I hear the Reverend Scarlet say that Tristram had passed away?' Mary asked.

Beatrice nodded. 'Very sadly, yes. Apphia is a little better, but I am still afraid that we might lose her, too.'

'Is it true that the Widow Belknap put a spell on them? That's what everybody's been saying.'

'No, Mary, I don't think it was witchcraft, although it's possible that the Widow Belknap was party to what happened. We should keep our tongues still, though, until we have proof.'

'Yes, ma'am,' said Mary. She went back to stirring the thickening curds in her cheese-kettle, but then she stopped and said, 'Is it all right to make cheese in a thunderstorm? It won't turn sour, will it?'

'No, Mary. It won't turn sour.'

Beatrice wondered if now was the time to tell Francis about the tests she had carried out on Kingdom's vomit and diarrhoea, and on the tarry hoof prints from Henry Mendum's field. She didn't yet have enough evidence to prove beyond doubt who might be responsible for all the disturbing events that had been taking place in Sutton over the past few days. In spite of that, she might be able to reassure Francis that it was not his faith that was lacking. All the prayers in heaven and on earth would not have deterred the kind of person who was capable of painting four naked slaves with pine resin and quicklime and saltpetre and setting them alight, or of killing a small child like Tristram, however that had been done, or of poisoning Kingdom with yew leaves.

She was almost sure that this was the work of man – or of woman – and not of demons.

She was tying on her apron when Francis called out, '*Bea*! Beatrice! Come here, my dearest, if you would!'

She went through to the hallway and Francis beckoned her out to the porch.

'There,' he said, grasping her arm, and pointing towards the end of the driveway. 'Is that the person you saw before? A brown cloak, you said, didn't you – with a hood, and carrying a staff? I didn't notice him at first but then a grouse broke out from the trees, as if something had startled it, and it was then that I saw him. Him or *her*, whoever it is. He's been standing there ever since, quite still. Is he looking in our direction or not? It's hard to say.'

Beatrice looked where Francis was pointing and through the rain she could just make out the brown hooded figure she had seen before.

'Yes,' she said, 'I believe it's the same.'

'Then I shall challenge him,' said Francis. 'If it's some maunder, then I shall give him a few pence and something to eat. But if it's some rogue, I shall chase him away on pain of calling the constable. Perhaps you were right, though. Perhaps it's the Angel of Death, looking this time for the soul of little Tristram.'

'Francis, don't. Leave him be. He could well be armed.'

'I'm not frightened of death, Bea, no matter how death might manifest itself. Robber, beggar or angel.'

'Francis – *please* – don't,' said Beatrice, but Francis gently but firmly pulled himself away from her. He marched off down the driveway, his coat collar turned up against the rain. Beatrice was deafened by a rumble of thunder like somebody rolling a hundred empty barrels down a cobbled street, and the rain began to beat down even harder.

'*Hoi*!' Francis shouted out, waving his arm. 'You there! Who are you? What do you want?'

He wasn't even halfway along the driveway, however, when the figure stepped back into the shadows beneath the trees and disappeared. Francis hurried up to the place where it had been standing and looked around, but even from a distance Beatrice could see that he had lost sight of the figure altogether.

Who in the world could he be? she thought, as Francis came trudging back. If he was somebody who wished them harm, then surely he would have attacked them by now. If he simply wanted alms, all he had to do was approach them and ask. But who had given her that bottle of expensive perfume? Was it him? Or had the perfume been left by some unknown admirer who was either too shy to give it to her directly, or somebody she knew only too well? She fleetingly thought of the looks that Jonathan Shooks was always giving her – sceptical and knowing, but also seductive, as if he were thinking, *I could have you, pretty goodwife, if I were so minded.*

'Well – whoever it was, they've made themselves scarce for now,' said Francis, wiping the rain from his face with his cravat.

'I have the feeling, though, that you might be very close to the truth when you called him the Angel of Death.'

'What do you mean?'

'I think he is not a real person but an apparition – a shade, a phantom, a spirit, call it what you will. He has come as an omen, or a warning, like a stopped clock or a picture that falls off the wall for no apparent reason, or a sudden flock of crows. Perhaps that is what all these terrible incidents have been – warnings that the people of this community should act more devoutly and not to be so concerned with wealth and creature comforts.'

'I still think you should tell Constable Jewkes about it,' said Beatrice. 'And you could put word around the parish for people to keep their eyes open. It might be an omen, but it could equally be a budger, or a footpad.'

Francis took hold of her hands and kissed her on the forehead. 'You are such a down-to-earth person, Bea, and I am so head-in-the-air! That very first morning I saw you, when I was coming out of Sunday prayers, I could almost hear a voice inside my head saying, "This is the one, this is the woman you will marry, this is the woman who will anchor your beliefs and make your life complete. This is the woman who will help you to fulfil the purpose for which God has put you here on this earth."'

Beatrice kissed him back. He looked so lean and handsome and saintly with his long dark hair all wet. The smell of warm rain blew in through the open front door, but the sun was beginning to break through the clouds. Yes, Francis could be unworldly, but she loved him for that. His faith always made her feel protected, as if it was enfolding them both, and Noah, too, in an iridescent cloak of light.

Francis had convinced her that there *was* a heaven. Sometimes she thought back to the frozen girl that she and her father had found that Christmas morning in the alley off Giltspur Street. Francis had made her confident that her soul *was* being cared for after all.

Beatrice drove back into the village on her own the following morning. She wanted to see if Apphia was any better, and Francis had also asked her to talk to the Buckleys about the funeral arrangements for Tristram. When she entered the Buckley house, however, she found that Judith was lying on her bed in the front parlour, with three or four of her neighbours around her. She looked as white as wax, and one of the women was vigorously fanning her.

'Judith? What's happened?' asked Beatrice. 'Are you unwell?'

'She's fainted from exhaustion,' said Goody Rust. 'Nicholas went out last night, saying that he had urgent business to attend to, and he has not returned since. Judith fears that he went back to see the Widow Belknap.'

'Has anybody been to the Widow Belknap's house this morning to ask her if she has seen him?'

'No, but do you think she would tell us, even if she had? *Especially* if she had!'

'How is Apphia? Is she any better?'

'A little. She has taken a feed of pap and she has kept it down so far, fingers crossed. I think the lungwort is helping to clear her chest.'

Beatrice went along the hallway to the children's bedchamber. Apphia was asleep, breathing through her mouth, but her cheeks were flushed a healthier pink than yesterday and she was wearing a clean white flannel pilch over her belly-band, which showed that she hadn't soiled herself for a while.

Back in the parlour, Beatrice asked Judith where she thought that Nicholas might have gone last night, on what kind of urgent business.

Judith's dark brown pupils darted from side to side, almost as if she were dreaming with her eyes open. 'I don't know. I don't know. All he said was that he had to settle it once and for all. That's what he had to do. Settle it.'

'Do you think he might have gone to see the Widow Belknap?'

'He swore to me that he would see her brought to justice. He was certain that it was she who made the twins so sick.'

'Well, let's wait upon him a little longer. If he doesn't return by the middle of the afternoon, we can arrange for a party to go out looking for him.'

Judith reached out and took hold of Beatrice's hand. Her own hands were surprisingly cold, considering how warm it was inside the house.

'He's dead, isn't he?' she said. 'I know it. I can feel it my water. I felt a chill last night when I was lying in bed, as if the Angel of Death had passed my window, and I haven't felt warm since.'

Beatrice sat down on the bed beside her. 'You're worn to a rag, Judith, that's all. You've had days of dreadful anxiety and hardly any sleep. Poor Tristram died only yesterday. It's not surprising that you're thinking the worst. But Nicholas will be back soon, you'll see. He cares for you too much to let you worry.'

'But where has he gone and why is he taking so long?'

'Judith – our husbands don't always tell us all of their business, do they? – and we can't expect them to.'

'He's dead,' said Judith, her pupils still flickering from side to side. 'I know he is. He's dead.'

*

As she came out of the front door, Beatrice found that Constable Jewkes was sitting outside on his huge brindled horse. He was leaning forward in his saddle and talking in low, earnest tones to William Rolfe and Thomas Woodman, the tailor, as if he were passing on some scandalous rumour. As soon as he saw her, however, he sat up straight and raised his hat and called out, 'A very good morning to you, Goody Scarlet!'

Beatrice went over to him. Constable Jewkes was very tall and lanky, with arms and legs that looked as if the disconnected parts of a man's body had simply been thrown into a soiled white shirt and a dusty blue coat and hurriedly buttoned up before they all fell out again.

He had a prominent nose but a sharply receding chin, which gave him the appearance of a sharp-shinned hawk, especially since his eyes were always so bloodshot from drink.

'I hear you visited the Gilmans yesterday,' he said. 'Deeply shocking, that was. Deeply! I'm surprised that you had the stomach for it.'

Constable Jewkes had a strong Welsh accent which made it hard for Beatrice to understand him, especially when he was drunk.

'Do you have any notion yet who might have done it?' she asked him.

'I have some strong suspicions, Goody Scarlet. But I was on my way there now to talk to the Gilmans' servants and their slaves. I want to know if any of them noticed anybody unfamiliar around the farm before those poor beggars were set afire.'

'Well, good. But with respect, you should be careful not to jump to any hasty conclusions. I believe that there's more to what's happening here in Sutton than we can guess at.'

'Oh, I'm never hasty, Goody Scarlet, you know me! Slow and measured, that's what I am. If the court is going to order somebody to be hanged by the neck, or pressed, or burned at the stake, then I like to make sure that it's the person what has actually perpetrated the deed.'

I'm sure you do, thought Beatrice. Five years before, three young sisters in Haverhill had been hanged for killing their father with a hatchet. Not everybody in Sutton knew it, but their fate had been sealed by the evidence given by Constable Jewkes, even though he had been so drunk on cider that he could hardly stand up. Later, it was discovered that a Penacook Indian had committed the murder when he was surprised by the girls' father during a robbery.

Constable Jewkes turned to William Rolfe and Thomas Woodman and said, 'Well, gentlemen, I must be on my way! Justice waits on no man, especially me.' He raised his hat again to Beatrice and clicked his tongue to start his horse.

He had gone no more than twenty yards, however, before another rider appeared at the top of the village green, and he was cantering very fast. He rode his horse straight across the grass at a steep diagonal and reined it in right in front of Constable Jewkes.

Beatrice recognized him as John O'Dwyer, a young Irishman who was indentured to Ebenezer Rowlandson, a farmer and forester on the far side of Henry Mendum's property. He was a stocky lad, gingery-haired and freckled from working out in the sun, and his forehead was bursting with perspiration.

'I've been looking for you all over, constable! They told me you was over at the Goodhue farm, but you're not, you're here!'

Beatrice could hear the distress in his voice and so she walked along the road to join them.

'John O'Dwyer, isn't it?' she asked him. 'What's wrong, John?'

Constable Jewkes twisted around in his saddle and looked down at her with an expression that seemed to mean, *I'm the one who asks the questions, Goody Scarlet, not you, even if you are the pastor's wife.*

'It's the fish in Master Rowlandson's trout pond!' John O'Dwyer blurted out. 'They've all come floating up to the surface! There's scores of them!'

'Dead?' asked Constable Jewkes.

'Some of them, sir, but only a few. Most are still breathing but it's like they're asleep.'

'What the devil are you talking about, boy? Fish don't *sleep.* They don't have eyelids, so how can they possibly sleep?'

'These ones seem to be sleeping, sir. You can pick them right out of the water with your hand and they set up no struggle at all.'

Constable Jewkes lifted out his pocket watch. 'Well, boy, I have to attend the Gilman farm on account of those slaves that were burned, which to my mind is more important than sleeping fish. I'll pay your master a visit when I'm finished up there.'

'There's another thing that Master Rowlandson said I should tell you, constable.'

'Oh, yes, and what would that be?'

'There are footprints on the wooden jetty at the side of the pond. Well, they're hoof marks, really, not footprints, as if they were made by a donkey or a goat.'

'Hoof prints?' Beatrice asked him. 'Can you describe them, John, these hoof prints?' Again, Constable Jewkes gave her a sideways look which meant, *Leave this to me, if you don't mind, Goody Scarlet. I represent the law in Sutton.*

'I don't know, ma'am,' John O'Dwyer told her. 'They're

brown and they smell strong and they're sticky, that's all I can say. Master Rowlandson said not to touch them because they could be have been trod by the Devil himself.'

'I think I need to come and take a look at them,' said Beatrice.

'Be sure not to tamper with them before I arrive,' cautioned Constable Jewkes. 'The Devil may come under *your* jurisdiction, Goody Scarlet, or that of your husband at least, but all other wrongdoers come under mine.'

He gave his horse an irritable smack on its rump with his whip and set off towards the Gilman farm. John O'Dwyer waited for Beatrice while she walked back to her shay. Then he rode beside her as she steered Uriel out of the village towards the Rowlandsons'.

'How long before you finish your indenture, John?' she asked him, raising her voice to make herself heard over the clattering of wheels and squeaking of leather straps.

'Another two years, seven months, and three days,' said John O'Dwyer.

'It sounds to me as if that won't be too soon, so far as you're concerned.'

'Master Rowlandson expects his money's worth, ma'am, that's all I'm going to say.'

Beatrice drove down the track that led between split-rail fences to the Rowlandson home-lot. Around the red-painted house and barns and outbuildings the fields were mostly given over to corn, which was tall and ripe and whiskery and almost ready for harvesting. A warm breeze was blowing across them, so that shining ripples ran from one side to the other.

Beatrice followed John O'Dwyer around the edge of the fields until they gave way to scrubby grass and rocky outcroppings, and she saw a pond glittering up ahead of them. When they came closer she saw that it was so wide that it was almost a lake, with several smaller ponds around it. On the far side of it stood acres of hardwood forest, mostly hemlock and yellow birch and sugar maple. There were tall pines, too, but these were reserved for His Majesty's navy. The trees were reflected in the water as if there was another forest, upside down, beneath their feet, with an upside-down sky and clouds.

Beside the pond there was a long wooden jetty with a small boat tied up to it. Standing by the boat was Ebenezer Rowlandson with three of his farm-workers. Ebenezer Rowlandson was a short, stubby man, with a wiry brown wig and a face like a cross little Boston terrier, with bulging eyes. He turned around when he saw Beatrice and John O'Dwyer approaching, one hand shading his face against the sun. Beatrice drew up the shay and one of the farm-workers came over and took Uriel's bridle for her.

'Goody Scarlet!' barked Ebenezer Rowlandson, obviously surprised to see her. Then, 'John – where's the constable?'

'He had first to attend to the Gilmans, sir, because of those four slaves that were burned,' said John O'Dwyer. 'He told me he'll be here directly.'

'I'd like to know which matter is the more pressing,' retorted Ebenezer Rowlandson. 'Gilman's slaves are dead and can't be resurrected, can they? – but look at my trout! They're still alive, most of them, but who can tell what mischief has been done to them or how much longer they can survive?'

Having said that, he turned to Beatrice and bowed his head and said, without much grace, 'Good day to you, Goody Scarlet. I trust you're keeping well. May I ask what brings *you* here?'

'The Reverend Scarlet is attending to other business at the moment,' said Beatrice. 'I have come here on his behalf to see if you needed any pastoral help.'

'You mean you came to see if this was the work of the Devil, too – like your own pigs and Henry Mendum's milk-cows and the Buckley twins and George Gilman's slaves?'

'Well, yes, that too, to be truthful. In the light of what's been happening lately, the pastor obviously needs to know if your fish have suffered some natural misfortune or whether somebody has poisoned them.'

'Oh, somebody has poisoned them, right enough, or put a curse on them, more likely, and we all know who that "somebody" is! The sooner we can find some evidence against that widow-woman, the better. As if we didn't already have evidence enough, just in the way she looks at us, and speaks about us, and talks to that devilish bird of hers, and sings to her goat!'

'Do you think that I could see your fish?' asked Beatrice. She paused, and then added, 'Please'.

'I don't know what earthly good that will do,' said Ebenezer Rowlandson, but he grudgingly led her over to the jetty. In the water below, scores of shining brown trout were lying on the surface, their gills still opening and closing and their tails still waving, but only feebly.

Ebenezer Rowlandson said, 'Here, I'll show you,' and with an effortful grunt he knelt down on the jetty and reached down into the water. He scooped up one of the trout and though it made a half-hearted attempt to wriggle out of his hand, it seemed to have hardly any strength at all, as if it were drugged.

Beatrice held out both hands and said, 'May I hold it?'

'For what purpose?' asked Ebenezer Rowlandson. 'Will you ask it who cast a spell on it? I would have done that myself, if only I could speak Troutanesian.'

All the same, he laid the slippery brown trout across her upturned palms. It was gasping even more desperately now that it was completely out of the water, but it could barely manage to flex its body from side to side or flap its tail. It reminded her of the gudgeon that she had sometimes found lying on the mud on the banks of the Thames, stunned by the bleach from London's riverside laundries.

Apart from its weakness, the trout was silvery-scaled and apparently healthy, so she guessed that it had been affected by some substance added to the water in the pond, rather than diseased. It might be oil of rhodium, she thought, which her father had sold to anglers to attract and stupefy fish, and to rat-catchers to do the same with rats, to lure them into a sack which could then be tied up and thrown in the river. Or perhaps it was *Cocculus indicus*, a climbing Asian plant that was also used by unsportsmanlike anglers, and by unscrupulous brewers to give their weak beer more 'giddiness'.

'Well?' asked Ebenezer Rowlandson. 'What has Master Trout told you? Did the name "Belknap" pass his lips?'

Beatrice returned the fish to him and Ebenezer Rowlandson dropped it with a plop back into the pond. 'Master Trout was quite helpful, as a matter of fact,' she said. 'Do you think you could show me the hoof prints?'

Ebenezer Rowlandson puffed out his cheeks. 'I'm not so sure about that, Goody Scarlet. Don't you think that we had better wait for your husband, and for Constable Jewkes? If laws have been broken here, either holy or human, they are the men appointed to deal with such things, after all.'

'I assure you I won't touch anything,' said Beatrice. 'I would just like to look at them, to see how they compare with the hoof prints we found at Henry Mendum's.'

'Well . . . very well,' said Ebenezer Rowlandson. He walked about thirty feet further along the jetty and then stopped and pointed down to the planks beneath his feet. 'They begin here and they run all the way down to the very end there, see?

Whatever made them – whether it was man or beast or Satan himself – it ran right off the jetty and into the water.'

He hesitated for a moment and then he said, 'Maybe, on the other hand, it *didn't* go into the water. Maybe it had wings and flew off into the air. Or maybe it ran right across the surface to the other side and into the forest.'

'And which of those do you think it did?' Beatrice asked him.

'I don't know, Goody, I'm sure. Every one of those possibilities puts the fear of God into me, I can tell you. Do you know what I keep thinking? I keep thinking that if by chance I had been here at the time, I would have come face to face with Satan himself. It makes me tremble to my very boots.'

Beatrice looked down at the hoof prints that ran from the middle of the jetty to the end. She found it curious that they started only halfway along, as if the creature that had made them had dropped right out of the sky, run down to the end of the jetty, and then either jumped straight into the water or flown away into the air, as Ebenezer Rowlandson had said. The only other alternative was that it had walked across the water, like Jesus when he rescued his disciples on the Sea of Galilee. That thought was not only blasphemous but very frightening.

The hoof prints appeared to be made of the same treacly substance as the prints at Henry Mendum's farm and the two upside-down crosses that had been daubed on the walls at the Buckleys' and the Gilmans'. What Beatrice thought was amazing, though, was that they ran in a dead straight line, with left and right hoof prints completely parallel, all the way down to the very end of the jetty, each one about a yard apart.

In shape they were cloven, like those of a goat, and yet they had clearly been made by a creature with two legs rather than four. A goat would have left its prints in pairs, with the hind hoof prints slightly in front of the fore hoof prints, but these hoof prints had been made singly, like those of a man.

What was even more curious was how evenly spaced they were. If the creature had launched itself into the air from the end of the jetty, its hoof prints would surely have been clustered closer together just before it had started to flap its wings. The same would have happened immediately before it jumped into the water – or *on to* it, if it had been able to walk across the surface. The water was at least two feet below the level of the jetty and she couldn't imagine that it had simply run off the edge without changing its gait at all.

'Well?' said Ebenezer Rowlandson. 'What do you see?'

'I see a great deal, thank you, Master Rowlandson.'

'Such as?'

'I'm sorry, but there is little point in my telling you now. I haven't yet been able to make sense of it all myself, and I'm quite sure that you won't be able to, either.'

'Oh, I see. Thank you for the compliment.'

'When I have a better understanding of what might have happened here, I'll be sure to explain it to you, have no fear.'

'Well, I thank you for that, Goody Scarlet, although I am much surprised that the pastor allows you to be so condescending.'

Beatrice turned to him. 'A wife can be assertive, sir, without being disobedient. Sometimes a wife has a duty to her husband to speak her mind.'

Ebenezer Rowlandson grunted again, as if he didn't really understand what she meant, and didn't want to – but if he did, he probably wouldn't like it one bit. His own wife, Emily, was one of the most timid women in Sutton and she was frequently in need of Solomon's seal for her bruising.

'Have you seen enough, then?' he asked her testily. 'Perhaps you can now take word back to the pastor and see what he makes of it all.'

'I will go and tell him post-haste, Master Rowlandson.'

'Good. If Satan *has* been at work here, I will urgently need his advice on how to protect my livelihood from any further depredation, don't you think? Unless, that is, *you* already know better.'

'I don't mean you any disrespect, sir. Don't think that.'

'Huh! Well, that's as may be.'

Ebenezer Rowlandson was now so impatient for her to leave that she could see that it was going to be difficult for her to take a sample of the hoof prints, as she had in Henry Mendum's field. She took a step to the side, so that her gown covered one of the prints, and then she jabbed two or three times with the heel of her shoe on to the hem of her petticoat, hoping that some of the tarry substance would stick to it.

She followed Ebenezer Rowlandson back along the jetty. As she reached the steps at the end of it, however, she noticed that the narrow channel of water between the pilings and the steep grassy bank was clogged with thick whitish foam. She had been remembering the fish poisoned by the laundries beside the Thames, and now here was a mass of bubbles that looked like soapsuds.

'Are you coming, Goody Scarlet?' called Ebenezer Rowlandson. 'I have much to do this afternoon!'

'Yes, of course,' said Beatrice and walked briskly back to her shay. She settled into her seat and took up the reins, but before she could leave Ebenezer Rowlandson held on to the harness and looked up at her with one eye closed against the sun.

'I will say this, Goody Scarlet. If you were a wife of mine, a few stripes would soon cure you of your boldness,'

Beatrice smiled at him. 'If I had chosen to be a wife of yours, Master Rowlandson, I think I would deserve them for my stupidity.'

Twenty-three

When she returned home Beatrice immediately ran upstairs and took off her petticoat. She had managed to impress almost half of one of the hoof prints on to the hem and it had stained the cream linen dark brown. She sniffed it and it smelled exactly the same as the tarry substance that she had taken from Henry Mendum's cow pasture: coal tar, civet oil, sulphur and something sweet, like molasses or dark treacle.

She wished that she had taken a sample of the thick white foam that she had seen beside the jetty. It had looked so much like soapsuds and yet where had it come from? She wondered if any of the Rowlandsons' maids had emptied soapy water into the pond after washing the laundry, but that didn't seem likely when Talbot Brook ran so close to the farmhouse. Even if they had, she didn't think that soap would have affected the trout like that, making them comatose.

She stepped into a clean petticoat and tied the laces, and then went back downstairs. She was well behind with her housekeeping now, even though Mary had done so much. She had at least two hours of plain-work to do: shirts and cravats to sew for Francis, and stockings to darn. Then she had aprons and bed-linen to iron, as well as making damson jam which was now nearly a week overdue, and she had beans and asparagus to preserve in stone jars filled with clarified butter.

She needed to have all these chores finished today because tomorrow morning she and Francis would go to Londonderry to buy six more pigs. Autumn would be here before she knew it, and she needed to have her bacon salted and smoked up the chimney and stored in barrels before the winter.

When she came into the kitchen she found Caleb there, drinking a mug of cider. He was so hot that his shirt was sticking to him and he smelled strongly of sweat.

'I fetched all the things from the village you asked me, Goody Scarlet. The flour and the vinegar and the candles and the side of beef.'

'Thank you, Caleb. Did you hear any news of Nicholas Buckley?'

'No, nothing – only that he's yet to come home. I saw Goody Buckley and she's almost distracted. She told me that Constable Jewkes is talking of sending out some fellows to search for him, but they don't even know where to start looking. They've already called on the Widow Belknap, but she says she's not seen hide nor hair of him – but then she would.'

'Who was the last person to see him?'

'Mr Bartlett, the farrier. That's what Goody Buckley told me. He was leading a horse out of his smithy after shoeing it and he saw Mr Buckley leave his house and walk quick towards the Widow Belknap's. He waved to him but Mr Buckley didn't wave back. Mr Bartlett didn't see him go to the Widow Belknap's door, though. He could just as well have walked straight past and kept on going.'

'That's really strange. Nicholas Buckley is usually such a considerate man. I can't imagine that he would allow Judith to fret about him so.'

'I don't know, Goody Scarlet. You have to admit there's been some real uncouth goings-on round Sutton of late. Maybe this is just one more of them.'

'Yes, maybe,' said Beatrice. 'How's little Apphia, by the by?'

'Much better. Goody Buckley said to thank you again for the confusion you gave her.'

'*In*fusion, Caleb.'

'Yes, ma'am. Whatever you say, ma'am.'

By the time Francis was brought home that evening by young John Jenkins it was growing dark and it was too late for him to go out to the Rowlandson farm. When Beatrice came out on to the porch to greet him she saw three comets in the eastern sky. She wondered if they were an omen.

During the afternoon she had boiled chicken with cream and onions, which they ate at the kitchen table out of large blue bowls. Francis had been sitting for most of the afternoon with Goody Jenkins, who was very close to death now, and Beatrice thought that he looked haggard and dispirited. She reached across the table and laid her hand on his.

'So what do you think affected those fish?' he asked her, dully, almost as if he didn't really want to know.

'I'm not at all sure, Francis. There was white foam on the surface of the pond, but I don't know what could have caused it. But of one thing I am practically certain. Those hoof prints were created by some human artifice, not by any kind of creature.'

Francis didn't say anything, but tore off a piece of bread and dipped it into his bowl and waited for her to continue.

Beatrice said, 'The substance that they are composed of is not a natural secretion. It does have civet oil blended in with it, which is natural. It comes from the glands of civet cats. There used to be a perfumier in our street in London and he used it to make scents.'

'Go on.'

'So far as I can tell from the odour, the hoof prints and the two crosses are a concoction of coal tar, cloves, civet oil, sulphur and some other ingredients, possibly molasses. I think that it's been deliberately mixed to make it smell like something from hell.'

'But, Bea,' said Francis, 'even if it wasn't naturally secreted by the demon itself, could it not still have originated in the underworld?'

'What do you mean?'

'If you and I trample through mud, we leave muddy tracks across the floor, don't we? If a demon has been trampling through the mires of hell before it enters *our* world, would its hooves not leave traces of whatever those mires are composed of? Remember that when Satan was cast out of heaven he was thrown into a lake of burning sulphur, and where else would that lake have been, except in hell? And what is the purpose of perfume, except to arouse our lust?'

'Francis, the hoof prints were far too evenly spaced out to have been those of a living creature. Each of them was almost exactly a yard apart, with no sign of hesitation whatsoever.'

'Yes, but we are not talking about a horse or a goat here, Bea, we are talking about a *demon*, and who can say how a demon may run?'

Beatrice took hold of his hand again and squeezed it. 'Why you are so determined to ascribe all of these incidents to Satan? Surely it is much more likely that some member of our community is working mischief?'

'It *must* be Satan, Bea, because his motive is so obvious! He wants to dispossess us of our farms and fields so that we leave New Hampshire and take our faith with us. He wants to reclaim this land for heathens. But that – *that* I can fight against, with prayer and with the help of God.'

'Supposing, though, it *isn't* Satan. Supposing it's somebody from the village?'

'Why should anybody from our village wish to commit such terrible acts? What could they possibly want? I'm even beginning to doubt that the Widow Belknap is in any way involved. Surely she can't feel so slighted that she would murder a baby and set men on fire?'

Beatrice didn't know what to say. She had never felt so torn in her life. She was devoted to Francis and she believed implicitly in God, but she couldn't ignore what she had clearly seen for herself. Her father had always said: God gave you eyes to observe and a nose to smell and a tongue to taste. Trust the senses that God gave you, because they will always tell you the truth.

After she had dressed in her nightgown, Beatrice went into Noah's little bedchamber and stood beside his crib watching him sleep. *My precious, only child*, she thought. *If there is a demon abroad, please may God protect you from it.*

She was still standing there when Francis came in and put his arm around her shoulders and kissed her cheek.

'I will go first to Ebenezer Rowlandson's tomorrow morning,' he said. 'If you care to, I will take you into the village so that you can visit Judith Buckley. Perhaps you could also go to the meeting house and see if Peter Duston has finished raising the bench at the back.'

'What about buying new pigs?'

'We should have time to go to Londonderry afterwards. If not, we will have to go on Friday. But I need to see how Ebenezer's fish are faring. I have a bad feeling about them. I hope I'm wrong, but it seems to me as if it's a deliberate mockery of the feeding of the five thousand. Instead of five thousand people being fed, five thousand fish are dying, or maybe are already dead.'

'Francis, don't let your fancy run away with you.'

'I'm trying not to, my dearest, but everything that has been happening seems to be some travesty of Christian belief. The pigs in that Devil's Communion, and Henry Mendum's cows arranged as a pentacle, and those three slaves hanging as if they had been crucified...'

It was still dark when Beatrice woke up the following morning. She sat up to find that Francis had already got out bed and was dressing.

'Did you sleep?' she asked him.

'A little,' he told her. His nose sounded blocked up. Then, 'Not much, frankly. Hardly at all. I am finding that this is all very stressful.'

In the kitchen Beatrice poured them each a mug of cider and spread some muffins thickly with butter. They hardly spoke at all while they ate and drank, and Beatrice could see that Francis kept drumming his fingers on the table.

By the time they had finished their breakfast it was growing light and Mary arrived to take care of Noah. Francis and Beatrice climbed into their shay shortly after six o'clock and headed towards the village. The grass was glittering with dew but it was warm already and Beatrice could tell that it was going to become very hot later.

Francis stopped outside the Buckley house and Beatrice climbed down. As she did so, Judith Buckley came out of her front door to beat one of her mats.

'Good morning, Judith!' Francis called out to her. 'Any news of Nicholas yet?'

Judith shook her head.

'I have to go to the Rowlandson farm,' Francis told her. 'Afterwards, though, I will come and see what we can do about raising some men to look for him. I know that Constable Jewkes has talked to you about it.'

'Huh!' said Judith, turning to Beatrice with undisguised bitterness. 'The only thing that Constable Jewkes can ever find is the stopper in a wine bottle.'

Uriel jerked forward and Francis almost lost his balance. The village horse-trough was only five yards away and Uriel was sweating and must have been thirsty. Francis let him amble forward until he reached the trough, but when he got there Uriel abruptly reared his head away and snorted.

'Go on, boy!' Francis coaxed him. 'Don't you want a drink after all?'

But Uriel not only turned his head away, he started to shuffle backwards, away from the trough, causing the shay to back up and swing around so that its wheels bumped into the hard-baked muddy ridges at the side of the grass.

'Uriel! Calm, boy! Calm! What's the matter with you?'

Francis pulled at Uriel's reins to bring him under control and then stood up in his seat and peered towards the trough to see what might have unsettled him so much.

'There's something in there,' he said.

'What?' asked Beatrice. 'What is it?'

She picked up the hem of her gown and walked across to the horse-trough. It was hewn out of rough local granite, at least ten feet long and four feet wide, with a pump at one end. Even before she reached it she could see that there was more than water in it. It looked as if it somebody had filled it with sticks and wet grey rags.

It was only when she came up close that she realized what

was lying in it, and even then it took her a few seconds to get over the shock The trough was nearly full, but not with water. Instead it was brimming with a pale yellow effervescent liquid from which an eye-stinging vapour was rising. It was the same colour as cider when it was fermenting, and it made the same singing sound, but when Beatrice breathed it in it burned her sinuses and the back of her throat and made her cough.

At one end of the trough, under the pump, a human skull was floating, eyeless and mostly fleshless, except for a few stray clumps of long brown hair. It was grinning, as if it had just been told some macabre joke. Next to it, a bony ribcage was protruding, draped with the sodden tatters of a Holland shirt. Below that, Beatrice could see a half-submerged pelvis beneath the surface, like a white basin in which the victim's bowels were simmering and bubbling as pale as porridge. Two thigh-bones were still tenuously joined to the pelvis by tendons and strings of connective tissue, although the shin-bones were no longer attached to the knees. At the other end of the trough two half-dissolved shoes were sticking up at right angles, each adorned with a shiny silver buckle.

'Beatrice! Bea?'

Francis climbed down from the shay. A young boy was running across the green bowling a hoop and Francis called him over to hold Uriel's reins for him. Then he came and joined Beatrice at the side of the horse-trough.

'Good God in heaven,' he said, pressing his hand over his mouth. 'It's a man, isn't it? It's a man!'

'Don't stand too close,' said Beatrice, catching his sleeve and pulling him back. 'That isn't water. I'm quite sure that it's concentrated oil of vitriol. If you breathe it in, it could scorch your lungs beyond healing.'

'He's *melted*,' said Francis. 'Look at him, he's actually *melted*!'

'That's what oil of vitriol can do to you,' Beatrice told him. She found it hard to catch her breath and her voice was shaking. 'Look – see how bright his shoe-buckles are! Jewellers use oil of vitriol for cleaning silver.'

Francis peered at the buckles and then he said, 'Oh, God. Those are Nicholas Buckley's. I'd recognize them anywhere.' He quickly turned around to see if Judith was coming over, and sure enough she was.

'Judith !' he said, stepping in front of her with both arms spread wide. 'This is something that you shouldn't see.'

'Why not?' she demanded, trying to circle round him. 'What is it?

Beatrice went up to her, too. 'We think it may be your Nicholas.'

'What, drowned? Drowned in the horse-trough? How can that be? I want to see him! How can he be drowned in the horse-trough?'

'It's worse than drowned,' said Beatrice. 'Francis is right. You really shouldn't see. You don't want to remember him like this for the rest of your days.'

'I'm not a child!' snapped Judith. She sidestepped both of them and went right up to the side of the trough.

There was a long moment when she simply stood there, her arms straight down by her sides, staring at him. Then, very gradually, with a thin whine like air leaking out of a bladder, she sank to her knees on to the ground and bent her head forward. Beatrice went over to her and laid her hands on her shoulders.

'What's happened to him?' said Judith. The acid fumes were irritating the back of her throat so that she spoke in a croak. She turned around and looked up at Beatrice and said, '*What's happened to him*?'

'Judith – it's too terrible for words.'

'*Tell me*! *What's happened to him*!'

Beatrice took a deep breath. 'It looks as if somebody has plunged Nicholas into concentrated oil of vitriol. It is very caustic and can dissolve almost everything organic.'

'*Alive?*' Judith demanded. 'Did they do it while he was alive?'

'There really is no way of telling. I would pray not.'

Judith held out her hand and Beatrice helped her back on to her feet. She didn't look around at the horse-trough again but she pointed with a stiff trembling finger towards the Widow Belknap's house.

'It was her, wasn't it? *She* did it!'

'Judith, we have no way of knowing *who* did it, not yet!'

'It was her! It must have been her!' Judith's voice was rising into hoarse, breathless yelps. 'When Nicholas went to accuse her of killing our poor little Tristram – what did she say to him? She said that she would turn him into broth, didn't she? Boil his bones and turn him into *broth*! And that's exactly what she's done, the witch! She should be locked up *now*! She should be burned!'

'Judith, you have to ask yourself how one woman could have done such a thing unaided.'

'Who says she was unaided? She had Satan to help her, or a demon, or one of her familiars! Who knows what that black bird of hers turns into, after dark? A man as black as a shadow, I shouldn't wonder! She's a witch! She can cast all manner of evil spells!'

'Let me take you back inside,' said Beatrice. 'You need to sit down and calm yourself. Francis will call for Constable Jewkes, won't you, Francis? And we must find some way of removing those remains.'

Beatrice was trying to stay calm and controlled, but when she looked back at Nicholas Buckley's dissolving body lying in the horse-trough her stomach tightened and her mouth was flooded with bile. It was all she could do to stop herself from retching. Judith was right: whoever was guilty of killing Nicholas, Satan or sinner, they *had* turned him into broth.

As she led Judith back to her house, with one arm around her, she heard carriage wheels. She looked up across the village green and saw Jonathan Shooks's calash driving past with its black top raised, very fast, so that it raised a high cloud of tan-coloured dust behind it. It was heading in the direction of Penacook, which was where Jonathan Shooks was staying, but the same road led to Ebenezer Rowlandson's farm, too.

Twenty-four

Constable Jewkes arrived. Although it was so early in the morning he smelled strongly of wine and when he saw Nicholas Buckley's remains in the horse-trough he promptly vomited on to the grass.

He was still sniffing and wiping his mouth with his cravat when he came into Judith's parlour, where she was sitting with Apphia in her lap. Beatrice was sitting close beside her: she had promised to stay with Judith and comfort her for as long as she needed her. Buying fresh pigs could wait until tomorrow, or another day.

'What ungodly thing has befallen your husband, Goody Buckley?' blurted out Constable Jewkes. 'I never saw the like of it! He looks like a storm-smashed row-boat, rather than a man!'

'*Please*, constable, try to be compassionate,' said Beatrice. 'Goody Buckley has seen him for herself.'

'But he's been *liqueficated*!'

'Yes, he has, God rest his soul. Somehow, somebody dropped him into oil of vitriol, or poured it over him. Whether he was still alive when it was done, we will never be able to tell.'

Constable Jewkes remembered that he still had his hat on and removed it. 'I'm sorry,' he said, tucking it under his arm. 'I was so much amazed by your husband's condition, that's all. You have my sympathy, Goody Buckley.'

He stood in the doorway for a moment, swaying slightly, and then he said, 'I gather that you have been accusing the Widow Belknap for his death, which is really why I'm here.'

'Who else it could be?' Judith demanded, with tears in her eyes and her chin tilted up defiantly. 'Nobody else in the village bore Nicholas a grudge of any kind, only her. He told me that she threatened to boil his bones and make him into broth – those exact words, and in front of witnesses. And surely she is the only one who would have the knowledge and the wherewithal to commit such an act. She is a *witch*, Constable Jewkes, and she should be tried for her witchcraft and face punishment according to the law.'

'Very well, Goody Buckley,' said Constable Jewkes. 'Since you have brought a formal accusation against her and there are witnesses to her intention to murder, I will detain her. It's high time the jailhouse had an airing in any event.'

He turned around and walked unsteadily back down the hallway, tripping on the front doorstep and only managing to save himself from falling by seizing the door handle. Beatrice stood up and said, 'I think I'd better go, too. We don't want this to turn into a pantomime.'

'You *do* believe that the Widow Belknap killed Nicholas, don't you?' Judith asked her.

'The court will have to decide that, Judith. But she did threaten him, I agree. I heard her myself.'

She left the house and walked quickly to catch up with Constable Jewkes. Francis was standing by the horse-trough while Rodney Bartlett pumped water into it, a red scarf tied tightly around his nose and mouth to save him from breathing in the fumes. It had been Beatrice's suggestion to dilute the oil of vitriol until Nicholas Buckley's remains could safely be lifted out. Acid and water were pouring down the sides of the trough, but fragments of clothing and human membranes were sliding down, too.

Four or five more men were gathered nearby, including William Rolfe, the shoemaker, and Peter Duston, the carpenter, who had crossed the green from the meeting house still wearing his long leather apron. It was Peter Duston who made coffins for Sutton's deceased and usually he had two or three ready, but this morning he had none spare. Instead, Thomas Varney, the weaver, had brought over his farm wagon with two empty tea chests on it.

Beatrice quickly went over to Francis and told him that she was following Constable Jewkes to the Widow Belknap's house.

'Very well, my dearest. I will keep my eye on you, but I have to stay here for the moment out of respect for poor Nicholas. It will not be a pretty sight when they lift him out.'

Constable Jewkes was walking so slowly and unsteadily that Beatrice quickly caught up with him. As she did so, they were joined by Goody Rust and Georgina Varney, a tall, flaxen-haired, wide-hipped girl with upper arms like two pale hams. She was Thomas Varney's youngest daughter, who helped Goody Rust with her scouring and her laundry. Goody Rust was clearly intent on seeing that justice was done.

They came to the Widow Belknap's front door and Constable Jewkes knocked three times with the wolf's-head knocker. They waited, but there was no answer, so he knocked again, much harder this time, and called out, 'Widow Belknap! This is Constable Jewkes! Open your door!'

There was still no response, only the mournful bleating of the Widow Belknap's goat from the side of the house.

'Widow Belknap! Do you hear me? I order you to open up your door, in the name of the governor!'

Still no reply, so Constable Jewkes said, 'I shall be obliged to force the door open. Goody Scarlet, if I cause any damage, will you bear witness that I had no alternative?'

He took a step back, trying to balance himself so that he could kick at the door, but before he could do so Beatrice had turned the handle and pushed it, and it silently swung wide open.

They stepped into the Widow Belknap's parlour. Beatrice had never been invited inside the Widow Belknap's house but it was not what she would have expected from a witch's lair. There was a bed in the opposite corner with linen curtains embroidered with roses and a counterpane to match, and a small fireplace with a vase of wild flowers in it. Three pine chairs were arranged around a table and on the table was a plate with two slices of bread on it, one of them half-torn, and a piece of yellow cheese, and a tipped-over cup which had spilled milk across the tablecloth.

'Widow Belknap?' called Constable Jewkes. 'Are you at home, Widow Belknap?'

He went through into the kitchen, which was very small and mostly taken up by the wide brick fireplace. The fire had died to grey powdery ashes, although it was still faintly warm. Above it hung an iron pot and Beatrice took a quick look inside it to see what the Widow Belknap might have been cooking. Immediately, she wished she hadn't. The pot was filled with peas and beans which had all boiled dry, but lying on top of them was the bedraggled body of Magic, the Widow Belknap's black parrot, its beak open and its grey eyelids closed.

'Constable Jewkes,' she said and beckoned him over. He peered inside the pot and the sight of the parrot seemed to sober him up on the spot. Goody Rust peeked inside it, too, and pulled a face.

'Well, the widow's not here, is she?' said Constable Jewkes. 'The bird has flown the nest. Well, not *this* bird. You know what I mean.'

'It looks as if she might have been taken,' said Beatrice. 'She loved this bird, she wouldn't have harmed it herself. And why would she leave her breakfast half-eaten, and not wipe up that milk when it was spilled? You only have to look around you to see what a careful housekeeper she is.'

'If you ask me, she was boiling that bird as a potion to make a spell,' said Goody Rust. 'She hasn't been taken. Who would want to take her?'

'It could have been Indians,' said Georgina. 'My cousin Susan was kidnapped by the Abenaki when she was only twelve and we never saw her again.'

'It's possible, I guess,' said Constable Jewkes. 'But Indians haven't taken any captives around here for two or three years now, have they? And if it *was* Indians, why did they take only her?'

'She killed Nicholas Buckley and then made good her escape,' said Goody Rust.

'With her breakfast half-finished?' asked Beatrice.

'It could just as well have been her supper.'

Constable Jewkes looked around the kitchen and then shrugged. 'Not much more that I can do, excepting put out the word that folks should keep their eyes peeled for any sight of her. Depending on when she left, she could be five miles away by now.'

They went back outside, just as Francis was coming up the path.

'Where is she?' he asked. 'Have you not arrested her?'

'She's gone,' Beatrice told him. 'Either she was abducted or else she has flown.'

'Well, maybe that will prove to be a mercy. If she really was Satan's procurator, as Nicholas Buckley suspected her to be, perhaps we will see an end to all of these terrible events.'

'Oh, poor Nicholas,' said Beatrice. She could see that Rodney Bartlett had stopped pumping and was emptying the diluted oil of vitriol out of the horse-trough with a pail. Thomas Varney and Peter Duston were carrying between them a drooping tarpaulin, which they swung up on to the back of the wagon and then emptied with a sloppy clatter into one of the tea chests.

'We will of course give him a decent coffin,' said Francis. 'I have prayed for his immortal soul, Bea, which is all I can do for him now. He was a very good man, pious and honest and hard-working. He certainly didn't deserve to die so horribly.'

He looked up to see how high the sun had risen. 'I must go to see Ebenezer Rowlandson now. I think we will have to leave Londonderry until tomorrow.'

Francis never showed his affection for Beatrice publicly, but at that moment Beatrice ached for him to hold her tightly in his arms, just hold her, and tell her that he loved her and cherished her.

He might believe that Sutton would return to normality now that the Widow Belknap had disappeared, but she suspected that there was far worse to come.

She stayed with Judith Buckley until Francis returned from the Rowlandson farm.

'You saw the fish?' she asked him as they started for home.

'Yes, I did,' said Francis. 'About a score of them have died, but no more than that. The remainder look quite lively.'

'Really? When I saw them yesterday they were all in some

kind of a trance. Ebenezer had no trouble in plucking one out of the water with his hand.'

'I asked him about that, but he seemed reluctant to discuss it. In fact, I have to say that he was more than a little short with me, as if he resented my coming to see him.'

'Why should he? You were only showing him your concern.'

'I don't know. But he said he was certain now that the fish had not been affected by anything satanic, but by green pond weed. It always blows in spells of very warm weather.'

Beatrice frowned at him. 'He seemed sure when I talked to him that some demon had poisoned his pond, if not Satan himself. In fact, he said that if he had been there earlier, he was afraid that he would have met Satan face to face. Did he show you the hoof prints? They were almost exactly the same as the hoof prints at Henry Mendum's, weren't they?'

'He said that you must have been mistaken.'

'Mistaken? What did he mean by that?'

'I could see no hoof prints on the jetty, Bea, and Ebenezer denied that there had ever been any. He said that you had probably seen the paw prints from his dog, which had been swimming in the pond just before you arrived.'

'You *really* saw no hoof prints?'

'None. But in any event, you said yourself that they were artificial.'

'They may have been artificial, Francis, but they were *there*. I saw them with my own eyes. I *smelled* them. I stepped on one of them and it stained my petticoat. I can show you.'

'Perhaps Ebenezer had them scrubbed off.'

'But why? Why would he tell me so insistently that it was Satan who had entranced his fish but then the very next day deny it?'

'Bea, you have constantly questioned if Satan is really among

246

us, so are you not relieved that Ebenezer's fish were affected by weed, rather than witchcraft? Perhaps my prayers have been answered at last and Satan has decided to leave us be. After all, the Widow Belknap has gone. Perhaps His Satanic Majesty has realized that our faith here in Sutton is too strong, and we have now seen an end to all of these horrors.'

When they arrived home Francis hung up his coat and went into the parlour to finish his sermon for Sunday and to write letters about what had happened to two of his fellow ministers in neighbouring parishes. Beatrice found Mary and Noah out in the yard at the back, where Mary was pulling radishes and Noah was sitting close by, solemnly eating a stick of cheese pastry with his right hand and allowing ants to run over his left hand and up his arm.

Beatrice picked up Noah and brushed the pastry crumbs and the ants from his pinafore. 'Look at you, silly boy! They're crawling all over you!'

Mary stood up straight and stretched her back. 'I saw that man again, Goody Scarlet, when you were gone. The brown cloak man.'

'Really? Where?'

'I was going back to the kitchen to fetch Jubal and Caleb a drink and I saw him hurrying away down the driveway. He was walking very fast.'

'Did you call out to him?'

'No. He was too far away. And besides I was afeared to.'

Beatrice flicked an ant away from Noah's hair. 'There's nothing missing, is there, from the house?'

'I don't know if he came into the house or not, but there was nothing stolen that I could see. There were cookies cooling on a rack in the kitchen, but none of those was gone, so I don't think it was food he was after.'

'Well, who can tell what he wants?' said Beatrice. 'I just pray that he will go away and leave us in peace. I must put my pie in the oven in any event. When you've finished here in the yard, can you come inside and help me with the vegetables?'

She went back into the house and gave Francis a little finger-wave as he sat writing in the parlour. She would tell him when he had finished that Mary had seen the brown hooded figure, but she didn't want to disturb him now, especially since nothing seemed to have been stolen. Francis always laboured with great difficulty over his sermons and he didn't like to be interrupted.

She went up to her bedchamber. As she climbed the stairs, she became aware of a sweet, strong fragrance. It grew even stronger as she reached the landing and when she entered the room she saw that a heap of wild flowers was lying on the bed, loosely tied together with a white silk ribbon. The sweet fragrance came from purple bergamot, but there were dark blue lobelias, too, and blanket flowers which looked like bright red daisies.

Beatrice slowly approached the bed, mystified. Surely Mary hadn't picked these. If she had, she would have arranged them in vases for the parlour. Perhaps Francis had asked Mary to do it, to show her how much he loved her, but she doubted it. Although he had such romantic looks, and told her frequently how much he adored her, he had never been given to romantic gestures like this.

It was true that the flowers had been laid on *her* side of the bed, but even a stranger would have known it was hers because her nightgown was folded on the left-hand pillow.

There was no note attached – nothing to give her any clue who might have left them there. If it wasn't Mary, then somebody had been very daring in entering their house while they were out. Trespassers were at risk of being stabbed, or beaten, or having boiling water poured over them, as Goody Buckley had once done to one of her interfering neighbours.

Again, Beatrice couldn't help thinking of Jonathan Shooks and the knowing, subversive way he always looked at her. She surprised herself by almost wishing that it *had* been him – even though she knew that she would never be untrue to Francis. But of all the men who might have had the inclination and the nerve to do this, and not be afraid of the consequences, Jonathan Shooks was the only one she could immediately think of.

It was then that Francis called out from the bottom of the stairs, 'Bea, my dearest! How long will it be before dinner?'

'Only an hour, Francis! It's a beef and turnip pie, which I have made already! I have only the beans and the carrots to prepare!'

There was a long pause from downstairs. Beatrice hoped that he hadn't caught the hint of guilt in her voice. But what was she going to do with these flowers, and how was she going to explain to Francis where she suspected they might have come from? And why should she feel so guilty about it?

Twenty-five

The next day was grey and hot and humid, and Beatrice felt as if she could hardly breathe. It was nearly seven miles from Sutton to Londonderry, but because some stretches of the road had recently been levelled and cleared of stones it took them only two and a half hours. All the way they could hear thunder mumbling behind the hills and a few spots of rain pattered on to them from time to time, as well as hazelnuts from the trees that bordered the road.

Francis seemed preoccupied and spoke very little, except to say that the funerals of both Nicholas and Tristram Buckley would be held the following morning.

'And what of the Gilmans' four slaves?'

'They will be buried by their families in a plot behind their shanties. I will go up there later and say prayers over them.'

'And there is still no evidence as to who might have killed them?'

'No. Nothing. Major General Holyoke has written to the governor that their deaths were caused by "supernatural acts of malice by persons as yet unknown" – if persons they were.'

'He didn't say "witchcraft"?'

'*Beatrice*,' Francis admonished her.

Major General Holyoke had been magistrate several years ago when a young Sutton girl called Lucy Parminter had been sentenced to death for witchcraft, a charge of which she was found to be innocent – but only at the very last moment before she was due to be hanged. Major General Holyoke might well be "known in the gates", but in common with Constable Jewkes he had made several embarrassing and potentially fatal misjudgements.

After a few moments Beatrice said, 'Mary saw that hooded figure again.'

'Oh, yes.' Francis didn't seem to be paying attention to her.

'It was yesterday, when we were down in the village.'

'What was he doing?'

'Walking away from the house, that's all.'

'Was anything stolen, or any damage done?'

'No, I don't think so. Mary couldn't see that anything was missing.'

She was about to tell him about the wild flowers, too, but it suddenly started to rain much harder and he stopped to put up the hood. Somehow, when he climbed back into his seat again she felt that the moment had passed. He seemed to have something on his mind that was much more important than a mysterious bunch of flowers. All he would probably want to know is why she hadn't told him about them immediately, and shown them to him – and if she were truthful with herself, she wasn't sure why she hadn't. She hadn't told him about the perfume, either, and now it was far too late to do that.

For some reason that she found difficult to understand, she found the secrecy exciting. Other men in the village had always treated her with the respect and deference that was due to the minister's wife, but now some unknown man was showing an interest in her as a desirable woman.

As they drove on further, the road began to deteriorate into ruts and potholes and they had to slow down. The rain was drumming on the hood now and Uriel kept shaking his mane.

'You're worried, Francis,' said Beatrice. 'What are you worried about?'

'It's nothing. Yesterday I felt as if everything might have been resolved, but now I'm not so certain.'

'Why? Tell me.'

'You will think me ineffectual if I do.'

'Of course I won't. Tell me.'

She waited, but he didn't answer. They trundled further along the road, and after a while the rain eased up, and the sun came out, intensely hot, and the dense forests of butternut trees on either side of them began to steam.

'Francis, what's wrong?' she persisted.

He gave a quick shake of his head and said, 'Later. I'll tell you later. We have pigs to buy.'

They bought three sows and a boar from the same ginger-haired Scottish-Irish pig farmer who had sold them their last five Berkshires and he promised to have them delivered the following day, sealing the deal by spitting into the palm of his hand and shaking on it.

They talked for a while, but Beatrice could barely understand the pig farmer's accent and she could hardly hear him over the grunting of his pigs.

Francis hardly spoke to her on the way back to Sutton. She was beginning to wonder if he had found out about the perfume and the wild flowers and was angry with her. He had said, after all, that he felt 'ineffectual'.

When they reached home, however, he said, 'Don't worry about preparing food for me, Bea. There is somebody I must talk to first.'

Noah came running out of the porch and clung to Beatrice's gown. Beatrice picked him up and kissed him. 'Who is it, Francis? Who must you talk to? You're beginning to disturb me.'

Francis reached inside his coat and took out a folded letter. 'Very well,' he said. 'I received this early this morning from Thomas Norton, the lawyer. One of his sons brought it here.'

She put Noah down and he passed her the letter. When she unfolded it she read:

My Dear Reverend Scarlett,

I believe it incumbent upon mee to inform you that Goodman Ebenezer Rowlandson has requested mee as a matter of Urgency to Deede 36 acres of his propertie to Mr Jonathan Shooks as a Precaution against Further Depredationes of Satan & his Representatives. He has requested Most Earnestlie that I should not inform you of this Matter & I am loath to be seen as an Intermedler but since Master George Gilman has also Deeded almost an Equalle acreage to Mr Shooks for the same Purpose I believe that as our appointed Minister you should be made Conscious of these Transactions.

Yrs Thos Norton.

Beatrice read the letter twice and then handed it back to Francis. 'Why did you say nothing until now?' she asked him.

'Why do you think? Two of my most prosperous and influential communicants have turned for help against the forces of evil to – to what? To whom? Not to me – to some itinerant quack! Some charlatan who has arrived from nowhere

253

telling me that I have no knowledge of the demonic presences in this country and that I am powerless to protect my own congregation!'

Francis was so agitated now that he had crumpled up the letter in his fist and Noah was looking up at him with an apprehensive frown on his face and his bottom lip quivering.

'George Gilman said nothing to me about deeding his land to Jonathan Shooks, and Ebenezer Rowlandson told me nothing but lies! Why didn't they both simply say to my face that they have no faith in my ministry, that my prayers have obviously come to nothing, and that I can't even save my own pigs from the Devil, let alone Nicholas Buckley and George Gilman's slaves!'

He paused for breath, and then he said, 'I don't know why we bothered to travel all the way to Londonderry to buy new pigs. What was the point? The Devil will probably kill those too, just to rub my impotence in my face!'

'Francis, Francis,' Beatrice soothed him. 'If Ebenezer Rowlandson and George Gilman choose to be so foolish, it is not your fault!'

'Of course it's my fault! I'm supposed to be their shield and protector! It wouldn't surprise me if Henry Mendum has given half his land to Jonathan Shooks, too, without telling me!'

'So what do you propose to do?'

'I could send Jonathan Shooks an ecclesiastical document warning him off, but I very much doubt if that would deter him. No – I'm going to find him and have it out with him, face to face! This is my congregation, my ministry, and he has wilfully led my communicants astray. It is just as humiliating for me as if they had left my parish and started to attend church in Dover instead.'

'You should be careful, Francis. Please, my love. Jonathan Shooks is not the kind of man to be crossed.'

Francis grasped her shoulders and looked into her eyes. His own eyes were glittering and dark and she had never seen him look so determined.

'I am not at all sure what I am confronting here, Bea – Devil or man, demon or deceiver. All I do know is that I am facing the greatest challenge of my entire career as a minister of God – perhaps of the whole of my life. In one form or another, Satan has come to Sutton, and it is my bounden duty to stand up to him.'

'Where will you find him?'

'I shall go to the village first to see if anybody knows of his whereabouts. If not, I will go to the inn at Penacook and wait for his return.'

'Francis, I beg you not to. The law should be dealing with this, not you.'

'How can the courts deal with Satan, Bea? And what law is greater than God's law?'

'Let me show you that stain on my petticoat made by that so-called demon's hoof print! It's nothing but a mixture of common substances, Francis! It's not supernatural at all! Kingdom was poisoned by yew leaves, which anybody could have fed him, and our pigs were probably killed by arsenic or perhaps some toxic plant like belladonna. As far as Ebenezer Rowlandson's fish are concerned, they could have been affected by oil of rhodium or something similar. The same goes for Henry Mendum's cattle.'

'Bea, you don't understand! *How* these atrocities were perpetrated, and what with, tells us nothing! What do witches use in their potions? The same common herbs that anybody can grow in their gardens! It's the way in which they prepare those potions that gives them their power! Just as we say prayers and appeal to the Lord to give *us* strength, they use rituals and incantations to be given strength by Satan.'

'Let me show you the stain.'

'Bea, it makes no difference. One way or another, I have to face up to Jonathan Shooks and take back authority over my own parish. How can I preach my sermon on Sunday, admonishing my congregation to honour the Lord God, when they cannot even honour me?'

'I honour you, Francis. You know that.'

Francis leaned forward so that their foreheads were touching and they were so close together that Beatrice couldn't focus on his face. 'I know you do, my dearest. But this time it isn't enough.'

Francis returned home a little after nine o'clock. She had been waiting at the window for him and she was relieved to see his two carriage-lamps jiggling in the darkness at the end of the driveway. When he came into the house he was dusty and exhausted and he smelled of sweat. He sat down at the kitchen table and she gave him a mug of cider, although he didn't drink it straight away.

'You didn't find him,' she said.

'No, I didn't find him. Everywhere I went he had only recently left, but nobody ever knew where he was bound for next. It was more like hunting a ghost than a man. I went to the Penacook Inn at the very last. He is still residing there, apparently, but I waited an hour and there was no sign of him, so I left.'

'You'll find him tomorrow. Somebody must have told him by now that you're looking for him.'

'I don't know if that's good or bad. If he knows that I'm looking for him he might do everything he can to avoid me.'

'I don't think he will,' said Beatrice. 'I don't think he's that kind of a man.'

The wild flowers, she thought, *and the perfume.*

*

When they went to bed that night, Francis held her very close, although he made no move to make love to her. She could feel his half-stiffened penis through his nightshirt, but she knew that his mind was full of demons and witches and incinerated slaves and Satan and Jonathan Shooks.

After a while he leaned across her to blow out the candle, but before he did so he said, 'What's this?'

'What's what?' she asked him.

He was holding a small purple petal between finger and thumb, like the wing that had fallen off a fairy. He sniffed it and said, 'It smells very sweet. What is it?'

'Bergamot,' said Beatrice.

'So where did it come from?'

Beatrice raised her eyebrows but said nothing. The last thing she wanted to do was tell him a lie.

'Perhaps it's a sign,' said Francis. 'A sign from God of sweet things to come.'

He leaned over again and blew out the candle. Beatrice lay in the darkness and she had never felt so guilty and confused in her life – and fearful, too. There was no moon tonight and she felt as if all around the house the scenery of her world was being furtively rearranged and that in the morning everything would seem different, unfamiliar, and that she would have no idea what to do next.

As it turned out, Jonathan Shooks took events in hand. She and Francis were eating a breakfast of flummery and dried plums when they heard a carriage outside and then a knock at their front door. Mary came into the kitchen and said, 'Mr Shooks is calling on you, reverend.'

Francis gave Beatrice a quick, surprised look and then stood up and went out into the hallway. Beatrice was tempted to say, '*Be careful, Francis*,' but she was afraid that Jonathan Shooks might hear her and question why she had said it.

Francis took Jonathan Shooks into the parlour. Beatrice took off her apron and left her breakfast to follow them. Jonathan Shooks bowed as she came in through the door, and smiled. He was wearing his pale grey linen coat and britches and shoes with silver buckles that reminded Beatrice of the buckles on Nicholas Buckley's shoes.

'The gracious Goody Scarlet, good morning!' said Jonathan Shooks. 'I was just asking the reverend why he has been looking for me here, there and everywhere.'

In a strained voice Francis said, 'I have been given intelligence, sir, that both George Gilman and Ebenezer Rowlandson have deeded you considerable tracts of their land.'

'Yes, very true,' said Jonathan Shooks, nodding his head as if Francis had said something very reasonable. 'And you know, of course, why they should have done so.'

'Your demons demanded it?' Francis challenged him.

'One demon in particular, as a fee for Satan's protection.'

'That is nothing short of extortion, Mr Shooks.'

'I realize that, reverend, but when a man is given a choice between ruination and possible death or surrendering some of his acreage, which do you think he will choose? Let me remind you that if it weren't for me, Gilman and Rowlandson wouldn't have even been offered such a choice. The demon would either have destroyed their livelihoods, so that they were forced off their holdings completely, or thought up some grotesque way of killing them.'

'So who is this demon? Or *what*?' asked Beatrice. 'Is it

a man or a woman or a two-legged beast with horns and hooves? Does it have a name?'

Jonathan Shooks smiled and touched the tip of his finger to his lips. 'I have said before, Goody Scarlet, that I cannot say the name. If I say the name, then all will be undone and Satan will take a truly terrible revenge.'

'Can I not come with you, next time you meet this demon, and reason with it?' asked Francis.

'If you come with me, reverend, then you will discover its identity, and as I say, all will then be undone. Once you know its identity your holy calling will oblige you to try to exorcize it, and that can only bring catastrophe. Whatever choice we make, whether we choose to defy the demon or to come to some arrangement with it, the consequences will be unpleasant, so I am opting for the lesser of those evils.'

All the time he was saying this Jonathan Shooks didn't once take his eyes off Beatrice, and although his voice was so serious he seemed to be smiling very slightly.

Francis vigorously shook his head. 'I cannot permit this to continue, Mr Shooks. Sutton is my ministry and while it remains under my authority I will not have bargains made with Satan here, nor with any of Satan's representatives.'

Jonathan Shooks still didn't take his eyes away from Beatrice. 'Would you condemn yet more of your congregation to an agonizing death, like Nicholas Buckley? Is that what you would do? Because that is what would surely happen, I assure you. Your ministry would become a ministry of martyrs simply because you were so inflexible.'

'Mr Shooks – I insist that you return the land that has been deeded over to you, every work-lot of it, and I also insist that either you desist from your dealings with this demon or else leave my parish altogether. I will take this matter to the highest church authorities if I have to, and to the courts.'

Jonathan Shooks didn't answer immediately, but turned his head and frowned out of the parlour window as if he had seen somebody quickly walk by. Beatrice looked, too, but she couldn't see anybody.

After a moment, he turned back to Francis and said, 'No, Reverend Scarlet, I will not desist. If members of your congregation decide that it is in their own best interests to hand over the acreage that this demon demands, then there is nothing you can do to stop them. They have seen for themselves what this demon can do to them if they refuse.'

'Is it the Widow Belknap, this demon?' Francis demanded. 'Or perhaps some malign spirit that has *possessed* the Widow Belknap?'

'I have told you, reverend. I will name no name.'

'Then you are warned. I will take this matter as far as I have to. I will take it to Governor Wentworth if necessary.'

Jonathan Shooks shrugged. 'Do what your conscience dictates. All I can tell you is that *I* have the ability recognize the demons that appear in this land on Satan's behalf, be they wizards or witches or Wendigos, even if you cannot. Since the only way to save the lives of innocent people is to do business with these demons, then do business with them I shall.'

With that, he bowed again to Beatrice and said, 'Good day to both of you. I hope when we meet again it will be under more amicable circumstances.'

Francis said, 'I'm serious, Mr Shooks. I will not allow this extortion continue. Good day to you, too!'

Beatrice escorted Jonathan Shooks to the front door. Outside, in the sunshine, Samuel was waiting with his calash and he waved when he saw her.

'I am not over-fond of wild flowers, Mr Shooks,' she told

him as he put on his hat.

He looked at her with one eyebrow lifted. 'Are you not, Goody Scarlet?'

'Some of them I like. It depends who gives them to me.'

'I suppose that would apply to almost every gift,' he replied.

What does he mean? She thought. Is he asking me if I was pleased by the perfume?

'Yes,' she said. 'No matter what it was.'

There was a long silence between them, as if both wanted to say something but both were too wary of committing themselves. Then Jonathan Shooks said, 'Your husband is a good and upright man, Goody Scarlet. Please try and dissuade him from doing anything rash. There are forces at work here in Sutton of which, for all of his rectitude, he has very little understanding.'

'The Reverend Scarlet is officiating this morning at two funerals, Mr Shooks – Nicholas Buckley and his baby son, Tristram. I think he is well aware of what these forces are and what they can do, as am I.'

'Oh, yes. I have heard it said that you are quite the amateur apothecary.'

'My father taught me, Mr Shooks, in London. Suffice it to say that I can distinguish the difference between a concoction from hell and one from New Hampshire.'

Jonathan Shooks kept on smiling. 'You are a very fair young woman, Goody Scarlet. Please have a care, and do try to speak persuasively to your husband. It would be tragic to see you a relict so young.'

With that he climbed with a creak of leather springs into his calash and Samuel gave one of his weird whoops and cracked his whip. Beatrice stood and watched him as he drove away under the trees. She was almost wishing that the brown-cloaked figure would appear out of the shadows as he went past, which would prove beyond doubt that it was neither him nor Samuel acting on his behalf.

She was still standing there when Francis came bustling out of the house. His cheeks were flushed and he was tugging on his cream linen coat.

'Caleb!' he shouted. '*Caleb!*'

Caleb came hurrying around the side of the house carrying a rake. 'Yes, reverend? Sorry I've took so long weeding the turnip bed. Hard as rock that dirt is!'

'Never mind that. Please harness Uriel for me as quick as you can!'

'Francis, where are you going?' asked Beatrice. 'You can't be too long – the funerals start at eleven o'clock!'

'I'm going after Shooks. I'm going to follow him.'

'Francis – don't!'

'You won't stop me, Bea. I'm going to follow him and see this demon for myself, and confront it! I refuse to surrender my authority to some crawling creature from hell, even if Shooks is prepared to give in to it!'

'Francis, don't you see? There *is* no demon!'

Caleb had brought Uriel round from his paddock and was fastening his trace buckle and adjusting his tugs.

Francis said, 'What? How can you say such a thing, Bea? How could an ordinary mortal have hung George Gilman's slaves so high up in the rafters, as if on Calvary Hill, and then set fire to them? Or melted Nicholas Buckley into broth? Or caused our pigs to die without any trace of sickness, like the Gadarene swine? Or stunned Ebenezer Rowlandson's fish?'

'I believe that every one of those events has an explanation, Francis – every one of them, even if we don't yet understand what all of those explanations are. That's what I've been trying to tell you. I have been loath to contradict you, my dearest, or to question your faith, and several times I have been close to being persuaded myself that the Devil must be to blame. But I'm sure that he's not. I'm convinced that we can put an end to all of this terrible mischief by other means apart from prayer.'

Francis looked down the driveway. Jonathan Shooks's calash was out of sight now, and even the dust from its wheels had settled.

'If you are saying that there is no demon, Bea, then by implication that means that there is no Satan.'

'Not necessarily. Satan can turn the hearts of men, he doesn't have to send demons to do his work for him.'

'No, Bea. You are still influenced far too much by what your father taught you. Not everything in this world can be explained by science, nor should it be. If everything can be explained by science, then how can there be miracles? Lazarus would not have risen from the dead, nor the water at Canaan turned into wine. Don't you understand, Bea? What has been happening here in Sutton is not just empirical proof of the existence of Satan, it is empirical proof of the existence of God.'

Beatrice didn't know what to say to him. She had always thought that his faith was shining, unquestioning and flawless. Did he really need *evidence* that God was real?

Caleb had finished harnessing Uriel and Francis said, 'Now, my darling, I have to go or I will lose him. I will be back as soon as I can.'

'Francis—' she began, but then she realized that nothing was going to stop him from going after Jonathan Shooks. It was as much to prove his manhood as it was to prove his belief in God.

Twenty-six

By a quarter to eleven, Francis had still not returned home, so Beatrice took Noah and Mary and walked down to the village. Both Beatrice and Mary wore black and Noah was dressed in his dark grey pinafore.

Beatrice was desperately hoping that Francis had decided to go to the village first, in order to make sure that the meeting house had been properly prepared for the funerals. As soon as she reached the village green, however, she could see that even though a large crowd of mourners had gathered outside the front doors, Francis was nowhere to be seen, nor Uriel, nor their shay.

'Goody Scarlet!' called out Major General Holyoke, as she crossed the grass. He was a short, stout man with wiry grey whiskers, ruddy cheeks and a black eye-patch over his left eye socket. 'Is the reverend not with you? Most of these people were here betimes but now we are more than ten minutes delayed.'

It was well past eleven now and the congregation were beginning to file into the meeting house and take their seats, with the men in the front benches and the women and children right at the back, although Peter Duston had raised the women's benches so that they had a better view. The only exception was Judith Buckley, who was sitting beside the two elm-wood coffins that stood on trestles in the centre of the aisle, her head covered with a black lace veil.

Inside the meeting house it was hot and airless and smelled strongly of musty clothes and warm people. The only sound was a low, reverential murmuring, the scuffling of children's feet, and the flap-flap-flapping of fans.

Both of the coffins were closed now because the weather had been so hot. Peter Duston had been concerned that if he delayed screwing down the lid of Tristram's little coffin before much longer, Tristram's body would become so bloated that he wouldn't be able to screw it down at all.

Outside, Beatrice said, 'Francis went off on an errand four hours ago and I have not seen him since. I'm worried that he may have met with an accident.'

'Did he tell you where he was going?'

'He didn't know himself.'

'I'm sorry,' said Major General Holyoke. 'I'm not sure that I quite understand you. He went off on an errand but he didn't know where to?'

'He was following Jonathan Shooks. He's mentioned Jonathan Shooks to you, I presume?'

'Yes – yes, he has. He has told me more than once that he suspects Shooks of being a mountebank, although he has no real proof of it. Is that why he was following him?'

Beatrice nodded. 'I'm very worried for him, general. Jonathan Shooks has always been the soul of courtesy to me, but I very much fear that he is not a man to be meddled with lightly.'

Major General Holyoke took out his pocket watch. 'We will give the reverend ten more minutes, Goody Scarlet, but if he doesn't arrive by then we will have to commence the funeral proceedings without him. We have to consider poor Goody Buckley, with both her husband and her infant son to commit to the ground. I'm sure that Goodman Lynch knows the words of the funeral service off by heart.'

Benjamin Lynch was Francis's sacristan and had frequently led prayers when Francis had been away on ecclesiastic business, or unwell. He was easily the oldest man in Sutton, nearly seventy, and Beatrice could see his white hair shining like a dandelion puffball on the opposite side of the graveyard.

'Very well,' she said. 'But if he doesn't appear by the end of the service, I think we should send men out to go looking for him.'

'Don't you worry, my dear,' said Major General Holyoke, patting her on the shoulder. 'I'm sure that no harm has come to him. His carriage may have lost a wheel, nothing more serious than that, or perhaps the traces have snapped.'

'If that had happened he would have unharnessed our driver and ridden him here.'

'You never know, your driver may have been lamed.'

Beatrice was looking around to see if Jonathan Shooks was among the crowd, but there was no sign of him, either. She could see Henry Mendum, all dressed in black with a black cocked hat, looking sombre but bored. His wife, Harriet, had her nose lifted as haughtily as ever and she was wearing a voluminous black silk hood which denoted her social status in the community. A woman of lesser standing would have risked a fine for wearing such a hood.

'Come on, Goody Scarlet, let's go inside,' said Major General Holyoke. 'Fretting will do you no good at all. There will be a good reason for Francis's delay, I'm certain of it, and he'll be back before you know it.'

But Francis didn't come back. Benjamin Lynch had to conduct the funeral service in his place, which he read from the pulpit in a high, scratchy voice like a crow cawing from a nearby tree. It seemed to Beatrice that it took him hours to get through it, with interminable quotations from the Psalms. '*You have made my days a mere handbreadth, O Lord.*' He ended with an uplifting verse:

Ye mourners who in silent gloom
Bear your dear kindred to the tomb,
Grudge not when Christians go to rest,
They sleep in Jesus, and are blest.

Afterwards, as the coffins of Nicholas and Tristram were lowered into their graves, Beatrice kept looking around, shading her eyes with her hand, but there was still no sign of Francis. She went across to the Buckley house to give her condolences to Judith, and to make sure that little Apphia was still improving, but she didn't stay for burnt wine and biscuits. She urgently needed to return home in case Francis had been hurt and had managed somehow to make his way back to the parsonage.

Hurrying back along the roadway, with her black gown lifted to help her to walk more quickly, she couldn't stop herself imagining all kinds of horrifying scenarios. Francis covered in blood. Francis brought back home unconscious in the back of the shay, his skull broken. Francis beaten by robbers and his dead or senseless body thrown into the porch.

She even began to think that he might have been right, after all, and that Jonathan Shooks *had* been meeting with a demon, and that when Francis had followed him he had been discovered and the demon had melted him like Nicholas.

Perhaps all the time she had been too pragmatic and hadn't allowed herself to accept that the world really was full of wonders and miracles and spirits both good and malevolent.

'Ma-*ma*!' called Noah, trying to keep up with her, but she only hurried all the faster.

When she arrived home, though, she found that Francis had still not returned. She heard squealing noises from the back of the house and when she walked round she found that the farmer from Londonderry had delivered their pigs. Caleb had already filled their trough with water and was feeding them with bran and cabbage stalks.

'Bacon's come, ma'am!' he called out to her.

Beatrice walked over to the pig-pen and said, 'Thank you, Caleb. Thank you.'

She started to ask him, 'The Reverend Scarlet hasn't been home, has he?' but before she could finish her throat tightened and she started to sob. Her eyes blurred with tears and she waved her hand uselessly because she simply couldn't speak.

Caleb dropped his pail of bran and let himself out through the gate.

'Goody Scarlet! Goody Scarlet! Whatever's wrong?'

'It's the Reverend Scarlet, Caleb,' Beatrice managed to tell him, smearing the tears from her cheeks with her fingers. 'He's been missing since early this morning. He didn't come to the Buckleys' funerals to officiate. I have had no word from him at all.'

'Did he tell you where he was going?'

Beatrice shook her head. 'He said only that he was going to follow Mr Shooks, to discover what manner of business he was up to. I cautioned him not to, but he insisted and now I don't know where he is.'

'Well, we'd best go look for him,' said Caleb. 'I'll fetch Jubal. He's down by the brook cutting back the bushes and he has two of Mr Barraclough's boys with him. They can go out looking, too.'

'Thank you, Caleb. I'm worried that he might be lying hurt somewhere and needs our assistance.'

'Did you see which direction he first went off in?'

'Left, towards the village, but after that I don't have any idea. Jonathan Shooks is staying at the Penacook Inn, so they might have headed that way, but he is very elusive. Like a ghost, the Reverend Scarlet called him.'

Jubal and Caleb and the two Barraclough boys went off to search for Francis. The Barraclough boys had come to the parsonage on one horse and they said that they would first ride back to their home-lot and saddle up another, so that they could widen their search even further. They would also try to enlist the help of as many people in the village as they could. Francis was well liked in Sutton and nobody in his congregation would wish to see any harm come to him.

Beatrice stayed at home. She knew that she would be of very little use trampling through the woods in her mourning dress. Better that she stay here, so that she could welcome Francis when he did return and tend to any injuries he might have sustained. She couldn't get the thought out of her mind that he was badly hurt, almost as if he were trying to communicate with her by animal magnetism.

The afternoon passed and there was still no news. The sun began to sink behind the pines. Beatrice fed and washed Noah herself, even though Mary had stayed on, and she tucked him up in his crib and sang him a lullaby.

Dear God let Francis be safe, she thought. *Don't let Noah become a fatherless child.*

Noah cried when she left the room, but she knew that he would soon fall asleep. As she reached the bottom of the stairs she heard horses outside, and a carriage. Immediately she opened the front door to see who was out there.

'Thank the Lord,' she said, because it was their own shay, with Uriel pulling it. When she hurried out of the porch, however, she saw that Henry Mendum's black stable-boy was driving it, and that Henry Mendum himself was riding beside it, still dressed in his black cocked hat and his funeral coat.

'Goody Scarlet,' he said, lifting his hat. He climbed down from his horse and handed the reins to his stable-boy.

'What's happened?' she asked him. 'Where's Francis? What's happened to him? Have you found him? Is her hurt?'

'I regret that we haven't yet found him, no,' said Henry Mendum. 'Less than an hour ago Bobbin turned up at my stables pulling your empty shay behind him. I don't know where your husband is, Goody Scarlet, but obviously he and the shay parted company at some point, so Bobbin made his own way home.'

Beatrice laid her hand against the horse's neck. 'Uriel, we call him, after the archangel Uriel. Could you tell how far he might have travelled, or where he might have come from?'

'There was steeplebush caught in the wheel spokes which caught my attention, because steeplebush grows mainly beside rivers and lakes, not close to the highway. In particular it grows around Johnson's Pond, and that's a good six miles off.'

'Can you send some of your men to Johnson's Pond, to see if Francis is anywhere nearby? I am so worried that he might be badly hurt and unable to walk.'

Henry Mendum looked towards the tall pines beyond the orchard. The sun had sunk behind them now and the evening air was whirling with bats.

'It's too late now, I regret. It will be so dark soon that we won't be able to tell if our eyes are open or closed. But I promise you that I'll have every available man out at first light tomorrow.'

'Thank you, Mr Mendum. I understand, and I appreciate it. And I thank you, too, for bringing Uriel back.'

'My heart is with you, Goody Scarlet,' said Henry Mendum. 'So soon as I have any news, I will let you know. I bid you good evening.'

With that, he heaved himself up into the saddle, turned his chestnut horse around and trotted off down the driveway, with his stable-boy trotting behind him on foot.

Mary came out and helped her to unbuckle Uriel from his traces. She led him to his paddock and opened the gate for him.

'There, Uriel. Good boy. If only you could talk.'

Mary stayed the night in Noah's bedchamber, so that as soon dawn broke Beatrice could harness Uriel again and get ready to leave for Johnson's Pond. She knew that any search she made for Francis would probably be fruitless, but she was too agitated to remain at home any longer, constantly going outside and looking down the driveway to see if anybody was coming, or listening for the sound of horses or carriage wheels.

She had hardly slept all night, and when she had she had been woken by the trickling of rain down the window, which she had thought at first was somebody whispering very quietly in her ear.

Mary had insisted on wrapping up a small crusty loaf for her in a cloth and giving her a stone bottle of apple juice, but she felt neither hungry nor thirsty. As she drove Uriel towards the village she could see from the clouds that the weather was going to be much more disturbed today, with strange streaky clouds, and cooler, too.

There was nobody in sight around the village green as she drove past it, although she could hear clanking coming from Ronald Bartlett's smithy. Because it had rained during the night the green smelled strongly of horse manure.

She passed by the Widow Belknap's house, but it didn't look as if the Widow Belknap had returned, either. Her curtains were half-drawn and her goat was gone. Either the goat had gnawed through its rope and escaped or else it had been taken into care by one of her neighbours.

The road to Johnson's Pond wended its way northwards for a little less than five miles, almost parallel to the Merrimack river. Then it turned sharply north-east, with the forests growing denser and the ground becoming rockier. At last it sloped to the north again, sharply downhill, until it passed through a thickly wooded valley with a large dark pond in the middle of it, as black and reflective as a sheet of glass.

This was Johnson's Pond, and as Henry Mendum had said, its banks were thick with fuzzy purple steeplebush, like the brushes that her father used to use for cleaning out bottles. Beatrice stopped the shay beside the water so that Uriel could rest and have a drink. The woods all around were dark and cool and aromatic, and every now and then the silence was interrupted by the repetitive whistling of nuthatches. She took a drink of apple juice herself and then tilted her head back and tiredly closed her eyes.

She almost nodded off to sleep for a moment, but then she heard a crackling sound, like somebody stepping on twigs, and she opened her eyes and turned her head in alarm. She gasped in surprise, because a figure in brown was stealthily creeping towards her and was less than thirty feet away.

Although it was dressed in brown, it didn't look the same as the brown-cloaked figure she had seen around the parsonage. Its head was covered so that its face was hidden, but it was wrapped only in a blanket, rather than a cloak.

'Who are you?' said Beatrice, trying to sound challenging. 'What do you want? I have no money!'

The figure came and stood beside the shay, not moving. Beatrice stared at it with her heart beating hard against her ribs – so hard that she thought the figure might be able to hear it.

Another nuthatch whistled and as it did so the figure swung its left arm so that it dropped its blanket to the ground. Beatrice jerked back in her seat, startled. The figure was the Widow Belknap, completely naked, skeletal and white-skinned except for a triangular suntanned V on her chest where she had worn her low-cut gown. Her tangled blonde hair was prickly with twigs and leaves and burrs and hung right down to her bony shoulders. Her breasts were flat and pendulous, with nipples as dark as raisins, and covered in criss-cross scratches. She had no pubic hair and her legs were as thin as broomsticks.

She stared up at Beatrice with those emerald-green eyes, although she didn't appear to be able to focus on her, and she was swaying very slightly from side to side, as if she were being blown by the wind, though there was no wind.

'Widow Belknap,' said Beatrice. 'What's happened to you? What are you doing here in the forest? Where are your clothes? Has somebody whipped you? You look as if somebody's whipped you!'

'*Who* did you say I was?' asked the Widow Belknap in a slurred voice.

'You're the Widow Belknap.'

'I'm nobody of the sort. My name – my name is *Bernice*.'

'Very well, you are Bernice. But what are you doing here, and where are your clothes? You cannot roam around here naked. I'm looking for my husband, Francis, the Reverend Scarlet. Have you seen him?'

'I am looking for revenge. I am preparing to wreak *havoc*!'

'Revenge against whom? And for what?'

The Widow Belknap lifted one finger and then looked around her as if she suspected that somebody might be eavesdropping.

'Revenge for all of their slanders, every one of them. Revenge for all of their hypocrisy, especially that brown one.'

'What "brown one"? Who are you talking about?'

'Oh, he seems to be so upright. He seems to be so blameless. But there are devils and then there are devils. At least Satan makes no pretence about what he wants, unlike *this* devil.'

'Who is it, Widow Belknap – I mean, Bernice? Can you tell me his name?'

The Widow Belknap frowned at her as if she didn't understand what she was talking about. She bent over and picked up her blanket from the ground, wrapping it around her shoulders. Then she spat emphatically, and after she had done so the spit dangled from her pointed chin.

'Who is it, Bernice?' Beatrice repeated.

'I haven't finished yet,' said the Widow Belknap. '*All* will suffer, I promise you! All will suffer! Goodmen, goodwives, children, babies, cattle and swine! The plagues of Egypt will be nothing to what will be visited on this community!'

'But I still don't understand why,' said Beatrice. 'If people in the village have been slandering you, you can always take them to court and have damages awarded against them. Don't you remember Goody Sanderson, when Abigail Belling called her a "Jewess" and a "hobbling Joan"? She received five shillings for that.'

'Goody Sanderson? Hah! She didn't deserve it. She was never pitiful to the poor. But it isn't money I want, Goody Scarlet. It's a settling of scores! Call me a slut and I will be a slut, that's vengeance for you. Call me a witch? I'll fly down your chimney at night and choke your children!'

'But who is this "brown one", Bernice? And what has he done to offend you so grievously?'

The Widow Belknap raised her left arm so that her blanket half covered her face, and winked at her. Then she started to laugh – a high, screaming, hysterical laugh that made Beatrice feel as if her skin were shrinking.

She lifted her blanket high over her head and danced around in a circle, still laughing. Then, without saying anything else, she went dancing off around the side of the pond, kicking her way through the steeplebush so that their fuzzy purple flowers scattered in all directions. There was nothing that Beatrice could do except sit and watch her disappear between the trees. She could still hear her laughing when she was no longer in sight, but then there was silence again, with no birds singing.

Beatrice had wanted to ask the Widow Belknap again if she had seen Francis, or at least if she had any idea what had happened to him, but now it was too late.

She had been deeply disturbed by the Widow Belknap's talk of 'that brown one'. Had she been referring to the brown-cloaked figure who had been haunting the parsonage? Did she want her revenge on him because he had mistreated her, or slandered her? Who had inflicted those cross-hatched scratches on her breasts? Even though it may have been 'that brown one' who had brought Beatrice perfume and wildflowers, could he possibly be dangerous?

Beatrice tied Uriel's traces to a tree and then walked all the way around the pond, which took her nearly two hours. She had brought a brass-topped walking stick with her and she used it to beat at the bushes and the weeds in case Francis was lying underneath them, hidden from view.

At last, however, tired and tearful and scratched by briars, she had to admit that she couldn't find him. Perhaps Jubal or Caleb or one of the Barraclough boys had met with better luck. She climbed back into her seat and turned the shay back towards Sutton.

Twenty-seven

She was still a mile away from the village when she saw the high plume of grey smoke rising above the treetops.

It was billowing up far too dark and dense for a bonfire, and it was coming from the wrong side of the village green for it to be another chimney fire from Rodney Bartlett's smithy. She snapped her whip in order to coax Uriel to trot faster, and he tried to, although he was tired from taking her all the way to Johnson's Pond and back.

When she drove into the village she saw that the Buckleys' house was on fire, and not just smoking. Huge orange flames were dancing out of the front parlour windows and the front door, and the whole framework of the house was blazing.

A crowd of thirty or forty villagers were gathered around the front of the house, and at least a dozen of them had formed a chain to pass buckets of water from the horse-trough pump and empty them on to the flames. The fire was so ferocious, however, that they seemed to be having no effect at all and each bucketful simply exploded into steam as soon as it was thrown.

Beatrice climbed down from her shay and quickly tied Uriel to the nearest picket fence. She hurried up to Thomas Varney and said, 'My God, Mr Varney! How did this happen? Is Judith safe? And Apphia?'

Thomas Varney's face was reddened and sweaty and there was a smudge of soot on his forehead. 'They're both of them still inside! Me and William Rolfe tried to get in to save them, but it was like trying to go in through the gates of hell!'

He was passed another bucket of water, which he swung back and emptied into the parlour window, but there was a crackle and a hiss and a fleeting cloud of steam and it was gone.

At that moment the upstairs window directly above the parlour was flung open and thick black smoke came pouring out of it, and a shower of sparks. Judith Buckley appeared, holding Apphia in her arms. Her face was blackened with smoke and Beatrice could see that the backs of her hands were scorched scarlet. Apphia was crying in a thin, high whine.

'Oh God, help us!' screamed Judith. 'Oh God, we are burning in here!'

Beatrice said to Thomas Varney, 'Ladders! Has anybody sent for ladders?'

Thomas Varney turned and pointed up towards the meeting house. Sure enough, Peter Duston and his apprentice, John, were hurrying down the slope carrying a long ladder between them.

Beatrice looked back to the upstairs window. '*Oh God, save us*!' Judith screamed, but as she did so there was a flare of flames right behind her as her petticoats caught alight. Within a few seconds she was blazing from head to foot, still screaming, and Apphia's nightgown caught fire, too. Apphia shrieked and struggled in her mother's arms as the flames engulfed them both.

Beatrice took two or three steps forward, but Thomas Varney caught hold of her arm. There was nothing anybody could do to save them. Peter Duston arrived with the ladder, gasping for breath, but he was seconds too late.

'Oh Lord God,' he said, and pressed his hand over his mouth.

As they watched in helpless horror, Judith threw Apphia out of the window. Apphia was already ablaze, so it looked as if Judith were throwing out a fiery effigy rather than a real child. To Beatrice, it seemed as if time slowed down and Apphia took minutes to fall rather than seconds. She somersaulted over and over, her arms and her legs waving, the flames making the softest of blurting noises as she dropped to the ground. Then she hit the grass in front of the house with a thump, and two men ran up to her and threw buckets of water over her.

Apphia lay on her back, shuddering for a moment, and then lay still. Beatrice looked up to the window, but Judith had disappeared now and flames were lasciviously licking out of it, like dragons' tongues.

Beatrice knelt down beside Apphia but she was clearly dead. Her hair was burned into clumps, her face was bubbled with blisters, and her nightgown was charred into brownish rags.

'You poor, poor girl,' Beatrice whispered.

'She's sleeping with Jesus now,' said Thomas Varney. Beatrice didn't turn around but she could tell by his voice that he was crying.

She stood up. 'How did this fire begin? Does anybody know?'

Judith's serving girl, Meg, was sobbing. 'Goody Buckley sent me to the dairy for milk and when I came back the house was already afire. I can't think how. There was only the fire in the kitchen, and that never caused us no trouble.'

The entire house was now in flames and with a loud lurch the interior collapsed. The upper floor dropped into the parlour, bringing down with it the loom that Judith had kept upstairs, and the staircase itself fell sideways. The fire was so intense that within less than twenty more minutes the whole building was nothing but the blackened skeleton of a house, with choking black smoke pouring from it.

There was nothing that any of them could do but stand and watch while the fire burned itself out. Goody Rust brought a grey blanket to cover Apphia, and two men lifted her on to a small barrow and wheeled her back to Goody Rust's house.

As the timbers continued to smoulder Beatrice went over to Peter Duston. His face was drained of colour and he was so upset that he could barely speak.

'I went for the ladder as fast as I could,' he wept. 'Fast as I could, I promise.'

'I know you did, Peter. But I have never seen a fire consume a house so quickly.'

'I reckon it was set deliberate. How else could it have taken hold so fast?'

'I can't think why anybody would have wanted to burn down Judith's home. I would have thought that she had been punished quite enough of late.'

All the same, she couldn't stop herself from thinking: *I wonder if this was the Widow Belknap's doing. She wasn't here when it started, but then she wouldn't have needed to be.* She remembered her father showing her how to set fire to cotton rags simply by soaking them in purple water and then pouring some thin yellow oil on them. The rags didn't always catch fire immediately, so he was always careful to throw them away before he left his laboratory in case they burst into flames later. Maybe the Widow Belknap knew how to do that, too, or had her own way of starting a fire.

'Early on, I saw that fellow with the black and grey horses outside Goody Buckley's,' said Peter Duston, wiping his eyes and sniffing.

'Jonathan Shooks?'

'I don't know what his name is, but he has a black calash and a nocky for a coachman.'

'Yes, Jonathan Shooks. What time was this?'

'Early, seven I'd say.'

'Hmm,' said Beatrice. She looked at the smoking framework of the Buckley house. A few small fires were still burning inside it and it was still too hot for Judith Buckley's body to be retrieved, whatever was left of it. 'You'll make coffins for them, won't you – Goody Buckley and Apphia?'

'Of course I will, and I won't charge for it, neither. I fetched the ladder as fast as I could, I swear to you.'

'I'm sure you ran as fast as you could, Peter. It wasn't your fault, but it still looks as if we'll be holding two more funerals.'

'Oh – I'm sorry, Goody Scarlet,' said Peter Duston, collecting himself. 'I should have asked you. Is there any sign yet of the pastor?'

'No, not yet. I went searching for him myself this morning, but I could find no trace of him.'

'I'm sorry, Goody Scarlet. I'm truly sorry. Pray God he comes home safe. It seems to me like this whole village is cursed at the moment Cursed! – though what we've done to deserve it, I simply can't think.'

Beatrice stayed in the village until mid-afternoon, doing her duty as the pastor's wife. All of the women and children who had seen Judith Buckley and Apphia burn to death were in shock, and she comforted them, and fetched a Bible from the meeting house to lead them in prayers, although she was equally shocked herself and her voice shook when she quoted from Job: '*After my skin has been thus destroyed, yet in my flesh I shall see God, for I know that my Redeemer liveth.*'

She stood on the edge of the green and watched as three men lifted Judith's body out of the ashes. She was completely black, with her arms and legs bent double like those of a clockwork monkey.

While she was standing there, Constable Jewkes came clopping up, his big horse snorting and snuffling and shaking its head. He dismounted and came over to join her.

'God's blood, Goody Scarlet, what's happened here? I saw the smoke all the way from Allen's Corners.'

'What does it look like, constable? The Buckleys' house has burned down and both Judith and Apphia are dead.'

'God's blood! If you'll forgive my language.'

Constable Jewkes high-stepped his way through the smoking timbers until he reached Judith's body. He bent over and peered at it closely and then he came high-stepping back again.

'How was the fire set? Was it deliberate? Does anybody know?'

Beatrice shook her head. 'It could have been an accident, although no candles would have been lit, not in daytime, and young Meg told me that the kitchen fire was never troublesome.'

'I can't arrest anybody for arson if I can't be sure that it was arson.'

'Even if you knew for sure that it *was* arson, constable, you still couldn't arrest anybody until you knew for certain who the arsonist was.'

'Let me tell you something, Goody Scarlet, a nod is as good as a wink to a blind horse. I know everybody for twenty miles around and what mischief they're capable of, so you don't need to tell me my business, with all respect.'

He paused, and unexpectedly sneezed, because the smoke had irritated his nostrils. 'Let me tell you this, too. I've been out this morning since first light searching for your husband, the minister, and that's why I wasn't here to attend this con – this conflagration. But no luck so far. I rode as far as Musquash in one direction and the Litchfield Bridge in the other, so you can't accuse me of shirking my duties.'

Beatrice didn't know what to say. She stood watching as Judith's cremated body was carried out of her house and it seemed incongruous that the sun should be shining so warmly and the sky so blue and the birds whistling so cheerfully.

'Are you all right, Goody Scarlet?' asked Constable Jewkes.

'Not really,' said Beatrice.

'Is there anything that I can do for you? Apart from finding the pastor, of course?'

'No – no, thank you, but it is kind of you to ask. If you have any news for me, I shall be at home.'

Constable Jewkes said, 'I'm sorry, Goody Scarlet – I didn't mean to—'

But Beatrice shook her head and lifted both her hands to show him that it didn't matter. Everybody in the village was distressed and feeling helpless and afraid. As Thomas Varney had said to her, 'I feel as if God has abandoned us. I really do.'

The rest of the afternoon seemed to last forever. Usually she would have spent it cooking and making preserves, but she had plenty of mending to do. She sat in the parlour stitching one of Francis's shirts where the sleeve was ripped and she couldn't help wondering if there was any point to her doing it – if he would ever wear it again. She had to stop for a moment with her sewing in her lap, her head lifted, trying hard to swallow the lump in her throat.

Eventually it grew dark and when she had put Noah down to sleep she went to bed herself. She took her father's notebooks with her and leafed through them to see if she could find any reference to chemicals that could start fires. What was so frustrating about her father's notes was that he had written them in no particular order, and there was no index, so every time she wanted to look up some experiment that he might have conducted, or some discovery that he might have made, she had to look through every one of his notebooks, page by page.

Still, with nobody to cook for, or talk to, she had the whole night to herself.

After almost an hour, when her bedside candle was beginning to flicker and burn low, she came across a reference to 'Spontaneous Fire Mixture'.

First, dissolve in water the crystals of permanganate of potash, according to the preparation by the German alchemist Johann Rudolf Glauber in 1659 (and described in his Opera Chymica). Soak cotton rags in the purple liquid that results and when saturated pour on the sweet oil residue from candle-making. Almost always, the result will be instant combustion, although be cautious if this does not occur and dispose of the rags carefully since they might ignite later when unattended.

That was the experiment she remembered, but she could find no other references to starting fires, although there was a warning about oily rags bursting spontaneously into flames in very hot weather.

Her candle had started to gutter when another entry caught her eye. 'Madness and Delusions Caused by Wormwood Oil'.

Wormwood oil is extracted from the herb Artemisia
absinthium and I have prescribed it in diluted form
for several digestive complaints as well as tapeworms.
I suspect also that some of my female customers
have purchased it for the express purpose of aborting
an unwanted foetus. In strong doses, however, it is
highly toxic and can bring on madness and delusions,
accompanied by convulsions which sometimes take the
form of fitful dancing.

That was all Clement Bannister had written about wormwood oil, but Beatrice thought about the Widow Belknap dancing in the woods around Johnson's Pond.

She finished reading just as her candle went out. At first, she laid the notebook beside her on the bed, where Francis should have been lying, but then she leaned over and dropped it down on the floor in case it was bad luck to assume that he wouldn't be coming back tonight.

In the first few hours the night seemed darker and more stifling than ever, but just after midnight the moon rose and shone through the pines and the bedchamber was filled with a cold, inhuman light. She hadn't been able to sleep in any case. Whether her eyes were open or closed, she hadn't been able to blot out the pictures in her mind of Judith Buckley screaming for help at her upstairs window and Apphia whirling down to the ground in flames.

Beatrice lay on her back with her fists clenched and her mouth tightly pursed and tears streaming from her eyes, in physical pain for the pity of it all.

*

Three more days went by and still there was no sign of Francis. Major General Holyoke sent out messages to all of the nearby communities and at the same time organized a search by more than fifty of the local men and boys. They covered all the surrounding area for three miles in every direction, but found no trace of Francis. In the woods to the south-east of Sutton they came across a makeshift camp, where a fire had only recently been burning and there were signs that somebody had been sleeping, but whoever had occupied it must have moved on.

In any event, Francis wouldn't have been camping in the woods, not unless he had lost his reason and forgotten who he was and where he lived.

Beatrice kept the parsonage and the ministry going as best she could. She helped Benjamin Lynch to organize funerals for Judith Buckley and Apphia, and on Wednesday morning they were buried in the graveyard next to Nicholas and Tristram. For once, Benjamin's address was short and moving, and he told the congregation that the Buckley family were now 'together with Jesus'. Afterwards, Beatrice and Goody Rust and Goody Bridges held a wake in the meeting house, with wine and cake.

Most wakes became quite animated after a few hours, even merry. After all, death was common enough and was sure to come to them all, and some of the women who had passed away in the past few years were much better off in heaven than in the arms of their husbands. But apart from some of the smaller children running around this wake remained sombre, with very few voices rising above a whisper. After they had exchanged their memories of Judith and Nicholas Buckley, the mourners talked about nothing but the strange and frightening events that had been taking place around Sutton of late, and how fearful they were of what might happen next.

'Locusts, it wouldn't surprise me,' said Goody Goodhue, looking all pinched and proper. 'You only have to read your Bible' – as if to suggest that nobody read it as assiduously as she did.

After the funerals Beatrice continued with her household duties – baking and cleaning and feeding the pigs and tending the vegetable garden – but as each day passed her chores seemed more and more pointless. On the morning of the third day, when she woke from yet another restless night, it occurred to her that she might never see Francis again and that she might never discover what had happened to him. She wasn't sure that she could bear that. She wouldn't even have a grave to tend.

For some reason, she was moved to open the drawer in the pinewood hutch and take out the bottle of perfume. She took out the stopper and sniffed it, and then she dabbed a little on each of her wrists and on her neck behind her ears. She didn't really understand why she did it, but perhaps it was something to do with attracting Francis back home, or making her feel more like a woman again. Some man had wanted to please her by giving her this bottle of perfume, so somebody cared for her, even if he was anonymous, and she wasn't entirely alone in the world.

Mary arrived at five past six, but she didn't come on foot as she usually did. She was driven by Peter Duston, the carpenter, in the wagon he used for carrying lengths of timber. He was wearing a large floppy hat and leather jerkin and he was looking distinctly grim.

'Mr Duston,' said Beatrice, stepping out of the porch with Noah in her arms. 'What brings you here? Is something amiss?'

Mary came up to her and held out her hands. 'Let me take Noah, Goody Scarlet.'

'What's wrong?' asked Beatrice, holding Noah even tighter. 'What's happened? Please tell me! Is it my husband?'

Peter Duston took off his hat and bared his bald sunburned head. 'I'm sorry, Goody Scarlet. I really am. It *is* the Reverend Scarlet, yes.'

'Is he dead? Where is he?'

'We believe you need to see this for yourself, Goody Scarlet. There is no way that words can describe it.'

'I'll take care of Noah,' said Mary, still holding out her hands.

'I can't believe you won't tell me what's happened to him!' said Beatrice. '*Tell* me!'

Peter Duston looked down at the ground, but said nothing. Realizing that she was going to get nothing more out of him, Beatrice passed Noah to Mary and went inside to fetch her shawl.

'Come on, then,' she said. 'You'd better show me the worst.'

Peter Duston helped her up on to the seat and then turned the wagon around and headed back to the village.

'He's dead, though?' said Beatrice, as they reached the end of the driveway, although she could hardly believe that she was saying it. Was it her, or some other Beatrice, in some dream or parallel existence? 'You can tell me that much. He must be dead, or he would have come home.'

'I can only show you, Goody Scarlet,' said Peter Duston. She noticed for the first time that two fingers were missing from his left hand, the index finger and the middle finger. 'You'll just have to see for yourself.'

Twenty-eight

The village green was already crowded when they arrived, but hushed. As Peter Duston drove Beatrice towards the meeting house, the crowd stepped back and several of the men took off their hats. Beatrice was filled with a terrible sense of dread because she couldn't even begin to imagine what must have happened to bring most of the village here this morning, so early, when almost all of them should have been working at their businesses or in their houses or on their farms.

Peter Duston stopped his wagon about thirty yards short of the meeting-house fence. He helped Beatrice down and as he did so Major General Holyoke came forward. He took her right hand between both of his and said, 'My dear Goody Scarlet. Beatrice, my dear. I am really so sorry.'

'Where is he?' Beatrice asked him. 'What's happened? Mr Duston wouldn't say.'

'We debated among ourselves whether to bring him down before you saw him,' said Major General Holyoke. 'In the end, it was my decision to leave him where he was. I believe you have the right to see exactly what has been done to him, and I know you to be a woman of considerable strength and character.'

'Bring him down? What do you mean, general, "bring him down"?'

'You can blame me if you want to, my dear. As I say, it was my decision and if I have in any way exacerbated your grief, then I can only beg for your forgiveness.'

He took Beatrice gently by the arm and led her round the front of the meeting house. When they reached the opposite end of the fence, where the graveyard was, he turned her round and pointed upwards, towards the roof.

Beatrice opened and closed her mouth, but she couldn't speak. She felt her knees weaken and her head fill with darkness, but she was determined not to faint. In spite of that, she held on tight to Major General Holyoke's arm and took six or seven very deep breaths.

Twenty-five feet above her, Francis was standing upright on the ridge of the roof with his arms stretched out wide, as if he were just about to dive off it. He was completely naked, white-skinned apart from his sunburned face and hands, with a crucifix of dark hair across his narrow chest. His head was crowned with wilting red roses, their thorny stalks twisted tightly around his temples.

Beatrice stared up at him in disbelief. When she spoke, she thought she sounded like somebody with phlegm in the back of their throat. 'Are you sure he's dead?' she said. 'How can he be dead? He's standing up by himself, there's nothing to support him!'

Major General Holyoke said, 'I'm sorry, Goody Scarlet. Two of my men have been up on the roof already and he is quite dead. His ankles are tied to two stakes that have been fastened to the roof, but that is all the support he needs. His body is as hard as wood, they tell me. In fact, he could be carved out of wood, except that he is unmistakably formed of flesh and he is unmistakably your husband, the Reverend Francis Scarlet.'

Beatrice turned to stare at him. 'Wood?' she asked. 'You say that he feels like *wood*?'

'Now we know for sure that it's witchcraft!' put in Goody Rust, who was standing nearby. 'One man turned to soup and another turned into timber! That's witchcraft, no mistaking it!'

Beatrice raised her eyes again. Francis was still standing there, utterly motionless, his arms spread wide. *Everything that has happened has been a travesty of Christian belief*, that's what he had told her. And there he was, as if his arms were held out to welcome his flock, or as if he had been nailed to an invisible cross.

After a few moments she turned away. She could no longer bear to look up at that naked body beside which she had lain so many nights in bed. He had been her lover and her husband and her closest friend, and yet here was all that intimacy exposed in front of the whole village, for anybody to gawp at. Whoever had taken his life had taken her life, too.

'We will bring him down now,' said Major General Holyoke. 'Believe me, I will have it done with all due reverence. I deeply apologize if this exhibition has caused you pain.'

'No, no, you were right to let me see him like that. I also want to see him after you have brought him down. Please have him taken to the parsonage as soon as you can.'

Major General Holyoke looked uncomfortable. 'The coffin may be problematical.' He paused, and then stretched out his arms. 'How can I put it? He is not at all *flexible*, and it is more than *rigor mortis*.'

'Then, please, have him covered with a shroud, or a sheet if no shrouds are available. We can decide later what we can do about a coffin.'

Major General Holyoke escorted her further along the green towards his own house. Most of the crowd nodded to her, and some called out their condolences, but they were making no move to disperse. The naked figure of their minister was about to be manhandled down from the roof of the meeting house, like Christ being taken down from the cross, and that was a sight they did not want to miss. They would be telling their grandchildren about it for years to come.

'Come in for a glass of sherry-wine, or perhaps some tea,' said Major General Holyoke. 'I must say that you have shown enormous fortitude. I will, of course, have my coachman drive you home afterwards.'

Beatrice gave him the weakest of smiles. 'I will come in, yes. I think I need to sit down for a moment.'

He opened the door and Beatrice stepped into the hallway where Marjorie Holyoke was coming forward with open arms to greet her.

Three things happened at once. Marjorie Holyoke said, 'My dear, *dear* Beatrice,' the long-case clock in the hallway began to strike seven, and Beatrice blacked out and collapsed, knocking her forehead against the floor.

The Holyokes begged her to stay. They would even send their coachman to fetch Noah if she wanted them to. But she needed to return home, where Francis had already been taken. She needed to be close to him, even if he was dead.

She arrived home to find, unusually, that the parlour door was closed. She didn't open it, but went through to the kitchen where Mary was feeding Noah his supper. Noah reached up his hands and flexed his fingers and said, '*Mama*! *Mama*!'

Beatrice picked him up and kissed him and cuddled him. He looked up at her and there was a question in his pale blue eyes, even though he wouldn't have understood her if she had told him what was wrong.

Mary said tearfully, 'They didn't know what to do with the reverend when they brought him back. They couldn't carry him upstairs on account of his arms held out stiff like that, so they laid him on the floor in the parlour.'

'I thought so,' said Beatrice. 'If you could just finish feeding Noah for me, and put him to bed.'

'Of course, Goody Scarlet. I'll stay with you again tonight if you need me.'

Beatrice shook her head. 'No, Mary. You'd be better off going home. Besides, I think I want to be alone for a while. I have to say my goodbyes.'

She returned Noah to his high-chair. He protested with a wail and said, '*Mama*! *Cuddah*!' but she smiled at him sadly and said, 'Ssshh, Noah. You can have another cuddle before you go to bed.'

She took off her shawl and hung it up in the hall. She stood outside the parlour door for a few seconds with her hands clasped together and pressed to her lips. She didn't know if she really wanted to see Francis's body or not, especially if it had been hardened like wood. After a few moments, though, she turned the door handle and opened the door and went inside.

The smell was unmistakable as soon as she walked in. Linseed oil. From that alone, she knew what had happened to Francis, even if she didn't know who had done it to him, or why.

He was lying on the carpet in between the chairs, covered with a white bed sheet. His arms were still outstretched and his left hand was showing. She saw with a terrible shrinking feeling that there was a deep hole in the centre of the palm, a stigma, where Christ would have been nailed to the cross.

She closed her eyes for a moment, gathering her strength. *This is why you became a minister, Francis, to fight the forces of evil, and even if you have become a martyr in your battle against Satan, your sacrifice will not be in vain, I promise you, I promise you, I swear to you, my dearest one.*

She bent forward, took hold of the edge of the sheet, and drew it back. Francis was staring up at her blindly. His eyes were open but as white as poached eggs. His hair was stuck flat to his head and there were scratches on his forehead where the crown of roses had been removed, although there was no blood.

A nail had made a hole through the palm of his right hand, too, and when she lifted the sheet away from his feet she could see that he had stigmata in both of his arches. This certainly looked like the work of Satan, or one of his demons – but then it was obviously meant to.

Beatrice looked down at Francis for a long time. When he was alive he had looked serious most of the time, even when she knew that he was very happy, but now he looked melancholy rather than serious, as if he had come to accept that his life was over but was saddened that there were so many days that he was never going to see.

She drew the sheet down further, down to his waist. It took all of her nerve to reach down and touch his chest, and when she did she gave a little reactive sniff. Major General Holyoke had been right: although he was still flesh-coloured, his body was as hard as oak.

She slowly stroked his chest. Even the hair between his nipples was crisp and it crackled when she touched it. She tapped his breastbone with her knuckle and it made a sound like a hollow wooden keg.

She knelt down beside him and held her face very close

to his and inhaled. There was no question at all. He smelled strongly of linseed. His body must have been treated in the same way as the rat that her father had turned into a wooden toy all those years ago.

She could hear him now, as he sharpened his carving-knife for their Christmas dinner. *I wonder if it would ever be possible to preserve your loved ones when they passed away, exactly as they were when they were alive?*

She stood up. She couldn't decide if this was a coincidence, Francis's body being hardened like this, or if somebody somehow had discovered what her father had done and used it to mock her. But whatever the reason, she couldn't even begin to understand why.

Of one thing, though, she was certain. Whoever had done this was neither witch nor demon. Francis's solidified body had finally convinced her of that. A witch or a demon would have used magic to do it, some spell or incantation, not days of painstaking simmering in linseed oil.

She was also convinced that all the terrible events that had been happening in and around Sutton over the past two weeks had been caused by the same malevolent person. But they were more than simply malevolent. They were well acquainted with the elements, and with chemical compounds, and with what extraordinary reactions those compounds could produce. They also had a comprehensive knowledge of poisonous herbs and other plants, and perhaps of their antidotes, too. Ebenezer Rowlandson's trout had recovered almost miraculously, and so had Henry Mendum's Devon cattle.

The Widow Belknap undoubtedly knew all about toxic herbs and was probably well versed in chymistry. But how, without assistance, could she have bound and set fire to George Gilman's slaves and hoisted them up to the rafters of his barn, and how could she have lifted Francis up to the roof of the meeting house and fastened him there?

Jonathan Shooks claimed to be dealing with a demon, and he blamed this demon for every misfortune, including the death of Nicholas Buckley. But if there *were* no demon, if Satan were not involved at all, in whatever guise, the only person responsible must be Jonathan Shooks.

She thought of the Chinese fire inch-sticks that he had doused in water and given to the Buckley twins. There was no doubt that the infusion had helped them to recover, although Beatrice didn't understand how. It had shown, though, that Jonathan Shooks knew his chymistry, too.

'Oh, Francis,' she said. She thought of how he had stared at her every Sunday morning in Birmingham when she was walking home from church, and how he had pushed over cousin Jeremy when he had been bothering her. She thought of their wedding night, and of their journey across the Atlantic, when she had been seasick for days.

She thought of the day they had first come to Sutton and reached the village green. The sun had been shining through the clouds so that the day brightened and faded, brightened and faded, and she thought they had arrived in paradise.

She covered Francis with the sheet. She would have to call on Peter Duston tomorrow and ask him to make a coffin. She would also have to ask him to sever Francis's arms.

She left the parlour and closed the door behind her. She didn't want little Noah toddling in there and discovering his dead father on the floor. Not only that, the smell of linseed was making her feel queasy.

She went to the front door and opened it so that she could breathe some fresh air. It was almost dark now and the insects seemed to be singing louder and more insistently than ever.

As she stood there, she thought she saw a movement at the end of the driveway. She peered harder, and as she did so the brown-cloaked figure stepped out of the shadows and stood in the middle of the driveway, holding its staff.

Maybe you are the Angel of Death, she thought. If so, you certainly know when to pay us a visit.

'You!' she called out, although her voice was weak from strain and tiredness. 'You – who are you? What do you want?'

The figure didn't answer. Beatrice didn't know if she should be frightened of it or not. After two or three minutes it turned around and walked back into the darkness and was gone.

She knelt beside her bed that night and said a prayer for Francis. She hoped so much that he was in heaven, walking with Jesus, and that he was happy. More than anything else, she wanted him to be happy.

She knew that Francis would have disapproved of her trying to take revenge on his murderer. *Vengeance is mine, saith the Lord.* But she was determined that the Lord should know who to punish, and then punish them with the utmost severity.

The next day she took the shay and drove to the village. The morning was warm but strangely foggy, so that Beatrice felt as if she were driving through some kind of ghostly dream. She called on Rodney Bartlett first, because he tended to so many horses and probably used more linseed oil than anybody else in the village. Linseed oil kept horses calm and made their coats and manes glossy and relieved them of the sweet itch, especially at this time of the year when the air was filled with midges.

'I still find it hard to believe what happened yesterday, Goody Scarlet,' said Rodney Bartlett. 'You know that the whole of Sutton is mourning, and feels for you.'

'Thank you, Mr Bartlett, you're very kind,' Beatrice told him. She looked around the gloomy, smoke-filled smithy. The furnace had just been lit and there were five or six horses tethered in the lean-to at the back, who were beginning to grow restless, as if they knew they were soon to be shoed. 'Has anybody bought any linseed oil from you lately?'

'I beg your pardon?' frowned Rodney Bartlett, as if she had asked him a question in a foreign language.

'Linseed oil, Mr Bartlett. I'm looking for somebody who might have purchased quite a large quantity of it – about a week ago, possibly, I'm not exactly sure. Or they might have taken it without you knowing.'

Rodney Bartlett slowly shook his head. 'I've sold none of mine, Goody Scarlet, and there's none missing that I'm aware of. You might ask Matthew Blackett. He uses linseed oil on his gunstocks. Or James Fuller, he uses it, too, when he's making his furniture. But, of course, I get all of mine from Robert Norton, over at Billington's Corners.'

'Robert Norton, the paint-maker?'

'That's right. We do an exchange. He brings over forty gallons of linseed oil to feed my horses and I give him forty gallons of horse piss to make his paint.'

'He makes his paint with—?'

'Horse piss, that's right. White lead and horse piss. The green paint anyhow, that's what goes into it. God knows what he uses for his Spanish brown.'

'All right,' said Beatrice. 'Thank you.'

She drove out to Billington's Corners, which was more of a small scruffy crossroads 'in back of no place at all', as Caleb would have put it, rather than a village. It was here, however, that Robert Norton and his brother Abel ran their paint shop, which mixed and supplied paints for most of the county. Their factory was a large grey barn set back from the Bedford road, with several wagons outside, and stacks of wooden barrels, as well as countless glass carboys with wickerwork casings.

The morning was growing hotter now and out of the paint shop's open doors came a pungent smell of linseed oil and a sour metallic tang of colouring mixtures. Beatrice tied up Uriel to a ring at the side of the building and walked inside. Several young men and girls in long aprons were grinding and sieving soil or scraping metal flakes from tall earthenware jars.

She found Abel Norton sitting at a desk in a small office on the left-hand side, in his shirt-sleeves, filling in account books. He was a plump little man, like a character out of a nursery rhyme. His pate was bald, but the rest of his hair was almost shoulder-length, and very white. He was wearing tiny eyeglasses, which he took off his nose as Beatrice came in.

'Goody Scarlet!' he greeted her, and stood up to clasp her hand. 'What brings you here? Are you thinking of painting the parsonage? I have a new taupe mixture which has just arrived from Europe, very *fashionable* if I may say so, but discreet, and uplifting at the same time. Just right for a minister's house!'

'You clearly haven't heard,' said Beatrice. Although the Nortons were members of their congregation they rarely came into the village on any day except Sundays for communion. She told him how Francis had been murdered and turned rigid and displayed on the roof of the meeting house, and he listened in shocked silence, chewing his lip.

'I don't know what to say to you, Goody Scarlet, except to give you my heartfelt condolences. What terrible, terrible news! But . . . you haven't come here only to tell me that?'

'No, Mr Norton, I haven't. I've come here to ask you if you happen to have sold a large quantity of linseed oil in the past few days. It would have been an unusually large quantity.'

Abel Norton looked at her oddly and clipped his eyeglasses back on to the bridge of his nose.

'Linseed oil? A large quantity, you say? An *unusually* large quantity?'

'That's right.'

'Ah . . . well, the problem is that my business transactions are always strictly confidential. I have to keep them that way for many reasons, but mostly because my customers wouldn't be at all happy if I were to divulge their financial affairs to others.'

'You *have*, though, haven't you?'

Abel Norton gave her an almost imperceptible nod, as if he were afraid that somebody might see him or overhear him.

'Please, Mr Norton, you *must* tell me to whom.'

'Goody Scarlet, I'm really not sure – well, to be honest with you, I'm really not sure what the consequences might be.'

'It's a matter of life and death, Mr Norton. I can put it no plainer than that.'

Abel Norton looked around. He even leaned sideways a little so that he could see over Beatrice's shoulder to the yard outside. Then he said, in a very low voice, 'I was out of my office when you first arrived. By chance I had left on my desk a bill of trade that referred to a certain unusual quantity of linseed oil. If by chance you happened to see it, then it was certainly not with my knowledge or permission.'

With that, he sat down and opened his left-hand desk drawer. He took out a bill of sale and laid it on top of his ledger. Then he turned his head away and stared up at the little window high above his desk, as if he had developed a sudden fascination for cloud formations.

Beatrice went over and picked up the bill of sale. It was for two hundred gallons of best-quality linseed oil, to be delivered to Rutger's Farm near Penacook. The price was twopence half-penny the gallon, making a total of two pounds ought and eightpence, with a carriage cost of fourpence.

The bill was addressed to 'J. Shooks, Esq.'

'I thank you, Mr Norton,' said Beatrice. Her hand was shaking as she put the bill back on his ledger. 'I have seen all I need to. You have been most accommodating.'

Abel Norton folded the bill and returned it to his desk drawer. 'I'm sorry, Goody Scarlet?'

As she left his office, however, he said, 'Was *he* responsible for what happened to your husband? That fellow Shooks? I thought him queer, I have to admit, him and that coachman of his.'

'I'm not entirely sure yet, Mr Norton. But I believe him to be implicated at the very least.'

'But what use would he have for such a quantity of linseed oil?'

'What is the principal quality of linseed oil, Mr Norton? Why do you mix into paint and into putty?'

'Oh, my dear Lord, Goody Scarlet. You don't mean—? Dear Lord, and I was the provider of it! Oh, I am mortified, I really am! If my knees were not so stiff I would get down on them and beg for your forgiveness!'

Twenty-nine

Beatrice went back home first to make sure that Noah was fed and changed, and that Mary was coping with all of her chores. After she had helped Mary fold some sheets she sat in the kitchen with a plate of cold roasted pork with bread and pickled cucumbers. She chewed her food slowly and deliberately, and drank frequent mouthfuls of cider to help her swallow it, even though she had no appetite and the meat seemed tasteless. She was grieving so much that it gave her a pain in her stomach, but she was filled with determination and she knew that she would need strength and stamina to do what she had to do next. Uriel had needed a rest, too, and water and a feed.

The parlour door was closed and she didn't open it. As far as she was concerned, the wooden man lying on the floor beneath a sheet was only a replica of Francis, not Francis himself. Francis was alive, and gentle, and loving – still alive inside her heart.

Peter Duston would be calling on her later to take measurements for a coffin and she had already talked to Benjamin Lynch about a funeral service.

Just after two o'clock she drove back through the village and out towards Penacook. She went first to Rutger's Farm, which lay about a mile and a half to the east of Penacook. She knew that it had been lying empty for almost a year. James Rutger had died of the black jaundice last March, and his widow

Jessica shortly afterwards, and since her death the estate had been furiously disputed in the courts between seven sons, three of whom had been the progeny of James Rutger's marriage to his first wife, Helen, who had died in childbed.

When she arrived there she found the fields overgrown with weeds, almost waist-high, and the orchards littered with rotting brown apples. The buildings were dilapidated, with peeling grey paint and broken windows. As she approached a dark cloud drifted across the sun which made the farm look even more derelict.

Behind the main farmhouse stood two large barns, although the nearer one was leaning at an angle, as if it were close to collapse. Beatrice climbed down from her shay and went across to look at them. It was evident that nobody had entered the nearer barn for months, because the doors had dropped on their rusted hinges and purple flowering lady's-thumb was growing thickly up in front of them.

The doors to the second barn, however, had been cleared of weeds and two semicircular scrape marks on the ground showed that they had recently been opened. Gasping with effort, Beatrice managed to tug the left-hand door a few inches ajar so that she could squeeze inside.

This barn had once been the farm's feed store. Bales of hay were still stacked up against the opposite wall, almost to the rafters, while forty or fifty sacks of oats were heaped up in a pyramid on the right-hand side. Most of the sacks had been gnawed open by rats or mice and oats had spilled across the floor. There was a strong musty smell in the barn of half-composted hay and rotting oats and rats' urine – as well as the smell of linseed oil.

Almost in the centre of the barn stood a large circular cheese-kettle, almost six feet in diameter, made out of tarnished copper.

As soon as Beatrice saw it the clouds must have moved away from the sun, because it was suddenly illuminated with shafts of light from the clerestory windows in the roof, as if the barn were a church and the cheese-kettle some kind of unholy font.

Beatrice had seen cheese-kettles like this before, in Haverhill, where they made Swiss cheese at Saltonstall's dairy farm. Not far away from it were scattered about a dozen empty demijohns. When she walked up to the cheese-kettle she could see that it was filled almost to the brim with amber-coloured linseed oil.

She knew that a demijohn held fifteen gallons, so the cheese-kettle must have contained at least two hundred gallons, which tallied with Abel Norton's bill of trade. The oil was glowing in the sunlight, but its surface was thick with dust and globules of fat and it was speckled with scores of dead flies.

There was only one reason why anybody would have filled up a cheese-kettle with two hundred gallons of linseed oil. Beatrice stood by its brim and stared at it numbly, trying to picture what had happened. She could only visualize it as some two-dimensional medieval painting, with Francis lowered naked into the oil like a martyred saint. She hoped to God that he had already been dead before they immersed him.

It puzzled her, though, that the cheese-kettle was still filled up. How could Jonathan Shooks have been so careless as to leave it like this? Had it not occurred to him that she might well understand how Francis had been solidified and that she might go looking for the source of his linseed oil? Or had he done it intentionally to taunt her, to show her that he wasn't in the least afraid of her?

He could easily have opened the spigot in the cheese-kettle and let the evidence soak away, or he could have set fire to the barn which would have destroyed it forever.

Beatrice slowly circled around the barn, brushing aside the

hay and the oats with the side of her foot, trying to find proof that Francis had been brought here. She picked up a filthy grey cravat with some dark brown stains on it that might have been blood, but she couldn't be sure it was his, so she dropped it.

Before she stepped back outside she paused at the door of the barn and looked back at the cheese-kettle. She felt like burning the building down herself, but she knew that would be nothing but a mindless act of vengeance and that she should leave vengeance to God. Besides, she had something much more important to do.

As soon as the Penacook Inn came into view she could see that Jonathan Shooks was still there. His calash was parked by the stables at the side and when she came nearer she could see Samuel outside in a long leather apron, rubbing down the grey.

The inn was a white-painted, double-fronted building, with maroon shutters, surrounded by dark green oaks. It overlooked an ox-bow lake in which it was reflected, although the reflection was rippled into white fragments by the loons that were swimming across it.

Samuel turned his head when he heard Beatrice approaching in her shay. He stayed where he was, though, with his hand resting on the horse's flank, and when she drew up outside the front of the inn and tied up Uriel he made no attempt to come over and greet her. She looked across at him as she mounted the steps that led up to the verandah, but he remained expressionless, as if he were waiting to see what would happen next.

Inside the hallway a small, beaky-nosed woman in a frilly white cap and pale yellow gown came up to her, smiling, and said, 'Good day to you, ma'am. Can I help you? Are you looking for some place to stay?'

The inn was light and sunny, with tall vases of white chrysanthemums standing in the hallway and yellow drapes at the windows embroidered with birds and butterflies. Beatrice could smell warm biscuits and beeswax floor polish. Somewhere at the back of the inn, a girl's high voice was singing 'The Raggle-Taggle Gypsies-O!' It gave Beatrice an unexpected pang because her mother used to sing it to her when she was small.

'I'm looking for a guest of yours, Mr Jonathan Shooks.'

'He's in the dining room, ma'am, taking his dinner. May I tell him who's calling?'

'That's all right. I can introduce myself, thank you. Through here, is it, the dining room?'

'Well, yes, ma'am, but I don't know if Mr Shooks would wish to be disturbed at the moment.'

'*Disturbed*?' said Beatrice. What a word, she thought, for a man who might be guilty of murdering her husband and turning him into a wooden statue. 'Don't worry, I intend to do very much more than disturb him.'

'*Please*—' said the woman as Beatrice stepped forward. 'I cannot permit you to walk in unannounced! It would not be proper!'

Beatrice said, 'I am the wife of the Reverend Francis Scarlet of Sutton and I have urgent business with Mr Shooks. Church business. So, if you don't mind—'

'Very well,' said the beaky-nosed woman, becoming even more flustered. 'If you'd care to follow me.'

She led Beatrice through into a large dining room, with three circular tables in it, all draped with long white linen tablecloths. Two young men who looked like travelling salesmen were sitting on the left-hand side, laughing over bowls of chicken stew. They stopped laughing when Beatrice walked into the room and followed her with their eyes, nudging each other.

In the far corner, beside a window that looked out over the gardens, sat Jonathan Shooks. The sunlight behind him made him look strangely blurry. In front of him was a plate of hogs' ears ragout with pumpkin squash, and when Beatrice came in he was just about to lift a glass of white wine to his lips. As soon as he saw her he put it down, without drinking.

He stood up as she came across the dining room and bowed. He was wearing his grey linen coat and the grey wig, which made him look much older than he must really have been, although he looked tired today, too, with plum-coloured smudges under his eyes.

He didn't hold out his hand. He obviously sensed from the look on Beatrice's face that she wouldn't have taken it.

'Well, well. Goody Scarlet,' he said. His voice was deep and soft and as blurry as his image, and he made her name sound almost like a question.

Beatrice said, 'The *Widow* Scarlet, as of yesterday, sir.'

'Yes, of course. You have my very deepest sympathy. If there is anything I can do to ameliorate your grief, please don't hesitate.'

'May I join you?' she asked him. 'I think we have matters to discuss.'

'But of course. Mistress Pitcher, perhaps you could bring us another glass.'

'There's no need,' Beatrice told her. 'I will not be taking wine.'

Jonathan Shooks came round and drew out a chair for her and then sat down himself. Mistress Pitcher hovered beside them for a moment, before saying, 'Should I return your dinner to the oven, Mr Shooks, to keep it warm?'

'Don't trouble yourself,' said Jonathan Shooks, keeping his eyes on Beatrice and giving her that mocking, self-reverential look that he always gave her – that look that seemed to imply, *I could have you, my lady, any time I wanted to.* 'I fear that when Goody Scarlet and I have finished talking I shall have lost my appetite altogether.'

Beatrice wondered why he had said 'altogether', until she looked down at his plate and noticed that one of the hogs' ears protruding from the orange ragout sauce still had bristles on it.

'I will not beat around the bush, Mr Shooks,' said Beatrice. 'I know that you were responsible for my husband's death.'

She spoke as calmly as she could, trying to keep her voice low so that the two travelling salesmen wouldn't overhear her.

Jonathan Shooks looked at her for a long time without saying anything. Then he picked up his wine glass and started to swirl it around and around. A curved reflection from the wine flickered across his lips so that he appeared to be smiling, and then not smiling, and then smiling again.

'That is a very damning accusation, Goody Scarlet. An accusation like that could send me to the gallows.'

She noticed that he hadn't asked, 'Why do you think that?' or 'Do you have evidence?' He hadn't even said, 'That's a damned lie, how dare you?'

'My husband was immersed in a vat of linseed oil, Mr Shooks, which had the effect of hardening his body until it took on the consistency of wood. About a week ago, you purchased from Abel Norton's paint shop two hundred gallons of linseed oil, which you had delivered to Rutger's Farm, and filled up a cheese-kettle with it. This cheese-kettle is about six feet in diameter, which is quite sufficient to accommodate the body of a man with both of his arms outstretched.'

Jonathan Shooks stopped swirling his wine and sat back in his seat.

'You are a very intelligent and astute young lady, Goody Scarlet. Considering that you lost your husband less than a day ago, I greatly admire your pluck in pursuing this matter. Most women would be wailing inconsolably and reduced to a jelly.'

'Believe me, sir, I am suffering pain so intense that I cannot even begin to describe it to you. But I *will* see justice for my husband, and I *will* know why he had to die in such a manner, and I *will* see an end to all of this pretended devilry.'

'*Pretended* devilry? Do you not believe, then, that Sutton is being persecuted by some agent of Satan?'

'Yes, Mr Shooks, I do, but I do not believe that this agent of Satan is some witch or wizard or some Indian spirit from the woods. Every misfortune that has been visited on Sutton since our pigs were killed in a Devil's Communion can be attributed to chymistry or botany. Some of the events I admit I have not yet been able to explain, but I shall. I believe, Mr Shooks, that the agent of Satan is *you*, and you alone.'

'Well, well, the apothecary's daughter,' said Jonathan Shooks. 'He taught you very well, your father, didn't he? Oh, don't give me that look! Of course I know who you are. Before I came to Sutton I made it my business to find out everything I could about everybody of any importance in the village – who they were, where they originally came from, what their background was. Their strengths and their foibles. How wealthy they were, or how destitute. You cannot properly protect people unless you know them intimately. Your late-lamented husband will have been aware of that.'

'*Protect*, Mr Shooks, or deceive? I think that you are nothing but a clever trickster – a charlatan who uses chymistry to frighten superstitious and God-fearing people into thinking that they are being threatened by the Devil. I think that my husband followed you and found you out and when he confronted you with your deception you killed him.'

'I see. Is that what you truly believe?'

'Yes, it is. What other explanation can there be?'

'What if I told you, Goody Scarlet, that there *is* a demon and that everything I have said since I came to Sutton is true? What if I told you that I *am* doing business with an agent of Satan and that I have been persuading the local people to surrender some of their land only to save them from a fate so ghastly that I could never describe it to you?'

Beatrice was trembling and underneath the table she was twisting the ends of her shawl around and around as if she were wringing them out.

'If you told me that, sir – if you told me that, then I would not believe you.'

'You *do* believe in Satan?'

'Of course. But what does Satan want with people's land?'

'It's very simple. He wants Christianity driven out of it. He wants demons to dance on it again. Satan has never encouraged evil for evil's sake, whatever you think. He advocates complete human freedom – that we should think what we like, say what we like, and if you are offended by the way your neighbour looks, go pluck out *his* damned eyes, rather than your own. If you want something, take it, says Satan, whether it's land or gold or pigs or a woman's body. All Satan is trying to do is to make sure that the this wild and virgin country never becomes so noisy with ecclesiastical cant that we can no longer hear ourselves think, and that its air never becomes so choked with Bible dust that we suffocate.'

'And do you agree with him?'

Jonathan Shooks stared at her, breathing quite noisily through his nostrils, as if he had been hurrying upstairs. 'Did you hear me *say* that I agreed with him? All I said was that I am acting as a go-between in order to protect the people of Sutton from a fate much worse than death.'

'Did you kill my husband?'

'No, I did not.'

'Who did, then? Was it this demon of yours?'

'No.'

'Why did you buy all that linseed oil if it was not to dehydrate my husband's body? Who did that to him? Was that you?'

'No.'

'I don't believe one word you say, Mr Shooks. Not one. I am going directly to Major General Holyoke and I am going to tell him what I have discovered about your buying linseed oil, and what you did with it, and if you are not arrested and tried and hanged after I have told him that, then there is no justice or humanity here in New Hampshire and Satan and his demons might as well take it back and dance on it for all eternity.'

She said this quite loudly and the two travelling salesmen, who had been preparing to leave the dining room, stopped to listen to her, open-mouthed. She turned around to look at them and they both said, 'Sorry, ma'am, good afternoon!' and stumbled out.

In spite of what Beatrice had said, Jonathan Shooks appeared completely unruffled. He sat back in his chair inspecting his fingernails and then he said, without looking up, 'You are placing yourself in great danger, Goody Scarlet. This particular demon waxes very wrathful if he is crossed.'

'I am not afraid of your demon, Mr Shooks, nor I am afraid of you, especially since I believe them to be one and the same.'

'Very well. In that case I will swear to you two things, and I will swear them on the Holy Bible. Mistress Pitcher!'

The beaky-nose woman reappeared in the dining-room doorway. 'Yes, sir? Can I fetch you anything?'

'Would you be kind enough to bring me a Bible, Mistress Pitcher?'

The woman looked perplexed, but disappeared and came back a few moments later with a large family Bible. Jonathan Shooks moved his plate of hogs' ears aside and set the Bible down right in front of him.

'Thank you, Mistress Pitcher,' said Jonathan Shooks, making it clear that he wanted her to leave him and Beatrice alone. When she had gone, he laid his right hand on the Bible and said, 'I swear, first, by almighty God, that I did not murder your husband, the Reverend Francis Scarlet. I swear, secondly, that I am not the instigator of the recent misfortunes that have been befalling the people of Sutton.'

He paused for a moment, staring at Beatrice as if he wanted to make sure that his words had sunk in.

Then he said, 'Thirdly, I swear to you that if you attempt to hinder me in my business or report what I am doing to any constable or magistrate, you will suffer the consequences, just as the Buckleys did, and just as your late husband did, too. This demon will not be hindered by anybody.'

'Mr Shooks—' Beatrice began, but Jonathan Shooks raised his left hand to indicate that he had not yet finished.

'Because your late husband was Sutton's pastor, Goody Scarlet, the demon was particularly insistent that he, too, deed over some of his acreage. You see his reasoning? If the representative of God is seen to be giving a tithe to Satan, in order to ensure that he and his loved ones are kept from harm, then who else in the village could possibly refuse to do the same?'

Beatrice's tongue felt as if it were coated with fine dry sand. She would have done almost anything for a drink, but she was not going to drink at the same table as Jonathan Shooks.

'You may swear that you are not the demon himself, sir, but I hardly see the distinction when your heart is just as black as his.'

'Don't you understand, dear young lady? I am doing everything I can to save you from contracting some disfiguring disease, or being hideously burned in a fire, or struck by lightning. I am trying to save your life, Goody Scarlet!'

'I care little for my life now that my beloved husband has been taken away from me. All I want is to see justice done.'

'Oh, come now! Of course you care about your life! What would your baby son do without you? He looks so much like his father! Don't you want to see him grow into the man that the Reverend Scarlet once was?'

Beatrice didn't answer that – couldn't. Jonathan Shooks leaned forward across the table and said, 'I know that the parsonage and its yards belong to the church. But you have title to a further seventy-seven acres that surround it, don't you? And, of course, that acreage is all yours now that your husband is deceased. I believe that the demon would be content with only forty of those acres, so long as they included half of your orchard and a stretch of your brook.'

'You have lost your reason, Mr Shooks. I will not give you that. I refuse even to consider it.'

Jonathan Shooks sat back again. 'You will, Goody Scarlet. Have no doubt of it.'

'Is that a threat?'

'Of course not. There is a world of difference between that which is threatened and that which will simply come to pass, no matter what.'

Beatrice stood up, and Jonathan Shooks stood up, too.

'I believe we are done here, Mr Shooks.'

'Very well, but I hope to see you again very soon, Goody Scarlet, so that we can talk some more about a transfer of title. Please don't let it be too long.'

'You can hope until your face is black, Mr Shooks, to match your heart.'

He smiled, as if that amused him, but then he said, 'Before you go, Goody Scarlet, please remember not to speak of any of this to anyone. I would not wish to see anything untoward befall you.'

'And you don't consider *that* to be a threat?'

'It is out of my hands, I'm afraid. As I keep trying to tell you, I am no more than the go-between. If the demon thinks that you are defying him, then he will do whatever he thinks fit to persuade you to change your mind.'

Beatrice looked at him narrow-eyed for one more moment and then turned around and walked out of the dining room without another word. The beaky-nose woman called out to her as she went down the steps, but she ignored her. She was too angry, and in spite of all her bravado in facing up to Jonathan Shooks, she was confused, and she was very frightened, too.

Thirty

When she arrived home she found Peter Duston's wagon in the driveway. As she drew up her shay beside it, she couldn't stop herself letting out a single loud sob. Jonathan Shooks had shaken her badly and the very last thing she needed now was to have Peter Duston explaining to her how he was going to fit Francis's rigid body into a coffin.

Jubal must have heard her coming because he came round the side of the house and helped her down. Under his wide floppy hat his whiskery face was very grave, and his grey eyes were full of sorrow. His hands were so callused that they felt like leather gloves that had been soaked in the rain and then dried in the sun.

'The finish carpenter is here, Goody Scarlet.'

'Yes, Jubal. I know.'

'I am very grieved for you, ma'am. The Reverend Scarlet was never a fingerpost. He lived the way he asked others to live. He was always the best of men who gave you his heart.'

'Yes, Jubal.'

She went inside the house just as Peter Duston was coming out of the parlour. He was about to close the door behind him but Beatrice said, 'It's all right, Mr Duston. You can leave it open. Have you completed your measurements?'

'Yes, Goody Scarlet. And I have some real fine basswood to make the coffin out of. You could have some fancy carvings on it if you'd care to.'

'No, thank you, Mr Duston. I think the Reverend Scarlet would have preferred plain.'

'Yes, ma'am. Whatever you say.'

Beatrice went into the parlour. Basswood for your coffin, my love. How sadly appropriate. Francis used to suffer from headaches, especially when he had been working on a sermon for too long by candlelight, and she used to make him an infusion of linden flowers to relieve them, linden flowers from the basswood tree.

'His arms, ma'am,' said Peter Duston, who was still standing close behind her. 'I've tried to think of another way, believe me, like steeping him in a mixture of water and maple syrup, maybe. To be honest with you, though, I don't believe we have much of a choice except to – you know.'

Beatrice turned around and Peter Duston was making a sawing gesture in the air.

'All right,' she said. 'Do it when you bring the finished coffin. How long will it take for you to make?'

'I'll start work on it today, Goody Scarlet. You will have it by Friday morning.'

'Thank you.'

She left the parlour without lifting the sheet to look at Francis's body. She had seen so many bodies in her lifetime, either bloated on the riverbank, or crouched in a doorway stinking of gin, or lying in their coffins in people's front parlours, their skin waxy and their lips pursed. She had never thought when she had seen those bodies that the people they had once been were still within them. Those people had gone – quietly closing the door behind them, as she was doing now.

*

She spent nearly two hours in the kitchen, writing letters to Francis's family and friends in England, and also to his fellow ministers in neighbouring parishes. Each letter began 'It is with a heavy heart . . .' and told them briefly that he had lost his life to a person or persons unknown.

She asked none of them for help. She was sure in her own mind that she was more than capable of discovering how Francis had been murdered, and who had murdered him. It might take some time, but she had more knowledge of potions and plants than anybody else she knew, with the possible exception of the Widow Belknap, and for all she knew the Widow Belknap was somehow involved in Francis's death. Perhaps she was the demon that Jonathan Shooks claimed was responsible for so much havoc, or perhaps she was possessed by a demon, or even by Satan himself.

In spite of her firm belief that there was a logical explanation for everything that had happened, she thought it would be unscientific to rule out altogether the possibility that there had been some supernatural influence involved.

Beatrice had just finished writing to Geoffrey and Lavinia Scarlet, Francis's parents, when she heard Noah crying in his crib upstairs. Mary was outside, pegging up the wash, so she put down her quill and went to see what was wrong with him. Mary had put him down less than a half-hour before and usually he slept for at least two hours.

When she went into his bedchamber she found him standing in his crib, hot and sobbing. His cheeks were bright red, so she could see that he had started teething again. She opened the drawer of the chest beside his crib and took out his amber teething-necklace. When he sucked it, it would gently soothe his gums with spirit of amber.

She picked him up and cuddled him for a while, but when she tried to lay him down he started crying again.

'Come on, then,' she said. 'Come downstairs and help mama to finish writing her letters. How would you like some apple sauce? Apple sauce always makes those nasty teeth feel better, doesn't it?'

She carried him downstairs, but as she did so she saw that the front door was wide open. Mary must have come into the house for something and forgotten to close it. She went along the hallway, but when she reached the open door she stopped in shock. The brown-cloaked figure was standing outside, only about thirty or forty yards away. He was right in the middle of the driveway, his face concealed by his hood, holding up his staff, not moving.

Beatrice was tempted to call out to him and demand to know what he was doing there, but Noah was still grizzling and she didn't want to upset him by shouting. She stood in the doorway for a few moments staring at the figure, and the figure was presumably staring back at her. With Francis lying rigid on the parlour floor, she thought that the figure looked more like the Angel of Death than ever.

She closed the front door very slowly and deliberately to show the figure that she wasn't frightened of him, even though her heart was fluttering like a songbird trapped in a cage. She went back into the kitchen and sat Noah in his high-chair. Dear Lord, she thought, please help me through this. *Please give me strength. Is there no way that You can turn back the days, like a prayer-wheel, so that none of this ever happened?*

She went to the cupboard and took out a jar of apple sauce. She placed a bowl on the table in order to spoon some out, but as she did so she saw there was a fresh sheet of paper lying across the letters that she had been writing and that her quill was lying beside it. A drop of ink had fallen from the nib and stained the pine wood beneath it.

Written on the sheet of paper were the words: *Your sorrow gives me sorrow but also hope. But be warie of those who seem to be freinds. There is ever a price to be paid.*

Beatrice picked up the sheet of paper. The ink was still wet and it smudged the ball of her thumb. She looked towards the front door and realized that the brown-cloaked figure must have quickly and quietly entered the house while she was upstairs seeing to Noah and written these words.

But what did they mean? Why did her sorrow give him sorrow, too, '*but also hope*'. Hope of what? And who were those '*freinds*' of whom he had warned her to be '*warie*'? And what was the price that had to be paid?

She put down the letter and stood staring at it as if more writing might magically appear to explain what it meant. Perhaps she ought to seek help, after all. Perhaps Major General Holyoke might understand it. It appeared to be a friendly warning, and yet she wasn't so sure. There was something threatening about it, too. *There is ever a price to be paid.* In other words, pay up or else.

More than anything else, Beatrice wanted to know who he was and why he was lurking in the woods around the parsonage. She didn't have any more time to think about it, though, because Noah had dropped his amber teething-necklace out of his mouth and was crying for some apple sauce.

Four more days passed. On the fifth day, Francis was buried in the graveyard outside the meeting house. It rained steadily and quietly all day and it was unseasonably chilly. There was a feeling in the air of time passing and of the summer being almost over. Some of the trees were already beginning to turn rust-coloured or red.

After the funeral the wake was held in the meeting house because there were too many guests to be accommodated in the parsonage. Some of the church dignitaries had come all the way from Salem, and some from Essex and Ipswich.

Beatrice stood by the door as the guests began to file out into the rain, thanking them for coming. Little Noah stood patiently beside her in a long black linen shirt that she had made for him, with a black ribbon pinned to his pudding cap. He kept nodding his head from side to side like a pendulum and singing his favourite nursery song under his breath, 'Hickory Dickory Dock'.

George Gilman came over to her, noisily clearing his throat. 'I shall miss your late husband very much, Goody Scarlet. He was a gentle man, wasn't he? Gentlest man I ever met. But very courageous, too. I believe he could have driven the Devil out of Sutton, had he only survived. Then none of us would have had to sacrifice so much.'

'I know that Ebenezer Rowlandson deeded over thirty-six acres to Jonathan Shooks, and you yourself almost as many.'

George Gilman looked surprised.

'I'm sorry,' said Beatrice. 'We were told in confidence by Thomas Norton. He was gravely concerned about what was going on.'

'Well, he had no right to breach our confidence, but I think he was justified in his concern – especially since Ebenezer Rowlandson and I have not been the only victims. I'm not sure exactly how much Robert Axtell has given him, but I know that it includes two thirds of his pine forest. Then there's

James Moody out at Fiddler's Lake and William Tucker at Billingshurst, and probably others.'

'I can scarcely believe it.'

'Oh, yes, By the time Satan is satisfied, we shall have lost between us nigh on five hundred acres to Mr Shooks, maybe even more.'

'Could you not have refused him?'

'Are you serious, Goody Scarlet? Look what happened to Nicholas Buckley when *he* refused him his twenty acres! Melted! Turned into soup! And as I understand it, Shooks went to visit Judith Buckley the day after her husband's funeral and made the same demand of her that he had made of Nicholas. She showed him the door, and what was the consequence of that?'

He shook his head and then he said, 'I have no idea to whom the Buckleys' property will have been bequeathed, that's if they made a will at all, but if I were that person I would be very compliant indeed if Mr Shooks were to come a-calling on me!'

Beatrice said, 'Thank you, Mr Gilman. I had no idea how many farmers were involved. You've been exceedingly helpful.'

'None of us had any choice,' said George Gilman. A muscle in his cheek was twitching. 'Either we sign over some of our land, or we face the prospect of our cattle dying on their feet, or our crops being blighted – or, worst of all, our wives and children being burned alive and hung up in front of us like – like—'

He was so angry and ashamed of himself that he couldn't find the words, but all Beatrice could think of was those three charred slaves, slowly rotating on the ends of their ropes.

George Gilman went to join his wife and left the meeting house, leaving Beatrice so agitated that she could barely speak when Henry Mendum came up to her.

'My deepest condolences, Goody Scarlet,' he told her, taking her hand between his. She thought his face looked redder than ever, and more congested, as if it were about to burst at any moment. His wife stood behind him in the same black silk bonnet she had worn for the Buckleys' funerals, trying her best not to look supercilious.

'Thank you, Mr Mendum,' said Beatrice, taking a deep breath. 'You are indeed very kind.'

'Harriet and I would like you to know that if there is anything we can do for you, you have only to ask.'

'Thank you.'

'Um, it may be premature of me to say so, but a new minister will obviously have to be appointed in due course, and at that time the church will have to ask you to vacate the parsonage and find new accommodation.'

'I take no offence, Mr Mendum. I realize that.'

'Um, I understand that you have title to some of the land beyond the parsonage, and I presume you may be thinking of building yourself a new home on it, in due course. In the meanwhile if you have any difficulty in finding yourself a place to, um, *rest your head*, as it were, then you and your young boy are more than welcome to come stay with us, for as long as is necessary.'

'That's very considerate of you both, thank you.'

'A great evil has come among us,' said Henry Mendum, his jowls wobbling dramatically. 'A great, great evil! However, I believe, as indeed your dear husband believed, that our faith is strong enough to carry us through these times of tribulation and everything will soon be settled again. One we have given Satan all he demands, I am sure that he will leave us be and we will all prosper as before.'

'I hope so, Mr Mendum. I sincerely hope so.'

*

When they returned home Mary suggested that Beatrice should rest for the remainder of the day. If she wanted to sit in the parlour and think about her life with Francis, and pray for his soul, Mary would bring her a cup of tea and look after Noah for her.

Beatrice said no. She didn't want to sit alone in the gloom of this rainy afternoon and grieve. She wanted to get on with all the chores she had to finish, and while she was doing them she could churn over in her mind everything that she had learned today about Jonathan Shooks and his land-hungry demon. She was deeply disturbed that he had taken so much acreage. For the people of Sutton, the land that they owned was everything. It not only fed them, it also represented their status in the community and the heritage they would pass on to their children and grandchildren. Even more fundamentally, it was having settled here in New Hampshire and having been able to buy their own land that had made it possible for them to live according to their strict and simple religious beliefs. They had made this into God's country. Yet now they had been terrified by Jonathan Shooks into surrendering acres of it to Satan.

She changed into a simple grey cotton bed-gown and apron and went outside into the vegetable garden. It was still drizzling, although the sky was beginning to clear, and now and then an anaemic sun showed its face behind the clouds, like an elderly relative peering hopefully through the curtains. She began to dig up parsnips with a trowel and drop them into a trug.

She had only dug up eight or nine when she stood up straight and closed her eyes and felt the drizzle prickling against her face. She couldn't believe that if she called out '*Francis!*' he wouldn't answer her now, or ever again. She slowly sank to her knees in the mud and opened and closed her mouth in a silent howl of anguish, the tears streaming down her face to mingle with the rain.

*

The next day was warm and sunny and she baked bread in the morning and fed the pigs and scoured all her cooking pots. Goody Rust and Goody Mayhew came to call on her during the afternoon and they had tea together in the parlour. They talked about Jonathan Shooks for a while, and the tragic deaths of the Buckleys, and then about Francis, but Beatrice found it impossible to speak when they started talking about Francis, her throat simply closed up. They changed the subject to young Goody Woodward, who had been encouraged by her parents to marry a prosperous fisherman eleven years older than herself, but who had been seen in the company of a much younger man when her husband was away at sea. It could well be a matter for the courts.

That night she lay alone again in bed and found it difficult to sleep. She whispered 'Francis' and reached across the quilt, but there was nobody there.

'Noah!' she called. She knew where he was hiding, behind the pantry door, but she pretended that she couldn't find him. 'Noah! Where are you! I shall go to the village without you!'

He burst out of the pantry, giggling. Beatrice hoisted him up and carried him through to the parlour to put on his smock. She was going to take him to play with Goody Willowby's two little boys, so that she could have some time to do some shopping. She was fastening his laces when she heard horses' hooves and the grinding of carriage wheels on the driveway. She knew who it was even before she looked out of the window.

She opened the front door and Jonathan Shooks was already standing in the porch with his hat under his arm. There were dark crescent-shaped sweat stains under the arms of his pale grey coat.

'Good day to you, Widow Scarlet,' he said and gave her a bow.

She didn't answer, so he cocked his head to one side as if to say, *Why aren't you speaking to me? Have I done something to offend you?*

'I must apologize for visiting unannounced,' he told her. 'Usually, well, I would leave my card. But this is a matter of some urgency, I'm afraid.'

'I have nothing to say to you, Mr Shooks.'

'Then you are placing yourself in considerable jeopardy, Widow Scarlet, as I said to you before. The demon with whom I am dealing will stop at absolutely nothing to get what he desires. And as you have already witnessed, he is horribly inventive in his means of persuasion.'

'You can leave this property now, sir, and I do not wish you to set foot on it again.'

'Of course, I quite understand your animosity towards me. But please don't blame the messenger for the message. I need to know for certain that you are prepared to make over that acreage of yours that we discussed at the Penacook Inn. That is all. As soon as you have agreed to that, I will depart *instanter* and leave you in peace and you need never set eyes on me again.'

'No,' said Beatrice. 'I will not make over so much as a single square inch. Now, if you would kindly go?'

Jonathan Shooks sighed and shook his head. 'You do understand that you are making a very grave mistake? Ask yourself, which is more important, life or land?'

'So, if I don't agree to deed you my land, you will kill me? Is that what you're saying?'

'My dear Widow Scarlet, I would not touch one hair of your very becoming head.'

'But your demon will?'

'Your late-lamented husband was a man of the church. You should know better than most what demons are capable of doing.'

'I also know what men disguised as demons are capable of doing. I have come across more than a few of those in my time as a pastor's wife. Drunks, thieves, wife-beaters.'

'Oh, now then. Every wife needs a thrashing now and again. Otherwise, think how disobedient they might become! You know what they say about women and asses and walnut trees.'

'*Go*,' said Beatrice.

Jonathan Shooks had been smiling at her, but now his smile dropped from his face as if he were never going to smile again.

'Widow Scarlet, I myself would never dream of harming you, and I have not harmed a single soul in Sutton since I have been here. You have witnessed me swear to that on the Holy Bible. But I caution you now that if you refuse to deed me those acres that I have requested, then you will suffer for it as surely as the night follows the day.'

'*Go*,' Beatrice repeated.

'Are you sure you mean that? I am giving you a last chance here.'

Beatrice said nothing this time, but folded her arms across her breasts and waited.

'Very well,' said Jonathan Shooks. 'But I am very saddened that you are so obstinate.'

He walked back to his calash and said something to Samuel, who nodded and made an odd whooping sound. Beatrice closed the front door, but after she had done so she stood with her back to it, hyperventilating.

Noah appeared in the kitchen doorway and frowned at her. 'Mama?' he asked her. 'Mama?'

Thirty-one

Just after the moon had risen that night she opened her eyes and was abruptly wide awake.

The moonlight was so bright that it could almost have been daytime, except that everything in the bedchamber had the colour bleached out of it. Beatrice turned over, and the oval framed portrait of Francis beside the bed was smiling at her, as if he were saying, *You clever girl, Beatrice.*

She had asked herself again and again what Satan would do with all the acres that he had extorted from the farmers around Sutton. She had confronted Jonathan Shooks about it directly but his answers had been either mocking or unbelievable. *Satan wants the land back so that his demons can dance on it again. Satan doesn't want the air in this virgin country to be polluted with prayers and thick with Bible dust.*

It's all nonsense, she thought, as she lay there in the moonlight. *It has to be.* Demon or human, whoever acquired that land wasn't going to leave it to grow wild again. It was much too valuable and there was too much profit to be made out of it. It had taken years of back-breaking labour to clear it of rocks and trees and shrubs, and irrigate it and plant it for crops. Not only that, it was almost harvest time now. The Indian corn and barley and alfalfa were all ripe for harvesting, as well as sweet potatoes and pumpkins and gourds, and the trees in the orchards were heavy with walnuts and hazelnuts and apples and plums.

Whether Satan was really behind it or not, she could see now that what was happening around Sutton was robbery on an unbelievable scale. Its people were not financially wealthy. They had very little in the way of gold or jewellery to be stolen. But they did have land and all the riches that the land could produce.

Jonathan Shooks had used the very religious fervour that had brought the colonists to Sutton to frighten them into handing over their only valuable asset. The more Beatrice thought about it, the more convinced she was that there *was* no demon, that his demon was simply *him*. He had sworn on the Bible that he wasn't, but what was that worth? For a man who could rob a whole village of its livelihood, and horribly kill all those who wouldn't give him what he wanted, lying on oath was hardly likely to leave him tossing and turning at night wondering how God was going to punish him.

She sat up. What she needed to do was to talk to all those farmers and landowners who had made over their acres to Jonathan Shooks and find out exactly which areas of land they had given away. A map of those areas might show her a pattern and give this robbery some meaning. Pieces of material were just pieces of material until a pattern made them into a petticoat.

She could almost hear her father saying to her: *Nothing in God's universe is random, Bea. There is logic and order and reason behind everything, even if you can't see it – and even if you* can *see it, but can't understand it.*

For the rest of the night she was unable to sleep, and as soon as the sun came up she dressed and went downstairs. Jonathan Shooks had frightened her yesterday with his threat that she would suffer. This morning, though, she felt that she had the strength to stand up to him.

*

The first farmer she visited was George Gilman. He was standing beside a gently sloping field with his hands in his pockets watching five of his slaves and two of his sons scything down timothy grass and heaping it on to a wagon. Beatrice went over to join him. The smell of the newly cut grass made her sneeze. George Gilman turned around when he heard her.

'Oh, it's you,' he said. 'I think I know what you're after.'

She came and stood beside him. The morning was hot and hushed, with only the swish of the scythes and the chipping call of blackbirds from the nearby trees. Blackbirds always gathered when the crops were cut.

'I need to know which particular acres you gave to Jonathan Shooks,' she told him.

'What you need to do is steer wide of that man.'

'How can I? He is stealing land from my husband's communicants right, left and centre. He's taking their property from right beneath their feet. My husband can no longer do anything to stop him, God rest his soul, but I can.'

George Gilman wiped the sweat from his forehead with his shirt-sleeve. 'You know me well enough. As a rule, I never concede nothing to nobody, not for nothing. But that Shooks is different. You can call me a coward if you like, but I don't intend to wind up as Gilman soup in some horse-trough. There's cowardice and then there's common sense.'

'Just give me a rough idea of what you gave him.'

George Gilman sniffed and then pointed over to the far side of the timothy grass field. 'You see them pines? Beyond them pines is a cornfield, and he's taken that, and off to the side of that there's a pumpkin patch, and he's taken that, too, right up to the boundary line on the top of that ridge. See those white oaks? There.'

Beatrice tried to draw a map of the fields in her mind's eye. They were almost hatchet-shaped, with a long handle and a large triangular head.

'Couldn't you just have told him no?' asked Beatrice. 'Surely you and some of your fellow farmers could have banded together and made it clear to him that you weren't going to give in to him. He's only one man, after all.'

'It's not him I'm afraid of. It's that demon he's doing business with. And that demon is the procurator of Satan himself.'

'Supposing there is no demon?'

'Well, try telling that to Prince and Cumby and Isum. There's nobody human who could have set fire to them and hung them up that high.'

Beatrice didn't argue with him, or try to explain that there had to be a way in which his slaves had been hoisted up to the rafters and cremated. She had got what she had come here for, and that was an approximate idea of the size and shape of the land that he had given to Jonathan Shooks.

She drove out next to Fiddler's Lake, which lay to the north and the east of Henry Mendum's property. The lake itself lay in a deep, forested valley, noisy with the plaintive squeaking of sapsuckers, but beyond the valley the land was high and undulating and it was there that James Moody grew Indian corn and alfalfa and grazed his cattle.

When she arrived at his farmhouse, Beatrice found James Moody in one of his outbuildings mending a broken plough. He was a lean, tall man with a long, lugubrious face and a pointed nose like a pickaxe. Beatrice had never seen him look anything but sad. When he saw her approaching he came out into the yard, one eye closed against the sunlight.

'Goody Scarlet! Good day to you.'

He took hold of Uriel's bridle and led him over to the side of the outbuilding and tied him up.

'This is not really a social call,' Beatrice told him.

'Under the circumstances, I didn't imagine that it was. Again – you have our sympathy, mine and Abigail's. The Reverend Scarlet was cut from the finest cloth.'

'I have to ask you a question,' said Beatrice. 'I have to ask you how much of your land you have given over to Mr Jonathan Shooks.'

James Moody looked away, as if he had seen somebody else in the distance.

'I realize that your transaction was supposed to be confidential, Mr Moody, but this is a matter that is affecting all of Sutton and I am determined to put an end to it.'

James Moody turned back to look at her. His eyelids were very droopy, like curtains that were sagging halfway down. 'You should tread very careful, Goody Scarlet, believe me. I was told what would befall my family and me if I refused to give Shooks some of my land, and I would hate to see such a thing happening to you.'

'So Jonathan Shooks threatened you?'

'Not himself, no. He promised that he would do everything within his power to keep us unscathed. But he did say that Satan would be unforgiving if I didn't give him thirty acres of my lower fields.'

'Did he tell you what he meant by "unforgiving"?'

'My family and me would be gathered together and sat in a circle, children and all, that's what he said. Our bellies would be sliced open and our bowels would be heaped together and burned in front of our eyes.'

'So you assigned him your fields?'

'Satan has done for your husband, Goody Scarlet. Turned him to wood by witchcraft, despite him being a minister. It's plain that God can't protect us, or *won't*. So wouldn't you have done the same?'

Beatrice didn't answer that. Instead she said, 'Show me which fields you gave him, Mr Moody.'

James Moody waved his hand in a southerly direction and said, 'Most of my lower fields, that way. I shall suffer for it, I can tell you, because they're all well watered and the grazing is good.'

'I thank you for telling me,' said Beatrice. 'I'm sorry if my intrusion has upset you.'

'So long as you don't let Shooks know that I spoke to you. He was quite insistent that our arrangement should remain confidential. But I am sorely aggrieved by it, as you can imagine. Sorely.'

'Nobody else shall learn that I came here, Mr Moody.'

She drove away from Fiddler's Lake Farm with James Moody standing in front of his outbuilding and watching her go. She turned around when she reached the entrance to the farm, over a half-mile away, and he was still standing there as if he had forgotten how to move.

She decided to return home now, and have something to eat and drink, and start to draw her map.

Back at the parsonage, she walked through to the kitchen where Mary was chopping up pumpkins.

'Oh, I'm so *hot*!' said Mary. 'I do believe I'm going to be nothing but a puddle of lard by the end of the day!' Beatrice smiled at her, although she couldn't help thinking of Nicholas Buckley, pinky-grey and glutinous, dissolved in the horse-trough.

'I'm just going to help myself to a slice of that chicken pie,' Beatrice told her. 'Would you like some? I have to go out again this afternoon, but I shan't be back late.'

Mary finished her chopping and tipped the pieces of pumpkin into a large copper pot which she filled up with water from the pump beside the sink. 'I'll bring little Noah in, shall I? I can mash up some pie with milk for him. He always likes that.'

While Mary went out into the garden, Beatrice took the pie out of the pantry and set out two plates and a bowl. Although it was so warm today, she was surprised how hungry she was. She almost felt as if her hunt to find out the truth about Jonathan Shooks and his demon had given her an appetite.

She poured out two mugs of cider, too, and a cup of milk for Noah.

While she was waiting for Mary to bring Noah in from the garden she went to the hutch and took out a sheet of paper and a stick of charcoal. She sat down at the kitchen table and began roughly to sketch the areas of land that George Gilman and James Moody had surrendered to Jonathan Shooks.

From outside she heard Mary calling, 'Noah! Noah! Come in for your dinner, Noah! Come along, Noah!'

This afternoon she planned to visit Ebenezer Rowlandson. She would probably have to leave William Tucker until tomorrow because Billingshurst was over four miles away and it would take her most of the morning just to drive there and back.

'Noah! Noah! Come on, Noah! Where are you hiding yourself? It's your dinner time, Noah! Come along!'

Another minute went past, with Mary continually calling, and then she came back into the kitchen looking flustered and even hotter.

'I can't find him, Goody Scarlet! I've been calling and calling and I've looked in all the places where he usually hides, like the tool shed.'

Beatrice stood up and followed her outside. The garden was empty and silent except for the sound of Jubal and Caleb chopping back bushes by the brook. Noah's go-cart was lying on its side by the bean beds.

'Noah!' called Beatrice as loudly as she could. 'Noah, where are you?'

No answer.

'Noah! Mama will be cross with you!'

Still no answer.

Beatrice began to feel a hurting sensation in her chest, the beginnings of panic. She picked up her gown and hurried through the field beyond the garden until she came to the slope that led down to the brook. She could see Jubal standing knee-deep in the swiftly running water, hacking at some of the overhanging branches.

'Jubal! Have you seen Noah?'

Jubal shook his head. 'Caleb!' he shouted. 'Have you seen Master Noah at all?'

Beatrice couldn't clearly hear what Caleb shouted in reply, but Jubal shook his head again. 'Sorry, Goody Scarlet.'

Beatrice ran back to the house as fast as she could. Mary was coming back around the side of the house next to the paddock.

'He's not in the front neither!' she said. 'I don't know where he could be! He went out only a half-hour since, just to play!'

'Oh dear Lord,' said Beatrice. 'Dear Lord, protect our little son from harm.'

'I thought he would be safe, Goody Scarlet. Honest I did! I couldn't see him but I could hear him singing and riding his little go-cart up and down.'

'Oh dear Lord,' said Beatrice, closing her eyes for a moment. She was trying very hard not think the worst, but she couldn't stop herself. *Our bellies would be sliced open and our bowels would be heaped together and burned in front of our eyes . . . children and all.*

They searched the orchard and the fields and all the surrounding woods until dusk began to gather. Caleb went down to the village to ask if anybody had seen Noah there, but nobody had.

Beatrice wanted to drive to the Penacook Inn to see if Jonathan Shooks had any idea where he was. By now, however, it was totally dark and the moon wouldn't rise until well after midnight. She stood in the garden holding up a lantern and calling and calling but still Noah didn't answer. She knew that it was futile. She knew that he couldn't hear her, either because he was much too far away or because he was dead.

Please be too far away, but alive, and not in any distress. Please. Please don't be dead.

She spent the night awake, not even bothering to undress. Mary offered to stay with her, but Beatrice told Caleb to take her home. There was nothing Mary could do to help and she was so upset that she was almost hysterical and she needed her sleep.

Several times during the night Beatrice went outside. A heavy bank of clouds had moved across the sky from the west, blotting out the moon, so that it remained dark all night. In spite of that she stood in the garden holding up her lantern and calling Noah's name, even though she could hardly make herself heard over the furious chirping of the crickets.

*

A grey dawn began to lighten the sky at last and Beatrice splashed her face with cold water and lit the fire so that she could make herself a cup of tea. The cup of milk that she had filled for Noah's dinner was still on the table. There was a fly floating in it, so she emptied it down the sink.

Losing Francis, and now Noah, she could almost believe that Sutton *had* been taken over by Satan. What had she done, after all, that she should be punished like this, except love her husband and her son and believe absolutely in God?

Jubal and Caleb arrived just after six o'clock. Caleb came in to tell her that Mary was running a fever and might not appear until later, if at all. Beatrice suspected that Mary hadn't slept, just as she hadn't, and that she was simply too tired and distraught to come to work.

When she had finished her tea she went into the parlour to brush her hair in the mirror. It was tangled and untidy, and she hadn't had time to put in curling-papers. She looked very white, but much more composed than she actually felt. In fact, the distortion in the glass made it appear as if one side of her mouth was raised in the slightest of sardonic smiles. Perhaps this mirror was possessed by Satan. Perhaps all mirrors were.

She pinned on her black mourning cap and went out to ask Caleb to harness Uriel for her. As she opened the front door, however, she saw Jonathan Shooks's calash coming briskly towards her down the driveway. She felt like slamming the door shut again, but she stayed where she was until Samuel had slewed the calash in a circle and brought it to a halt.

Jonathan Shooks was dressed in black today. His coat was black and his britches were black, although his waistcoat and his stockings were grey.

He came up to the porch with his hat tucked under his arm but said nothing, not even 'good morning'.

'You had better come inside,' said Beatrice. She turned and went along the hallway to the parlour and he followed her, closing the front door behind him.

Inside the parlour, in front of the looking-glass, they stood face to face, staring at one another. Beatrice could almost feel static electricity crackling between them, like the glass globes in her father's laboratory.

'My son Noah – my son Noah is missing,' she said, trying hard to keep her voice steady.

'I know,' he replied in that low, controlled voice.

'Have *you* taken him?'

'Yes.'

Beatrice could hardly believe what he had said. She started to breathe more quickly, practically panting with anxiety.

'*You've* taken him? Is he safe? You haven't hurt him, have you?'

'Of course not. He is quite unharmed, and fed. He has wept a little and asked for his mama, but that is only to be expected.'

'Where is he? How could you do such a thing? I demand that you bring him back to me *now*!'

'Please, Widow Scarlet, calm yourself. The only reason I took him was to protect the both of you.'

'To *protect* us? You've abducted my baby son! How could that possibly protect us?'

'Because it is the only way in which I can persuade you to change your mind and deed me those acres I have asked you for.'

'*What*? What are you talking about? Haven't I made it clear enough that I refuse to give you any of my land?'

'Indeed you have, Widow Scarlet, and that is why I have taken Noah, and I will only return him to you when you sign a deed of land transfer.'

'You, sir – you are nothing but a monster!'

Jonathan Shooks shrugged. 'I admit that I am doing business with a monster, but I am only trying to save you and your son from torture or death, or both. I am the only one who can keep this demon at bay. He grows more and more impatient by the hour to complete the task that Satan has set him. It was an extreme measure, I agree, taking your son, but I could see no other way of saving you.

'Widow Scarlet, you are far too fair of face and figure to be burned, or gutted, or bathed in caustic. Do you want to have your hands and feet amputated? Do you want to be force-fed your baby son's heart before it has stopped beating? Do you want to see him blazing from head to toe in front of your eyes? The demon has been known to do such things, and worse. His evil inventions know no bounds, believe me.'

'There is no demon.'

'I assure you there is.'

'You are well aware that my father was an apothecary and that he taught me much of his skill in chymistry?'

'Of course. I was a yeoman in the Society of Apothecaries myself. Your father didn't know me, of course, and we never met, but I knew much about your father, as most apothecaries did. It was quite a surprise for me to find his daughter here in Sutton.'

'I don't believe you.'

'It's quite true, I assure you. It's a very small world, after all. Your father earned himself quite a reputation from some of the papers he published, didn't he? Very unusual, most of them, such as *Spontaneous Combustion with Oil of Potash* and *The Preservation of Organic Bodies by Means of Dehydration by Linseed Oil.*'

'You are mocking me, Mr Shooks. My husband has been murdered and his body subjected to just such a process and you have the gall to say that to me.'

'I am not mocking you, Widow Scarlet. Why would I? I was a very capable young apothecary, as a matter of fact. You accused me of being a charlatan, but I can assure you that I'm not and never have been.'

'You are a charlatan and a monster, too. I insist that you return my son.'

'You can call me what you like. But I was so good an apothecary that I was employed by a London shipping company to travel the world and seek out new cures from various cultures all around the globe. I was sent to India and to China and to Peru and to Valdivia. I was the first person to bring back wild American ginseng to London, which made me quite wealthy at the time.

'Of course, medicine in almost all cultures is inextricably mixed with religion and superstition. How else do you think I acquired my knowledge of spirits and demons, and the various guises in which Satan appears in different countries?'

Beatrice slowly shook her head. 'If you are such a well-qualified apothecary, Mr Shooks, you have convinced me even more that all of the so-called supernatural events that have been terrifying the people of Sutton were created by you, and you alone.'

She took a breath and then she said, 'I demand to have my son returned to me, and I demand to have him returned to me immediately, and if I discover so much as one single bruise on his body, your demon's evil inventions will seem like *nothing* compared to what I will personally do to you.'

'There *is* a demon, Widow Scarlet,' said Jonathan Shooks. 'Even now, as we speak, that demon is holding your son, and if I go back to him without your assurance that you will make over your land, then the demon will hurt him, and badly. Perhaps he won't kill him. Perhaps he will only cut off his arms, or his genitals, or blind him. Perhaps he will dip his head in a pot of scalding water. I really don't know. But I do know that if you persist in your refusal, you will never see your son again the way he once was.'

Beatrice stared back at him, her eyes narrowed, searching his face for the tiniest flicker of insincerity. But he held her stare steadily, and apart from that his voice was deep and measured, almost warm, as if he were counselling her rather than trying to frighten her.

She still found it impossible to believe that there was a demon, but she did believe now that Jonathan Shooks was not going to give Noah back to her unless she agreed to sign over her land.

She turned her head to the side and looked at herself in the mirror. 'Very well, then,' she saw herself saying. 'I will need to go the village and discuss the wording with Mr Norton, the lawyer.'

'A letter of intent will suffice for now. We can go over the finer legal points later, as well as the exact location of the land to be deeded and its dimensions.'

'Very well. If you return at noon I will have a letter drawn up for you.'

'Can you not write one now?'

'I need to think about it very carefully, Mr Shooks. My son's life is at stake here, remember. To whom should I address it?'

'You need write no name on it. For you to know the demon's name would be catastrophic. Simply say that you are prepared to transfer your land to me, acting as proxy for a client who wishes to remain anonymous.'

He paused, and then he, too, looked at the reflection of her face and added, ' You have come to a wise decision, Widow Scarlet, believe me.'

'I don't wish to discuss it any further, thank you. When you return, will you be bringing Noah with you?'

'Well, we shall see. If the letter is satisfactory, then I will ensure that little Noah is back in your arms before you know it.'

'You can call him my son. I would rather not hear his name on your lips, thank you.'

'Whatever pleases you, Widow Scarlet. Whatever pleases you.'

Thirty-two

For more than twenty minutes after Jonathan Shooks had left Beatrice sat in the parlour thinking. She could have followed him to see if she could discover where he was holding Noah, but it would be almost impossible to do that without him becoming aware that she was close behind him, and in any event what could she do even if she did manage to find out where Noah was?

Francis had followed him and although Francis had not been a weak man he had been overcome and killed.

She could call on Constable Jewkes. He was armed, at least, but he was probably drunk already and even when he was sober he was clumsy and incompetent. With Noah's life at stake she couldn't risk him barging in and giving Jonathan Shooks the chance to kill or injure him. Whatever Jonathan Shooks had sworn to her, she still found it hard to believe that there really was a demon with whom he was doing business.

Unless, perhaps, that demon was somebody who believed themselves to be possessed. She couldn't help thinking of the Widow Belknap, dancing naked in the woods and screeching for vengeance.

She supposed that she could appeal to some of Sutton's congregation to help her, such as Rodney Bartlett and Peter Duston and William Rolfe, but they were all family men, and after what had happened to Nicholas Buckley and Francis it was really too much for her to expect of them. Not only that, there was a risk that they would rush in as a mob and give Jonathan Shooks the chance to escape and take Noah with him, or to do him terrible harm.

After a while she stood up and went to the hutch in the kitchen for her writing materials. Before she started writing, though, she went to the trunk in the hallway and took out her father's notebooks.

When Jonathan Shooks came back she led him into the parlour and handed him the letter, rolled up and tied with string and sealed with crimson sealing wax.

'This is for your client, whoever he is. I have also made a copy for you, identical in every respect, so you can be certain that I am not trying to deceive you. Not that I would dare, with you holding my son as your insurance.'

Jonathan Shooks took the rolled-up letter and tucked it into the side pocket of his coat. Beatrice handed him the copy that she had made and he unfolded it and read it carefully, his lips moving slightly as he did so.

> *I Beatrice Anna Scarlet being the relict of the*
> *Reverend Francis Keyes Scarlet do hereby declare and*
> *pledge that I intend willingly and irrevocably to deed*
> *and transfer to Mr Jonathan Shooks acting as proxy*
> *for a person whose identity by our common consent*
> *is to remain confidential thirty acres at least of that*
> *demesne lying adjacent to the Sutton parsonage*
> *which I have been bequeathed by my late husband,*
> *this acreage to include both part of the orchard and*

the Sutton Brook. The exact dimension and specifics
of the said acreage to be determined by mutual
agreement.

When he had finished reading it, Jonathan Shooks nodded. 'Very good, Widow Scarlet. You should have been a lawyer yourself. I believe my client will be well satisfied with this.'

'If I were not the widow of a man of God, Mr Shooks, I would damn you to hell.'

Jonathan Shooks said, 'Do you know, Widow Scarlet, you excite me more than any woman I have met for many years.'

'What?'

He carefully put down the letter on the occasional table beside him and took a step towards her. 'I said that you excite me, Widow Scarlet. You stirred my blood the very first moment I set eyes on you, and your spirit and determination have stirred it all the more.'

'You had best leave now, Mr Shooks. I want my son returned to me as quickly as you can, and that is all.'

'I'm afraid that there is one more gift I want from you before I bring back your son.'

'You already have my word that I will give you thirty acres of my land. What more do you want?'

Jonathan Shooks took another step forward, until he was close enough to touch her. 'I want you, Widow Scarlet. I want to enjoy with you the pleasure that your late husband enjoyed, God rest his soul.'

'Mr Shooks, I must ask you to leave. Please go and fetch me back my son.'

'Not until you have given me what I desire. What better way could there be to seal a bargain? It would prove your sincerity beyond a shadow of a doubt.'

'I am widowed only a matter of days,' said Beatrice. Her heart was beating so hard that she could hear the blood rushing in her ears. 'You cannot ask this of me.'

'Do you want your son returned safe and well?'

'Of course. But what you are suggesting – it's monstrous!'

Jonathan Shooks smiled and raised one eyebrow. He stayed where he was for a moment and then he turned around and left the parlour without another word. He opened the front door and Beatrice felt light-headed with relief. He had simply been playing with her after all.

'Samuel!' he shouted. 'Samuel, come here!'

She heard Samuel make one of his whooping noises and then Jonathan Shooks came back into the parlour, with Samuel shuffling close behind him. Samuel smelled strongly of horses and saddle soap.

'What are you doing?' Beatrice demanded. 'I thought you were going to go to fetch my son. I have already given you my written promise.'

'As I said, Widow Scarlet, you need to prove your sincerity in deeds as well as words.'

'You dare to touch me!'

Jonathan Shooks grinned at her and started to tug at his cravat. 'Yes, Widow Scarlet, I *do* dare!'

'Get out of this house, sir, at once! And take this fond mute with you!'

'Samuel,' said Jonathan Shooks. 'Restrain this firebrand for me, if you will.'

'Don't you touch me!' screamed Beatrice. 'Don't you dare to lay one finger on me! Caleb! Jubal!'

'You know and I know that your men are down by the brook cutting wood and that they cannot possibly hear you, no matter how loudly you call for them.'

He took off his coat and dropped it on to the floor. Then he started to unbutton his britches.

'Get away from me!' Beatrice shouted at him. And then, when Samuel took a step towards her, 'You, too! I shall see you in the jail for threatening me like this!'

'You want to see your precious son again, don't you? Then this is the price of his safe return. Samuel!'

Samuel seized Beatrice by her right wrist and wrenched her towards him, so hard that she almost lost her footing on the rug. She slapped at him with her left hand, but he was far too big and strong for her, and he twisted her around and pinned both of her arms behind her back, forcing them up so hard that she felt he was going to tear them out of their sockets.

'Leave go of me! Leave go of me!' she screamed, but Jonathan Shooks slapped her cheeks, first one way and then the other, and said tersely, 'Hold your peace, Widow Scarlet, or I will cut out your tongue and render you as mute as Samuel.'

Beatrice struggled and kicked but Samuel's grip on her arms was relentless, and no matter how furiously she kicked beneath her petticoats it had no effect at all except to make her bedgown billow out.

Without warning, Samuel pitched her forward, first on to her knees and then face-down flat on the drugget. Kneeling down beside her, he rolled her over on to her back, levering out her arms one after the other, but still gripping both of her wrists so that he was holding them together above her head. The strain on her shoulder muscles was agonizing and she cried out, 'No! Dear God, you're hurting me!'

'Pain and pleasure are inseparable, my beautiful young widow,' said Jonathan Shooks. 'Surely you have read enough of your Bible to know that.'

'You devil!' she panted.

Jonathan Shooks took off his silver-buckled shoes and then rolled down his stockings. Next he stepped out of his britches, although he kept his thigh-length shirt on. Finally, he took off his grey-haired wig. His own hair underneath it was dark but cut very short and bristly, He knelt down, too, but between Beatrice's legs, with both knees on her gown to restrain her from kicking so violently. He leaned over her until his face was only inches from hers and their noses were almost touching. She turned her face away. She could smell something bitter on his breath, like wormwood.

'Don't you want to kiss me?' he asked her in his low, coaxing voice. 'Surely you don't want to make love without kissing me.'

She kept her face turned away and her lips tightly clenched.

'Such a reluctant mistress!' said Jonathan Shooks, and Samuel hissed with laughter, pulling her arms up even higher so that she couldn't stop herself from letting out a little mewl of pain.

'To Satan, it is a sin for a woman to be reluctant in fornication, did you know that? How can you not offer yourself willingly to a man who lusts for you like I do?'

Saying that, he grasped the neck of her gown with both hands and tried to tear it apart. At first the stitching held firm, but he tugged at it again, and then again, and then the black linen ripped and her white breasts spilled out. Jonathan Shooks took a breast in each hand and cupped it, to feel its weight and its tautness, and then rolled both of her nipples between finger and thumb until they knurled and stiffened.

She kept her face turned away while he was caressing her, but she could sense that he was staring at her all the time to see if he was exciting her.

'*Her tempting breasts the eyes of all command*,' he quoted, '*And gently rising, court the amorous hand*.'

Beatrice knew that there was nothing she could do to stop him from doing what he wanted, so she closed her eyes and lay absolutely still, in spite of the pain in her shoulders. As Jonathan Shooks continued to massage her breasts, around and around, and Samuel sniggered and snorted as he watched him, she tried to think of Francis, and how much she had loved him, and of Noah, and to forget that she was even here, lying outstretched on the parlour floor, unable to break free.

Jonathan Shooks eased himself up a little, taking his knees off her gown. She could have kicked out again, but she thought that would only arouse him even more, and so she remained utterly lifeless. He took hold of the hems of her gown and her petticoats and forcibly wrestled them upwards, a few inches at a time, until they were bunched around her waist.

Samuel let out a whoop and then a whirring sound like a wooden rattle, which for some reason made Beatrice feel nauseous. Her mouth filled with bile, which she had to swallow. She wasn't even going to give Jonathan Shooks the satisfaction of knowing that he was making her feel sick.

She could feel him stroking her pubic hair, over and over again, with the palm of his hand. Although he was doing it so softly and so gently, she could hear him breathing harder and harder. Then she felt his fingertips opening up her lips. She shuddered, and every nerve-ending in her body shrank as if she had opened up her front door naked in the middle of winter.

'So liquid,' said Jonathan Shooks in little more than a murmur. 'She feigns not to want me and yet her juices say that she is brimming with desire.'

Oh dear Lord, let this be over with, thought Beatrice. *Oh dear Lord, don't let him hurt me. Forgive me, dear Lord, for this sin, because I have no choice.*

She heard a soft rustle as Jonathan Shooks lifted up the front of his shirt and then she felt him position the glans of his penis between her lips. It seemed to be enormous, like a bull's penis. How was she possibly going to take that inside her? It was huge. She closed her eyes and prayed again that he wouldn't hurt her. She waited for what seemed like almost a minute and then he slowly started to push himself into her.

She felt his penis go in about two or three inches and then he retracted it a little because she was so tense and her vagina was so tight. He paused, and then pushed it in again, and this time he went in so far that he made her jump and she felt as if he was almost touching her heart. She still kept her eyes tightly closed but that couldn't blot out her other senses. She could still hear him breathing and grunting, and she could still feel his wiry pubic hair pressing up against hers, and his testicles nodding between her thighs.

'Ohhhm' he groaned. 'There is nothing to compare with this, Samuel! Taking a young woman in her widow's weeds!'

He kept up a steady, tireless rhythm, and with every stroke he pushed his penis into her as far as it could possibly go, until her pubic bone began to feel bruised.

Please, dear God, let it be over. Please, dear God, let this not be me.

Quite unexpectedly, Jonathan Shooks said, 'Samuel,' and drew his penis completely out of her.

Has he finished? Has he relented? Why has he stopped?

She allowed herself to open her eyes for a split second and she saw him kneeling upright, holding his erect penis in one hand, as if it were a thick red sceptre. With the index finger of his other hand he was making a circular motion in the air.

'Samuel, turn her over.'

'No!' she screamed, and kicked out wildly, like a bucking pony. But Jonathan Shooks immediately snatched at her ankles and Samuel gripped her wrists even more tightly. Between them, they rolled her over until her face was pressed against the carpet. She could smell the bull's gall that Mary used to clean it and it made her retch. All the same, she managed to choke out, 'You will go to hell for this, Mr Shooks!'

Samuel made the most hair-raising of noises, a high-pitched screech that ended with a gargle that hardly sounded human.

'Hold her fast, Samuel!' said Jonathan Shooks, and then he clasped the cheeks of her bottom and parted them as wide as he could. He snorted with effort as he drove himself into her, but Beatrice was conscious of nothing except how much it hurt. He leaned forward so that almost all of his weight was on top of her and buried himself into her as deep as he could. In spite of herself, she began to sob. This was so painful, and so humiliating, and it made her feel so miserable.

Jonathan Shooks was breathing hard against her neck. He drew aside her long tangled hair and reached around to dab at her cheeks with his fingertips. He felt the tears sliding down her cheeks and then he ran one finger across her lips so that she could taste their saltiness.

'Oh, *Widow Scarlet*,' he said as he did so, and inside herself she felt him shudder, and quake, and shudder again.

Afterwards, he stood up and dressed himself as unhurriedly as if he were in his own room at the Penacook Inn, admiring himself in the looking-glass as he replaced his wig and tied up his cravat. Beatrice remained lying on the floor, although she had pulled down her petticoats and her gown to cover herself.

When he had put on his shoes Jonathan Shooks stood over her and held out his hand. 'May I help you to your feet, Widow Scarlet?'

Beatrice refused even to look up at him. Instead, she stared at the turned mahogany leg of the chair next to her.

'Very well, whatever you wish,' he told her. 'But I will be as good as my word and bring your son straight back to you. It has been a pleasure to do business with you, Widow Scarlet, and if at any time you would care for more pleasure, you have only to send for me.'

Beatrice stayed where she was and didn't answer him. Eventually, Jonathan Shooks said, 'Come along, Samuel. It's time for us to leave this young lady in peace.'

They left the house and Beatrice heard them driving away. When they were out of earshot she reached out for the chair and painfully pulled herself on to her knees, and then to her feet. She wanted to cry, but she told herself not to. Crying could come later, at night, when Noah was safely home. She went into the kitchen and pumped some water into a bowl. Then, lifting her gown and her petticoats, she washed herself, wincing because she felt so sore. There were blood-spatters on her petticoats, so she would have to change them.

She slowly crept upstairs, clinging on to the banister rail like a woman three times her age. She had always thought of herself as outspoken. It was her father who had taught her that, because he had been obliged to deal daily with people who were stupid and feckless and ignorant. Until now, however, she had never thought of herself as vengeful. Not as vengeful as this. Not so vengeful that she could happily have seen somebody whipped until their spine appeared through the flesh on their back, or hanged.

Thirty-three

Even though her hands wouldn't stop trembling, she carefully stitched the neck of her black mourning gown where Jonathan Shooks had torn it apart. When she had dressed again, she carried one of the kitchen chairs out to the front porch and sat there to wait for Noah to be brought back to her.

She could hear Jubal and Caleb chopping away at the trees beside the brook, but she couldn't face seeing anybody at the moment, let alone telling them what had just been done to her. After the first wave of disgust and vengefulness had subsided, she now felt as numb and as cold as the frozen girl that she and her father had found kneeling in a doorway that long-ago Christmas Day in London.

She sat there for nearly two hours while the day turned around her, and the huge white clouds rolled over, and the shadows from the oak trees along the driveway gradually shrank. She could hear the birds chattering and the leaves rustling, but all she could think of was Noah.

At last, at the far end of the driveway, she saw Jonathan Shooks's calash. It stopped and she could see Samuel lifting Noah down and setting him on the ground. The calash drove off, leaving Noah standing there by himself.

Beatrice stood up, knocking over her chair with a clatter. 'Noah!' she called out. 'Noah!' She gathered up her gown in one hand and ran towards him, waving. '*Noah*! *Mama's here, my darling*! *Noah*!'

Noah started to toddle towards her, too, both arms lifted, crying as he came.

There was still fifty yards between them, though, when Beatrice saw somebody step from out of the shadows of the oak trees. It was the brown-cloaked figure with the staff. He was heading towards Noah as if he intended to intercept him, poling himself along with his staff so that he could walk more quickly.

'No!' screamed Beatrice. 'Don't touch him! Leave him alone!'

She ran even faster, although her petticoats made her stumble and almost trip over. But the figure had obviously heard her, because he stopped and stood motionless, and then he bowed his hooded head, turned round, and made his way swiftly back towards the trees. Beatrice scooped Noah up into her arms just as the figure disappeared.

'Mama,' sobbed Noah, clinging tightly round her neck. His face was dirty and his hair smelled of grease and his clout was sodden. She carried him into the house and through to the kitchen where she undressed him and gently washed him. She examined him very carefully but there were no bruises on him.

She carried him up to his bedchamber and dressed him in a clean white smock and combed his curls. He still clung to her, but he had stopped crying now and at least he smelled clean. She carried him back down to the kitchen and sat him in his high-chair and warmed up some milk for him. He was too little for her to ask him what had happened, and how he had been treated, so all she could do was smile at him and kiss him and sing him 'Hickory Dickory Dock'.

*

Shortly after three o'clock Mary appeared. Her face was flushed and her eyes were puffy, but she insisted that she was well enough to work.

'I have to go into the village myself,' said Beatrice. 'Why don't I take you back home? There is only plain-work to do. I was going to start boiling those cows' hooves for gelatine, but that can wait until tomorrow.'

'May I not stay here and sew?' asked Mary. 'If you take me back home, my mother will have me doing laundry and scrubbing the floors.'

'Of course you can stay. You needn't have to sew if you don't feel well enough. Take the bed in the back room if you need some sleep.'

Mary stared at Beatrice closely and said, 'Has something happened, Goody Scarlet?'

'What do you mean?'

'You have a bruise on your cheek, ma'am, and – please forgive me if I'm being disrespectful – you seem to be not quite yourself.'

Beatrice lifted her hand self-consciously up to her left cheek, which Jonathan Shooks had slapped much harder than the right. 'It's nothing. I was going out to feed the pigs and I tripped over and fell against the gate.'

Mary continued to stare at her as if she didn't believe her for a moment, but then she gave a little curtsey and said, 'I see. I'm sorry if I spoke out of turn. Thank you. Thank you for allowing me to stay. I'll go and get the sewing basket. Are you going to the village now?'

'Yes, and you won't have to worry about minding Noah, because I'll be taking him with me. He's a little upset today and I think he needs to stay close to his mama.'

'You're upset yourself, aren't you?' said Mary. 'And it's not just the tripping over. You're really distressed.'

Beatrice tried to smile but couldn't. She felt very close to tears and the very last thing she needed at this moment was sympathy. 'Yes,' she said. 'I can't tell you about it now but I promise I shall. You're a very perceptive girl.'

Mary didn't answer, but curtseyed again and left the room. It was only when she had gone that Beatrice realized that she probably didn't know what 'perceptive' meant and thought that she was being scolded.

She lifted Noah out of his high-chair and said, 'Come on, my little man. Mama has a very important call to make. It's time for *us* to start making some black magic.'

That Sunday morning, the meeting house was crowded. Bishop Coker had come from Dover to hold a special memorial service for Francis, and also to introduce the Reverend Miles Bennett, who would be acting as Sutton's pastor until a new minister could be sent over from England.

Bishop Coker was a very large, grand man, whose majestic progress down the central aisle of the meeting house was like a man-o'-war under full sail, and whose voice when he spoke was like the booming of a broadside.

He knew nothing of the troubles that had been plaguing Sutton, mostly because Francis had been reluctant to admit to his superiors that he was unable to cope with Jonathan Shooks and the demands he had been making on behalf of Satan, or the demon who was acting as Satan's procurator. No gossip had reached the ears of the church elders, either, as it would normally have done if there were suspicions of witchery or Satan-worship in the village. The people of Sutton had been too frightened to speak openly about what had been happening – especially after the ways in which Francis and Nicholas Buckley had met their deaths. They also didn't want the inhabitants of the neighbouring communities to think that God might have picked them out for punishment, for whatever sins they might have committed, or their lack of faith, and allowed Satan to strip them of their precious property.

'Truly, the Reverend Francis Scarlet was a light that shone in our darkness,' bellowed Bishop Coker. 'But his was a light that will never be extinguished, only passed on to his successor, and his successor's successor, and indeed to his successors' successors' successors.'

In murmuring voices, the congregation prayed that Francis's soul would find eternal peace in heaven, and they also prayed for the Buckleys. Some of them were wiping their eyes as Bishop Coker gave the final blessing.

When the service was over, Bishop Coker stood by the door to say a few comforting words and shake hands with all of the communicants, while Beatrice and Benjamin Lynch stood on either side of him. Close behind Beatrice stood Major General Holyoke, with his wig slightly too low over his forehead, which made him look as if he were frowning, or deep in thought. Every time one of the congregation took hold of Beatrice's hand, he would stand on tiptoe and peer expectantly over her shoulder.

George Gilman said to Beatrice, 'A fine tribute, Widow Scarlet. The Reverend Scarlet more than deserved it.'

Even Ebenezer Rowlandson took her hand between his and nodded tearfully, his lips puckered with emotion. 'What can I say to you, Widow Scarlet? We are all much poorer for having lost your husband. Much, much poorer.'

Henry Mendum was almost last to come out of the meeting house, wearing a black tailcoat and grey britches, arm in arm with his wife. He bowed his head to the bishop, and then to Beatrice, but he didn't hold out his hand to either of them.

Beatrice said sharply, 'A very warm day for wearing gloves, Mr Mendum.'

Henry Mendum held up his right hand as if he were surprised to see it on the end of his arm. He was wearing grey kid gloves, but they must have been too tight for him, because they were unbuttoned.

'Out of respect for your late husband, Widow Scarlet, I dressed formally today. Unlike some others I see around us.'

He nodded in the direction of William Rolfe, who was wearing a dark green coat with fraying cuffs, and his wife, who was dressed in a blue and white floral print gown.

'Of course, Mr Mendum,' said Beatrice. 'And I appreciate it very much. But here . . . you're undone . . . let me help you.'

She took hold of his hand and twisted the button of his glove as if she were trying to fasten it.

'That's quite all right, thank you,' said Henry Mendum. 'I confess that I've put on a little weight since I last wore these gloves, so they fit somewhat snug.'

He pulled his hand away from her, but as he did so Beatrice, quite forcibly, tugged it right off, so that all of the fingers were turned inside out. Henry Mendum tried to grab it from her, barking out, 'Here! Give that here, if you please! What are you doing?'

Beatrice held the glove up as high as she could and as Henry Mendum reached for it she could clearly see that the tips of his fingers and the ball of his thumb were all stained black.

'It is *you*!' she said breathlessly.

Henry Mendum tried to snatch his glove again, but Beatrice swung it out of his reach. 'It is *you*!' she repeated, much louder this time, although she was so shocked that she couldn't stop her voice from sounding shrill. '*You* are the demon! You are the one who has been terrorizing everybody in Sutton! You are the one who has been stealing their land!'

'What the devil are you talking about?' Henry Mendum snapped at her. 'Give me back my glove, woman! Have you lost your reason?'

'Your guilt is there for everybody to see, on your fingers!' said Beatrice. 'Look how black they are!'

'What?' said Henry Mendum. He stopped trying to snatch his glove and jammed his hand underneath his armpit, out of sight.

'It is no good trying to hide it, Mr Mendum,' said Beatrice. 'It is the indisputable proof that you are the representative of Satan that Jonathan Shooks has claimed that he is doing business with.'

'This is absolute *madness*!' said Henry Mendum. 'You're raving! You're insane! Do you hear what she's saying, bishop? Do you hear the babbling nonsense that's coming out of her mouth? She should be taken to a lunatic asylum and locked up for life!'

'Oh, no,' said Beatrice. 'Your fingers tell the truth, Mr Mendum. Your blackened fingers say that you have been terrifying the people of Sutton into handing over their land to you. They also say that you killed the Buckley family, and George Gilman's four slaves, and that you killed my dear husband, too.'

'That's a slander!' shouted Henry Mendum with spittle flying from his lips. 'It's a damnable out and out slander! I have never killed anybody in my life!'

'Perhaps you didn't murder them with your own hand. I believe that it was Jonathan Shooks who did that. I strongly suspected him right from the start, but now I'm sure of it. Even if he carried out the killings, though, he did it on your instructions. Sutton *has* been menaced by Satan, yes! But Satan's real name is Henry Mendum!'

'How dare you to speak to my husband like that!' snapped Harriet Mendum. 'He is the wealthiest and most respected member of this community! He has friends in very high places! In commerce! In the church! In politics, even! He has been charitable to a fault! How *dare* you accuse him of such a crime!'

'His fingers give him away,' said Beatrice. 'The black on his fingers.'

Henry Mendum took his hand out from under his armpit and held it up so that everybody could see it.

'I have black stains on my fingers? What does that prove? Nothing – except that I spilled some ink across my writing-desk this morning while composing a letter to the president of New Hampshire – with whom I have a very close and amicable relationship, I might add.'

'That is partly ink, yes,' said Beatrice. 'Ink, however, can be washed off. What you have on your fingers is a mixture of ink and lunar caustic, which is almost indelible. You may wash your hands a hundred times over and you will still have those stains.'

She looked around at the silent crowd that had gathered around them. 'Yesterday Mr Jonathan Shooks came to the parsonage and demanded that I prepare a letter for him, promising that I would hand over a large part of my land to this supposed demon who has been terrorizing us so much of late.

'Mr Shooks had abducted my little son, Noah, in order to force me to agree, and so of course I did agree. I duly wrote him a promissory letter, one copy for him and one for the demon.'

By now, Beatrice's voice was shaking, but she was determined to carry on. Henry Mendum kept on making explosive noises of disagreement and blurting out '*Nonsense*!' and '*Slander*!' while his wife gave out one scornful cry after another, like a crow. But Beatrice refused to be silenced. She had lost too much to be silenced.

'The copy I wrote for Jonathan Shooks I wrote in ordinary ink, but the copy I wrote for this demon with whom he said he was bargaining I wrote in a special mixture of ink and lunar caustic which stains the fingers when touched. The stains are almost indelible and cannot be removed by washing.

'I came to this service today because I knew that everybody in the village would be expected to attend, to pay their respects to Bishop Coker and to welcome our new minister. I hoped very much that I would see none of you with stains on your fingers, because that would mean that we had a murderous extortionist among us, somebody who would be prepared to threaten his own friends and neighbours with death in order to misappropriate their land, and who would carry out his threat if they resisted him.

'I hoped in vain, because here he is – Mr Henry Mendum, a demon in the shape of a dairy farmer.'

Henry Mendum held up his hand so that everybody in the crowd could see the black stains on his fingers. 'These mean nothing at all! These mean only that I have accidentally spilled a bottle of ink! I deny and refute everything that the Widow Scarlet is suggesting!'

It was then that Major General Holyoke stepped forward. 'Mr Mendum!' he said, very loudly, so that everybody could hear him. Then, more quietly, '*Henry*,' because they had known each other for more than a decade. In spite of that, he was a magistrate and he had solemnly promised Beatrice that whoever was suspected of having murdered Francis and the Buckleys and the Gilmans' slaves, they would not escape justice.

'The Widow Scarlet came to me yesterday afternoon and advised me of how she had treated the letters that she had written. The letter that was intended for the demon was rolled up and sealed so that only the person to whom it was addressed would have their fingers marked in the way that yours are marked.

'Had she not told me this yesterday, well before you allege that you stained your fingers with ink, I might have found your excuse plausible. But I do not, Henry, I regret. The fact that you found it necessary to conceal the stains with gloves shows that you could not remove them, as the Widow Scarlet has suggested.'

Henry Mendum opened and closed his mouth, but no words came out. His wife tossed her head and said, 'Huh!' and 'huh!' and '*huh*!' but she, too, had nothing else to say.

Major General Holyoke cleared his throat and said, 'There is one more item of supporting evidence that the Widow Scarlet showed me yesterday. She herself was not sure what it meant, although she had her suspicions. In the light of this morning's events, however, it has drawn me irresistibly to conclude that you, Henry, are more than likely to be the man responsible for the fear and misery and grief that has been brought upon this village.'

'What "item of supporting evidence"?' Henry Mendum protested. 'This is not a trial and you are not a magistrate. Well, you are a magistrate, but this is not a trial!'

Major General Holyoke reached into the inside pocket of his coat and produced a folded sheet of paper. He unfolded it and held it up in front of Henry Mendum's face.

'This is a sketch-map of the various acres that Mr Jonathan Shooks persuaded various farmers to assign to his "demon". This was on pain of having their crops or their livestock destroyed, or even their families injured or killed.'

'Now, wait!' Henry Mendum interrupted him. 'You are

forgetting that my finest Devon milkers were poisoned by this demon. Its hoof prints were first found in my field! The Widow Scarlet saw them for herself! I was just as much a victim as anybody else, and equally terrified, I might say!'

'Your cows suffered no lasting ill-effects, Mr Mendum,' Beatrice put in. 'They all recovered completely and no lasting harm was done to your livelihood. As for the hoof prints, I am sure that they were made artificially. Not only that, they were composed of substances that anybody can purchase at any pharmacy.

'More than anything else, did *you* deed any of your land to this demon in return for your cows' recovery?'

Henry Mendum's eyes bulged with fury. He turned to the crowd of villagers who had gathered around to hear what all the arguing was about, and shouted out, 'Well? Do you believe this slander? You all know me! You all know that I have always been honourable! I have always helped you through difficult times, both with money and with words of comfort! Who will speak up for me? Come on! Who will speak up for me?'

At first none of the villagers answered, but stared at him with undisguised curiosity, as if he were Minotaur the Bull-headed Man in a travelling freak show. But then Ebenezer Rowlandson raised his hand and said, 'You came to me not two years ago, Henry, did you not, and asked me if you could purchase thirty acres from me to increase the size of your farm?'

'I did, yes. But I offered you a very generous price for it, did I not? And did I threaten you? No, I did not – in no respect whatsoever!'

'But I said no to your offer, didn't I? And I recall that you were not best pleased about that. You hoped that I would not live to regret it, that was exactly what you said.'

'I think your memory is playing tricks on you, sir!'

'I have an excellent memory, Henry. I even remember the day – May the fourteenth, Saint Matthew's Day.'

Major General Holyoke held up the sketch-map again. 'Although this map is by no means complete, it shows beyond a doubt that a pattern is emerging! All of the land that the "demon" has so far acquired adjoins Mr Mendum's farm on one side or another. The effect of this acquisition has so far been to double the size of the Mendum holding and to make it one of the largest properties in the county.'

Somebody shouted out, 'Mendum! Is this true?'

Henry Mendum said nothing, but took hold of his wife's hand and pulled her away down the meeting-house path, past the freshly mounded graves of Francis and the Buckley family, heading for the gate. The crowd of villagers called out angrily, 'Shame!' and 'Shame on you, Henry Mendum!' and 'Where are you running to?' and one woman screamed out *'Demon!'*

Constable Jewkes was standing outside the gate, untethering his big brindled horse. Major General Holyoke called out, 'Jewkes! Constable Jewkes! Detain Mr Mendum!'

Constable Jewkes looked up and around, bewildered, as if his name had been called out of the sky by God.

'Detain him!' shouted Major General Holyoke, pointing frantically to Henry Mendum as he reached the gate.

Constable Jewkes took two steps forward with his right hand raised and said, 'Stop! Stop, sir! You are arrested!'

Henry Mendum pushed Constable Jewkes so hard in the chest that Constable Jewkes staggered back and almost fell over on to the grass. But as the Mendums hurried away, hand in hand, heading for their carriage, Constable Jewkes went over to his horse and drew out the yard-long mahogany baton that he kept in a leather holster beside his saddle. Half running and half hopping, he caught up with the Mendums, raised his baton and hit Henry Mendum so hard on the back of the head that Beatrice could hear his skull crack like a pistol shot.

Henry Mendum pitched face-first on to the road, still gripping Harriet Mendum's hand so that she tumbled over beside him, her gown flying up to show her petticoats and her piano-like legs in black silk stockings.

'*Henry*!' she shrilled as she climbed to her feet. '*Henry*!'

But Henry Mendum lay still, his face against the dry rutted mud, his eyes closed and blood sliding out of both nostrils.

'May the saints preserve us!' thundered Bishop Coker. 'Don't tell me that you have killed him, constable, right in front of our very eyes?'

Beatrice hurried out of the gate and knelt down in the road to feel Henry Mendum's pulse. Harriet Mendum hovered close to her, saying 'Well?' '*Well*?' 'He's not dead, is he?' 'Don't say that he's dead!'

'No, not dead,' said Beatrice after a few moments. 'Is Doctor Merrydew still here? Doctor Merrydew!'

Harriet Mendum let out an extraordinary wail and then struck Beatrice on the shoulder with her black parasol. 'If anybody in Sutton is a demon, Beatrice Scarlet, it is you! Look what you have done to my beloved husband! Look at him! You are a witch in widow's clothing!'

Thirty-four

That evening, just before sunset, Major General Holyoke came to the parsonage and knocked at the door. Mary let him in and led him through to the parlour, where Beatrice was writing up the church accounts, so that she could hand them over to the Reverend Miles Bennett. She was framed in a rectangle of crimson sunlight from the window, as if she were a portrait of herself painted only in shades of red.

'Major General Holyoke,' she said, laying down her quill and standing up. 'How is Henry Mendum?'

'Not at all well,' said Major General Holyoke. 'Doctor Merrydew fears that he may be bleeding beneath the skull which will either bring about his death or leave him permanently comatose. Even if he does regain consciousness, he will more than likely be a jingle-brains for the rest of his life.'

'It shouldn't have ended like this,' said Beatrice. 'He should have been fairly tried by the court for what he did and punished accordingly.'

'I came to tell you that I have talked with Harriet Mendum,' said Major General Holyoke. 'She has confessed to me that she knew of her husband's ambition to extend his farm. He wanted it to be the most extensive and most profitable dairy farm in the whole of New Hampshire, and he had ambitions beyond that, too, such as standing for state president.

'Two years ago he approached most of the farmers whose property abutted his and offered to buy large tracts of their land, but in almost every case he met with refusal. Mistress Mendum told me that one farmer showed some interest – John Tufnell, I think she said – but Mr Tufnell demanded twice the price for his acreage that her husband was willing to pay.'

'So instead he decided to terrify his neighbours into giving him their land?'

'That's right. According to Mistress Mendum, the idea came to him when he met a ship-owner on one of his business trips to Salem, and the ship-owner introduced him to Jonathan Shooks. Mr Shooks had acquired for this ship-owner three sloops from rival shipping companies by causing all manner of hideous accidents aboard their vessels. He had persuaded these rival companies that Satan was responsible for these mishaps, as a punishment for bringing Christian missionaries to America from England. He told them that the only way in which they could save their entire fleets from disaster would be to forfeit some of their ships.'

'Jonathan Shooks is a devil,' said Beatrice. 'He is clever and skilled in all manner of chymical tricks and his knowledge of herbs is extraordinary. He also has no soul and no conscience whatsoever.'

Major General Holyoke hesitated for a moment, blinking, as if he sensed that Beatrice's hatred of Jonathan Shooks ran even deeper than her grief for the death of her husband.

Slowly, and keeping his eyes on her as he spoke, he said, 'Mr Shooks had also extorted land on behalf of three other farmers, in Maine and Massachusetts. No news of those extortions was ever spread abroad because their victims were cautioned that they must keep silent about them or they would face even further horrors.

'Henry Mendum offered Mr Shooks a great deal of money to come to Sutton and extort hundreds of acres of land for him.' Here Major General Holyoke smiled and laid his hand on Beatrice's arm. 'What Mr Shooks clearly didn't realize is that in Sutton he would be confronted by a woman whose knowledge of alchemy and herbs was almost as great as his own, if not greater.'

'Oh, I think he knew it only too well,' said Beatrice. 'He was trained as an apothecary himself, in London, and he was aware of my dear father's reputation, and of who I was. He told me so. No – before he started to terrorize our community, he made a careful study of everybody with any influence, and where each of us came from, and what our weaknesses were likely to be.

'I believe he knew all about the skills my father had taught me and that right from the very beginning he regarded me as a challenge rather than a threat. He has tried with every fresh atrocity to baffle me and outwit me, and most of the time he has succeeded. I still don't know how he killed our pigs, or what he gave to Henry Mendum's cows to make them appear to be dying, or what he used to drug Ebenezer Rowlandson's fish. Yet I don't doubt now that he did it.'

'Let me ask you this,' said Major General Holyoke. 'Are you sufficiently certain that Jonathan Shooks was responsible for at least some of these outrages to be able to give evidence to a jury?'

Beatrice nodded. She could prove that Jonathan Shooks had purchased two hundred gallons of linseed oil and she was sure that alone would be enough to convict him, even if it meant exhuming Francis's body to show a jury how he had been dried like wood.

'Excellent,' said Major General Holyoke. 'In that case I shall issue a warrant for the arrest of Mr Shooks, and perhaps we can exorcize Satan from our village for good and all. You are a brave and clever woman, Beatrice Scarlet, and I commend you for what you have done.'

All the time they had been talking the parlour had been growing increasingly shadowy, and now it was so dark that Beatrice could hardly see Major General Holyoke's face. She felt as if they were standing in the shadows of days that had gone and would never return. Tomorrow everything would dawn new and bright and different, and she would start her life again, but just for now she felt as if Francis were standing close beside her, as well as Major General Holyoke, and the feeling was so sweet and so painful that her eyes filled with tears.

Major General Holyoke must have seen her tears glittering in the gloom because he reached out and took her hand and squeezed it, and said softly, 'Beatrice, my dear. Beatrice, my poor, poor dear.'

The following day did start bright, although a chilly breeze was blowing from the north-west. The tall pines swayed like dancers and the air smelled of autumn.

Beatrice woke early and started her morning by mixing dough. When Mary arrived she would enlist her help in killing one of the pigs and butchering it ready for the winter. She had seen signs already that this winter was going to be exceptionally cold: the corn husks were thicker than usual, and the raccoons had much bushier fur and brighter bands than last year. The cows, too, had thicker hair on the napes of their necks.

She kneaded the dough for four large loaves and then covered them with cloths and left them to prove. She was washing the flour from her hands when she heard Noah crying upstairs.

She went out into the hallway and there, standing in front of her, was Jonathan Shooks. She jolted in shock.

This was not the smart, suave Jonathan Shooks who had first visited the parsonage. This Jonathan Shooks had lost his silver wig and one of the sleeves of his tailcoat was hanging down in shreds. His face was smudged with dirt and he hadn't shaved. He had even lost one of his silver-buckled shoes. He stood staring at her and he was wild-eyed with rage.

'You *trull*!' he spat at her. 'You *whore*!'

'Get out of my house at once!' said Beatrice. 'There is a warrant out for your arrest and if you much as *breathe* on me again I shall happily make sure that you are hanged!'

'You betrayed me, Widow Scarlet. You, the widow of a pastor! They came for me at the Penacook Inn and Samuel and I were lucky to escape with our lives! As it is, I have lost my calash and my horses and all of my possessions! Everything!'

'You killed my husband, Mr Shooks. You kidnapped my child and you took me by force. What on earth led you to suppose that I would keep my word to you?'

'I fondly imagined that you would keep your word to me because you were afraid of me, and of what I might do to you if you did not.'

'I am not afraid of you,' she said, even though her voice was shaking. 'There is nothing that you can take from me now that you have not already taken. You disgust me. Apothecaries are supposed to use their knowledge to cure people and to ease their suffering, not to terrify them and steal their property and murder them. You are not even worthy of being called a demon. You are a slug.'

Jonathan Shooks sniffed loudly in his right nostril, then wiped his nose with the back of his hand. 'You think that I can't take any more from you, you whore? You think that you have nothing more to give me? I'll tell you what you can give me. You can give me my revenge.'

With that, he strode towards her and seized hold of her arm, whirling her around so that she lost her balance and throwing her on to the kitchen floor. Her left shoulder was jarred by one of the table legs and she knocked her forehead against the rung of a chair. She twisted herself around, making a grab for the back of the chair so that she could pull herself up, but Jonathan Shooks kicked the chair over and then kicked her hard in the hip. When she tried again to sit up, he kicked her again, in the thigh this time.

'Did you really think that you could outsmart Jonathan Shooks? Did you really believe that some mousy minister's wife could prove herself to be cleverer than me? So your father was Clement Bannister and he taught you some of his tricks and how to brew up some of his possets. But your father never travelled like I did. He never got to know half of what I know.'

'Let me up,' said Beatrice. 'My son is crying. Can't you hear him? I must go up to comfort him.'

'You are going nowhere at all, Widow Scarlet, ever again. Where you lie now is where your life will come to its well-deserved conclusion.'

Noah was screaming now and between each scream he could hardly catch his breath.

'Please,' begged Beatrice. 'It will make him sick if he cries any more.'

'Isn't life tragic? I thought you would have learned that much – you, an apothecary's daughter. Life is nothing but sickness and worry and pain and cruelty, and then we die. Do you want to know how I made those little Buckley twins sick? I gave them each a spoonful of boar's taint to clog their lungs. But the effects of boar's taint can be cured with sulphur dissolved in water, which is why I gave them a drink made from Chinese fire-sticks.

'And poor Ebenezer Rowlandson's trout! All it needed was some soap-root in the water and they were stupefied. The Indians use it in the west. Too lazy to catch their fish with spears.'

'You killed our poor horse, Kingdom, with yew leaves,' said Beatrice. 'Why did you have to do that?'

Jonathan Shooks shook his head. 'I did nothing to your horse! Your *horse*? Why would I? Did I not do enough to show your late husband how ineffectual he was by poisoning your pigs, and all *that* needed was fiddleneck seeds. Did you not guess that from their symptoms?'

'It must have been the Widow Belknap who fed him those leaves,' said Beatrice. At that moment she didn't really care who had poisoned Kingdom, but Noah was still screaming and she was trying to keep Jonathan Shooks talking in order to give herself time to think how she could get away from him.

'The Widow Belknap! Well, it's possible, I suppose! In fact, it's not only possible, it's very likely. She's a very vengeful woman, that Widow Belknap. I'm surprised her parents didn't christen her "Resentment". Still, it's a pity she witnessed what we did to Mr Buckley.'

'She *saw* you?'

'Regrettably, yes. We didn't expect anybody to be walking around the village green at that ungodly hour, but there she was, watching us. What choice did we have? We force-fed her wormwood to make her lose her mind, and then we took her away and left her in the woods. Whether she lived or died, we assumed that everybody in the village would blame her for every misfortune that had blighted their pathetic, obstinate lives – especially since most of them blamed her already. And they did!'

'Please, let me go. I promise that I will tell no one that you have been here.'

'How can I believe *anything* you say, Widow Scarlet? You betrayed me once and you will betray me again. Because of you, I now have to flee from Sutton as a fugitive, without my calash or my horses or any of my possessions, and more importantly, without any of the money that Henry Mendum was going to pay me for acquiring so much land for him. Samuel will probably have to go back to sea and start hoisting up sails again.'

'Better to be hoisting up sails than slaves,' Beatrice challenged him.

'Aren't *you* the sharp one, Widow Scarlet! No mistake about that! But now I'm going to show you how sharp *I* can be.' He reached across the kitchen table and picked up Beatrice's boning knife. Its blade was eighteen inches long and she had taken it out to sharpen it in readiness for killing one of the pigs.

'What are you going to do to me?' asked Beatrice. 'Whatever it is, please don't let it hurt. And don't harm Noah, I beg you.'

Jonathan Shooks ran the ball of his thumb down the blade of the boning knife and a thin trickle of blood ran down the inside of his wrist. 'I intend to do something demonic to you, Widow Scarlet, since you don't seem to think that I am worthy of being called a demon. I could cut your throat, but that would be altogether too humane. I could stab you in the heart, but that would be much too quick. For what you have done to me, I am going to suffer for years, so I believe that you should suffer, too – not for years, of course, but for as long as possible.'

Beatrice closed her eyes. She tried to imagine that she wasn't there at all, lying on the kitchen floor, listening to Jonathan Shooks talking to her in that low, measured voice. Although he was threatening her, he sounded as if he were trying to seduce her, and that made his words even more chilling.

'I am going to slice through your Achilles tendons, so that you are unable to walk. Then I am going to fetch down your little son and dangle him up in front of you and cut open his belly so that his bowels drop into your lap. Then I shall cut open *your* belly, too, and force him back inside you, so that mother and child can again be as one, joined as you were at the start of his life and now reunited at the end.'

Beatrice seized the edge of the table top and again tried to pull herself to her feet, but this time Jonathan Shooks kicked her in the ribs – so hard that she was winded and couldn't speak. He pushed her on to her back and then forced her over on to her face. He grasped her right foot and raised her leg, lifting the boning knife to cut through the tendon at the back of her ankle.

'*Please God, no!*' she screamed, kicking and struggling and trying to twist herself on to her back again. '*Dear God, don't do this! I'll give you anything! You can have all of my land! All of my money! Anything!*'

'What good to me now is your land or your money? You have made me a hunted man, Widow Scarlet! You can pay me now only with your miserable life – that and the life of your miserable squawking son!'

Beatrice made a last effort to pull herself free, but Jonathan Shooks was gripping her foot with such ferocity that the bones in her toes crackled. He wrenched her leg up even higher, but as he did so she heard the front door bang open and footsteps rushing along the hallway and somebody collided with Jonathan Shooks so hard that he was sent sprawling across the kitchen floor, thumping his back against the iron stove.

Beatrice turned around and with a thrill of alarm she saw that the brown-cloaked figure was standing over her. Inside the kitchen he seemed even taller than he had when he was lurking at the end of the driveway under the trees. His hood had dropped back, revealing a man with wild brown hair and staring brown eyes and a bushy brown beard.

'What? Who are you?' was all that Beatrice could manage to gasp out before Jonathan Shooks had heaved himself up from the floor. Jonathan Shooks obviously didn't care who the man was, only that he had violently pushed him over, and without saying a word he came stalking across the kitchen, his face contorted with anger. He was holding up the boning knife, stabbing it upwards into the air, *stab, stab, stab*, as if he were daring the brown-cloaked man to come any closer.

The brown-cloaked man feinted to the left and Jonathan Shooks caught his sleeve with the point of the knife. The brown-cloaked man tried to snatch at his wrist, but Jonathan Shooks was too quick for him and stabbed him in the back of his right hand. Blood flew in a red fan pattern across the floor, but the brown-cloaked man was undeterred and tried to grab the knife again.

Jonathan Shooks swept the knife from side to side, cutting at the brown-cloaked man's fingers again and again, and when at last the brown-cloaked man took a step back, holding up both of his bloodied hands, Jonathan Shooks lunged forward with a hog-like grunt and stabbed him in the side. The blade must have lodged between his ribs, because at first Jonathan Shooks couldn't pull it out.

As Jonathan Shooks tried to tug the boning knife out of him, the brown-cloaked man seized his moment and grasped his wrist with both hands. Grunting and struggling together, they pulled out the knife, but now the brown-cloaked man twisted Jonathan Shooks's wrist backwards and upwards and forced him to stab himself twice in the side of his neck. Blood abruptly sprayed over both of them, and as they wrestled and danced around the kitchen they began to look like life-size marionettes with their faces varnished scarlet.

Jonathan Shooks swayed violently from side to side, trying to break the brown-cloaked man's grip on his wrist, but the brown-cloaked man was taller and bigger and younger. He forced Jonathan Shooks to stab himself in the face again and again. The boning knife sliced his right cheek open, and then cut his upper lip apart so that it looked like a harelip, and then stuck right up his nostril.

Both men were grunting, but neither of them spoke. Beatrice climbed unsteadily to her feet. She could still hear Noah crying, but the two men were lurching from side to side in front of the kitchen doorway and she couldn't get past them. They crashed together into the hutch, so that half a dozen china plates fell to the floor and smashed. Then they stumbled into the stack of copper saucepans beside the stove, with a clatter like the bells of hell. All the time droplets of blood were flying in all directions, and the kitchen floor was becoming dahlia-patterned with bloody footprints.

At last the brown-cloaked man pushed Jonathan Shooks up against the open kitchen door. Very gradually he levered Jonathan Shooks's arm upwards until the point of the boning knife was only a half-inch away from his right eyeball.

There was a long quivering moment when both men were straining their utmost. Jonathan Shooks was already wearing a beard of blood and whenever he grunted he sprayed blood into the brown-cloaked man's beard.

Beatrice wanted to shout out, 'No!' but she could only watch them in horror. She didn't even know who the brown-cloaked man was. He could be a madman. If he were to kill Jonathan Shooks, he might very well come for her next.

The moment of impasse seemed to go on and on. But Jonathan

Shooks was losing so much blood that his knees were starting to sag and his head was dropping forward. With a last grunt the brown-cloaked man pushed the point of the boning knife deep into his eye. His eyeball popped, but the brown-cloaked man didn't stop pushing. The blade slid in at least four inches and must have pierced his brain.

Now, however, the brown-cloaked man released his grip. He took two steps back, his chest rising and falling with exhaustion. Jonathan Shooks feebly raised his left hand, pawing at the air, but he was too weak now to reach the knife handle that was protruding from his eye socket. He slid sideways on to the floor, leaving a semicircular smear of blood on the pinewood door. He twitched once, and then again, but then he lay still and his left eye misted over.

The brown-cloaked man turned to Beatrice, showing her his bloodstained hands.

'I should wash this off,' he told her, in a voice that was little more than a croak.

'Who are you?' she said. 'You're not going to hurt me, are you?'

'Hurt you?' said the brown-cloaked man. 'I thought I had just saved your life.'

He limped to the sink, holding his side. He stared at the pump but he didn't seem to have the strength to draw himself any water.

Beatrice approached him cautiously. 'I have seen you again and again, among the trees,' she told him.

'Among the trees, yes. That's where I've been living most of the time.'

'But who are you? What have you been doing here? Was it you who left me that perfume, and those wild flowers, and that message?'

The brown-cloaked man nodded.

'You're hurt,' said Beatrice. 'I'd best take a look at it. Take off your cloak.'

'Don't worry. I'll live.'

'No, I insist. Take off your cloak.'

Wincing, the brown-cloaked man lifted his cloak over his head. Beatrice helped him to pull it over his head and then she dropped it on the floor. Underneath, the man was thin and white-skinned, and he smelled as if he hadn't washed in a very long time. All he was wearing beneath his cloak was a pair of stained white cotton britches and sandals.

The knife wound between his ribs was oozing blood. Beatrice wiped it and then handed him the rag and said, 'Keep that pressed against it. I'm going to go upstairs and fetch a sheet to bind it with. Also, I have to rescue my son. He must think that I have deserted him forever.'

She dragged out a kitchen chair for him and said, 'There. Sit down. The less you exert yourself the better.'

She stepped past the body of Jonathan Shooks and then hurried upstairs. Noah had been crying so much that his face was red and smothered in tears. Beatrice picked him up and then went to the linen chest at the end of her bed and took out one of her older sheets. She carried Noah back down to the kitchen. The man was still sitting at the kitchen table but he was looking glassy-eyed now and leaning on his elbow as if he were close to collapse.

Beatrice put Noah in his high-chair and gave him a biscuit to keep him quiet for a few minutes. Noah turned his head and looked in bewilderment at the bloodied body of Jonathan Shooks lying sideways on the floor, and then at the skinny, grubby, half-naked man with his long brown hair and his big brown beard. Beatrice tore strips off the sheet and bandaged the man's chest as tightly as she could. While she did so, he stared at her but said nothing.

At last, when she had pinned the bandage together, she stood back and said, 'There. Once the bleeding has stopped, I'll apply some goldenseal tincture to it and that will guard against any infection.'

'Thank you,' he said. 'I knew that you would know how to treat me.'

'You *know* me?'

He nodded and then squeezed his eyes tight shut as he felt a stab of pain in his side.

'So how is it that you know me? Who are you? Do *I* know *you*?'

'It was all a long time ago, Beatrice. You probably never thought that I was worthy of being remembered.'

'Should I remember you? From where?'

' I was very foolish then, and reckless, but in my own way I fell in love with you the moment I first saw you, and I have always loved you, ever since.'

'You know my name,' said Beatrice. She sat down in the chair next to him and stared intently at his face. It was then that he looked up and sideways and she recognized who he was.

'*Jeremy*! Dear Lord, you're *Jeremy*!'

He tried to laugh, but all he could do was cough and nod his head again.

'But I don't understand! What are you doing here in New Hampshire? I thought you were in Manchester, working with your brothers! Why are you dressed like that? Why didn't you come to the house sooner? Have you been living in the woods? You're so *thin*!'

Jeremy gave her a regretful smile. 'You know what I used to be like. Always drunk, always thieving, never caring for anything or anybody. The only person I ever really cared for was you, and what a mess I made of that. Francis was much your better choice for a husband.'

'But what happened, Jeremy? How did you get here, for goodness' sake?'

'I fell out with my brothers because I was always drunk and never did any work. In the end I decided to follow your example and come to the colonies to make a fresh start. I used my inheritance to start up a trading company in Ipswich with a fellow I knew from Birmingham. We didn't do too badly until my partner skipped off with all of my money and left me high and dry.'

'Why didn't you come and ask us for help? We would have helped you!'

'I love you, Bea! But look at me! Look at my condition! This cloak is all I have in the world. How could I approach you like this, like some cadge-gloak? I nearly came to your door but each time I lost my nerve, and in any case Francis wouldn't have been happy about it, would he?'

'You could afford to give me perfume.'

'I stole it, what do you think? That's how low I am.'

'But you came here today and you saved my life, and little Noah's life, too.'

Jeremy looked across at Noah playing with the crumbs of his broken biscuit. 'Is that his name? Noah? That's a good name. Noah, who saved whatever he could when his whole world was drowned.'

Beatrice stood up. 'I'm going to call my labourers and have them take away this – this—' she nodded her head towards Jonathan Shooks, but she couldn't bring herself to say his name. 'I'll send to the village, too, to the magistrate, and let him know what's happened. I will testify that you saved my life,

Jeremy, don't worry. In any event, he was wanted for murder and extortion and they will thank you rather than condemn you.'

'Thank you, Bea.'

'Our first priority must be for your wound to heal. We must feed you properly and make sure that you rest, and clothe you properly, too. I am sure that Francis would not have begrudged you some of his shirts and britches, even if he were still alive.'

'Bea, you owe me nothing. Everything that has happened to me has been of my own making. I was a drunk and a fool. Had I not been so blind I would have seen that my partner was cheating me, right left and centre. I am simply glad that I was close by when I saw that man approaching your house. Ever since Francis passed away, I have been keeping a watch on you. I know – that sounds as if I am obsessed with you, doesn't it? Perhaps I am. But I will not be a burden to you, nor an embarrassment. I love you too much for that.'

Beatrice said, 'Jeremy, you are my cousin and you are going to stay here and get well, and only after that will we decide what you can do next.'

She lifted Noah out of his high-chair and said, 'Noah, I want you to meet your Uncle Jeremy. Can you say "Uncle Jeremy"?'

Thirty-five

Three days later, when Beatrice was weeding the garden, Major General Holyoke came around the side of the house.

'Beatrice!' he called out. 'Good morning to you!'

Jeremy was sitting on a kitchen chair by the side of the vegetable patch, wearing a wide-brimmed straw hat that used to belong to Francis, and one of Francis's shirts and a pair of his pale blue britches. He had shaved off his beard and Beatrice had cut his hair, and although he was still pale he looked at least human, not like the wild beast in the brown cloak who had rescued Beatrice from Jonathan Shooks.

Beatrice had been applying goldenseal tincture and garlic to his wound and had dressed it freshly twice a day, and it seemed to be healing well, although he still complained of a pain in his chest.

'Major General Holyoke,' Beatrice greeted him. 'You haven't met my cousin Jeremy. He was the hero who saved us when Jonathan Shooks came here to murder us.'

Major General Holyoke shook Jeremy's hand. 'You did this community a great service, sir. I thank you. How are you, Beatrice? Are you well?'

Beatrice laid down her hoe. 'I am quite well, thank you. Can I offer you tea, or cider?'

'I thank you, but no. This is not really a social visit. I have come to show you two things. If you would be kind enough to follow me back to my carriage?'

Beatrice wiped her hands on her apron and followed Major General Holyoke around to the front of the house. His shiny maroon chaise was standing there, with his coachman standing beside it talking to Mary. Sitting in the chaise, wrapped in a shawl, was the Widow Belknap. When she saw Beatrice she smiled and weakly raised her hand.

'Widow Belknap!' said Beatrice. 'I am so delighted they found you! How are you?'

'My mind is still full of fancies,' said the Widow Belknap hoarsely. 'I still believe that I can see people who are not really there, and hear voices in my head. I still believe sometimes that I can fly, or walk on water. But Doctor Merrydew says that will pass in time.'

'Where did they find her?' Beatrice asked Major General Holyoke.

'Not far from the lake where you said that you had seen her. She was quite naked and chewing tree bark. I doubt if she would have survived very much longer. Thank the Lord you sent us out looking for her.'

'There is no way that I can thank you, Goody Scarlet,' said the Widow Belknap.

'I am a relict now, as you are,' said Beatrice. 'You should call me Widow Scarlet.'

The Widow Belknap nodded. 'Yes . . . yes, they told me that the Reverend Scarlet had passed away. I am very sad for you. I know what grief is like. It is a kind of madness. In some ways it is even worse than the madness that I am suffering now. At least I know that my sanity will soon return to me, but not my dear dead husband.'

She paused, and then she said, 'I have to confess to poisoning your horse, Goody Scarlet. I fed him with yew leaves even as you and the Reverend Scarlet spoke to me. I was angry with you for suggesting that I would cast such wicked spells on my neighbours. I meant only to make the animal sick and cause you to have to walk home. I did not think for a moment that it would die. I apologize, from the bottom of my heart.'

'It's forgotten,' said Beatrice. 'Just as so much else should be forgotten, and forgiven, too.'

She turned to Major General Holyoke. 'Did you not say that you had *two* things to show me?'

'Aha!' said Major General Holyoke. He went round to the trunk at the rear of his chaise and opened it up. 'This contraption we discovered in Mr Shooks's calash. I would say that this is all the evidence we require for a posthumous conviction, wouldn't you?'

He lifted out a two long rods made of oak, which were joined together by a short crossbar, like a pair of legs. On the end of each rod was a cloven hoof, which looked as if it had been cut from a goat. Each hoof was stained with a dark, sticky-looking substance. Beatrice didn't have to smell it to recognize what it was.

'The Devil's hoof prints,' said Major General Holyoke. 'A very simple device indeed, but one that very successfully played on our fears.'

Beatrice heard Noah calling out. She looked around and saw Jeremy walking around the house, holding Noah's hand.

We came here to make a new life, she thought. *We wanted to leave behind all the myths and superstitions of the Old World. But we brought our fears of devils and demons along with us.*

She promised herself then that she would bring Noah up to fear nobody and nothing.

Six weeks passed. Jeremy grew stronger every day and was soon able to help in the garden, and with feeding the pigs, and with painting the parsonage ready for winter. Beatrice, on the other hand, began to feel increasingly tired, and her breasts and her ankles were swollen. She hadn't had a period since the week before Francis was killed.

She had no way of proving it, but she was sure that she was pregnant. She stood looking at herself in the mirror in the parlour and because of the distortion in the glass she was unsure if she was expressionless or if she was secretly smiling to herself.

If she was pregnant, she couldn't be sure whose child she was carrying. With Francis, she hadn't conceived since Noah, and Jonathan Shooks had taken her in such a way that conception seemed remote.

She looked out of the parlour window and she could see that the leaves of the oaks along the driveway were already turning yellow. Even with Noah and Jeremy and all her friends in the congregation, she had never felt so alone in her life.